THE GOLD COLLECTION

CHANTELLE
Shaw

SURRENDER TO THE TYCOON

THE GOLD COLLECTION

June 2016

July 2016

August 2016

September 2016

THE GOLD COLLECTION

CHANTELLE

Shaw

SURRENDER TO THE TYCOON

First Published in Great Britain 2016
By Mills & Boon, an imprint of HarperCollins*Publishers*
1 London Bridge Street, London, SE1 9GF

SURRENDER TO THE TYCOON © 2016 Harlequin Books S.A.

At Dante's Service © 2012 Chantelle Shaw
His Unknown Heir © 2011 Chantelle Shaw
The Frenchman's Marriage Demand © 2007 Chantelle Shaw

ISBN: 978-0-263-92209-7

24-0916

Our policy is to use papers that are natural, renewable and recyclable products and made from wood grown in sustainable forests.
The logging and manufacturing processes conform to the legal environmental regulations of the country of origin.

Printed and bound in Spain
by CPI, Barcelona

AT DANTE'S SERVICE

Chantelle Shaw lives on the Kent coast and thinks up her stories while walking on the beach. She has been married for over thirty years and has six children. Her love affair with reading and writing Mills & Boon stories began as a teenager, and her first book was published in 2006. She likes strong-willed, slightly unusual characters. Chantelle also loves gardening, walking and wine!

CHAPTER ONE

HE STOOD out from the crowd. Exceptionally tall and impossibly good-looking. Rebekah's gaze was drawn to the man standing on the other side of the garden and her heart gave a jolt. Handsome did not do justice to the sculpted perfection of his features. He looked Mediterranean with olive-gold skin stretched taut over chiselled cheekbones and his black hair gleaming like raw silk in the sunshine. His jaw was square and determined; the curve of his mouth innately sensual. Heavy black brows arched above eyes that Rebekah knew were light grey and could sometimes resemble cold steel when he was annoyed, but at other times, when he was amused, gleamed like silver.

He was chatting to one of the guests but perhaps he sensed her scrutiny because he turned his head and their eyes met across the distance of the wide lawn. She tensed beneath his brooding stare. But then he smiled, and she felt a fierce surge of delight. Her lips curved into a tentative smile in response. The low hum of chatter from the guests who were milling around the garden and gathered in the marquee seemed strangely distant. To Rebekah it seemed as though only she and Dante existed on this golden summer's day with the sun beating down from a cloudless blue sky and the sweet scent of honeysuckle filling the air.

From behind her she heard the faint rustle of silk, and out of the corner of her eye she caught sight of a willowy blonde wearing a low-cut scarlet dress that clung to her reed-slender figure like a second skin. The woman was looking across the garden, and it suddenly dawned on Rebekah that Dante was not smiling at *her*, but at his mistress, Alicia Benson.

Flushing hotly at her mistake, she turned her back on him and forced a bright smile as she offered the tray of canapés she was holding to the group of guests standing close by. *Idiot*, she told herself, praying he had not noticed that she had been staring at him like a lovesick adolescent. In fact there was no reason why Dante Jarrell might not have been smiling at her. Over the past two months they had established a harmonious and friendly working relationship. But that relationship had never crossed the invisible boundary between an employer and a member of his staff.

She was Dante's chef; she cooked his meals and catered for the many dinner parties and social events he hosted. Rebekah was sure he regarded her as a functional object necessary to help his busy life run smoothly, like his computer or his mobile phone. She was embarrassed by her intense awareness of him and was always on her guard to hide how she felt about him, which was why she was so annoyed with herself for thinking that his sexy smile had been directed at her.

Unlike the lovely Alicia, she hardly warranted the attention of a gorgeous multimillionaire playboy, she thought, with a rueful glance down at her uniform of black and white-checked trousers and pristine white jacket. Her clothes were practical but did not flatter her curvaceous figure; rather they seemed to emphasise the fact that she was not beanpole-thin as fashion dictated. Beneath her chef's hat her hair was tightly braided and pinned on top of her head, and she knew that after spending hours in a hot kitchen her face was pink and shiny. If only she'd put on a bit of make-up. But it was still unlikely that Dante would have taken any notice of her, she reminded herself as she shot another glance across the garden and watched his beautiful mistress wrap her sinuous body around him.

'I've already eaten far too much, but I can't resist one of these pastries. What's the filling made of?'

The sound of a voice dragged Rebekah from her thoughts and she smiled at the man who had halted in front of her.

'It's smoked salmon with hollandaise sauce, cooked in a filo pastry case,' she explained.

'They're absolutely delicious, as all the food you have provided today has been,' the man said when he had finished his second canapé. 'I can't thank you enough, Rebekah. And, of course, I'm hugely grateful to Dante for allowing Susanna and I to hold the christening party for our son at his home. I was worried we would have to reschedule the whole thing, after the venue we'd booked cancelled at the last minute,' James Portman admitted. 'But Dante organised the marquee and the waiting staff, and assured me that he employed the best chef in London.'

Rebekah could not suppress a flare of pleasure. 'Did he really say that?'

'He was full of praise for your wonderful cooking. Dante's a great guy.' James looked self-conscious as he continued, 'When he took over from his father as head of Jarrell Legal, after Sir Clifford retired, the other lawyers, including myself, wondered what he would be like to work for. He has a reputation for being ruthless, but he's proved to be an excellent boss, and I'd like to think a friend. He didn't hesitate to offer his help with the christening party and he's been very supportive these past few months while Susanna has been suffering from post-natal depression.'

James glanced around the large garden of the beautiful Georgian townhouse which stood opposite Regent's Park. 'The day has been perfect,' he murmured. 'I really am indebted to Dante. Especially as I know the christening must have stirred painful memories for him.'

Rebekah gave him a puzzled look. 'What do you mean?'

Once again James's rather florid complexion turned pinker and he looked awkward. 'Oh, nothing—at least, just something that happened years ago, when he lived in New York.'

'I didn't know Dante had lived in America.' But there was no reason why she would know. Dante did not confide in her and Rebekah had only learned a few facts about him from the Internet after she had accepted his offer to work for him.

On a page entitled 'Britain's Most Eligible Bachelor' she had discovered that he was thirty-six, the only son of a High Court Judge, Sir Clifford Jarrell, and the famous Italian opera soprano, Isabella Lombardi. According to the article, the Jarrells were a hugely wealthy aristocratic family and in previous generations there had been two notable marriages with distant members of the Royal Family. But now Dante was the only heir and stood to inherit a historic manor house and vast estate in Norfolk. Aside from the huge fortune that would one day come to him, he was wealthy in his own right from his successful career as a divorce lawyer. He had gained a reputation as a tough, no-nonsense lawyer and had represented several A-list celebrities in their divorce cases.

As for his private life—busy was the best way to describe it, Rebekah thought wryly. The list of women he had been associated with was a roll call of top models, beautiful actresses and sophisticated socialites with impeccable pedigrees. Evidently Dante preferred blondes. There had been several pictures of him with leggy, platinum-haired beauties hanging on his arm. But, tellingly, he never seemed to be photographed with the same woman twice.

She was intrigued by the notion that her tough, cynical boss might have a softer side. Admittedly she had found him to be a fair and considerate employer, but she had heard a note of genuine admiration in James Portman's voice.

'So, how did you come to work for Dante?' James interrupted her thoughts.

'I used to work for a catering company, mainly providing business lunches in the City,' she explained. 'Dante attended one event and immediately after the meal offered me a job as his private chef.' The salary and the fact that the job came with live-in accommodation had been too good to turn down, Rebekah mused. But, if she was honest, one reason why she had accepted Dante's offer was because she had been blown away by his stunning looks and charisma so that for once in her life she had ignored the voice of caution inside her head and moved into the staff apartment at Hilldeane House.

'Well, if you ever decide to change your job and would consider working for a busy professional couple and their baby son…'

'Are you trying to steal my chef, James?'

There was amusement in Dante's voice but also a faint edge of steel that caused his junior lawyer to jerk guiltily away from Rebekah.

'Not at all.' James relaxed a little when his boss gave a lazy smile. 'Although from the sound of it you poached her from her previous employer.'

'I don't deny it.' Dante gave a shrug which drew Rebekah's eyes to the formidable width of his shoulders. She had been unaware of his presence until he had spoken and she hoped he had not heard her swiftly indrawn breath when she had turned her head and discovered him standing beside her. Being this close to him she was conscious of his height and the raw sexual magnetism he exuded. His jacket was undone, and beneath his white silk shirt she glimpsed the shadow of dark hairs and the faint delineation of his abdominal muscles.

For a shocking, heart-stopping moment she pictured him naked, imagined skimming her hands over his bare skin. Was his body as darkly tanned as his face? The way his trousers were drawn tight over his hips emphasised his powerful thigh muscles. A quiver of awareness shot through her and she could feel heat rise to her face. Terrified that he would realise the effect he had on her, she tried to edge away from him, but to her shock he placed a firm hand on her shoulder.

'I know a good thing when I see it,' he drawled, slanting an amused smile at her. 'I recognized the minute I sampled her food that Rebekah is a talented chef, and I was determined to persuade her to work for me.'

Rebekah stiffened. Dante's words confirmed what she had already guessed, she thought heavily. To him she was simply a cog in the wheel of his busy life. When they had first met he had been impressed by her cooking—while she had fallen in lust with him. It wasn't love, of course. She wouldn't be that stupid. But her inconvenient attraction to him was all the more surprising because after the way Gareth had treated her she had vowed to steer clear of men and allow her bruised heart to recover from the battering it had received.

Maybe after two years of being single her body was coming out of its self-imposed hibernation, she mused. And perhaps she had hit on Dante because, like the pop star she'd had a crush on when she was thirteen, he was way out of her league and therefore she could safely fancy him without the risk that he would ever notice her. Why would he, when he was used to dating beautiful women like Alicia Benson? she thought wryly as she watched the stunning blonde walk across the lawn towards them, accompanied by Susanna Portman, who was carrying a baby.

'Here he is—the star of the show!' James declared as he lifted his seven-month-old son from his wife's arms. 'You're too young to appreciate it, Alexander, but Dante and Rebekah have made your christening day very special.'

At the sound of his father's voice Alexander gave a wide grin, revealing his pink gums and two tiny front teeth.

Rebekah felt a sudden, intense pain in her chest and drew a sharp breath.

'He's gorgeous, isn't he?' James said proudly. 'Would you like to hold him?' he asked, noticing how she was transfixed by the baby. 'Let me take that tray from you so that you can give Alexander a cuddle.'

Alexander was indeed adorable, with chubby arms and legs and wispy golden curls covering his head. Rebekah knew his skin would be as soft as satin, and the scent of him, a unique perfume of milk and baby powder, was so evocative that the pain inside her became an ache of longing—and loss.

She gripped the tray in her hands so tightly that her knuckles whitened as she fought to suppress the agonising emotions surging through her. An awkward silence had fallen over the group and, realising that James was waiting for her to reply, she somehow forced a smile.

'Alexander looks very happy with his daddy, so I won't disturb him,' she mumbled. She looked over at the marquee and added in a brisker tone, 'The waiters are clearing the tables. I'd better go and help them. Please excuse me.'

What had that been about? Dante wondered with a frown as he watched Rebekah practically run across the lawn. His hand had been resting on her shoulder and he had felt the fierce tension that had gripped her when James had invited her to hold his son. At first he had assumed she was one of those women who could not bear the idea of getting baby dribble on her clothes—he'd noticed Alicia had kept her distance from Alexander, no doubt terrified he might leak from one end or the other and ruin her designer dress, he thought derisively.

He was surprised by Rebekah's reaction, though. She did not strike him as someone who cared about getting messy. He had watched her in the kitchen a few times and seen how she clearly enjoyed touching food, mixing ingredients with her hands and kneading dough when she made bread. In fact he had found her earthiness curiously sensual and had found himself imagining those firm fingers kneading and stroking his flesh.

Dio, where had that thought come from? He dismissed the image from his mind with an impatient shake of his head. Far harder to dismiss was the *devastated* expression he had just glimpsed in Rebekah's eyes. He was tempted to follow her and ask what was wrong. But it was unlikely she would confide in him, Dante acknowledged. She had worked for him for two months but, although she was unfailingly polite, her reserved nature meant that he had not really got to know her and usually he did not spare her much thought other than that he was pleased with the way she did her job.

Today's christening party that he had hosted for the Portmans was a prime example of Rebekah's admirable work ethic. He knew she had spent all the previous day preparing the food, and she'd been hard at work when he had walked into the kitchen at seven this morning. Since then she had been rushing about making sure that the party ran smoothly. He had tried to catch her eye earlier, hoping to express his thanks, but she had simply given him a cool look and turned away from him, leaving him feeling strangely irritated.

But there were other reasons for his dark mood, he accepted. The christening had stirred up memories he thought he had buried, and watching James with his baby son had evoked a dull ache in his gut. He remembered how proud he had felt at Ben's christening. At the time he'd believed he had everything a man could want—a beautiful wife and child, a successful career and an expensive home. He still had two out of the four, Dante reminded himself grimly.

'Darling, how much longer do you think it will be before the guests leave?' Alicia's bored voice interrupted his thoughts. 'Surely the party can't go on for much longer.'

Dante stiffened when his ex-mistress placed a possessive hand on his arm. Her unexpected presence today was another reason for his bad mood. He had been unaware that she was an old school friend of Susanna Portman until she had turned up at the church for the christening service.

He had ended his affair with Alicia several weeks ago, but she seemed determined to hang on to him—literally—he thought impatiently when she tightened her grip to prevent him from moving away from her.

'You are here as James and Susanna's guest, so I assume you read the invitation, which states that the event finishes at six p.m.'

The blonde seemed undeterred by his curt tone. 'I thought you might like to come back to my place this evening. We could have a few drinks and relax…' She ran her long scarlet-painted nails down the front of Dante's shirt and for some inexplicable reason a memory flashed into his mind of Rebekah's short, neat, unpolished fingernails. He doubted Alicia had ever kneaded dough or made pastry with her perfectly manicured hands, he thought sardonically, and at this moment he was concerned by the fact that his chef had seemed upset about something.

'I'm afraid not,' he said, firmly removing Alicia's hand from his arm. 'I'm in court tomorrow to represent a client and I need to read through the case notes tonight.'

She frowned petulantly but, perhaps sensing that his patience was running low, she did not argue. 'Can you at least drive me home? I hate travelling by taxi.'

Dante was willing to do anything to get rid of her. 'Of course,' he agreed politely. 'Are you ready to leave now?'

'I'll just collect my wrap,' she told him.

Half an hour later, James and Susanna Portman and their guests had all departed but Dante was still waiting to give Alicia a lift. With escalating impatience, he strode into the kitchen and found Rebekah still at work. Pages of recipe notes were spread over the worktop and a tempting aroma that he hoped was his dinner drifted from the oven.

She glanced at him as he entered the room and his sharp eyes noted that she still looked pale, although her face was not as bloodless as it had been when she had reacted so strangely in the garden.

'Are you all right now?'

She gave him a surprised look, but he noted that she had stiffened defensively at his question.

'Yes, of course. Why shouldn't I be all right?'

'I don't know.' He shrugged. 'I got the impression when we were admiring James's little boy that you were upset by something. You turned as white as a ghost when he asked if you wanted to hold the baby.'

'Oh—I had a migraine,' Rebekah said after a long pause. 'It came on suddenly and I had to rush away and take some painkillers.'

Dante's eyes narrowed on the twin spots of colour that had flared on her cheeks. She was possibly the worst liar he had ever met, he mused. But she clearly was not going to tell him what had bothered her and he had no option but to drop the subject. He did not even understand why he was curious about a member of his staff.

For some reason he felt more irritable than ever. A glance at his watch revealed that it was nearly seven o'clock. He had a couple of hours' work to do tonight and he wished now that he had not agreed to drive Alicia back to her home on the other side of London.

'Have you seen Miss Benson?' he asked tersely.

'I certainly have. She's in the front sitting room, in floods of tears—poor woman.'

Dante did not miss the tart edge to Rebekah's tone. He frowned. 'Do you know why she's upset?'

'Obviously you upset her.' Rebekah compressed her lips. 'She told me that the two of you had had an argument. She was crying, so I suggested she should try and calm down. I think you should go and talk to her.'

Dante felt his temper begin to simmer. What the hell was Alicia playing at? He strode across the kitchen. 'I'll talk to her,' he muttered, 'but I doubt she's going to like what I have to say.'

'I've prepared dinner for you and Miss Benson.'

He halted in the doorway and swung back to Rebekah, his eyes glinting dangerously.

'Why on earth did you do that? Did I ask you to?'

'Well, no. But I thought, with Miss Benson being so upset, that you might invite her to stay.' There was an infinitesimal pause, and then Rebekah said sharply, 'You know, you really should treat your girlfriends with a little more consideration.'

With an effort, Dante controlled his anger. He was infuriated by the behaviour of his clingy ex, but even more annoyed that Rebekah seemed to think she had the right to interfere in his private life.

'Can I remind you that you are my cook, not the voice of my moral conscience,' he said coldly.

He had expected her to apologise but, although she flushed, she lifted her chin and glared at him with what could only be described as a challenging expression. The first time he had met her he had been struck by her beautiful violet-coloured eyes. At this moment they had darkened to a shade that was almost indigo.

'I didn't realise you had a moral conscience. And there's no need for you to remind me of my role. But I'd like to point out that it was not part of my job description to have to deal with your girlfriends when they phone the house because you won't answer their calls to your mobile. Nor is it my job to console them when they sob their hearts out because they thought they meant something to you and they can't understand why you've dumped them.'

Dante frowned at the unmistakable criticism in her voice. 'That happens often, does it?' he demanded.

Rebekah hesitated, aware from the rigid line of Dante's jaw that she had angered him. 'Not often,' she admitted. 'But it has happened once before, with that red-haired actress who stayed for the weekend just after I started working for you. And now there's Miss Benson.'

'No, there isn't,' he said grimly. 'Alicia is a drama queen, which is one reason why I finished with her weeks ago.' His jaw tightened. 'You and I will continue this discussion once I've dealt with her.'

He slammed the kitchen door so hard that the sound ricocheted off the walls. There had been an ominous nuance in Dante's tone, Rebekah thought, biting her lip. The furious look he had given her had warned her she had overstepped the boundary of their employer/employee relationship and she could expect trouble when he returned.

She was regretting her outburst. As he would no doubt point out, his private life was none of her business and she had no right to comment on his playboy lifestyle. Maybe he would decide that he no longer wanted her to work for him. Her heart plummeted at the thought. *'Idiot,'* she muttered to herself. This was the best job she'd ever had. Why *hadn't* she kept her opinions to herself?

The reason was complicated, she thought bleakly. She had been feeling low all day since her mother had phoned with the news that Gareth and Claire's baby had been born. 'A little girl,' her mum had said in a brisk voice tinged with an underlying note of sympathy that had made Rebekah ache to be home with the people she loved. 'I thought it best if I told you, as you were bound to find out.'

So Gareth was now a father. Presumably he had wanted this baby, she thought bitterly. Following the conversation with her mother, she had been swamped by memories of the past. Seeing the Portmans' baby today had been so painful. She had coped by keeping busy with the party preparations and helping the waiters serve the food, but when James had suggested she might like to hold adorable little Alexander she'd had to hurry away before her tenuous hold on her composure shattered.

She had still been in a highly emotional state when Alicia Benson had walked into the kitchen and burst into tears as she confided that Dante had led her to believe their relationship was serious. Of course she had been sympathetic to Alicia, Rebekah assured herself.

She knew what it felt like to have your dreams dashed and your heart broken.

She began to stack the dishwasher with the pots and pans she had used to prepare Thai-style coconut chicken, her movements automatic while her mind dwelled, as it so often did, on Dante. His cavalier attitude to relationships made her infatuation with him even less comprehensible, she thought ruefully. She assumed that one day she would come to terms with everything that had happened with Gareth and want another relationship, but it would take her a long time to trust a man enough that she would risk her emotional well-being and she certainly would not consider becoming involved with a womaniser like Dante.

The sound of footsteps striding down the hall made her stiffen and she lifted her chin with a touch of defiance as the kitchen door swung open and he walked in. She had been perfectly within her rights to remind him that her duties did not include coping with the fallout from his fast-changing love life, she assured herself. It was important to establish boundaries, and if he did not like them then maybe it would be better if she handed him her resignation.

She shot him a lightning glance and saw that he had removed his tie and undone the top few shirt buttons to reveal his tanned throat. The musky scent of his aftershave teased her senses and, to her disgust, her heartrate quickened.

'Miss Benson has gone and won't be back,' he informed her curtly.

Not now he had made it clear to Alicia that the tears she was able to turn on when it suited her left him completely unmoved, Dante thought. He had done nothing to feel guilty about. There had never been any question that he would want more than a casual fling with her. Far more troubling was Rebekah's attitude. He had no wish to lose an excellent cook but he would not tolerate her interference in his private life.

He ran a hand through his hair and stared exasperatedly at her. 'What the hell was all that about?'

The sensible thing to do would be to apologise for poking her nose into matters that did not concern her, but the gremlin inside Rebekah had other ideas. The phone call from her mother had triggered memories of the day Gareth had called off the wedding. She still remembered the gut-wrenching shock she'd felt when he had admitted that he had been secretly sleeping with Claire for months. Was it too much to ask for men to be honest and truthful with women? she thought bitterly.

'I won't apologise for feeling sorry for your girlfriend,' she said stiffly. 'I realise you don't give a damn about the feelings of the women you have affairs with. But I think it was despicable of you to lead Miss Benson on and make out that you wanted a serious relationship with her.'

Dante uttered an oath, instinctively reverting to his first language to express his anger. 'I did not lead her on. I made it clear from the start, as I always do, that I wasn't looking for a long-term relationship. I don't know what rubbish Alicia spouted to you, but if she told you I had promised to make a commitment to her then she was lying.'

Rebekah did not know why she was so certain Dante was speaking the truth but he had spoken so forcefully and she felt instinctively that he was not a liar. She tore her eyes from him and became very busy tidying up her recipe notes that were strewn over the worktop. 'I see. Well, it's nothing to do with me. I shouldn't have said anything,' she mumbled.

'You're right—you shouldn't. I pay you to cook for me, not give me a sermon on morality.' Dante was furious, but he was also intrigued as he watched the rosy-pink flush spread across Rebekah's cheeks. 'Why do you care who I sleep with, anyway?'

'I don't. I have absolutely no interest in your bedtime activities.'

'No?' Dante's eyes narrowed speculatively on her face. He could feel the vibes of tension emanating from her and his curiosity was aroused. He knew very little about her, he realised. She had told him a few basic facts, such as that she had grown up on her family's farm in North Wales and had trained as a chef at a hotel in a town with an unpronounceable name. But he knew nothing about her personal life. He'd seen no evidence that she had a boyfriend, yet why would a young and attractive woman choose to be single?

'Maybe you're jealous,' he suggested idly. He was still annoyed with her, and had made the comment with the deliberate intention of riling her. But her reaction surprised him.

'Of course I'm not jealous,' she snapped. 'What a *ridiculous* idea. I want more from a relationship than to be a rich man's plaything.'

'I don't get any complaints from my playthings,' Dante drawled. He knew he was being unfair to tease her, but he could not deny a certain satisfaction as he watched the rosy flush on her face deepen to scarlet. He wondered if she was a prude. She certainly dressed like a woman determined to quash any hint of her sensuality. Occasionally he had found himself imagining unbuttoning her, literally, and removing her shapeless chef's jacket.

With a derisive shake of his head, he dismissed his inappropriate thoughts. He leaned his hip against the kitchen table and crossed his arms over his chest while he debated how he was going to deal with the situation that had arisen between them. He did not want to terminate her employment, but she would have to understand that he had every right to live his life the way he chose.

'I don't want to know about your love life.' Rebekah shoved her recipes back into their folder, praying Dante would not notice that her hands were trembling. She sensed he was still angry and she felt sick inside as she waited for him to dismiss her from her job.

'Then in future don't pass judgement on how I choose to live my life,' he growled.

Dante stared at her stiff shoulders and felt a sudden urge to pull the pins from her hair and release it from its tight knot on top of her head. He sighed, his temper cooling as quickly as it had flared.

'I'm going to forget what happened tonight on the understanding that you won't interfere in my personal affairs again. You said you had prepared a meal for two?'

Relief swept through Rebekah when she realised that Dante did not seem about to sack her. 'Yes, but I can freeze the spare portion.'

'I have a better idea. You can join me for dinner.' The steely glint in his eyes warned her against arguing with him. 'This is a good opportunity for us to get to know one another. I've been involved in a difficult divorce case in recent weeks and haven't taken the time to check if you've settled in. Now is your chance to tell me if you have any problems.'

CHAPTER TWO

WHAT would Dante's response be, Rebekah wondered, if she revealed that the only problem she had was when he strolled into the breakfast room at weekends, wearing nothing more than a black robe? On weekdays he was always dressed in one of his superbly tailored suits, and quickly gulped down coffee and toast as he skimmed through case notes. But on weekends he enjoyed a cooked breakfast and spent a leisurely hour reading the newspapers.

The first morning that she had been faced with his half-naked body, his hair damp from the shower and his jaw covered in dark stubble that added to his sex appeal, her heart had slammed against her ribs. Even now, the memory of his long tanned legs, and the mass of crisp dark chest hairs revealed when the front of his robe gaped slightly, evoked a molten sensation in the pit of her stomach.

She dared not look at him and quickly turned away to open the oven. 'If you go through to the dining room, I'll bring the food in.'

Minutes later, she pushed the serving trolley into the dining room and halted when she saw Dante's angry expression.

He stared at the table, set with candles and roses that she had picked from the garden. 'If I ever want you to play cupid, I'll let you know,' he said sarcastically. 'What were you thinking of?' His eyes narrowed. 'Did Alicia put you up to it, and ask you to arrange for her to have a romantic dinner with me?'

'No, I just thought…' Rebekah's voice tailed away. It was impossible to explain that she had hoped Dante's relationship with Alicia Benson was serious. If he was in a committed relationship then she would have to accept that her own attraction to him was pointless, she had reasoned. And instead of wasting time fantasising about him, she would get over her ridiculous infatuation.

She tore her eyes from Dante's handsome face, hating herself for the ache of longing she could not suppress. 'I'll take the flowers away,' she muttered as she set his dinner in front of him.

'You may as well leave them. Sit down and eat your food before it gets cold,' he said tersely when she leaned across the table to pick up the vase of roses. 'Do you need to wear your apron while we're eating?'

'Sorry!' Rebekah's voice was as curt as his as she reached behind her to unfasten the apron. She tugged it off and dropped it onto the chair beside her.

She sat down and stared at her plate of Thai chicken. While it had been cooking it had smelled so tempting that she had decided to forget her diet for one night and have some. But she hadn't expected Dante to ask her to eat with him—well, he had ordered, not asked, she thought, feeling infuriated by his arrogance. Sometimes she wondered why she was so attracted to him, but a quick glance at his handsome profile caused her heart to slam against her ribs. Every nerve-ending in her body seemed to be finely attuned to him and she felt so tense that the idea of swallowing food seemed impossible.

Dante leaned back in his chair and studied Rebekah. Today had been full of surprises, he mused. There had been that strange incident at the christening party when she had practically recoiled from James Portman's baby, and then her puzzling behaviour regarding his ex-mistress. And now, for the first time since he had known her, she was not dressed in her chef's jacket but had changed into a plain white T-shirt that moulded her breasts. Her curvaceous figure was a pleasant surprise.

To his shock, he felt his body stir as a hot flood of desire swept through him. It was a predictable male reaction to the feminine form, he told himself. Perhaps it was the Italian blood in him that made him find a woman with full breasts and shapely hips more attractive than the current fashion to be stick-thin and bony.

He cleared his throat. 'Would you like red or white wine?'

'Oh, I won't have any, thanks.' Rebekah grimaced. 'I'm really hopeless with alcohol. Half a glass of wine is all it takes to make me drunk.'

'Is that so?' Dante found himself picturing his chef after she'd had a couple of glasses of wine—all bright eyes, flushed cheeks and discarded inhibitions. He poured himself a glass of Chianti. 'Getting drunk doesn't sound a bad idea after having to deal with Alicia's unacceptable behaviour,' he said grimly.

'Don't you ever worry that you'll end up alone and lonely? Surely even playboys grow bored of sleeping around?' Rebekah's common sense warned her not to antagonise him, but she felt rebellious tonight, angry with the male species in general and Dante in particular—although if she was honest she was angrier with herself for her stupid crush on him.

'It hasn't happened to me yet,' Dante drawled, annoyed that she had the audacity to question his lifestyle. He was not going to admit that lately he had been feeling jaded. There was no thrill in the chase when you knew at the beginning of the evening that you were guaranteed to bed your date by the end of it, he thought sardonically.

'What do you suggest as an alternative to casual sex?' he demanded, posing the question partly to himself. Marriage wasn't for him—he had tried it once and had no intention of ever repeating the experience. But surely there had to be something more than meaningless affairs with women who did not interest him outside the bedroom? 'I grew out of believing in happy ever after at about the same time that I stopped wearing short trousers,' he said abruptly.

'Why are you so cynical? It's your job, I suppose,' Rebekah murmured. 'But not all marriages end in the divorce courts. My parents have been happily married for forty years.'

'How nice for them, and for you,' he said drily. 'Unfortunately, I was not brought up in a stable family unit. My parents split up when I was young and for most of my childhood they fought over me like two dogs over a bone. Not because they loved me particularly, but because I was something else to fight about and winning was all that mattered to either of them.'

Rebekah heard the underlying bitterness in Dante's voice and felt guilty that she had brought up a subject that he clearly found contentious. 'That can't have been much fun,' she said quietly, trying to imagine what it had been like for him as a young boy, torn between his warring parents. Her own childhood had been so happy, and she had always hoped that one day she would have children and bring them up in the same loving environment that she and her brothers had enjoyed.

Silence fell between them while they ate. Dante gave a murmur of appreciation after his first mouthful but Rebekah's appetite had disappeared and she toyed with her chicken.

'I'm surprised you're not married,' he said suddenly. 'You seem the sort of woman who would want to settle down and have a couple of kids. But you're what—late twenties? And you're still single.'

'Twenty-eight is hardly over the hill,' she said tersely. He had touched a raw nerve, especially when he had mentioned children. She was unaware that Dante had noticed her fingers clench around her knife and fork. He could almost see her putting up barriers and once again he asked himself why he was curious about her.

As the silence stretched between them Rebekah realised Dante was waiting for her to continue the conversation. 'I would like to marry and have children one day,' she admitted. She did not add that her longing for a baby sometimes felt like a physical ache inside her. 'At the moment I'm concentrating on my career.'

'What made you decide to train as a chef?'

'I suppose cooking has always been part of my life and, when I left school, training to be a professional chef seemed a natural progression. My grandmother first taught me to cook, and by the age of seven or eight I could make bread and bake cakes and help my mother prepare the dinner. It was a matter of expediency,' she explained. 'I have seven brothers—six are older than me and Rhys is younger. When we were growing up, the boys helped my father on the farm, and they're all huge rugby players with enormous appetites. My mother says it was like feeding an army when they all came in from working in the fields. I think she was relieved when she finally gave birth to a girl. Even when I was a small child I used to help her around the house.'

'I don't have any siblings and I can't imagine what it's like to be part of such a large family. Didn't you resent being expected to help with domestic tasks rather than work on the farm with your brothers?'

Rebekah laughed. 'My family is very traditional, but I've never minded that. We're all incredibly close, even now that most of the older boys are married and have families of their own. Mum was too busy to teach me how to cook, but my grandmother loved showing me recipes she had collected over many years, and others that she had created herself. Nana Glenys is in her nineties now, but when she was young she worked as a cook for a top military general and his family, and she travelled to India and the Far East. Much of her cooking was influenced by the food she experienced abroad, as well as traditional Welsh dishes.'

She hesitated, wondering if she was boring Dante. Although she had worked for him for two months she had never talked to him on a personal level and she was conscious that the details of her life were mundane and unexciting. But when she glanced at him she found he was watching her and appeared interested in what she was saying.

'Actually, I'm compiling a cookery book of Nana's recipes. I've been working on bringing the dishes up to date and replacing items such as double cream with low-fat ingredients that are available today. A publisher has shown some interest in the book, and Nana would be thrilled to see her recipes in print. But she's very frail now and I'm aware that I need to hurry and finish the book.'

Her eyes softened as she thought of the tiny elderly lady who had only recently been persuaded to leave her remote cottage and move into Rebekah's parents' farmhouse.

'It sounds like you are close to your grandmother.'

'Yes, I am. She's a wonderful person.'

Dante found himself transfixed by Rebekah's gentle smile and he wondered why he had not noticed before how pretty she was. Perhaps it was because her dull clothes and the way she wore her hair in that severe style, scraped back from her face and tied in a braid which she pinned on top of her head, did not demand attention.

But it wasn't quite true that he had not noticed her, he acknowledged. He knew from the subtle rose scent of her perfume the moment she walked into a room, and sometimes he felt a little frisson of sexual awareness when she leaned across him to serve a meal. Her violet eyes were beautiful, and her dark lashes that brushed her cheeks when she blinked were so long that he wondered if they were false. He quickly discounted the idea. A woman who was not wearing a scrap of make-up was not likely to bother with false eyelashes.

'I was close to my grandmother. In fact I adored her.' As the words left his mouth he silently questioned why he was sharing personal confidences with his cook when he had never felt any inclination to do so with his mistresses. 'She died a year ago at the grand age of ninety-two.'

'Did she live at your family's estate in Norfolk?

I looked you up on the Internet and learned that the Jarrells own a stately home near Kings Lynn,' Rebekah admitted, her cheeks turning pink when he looked surprised.

'No, Nonna Perlita was my Italian grandmother. She lived in Tuscany, where I was born. Years ago my grandparents bought an ancient ruined monastery with the idea of restoring it and making it their home. When my grandfather died shortly afterwards, everyone assumed Perlita would sell the place, but she refused to move, and oversaw all the renovations my grandfather had planned. She said the Casa di Colombe—which means The House of Doves—was a lasting tribute to her husband.'

'That's lovely,' Rebekah said softly. 'You must miss her.'

'I always spend July in Tuscany. This is the first year that she won't be there and I know the house will feel empty without her.'

Thinking about his grandmother evoked a tug of emotion in Dante's gut. After he had discovered the truth about Ben and learned how Lara had deceived him, Nonna was the person he had turned to and he had poured out his pain and anger to her.

'Dante…is something wrong?'

Rebekah's hesitant voice forced him to drag his mind from the past and, catching her puzzled look, he glanced down and saw that he had tightened his grip on his wine glass so that his knuckles were white.

'Is it the sauce?' she asked anxiously. 'It does have quite a unique flavour. Maybe I used too much lemongrass.'

'No, it's fine,' he reassured her. 'The dinner is superb, as usual. You said you have been concentrating on developing your career—' he determinedly steered the conversation away from himself '—is that the reason you left Wales two years ago and came to London?'

'Yes,' she said after a long silence.

Dante lifted his brows enquiringly.

'I…was in a relationship,' Rebekah explained reluctantly, realising she would have to elaborate. But she could not tell him the full truth. Maybe one day she would come to terms with what a fool she had been, but she felt ashamed of the way she had blindly trusted Gareth. 'It didn't work out, and I decided to move away and make a new start.'

'Why did you break up with the guy?'

Dante knew he should back off. He had heard the tremor in Rebekah's voice and sensed that she had been hurt. He did not need to be a mind-reader to realise she was uncomfortable with him probing into her private life, but for some reason he could not control his curiosity about her.

'He…met someone else,' she muttered.

'Ah, that explains a lot.'

'What does it explain?' Irritation swept through Rebekah at Dante's complacent expression.

'Why you got involved in the situation with Alicia, for a start. Your boyfriend let you down—I assume he was unfaithful with the "someone else"—and now you think all men, including me, are untrustworthy like him.'

'You *are* untrustworthy.' Rebekah did not know how they had got into this conversation, or where it was leading, but she recognized the truth in what Dante had said. Gareth's betrayal had rocked her comfortable world and made her doubt her judgement. 'In fact, you are a hundred times worse than Gareth,' she said hotly. 'You never stay with one woman for longer than five minutes.'

'True,' Dante agreed unrepentantly. 'But I never cheat. I have a strict rule of one woman at a time, and I always end a relationship before I start another one. I'm completely upfront at the beginning of an affair that I'm not looking for permanence. Surely that's better than stringing a woman along and building up her hopes that I might make a commitment to her?'

'In other words, you're a paragon of virtue when it comes to relationships,' she said sarcastically.

'I'd like to think so,' he replied seriously. 'I certainly don't deliberately set out to hurt anyone.'

Morosely, Rebekah pushed her plate of barely touched dinner aside. Maybe Dante was right. Maybe it was better to have an affair with someone who was adamant they did not want a deeper relationship than to trust that if a man said he loved you he meant it.

Dante's voice intruded on her painful thoughts. 'Your relationship must have ended some time ago, and you moved to London. How's the new start going—are you seeing anyone?'

'Not currently,' she muttered, wishing she could turn the conversation away from her personal life.

Dante leaned back in his chair and sipped his wine while he appraised her. 'Don't you think you've spent long enough moping over the guy in Wales? You need to get out and socialise. And I suggest you update your wardrobe. Without wanting to be rude, you're never going to attract a man in the frumpy clothes you wear.'

Anger boiled inside Rebekah like molten lava. 'My clothes are not frumpy; they're smart and professional.

Would you rather I served your dinner dressed like a burlesque dancer?'

'Now there's a thought,' he said softly.

The wicked glint in Dante's eyes caused a flush of rosy colour to spread across Rebekah's cheeks and the atmosphere in the dining room prickled with an inexplicable tension. Her breath caught in her throat and she unconsciously moistened her lower lip with the tip of her tongue. She watched Dante's eyes narrow and, to her shock, she felt a spark of electricity sizzle between them.

Startled, she dropped her gaze, and when she looked at Dante again his expression was shuttered and she wondered if she had imagined the flash of sexual awareness in his eyes. She shoved her hands under the table to hide the fact that they were trembling. 'Anyway, I do socialise,' she told him, annoyed by his accusation that she spent her free time moping about the house.

'You're hardly likely to meet a new man at an evening class in pottery,' he said sardonically.

'I don't recall saying I wanted to meet a new man.'

'So are you going to allow one failed relationship to affect the rest of your life?'

'No…but…'

'You can't live in the past, Rebekah. You need to move on.'

She frowned. 'Are you speaking from experience?'

He gave her a bland smile, but she noticed that his eyes had hardened. 'I'm a playboy, remember?' he mocked her. 'I don't have a problem moving on to the next affair. Seriously, though, I'm sure it can't be easy to move to a big city and make new friends. I could introduce you to a few people. In fact I'm attending the first night of the new musical that's opening in the West

End tomorrow, and the after-show party. Why don't you come with me?'

It made sense to help Rebekah feel more settled in London, Dante told himself. She was a fantastic chef and he did not want her to be tempted to return to Wales. Maybe if he took her out a couple of times she would find her feet on the social scene.

Rebekah swallowed. Perhaps that flash of sexual awareness had been in his eyes after all.

'You're inviting me to spend the evening with you?' She wanted to make sure she had not misunderstood him.

'It will do you good to get out,' he said briskly, as if he thought she needed to be encouraged to buck her ideas up.

Her stomach swooped as the realisation dawned that he had asked her out because he felt sorry for her. The words hovered on her lips to decline his invitation, but a spark of pride made her reconsider. She was not moping over Gareth and she was certainly not the pathetic victim of a failed relationship that Dante seemed to think. There was no reason not to go to the theatre with him. Her only plan for tomorrow night was to wash her hair. It was true that her social life was unexciting. She had kept in touch with a couple of friends she had made when she had worked for the catering company but they led busy lives and she'd only met up with them twice since she had started working for Dante.

'All right, I'd like to go with you,' she said quickly, before she could change her mind. 'I've never been to a first night before. What do you think I should wear?'

'These events are usually formal affairs and I imagine most women will wear full-length evening dresses.'

Rebekah ran her mind through the contents of her wardrobe and realised she had nothing suitable. 'In that case I'll have to go shopping.'

Dante took his wallet from his pocket, pulled out a credit card and pushed it across the table. 'Take this and buy whatever you need.'

'Certainly not,' she said frostily, and pushed the card back to him. 'I'm not a charity case and I can afford to buy my own clothes.'

He had never met such a proud and prickly woman, Dante mused as he returned the card to his wallet. All the women he knew would have seized the credit card and bought a dozen designer dresses with it, but Rebekah was looking at him with an outraged expression, as if he had suggested selling her grandmother. He felt a flare of irritation but also a grudging respect for her.

She stood up from the table and, as she leaned forwards to pick up his empty plate, his eyes were drawn to the sway of her breasts. His body tautened and, to his surprise, he felt a heady sense of anticipation at the prospect of taking her out tomorrow evening that he had not experienced for a long time.

If her mother knew how much she had paid for the dress she would have a fit, Rebekah thought guiltily the following evening as she got ready to go out with Dante. She still couldn't quite believe herself that she had spent so much money on an impractical slither of silk that she would probably never have the opportunity to wear again. But she did not regret buying it. She had spent all morning traipsing up and down Oxford Street and had tried on dozens of evening gowns that hadn't suited her. It had made her realise how much she relied on her chef's uniform to disguise her unfashionably curvaccous figure.

Finally, as she had been on the brink of giving up and phoning Dante to say she had changed her mind about going to the theatre, a dress displayed in the window of an exclusive boutique in Bond Street had caught her eye. Initially the price tag had put her off, but the shop assistant had persuaded her to try it on.

'The colour is the exact shade of your eyes,' the woman had enthused. And so Rebekah had pulled off her jeans in the changing cubicle and stepped into the dress. The assistant had run the zip up her spine, and they had both stared at her reflection in the mirror.

'It looks quite nice,' Rebekah had ventured at last, finding it hard to believe that the person in the mirror was actually her.

'You look absolutely stunning,' the assistant had assured her. 'The dress fits so perfectly it could have been made for you.'

It was the first time in her life that she had ever been called stunning, Rebekah had thought wryly, but to her amazement the dress really did suit her. The bodice had some sort of built-in support so that it was not necessary to wear a bra and the low-cut neckline was more daring than anything she had ever worn before. The delicate shoulder straps were decorated with sparkling crystals but, other than that, the dress was a simple sheath of violet silk that caressed her curves like a lover's hands. Her cheeks had flushed hotly as she had imagined Dante's hands sliding over the silky dress. But the sensuous material made her feel like a beautiful and sensual woman.

She had bought the dress, and also the silver stiletto sandals and matching purse that had been displayed with it. And, having spent so much money, she had decided to go completely mad, and had visited the beauty salon at Harrods and had an array of treatments that had left her looking and feeling as though she had discarded the dull, tired Rebekah Evans she had been for the last two years and transformed into a new Rebekah who was seductive and self-confident.

Perhaps, when he saw her in the dress, Dante would realise he did not need to feel sorry for her, she thought, remembering her humiliation the previous evening. She made her way carefully up the stairs from the staff apartment in the basement of the house, discovering that walking elegantly in high heels and a long skirt was an art she needed to learn quickly. Her new-found confidence wavered slightly and she hesitated outside the sitting room while she took a deep breath before she opened the door and walked into the room.

Dante was in the process of pouring himself a drink. He had told Rebekah to be ready for seven p.m., but it was only five to and he assumed she would not appear for at least another fifteen minutes. In his experience, women were rarely ready for a date on time.

He glanced round in surprise when he heard the door open and was so astonished at the sight of her that he froze with his glass midway to his lips.

'Rebekah…?' His voice deserted him as, for one crazy second, he wondered if the exquisite creature standing across the room was really his chef, who he had only ever seen wearing an unflattering uniform that made her appear as shapeless as a sack of potatoes. She walked towards him, moving with a fluid grace that held him mesmerised. As she came closer he noted that her incredible violet eyes were the exact same colour as her floor-length gown.

It was definitely Rebekah, but what a transformation! He had never seen her hair loose before and he could not take his eyes from the glossy chocolate-brown mane that rippled down her back. Soft grey shadow on her eyelids emphasised the colour of her eyes and her lips were defined with a slick of rose-coloured gloss.

As for her dress—Dante took a gulp of his drink to ease the sudden dryness in his mouth. She looked as though she had been poured into it and the silky material moulded her voluptuous figure. He stared at the creamy upper slopes of her breasts and felt a fierce throb of arousal in his groin that made him catch his breath. Utterly disconcerted, he was conscious of heat flaring along his cheekbones. He was not usually lost for words, but he did not know what to say and the casual greeting he had been about to make died on his lips.

Only once before in his life had he been so overwhelmed by a woman, and the memory caused his jaw to tighten. He did not want to feel this powerful attraction to Rebekah. He had asked her to accompany him tonight on a whim, thinking that it would be nice to give her a treat by taking her to the theatre in thanks for her hard work at the christening. He had been intrigued by the idea of her wearing an evening gown, but he had not expected her to turn into a gorgeous sex siren who made his heart race and had a disturbing effect on another pertinent area of his anatomy.

Dante's silence stretched Rebekah's nerves until she blurted out, 'If the dress is not suitable then I won't come with you tonight. I...I don't have anything else to wear.' She felt crushed by his reaction—or rather lack of it—to the dress. And that made her feel angry with herself because deep down she admitted that she had wanted to impress him.

'The dress is fine. You look charming.' Dante forced himself to speak. But as soon as the words were out and he saw the little flash of disappointment on her face he cursed himself that his tone had been unnecessarily brusque. He walked over to her, smiling with the careless charm that came so easily to him, but the delicate rose scent of her perfume filled his senses and it took all his willpower to resist the urge to run his fingers through her long satiny hair.

Flicking back the cuff of his jacket to check his watch gave him something to do with his hands. 'We should go,' he murmured. 'The traffic is usually hellish along Shaftesbury Avenue.'

With a nod of her head she spun round and preceded him out of the sitting room. Dante could not prevent his eyes from following the gentle sway of her bottom beneath its covering of shimmering silk, and as they walked down the hall to the front door he glanced towards the stairs and almost gave in to the fierce urge to sweep her into his arms and carry her up to his bedroom. He had been looking forward to the evening, but now he felt tense and frustrated and not in the mood to act the role of urbane playboy that was the façade he presented to the world.

CHAPTER THREE

THE show was spectacular—an extravaganza of music, dancing and amazing costumes that earned the cast and director a standing ovation when the curtain fell. Rebekah had enjoyed every moment of it, especially as she'd had an excellent view of the stage from the private box she had shared with Dante.

In the car on the way to the theatre she had sternly told herself to stop being stupid about his lukewarm reaction to seeing her dressed up. He quite clearly wasn't interested in her, and the sooner she accepted that fact the better. Following her silent pep talk she had been determined to make the most of the evening. She had never been to a top London show and she knew her grandmother would want to hear all the details.

And so when she had taken her seat next to Dante at the theatre she had willed herself to ignore the fierce tug on her senses as she breathed in the spicy tang of his aftershave. In the twenty minutes before the lights dimmed she studied the programme with him and peered over the balcony to spot the celebrities in the audience, many of whom Dante knew personally and a few he had represented in their divorce petitions.

'I hear the game show host Mike Channing has recently married for the third time,' he told her, directing her gaze to a man with an alarming orange tan. 'Against my advice, he didn't bother with a pre-nup. That's going to be expensive when his new wife decides to become the next ex-Mrs Channing.'

Rebekah shook her head. 'I feel sorry for you that you are so cynical.'

'I prefer realistic,' he replied with an amused smile. 'And you don't need to feel sorry for me. I'd rather be a cynic than a sucker. It's a fact of life that some women make a career out of divorcing rich husbands.'

There had been an edge of bitterness in Dante's voice that had puzzled her, Rebekah recalled later, when they were at the after-show party. Why would a self-confessed serial playboy have such a scathing view about marriage?

Perhaps he had been badly affected by his parents' divorce when he had been a child, she mused. From across the room she watched him chatting to an attractive blonde in a skimpy gold dress and thought wryly that his determination to avoid commitment did not stop women flocking to him. But, in a room packed with A-list celebrities and London's social elite, his stunning looks and virile sex appeal made all other men fade in comparison.

From the moment she had seen him dressed in a tuxedo she had been blown away by his sexy charm and had longed to trace his chiselled jaw and run her fingers through the lock of dark hair that fell across his brow. Her infatuation with him was becoming a serious threat to her peace of mind and her common sense told her that the only way to end her fascination with him would be to look for another job.

At that moment he glanced over at her and she hastily

turned her head, hoping he had not been aware of her staring at him. A waiter paused in front of her to offer her a drink. She briefly contemplated risking one glass of champagne, but she knew it would give her a headache and instead she chose the fruit punch that she had already discovered was deliciously refreshing, with a zing to it that she thought might be sherbet.

'Rebekah.' Dante appeared at her side. He gave her an intent look. 'Are you enjoying yourself? I noticed you've been chatting to a few people.'

'I'm having a great time,' she assured him brightly. 'Please don't feel you have to stay with me all evening. You're highly in demand,' she added drily, aware, as she was sure he must be, of the numerous predatory female glances directed his way.

'Someone would like to meet you,' he explained. He turned to the lean-faced, silver-haired man who had just joined them. 'This is Gaspard Clavier.'

'Yes…I know,' Rebekah said faintly. She knew she was gaping, but she could not help it. The world-famous French chef was an iconic figure and her personal hero. She couldn't believe he had asked to be introduced to her but, to her astonishment, the Frenchman lifted her hand to his lips with a Gallic flourish.

'So this is the Rebekah Evans I have heard so much about.'

'Have you?' she said blankly.

'Certainly. I believe you prepared the wedding lunch for Earl Lansford's daughter?'

'Yes.' Rebekah remembered cooking the four-course lunch for three hundred guests at the Earl's manor house in Hampstead when she had worked for the catering company. It had been manic in the kitchen but, to her

relief, everything had gone to plan and she had been
proud of the menu she had created.

'Dante!'

At the sound of his name Dante looked round and
waved to someone across the room. 'I'll leave you and
Gaspard to chat,' he murmured to Rebekah. 'Please excuse me.'

She watched him walk over to a statuesque blonde
and stifled a sigh, before resuming her conversation
with Gaspard Clavier.

'I was a guest at the wedding,' Gaspard told her. 'The
food was a triumph. Every dish was divine. You can
really cook, *ma chérie*, and that is not something I say
lightly. You understand flavours, and your passion for
food is evident in the dishes you create.'

Rebekah's cheeks flooded with colour at the Frenchman's
fulsome praise. Earning Gaspard Clavier's approval was
the highest accolade she could have dreamed of.

'Thank you,' she said shyly.

'You have heard, perhaps, of my restaurant, La Petite
Maison, in Knightsbridge?'

'Oh, yes, I visited it once when I first began my training and I was inspired by your food, Monsieur Clavier.
It confirmed for me that I definitely wanted a career
as a chef.'

'After tasting your wonderful food at Olivia Lansford's
wedding, I decided that I would like you to work for me.'

For a few seconds Rebekah was speechless. 'Cook
at your restaurant, you mean?'

'*Oui*. Not at La Petite Maison, but at my new restaurant that I hope to open soon in St Lucia.'

Once again Rebekah was lost for words. 'St Lucia

is in the Caribbean,' she said slowly, and then blushed when she realised she had spoken out loud.

Gaspard looked amused. 'It is indeed. My restaurant is on the beach. Imagine miles of white sand, turquoise sea and palm trees. How would you like to work in paradise, Rebekah?'

'I don't know…I mean, it sounds wonderful.' She pressed her hands to her hot face. 'It's just a shock. And I already have a job here in England.'

The Frenchman shrugged as he pulled a business card from his pocket. 'The new restaurant will not be ready to open for a few months, so you do not need to make an immediate decision. Think about it and, if you are interested, phone me and we will discuss it further.'

'Yes…yes, I will.'

'Bon.' Gaspard smiled. 'And now perhaps I can persuade you to dance with me?'

Later, Dante fought his way through the crowd on his way to the bar, wondering where Rebekah had disappeared to. He had glimpsed her periodically during the evening, dancing with Gaspard Clavier and then with a couple of other men. Now, as he scanned the ballroom, he caught sight of her partnering a handsome young actor from one of the popular TV soaps. The guy was a notorious womaniser and, from the way he was laughing and *flirting* with Rebekah, it seemed that he had decided to make her his next conquest.

But perhaps Rebekah had decided to seduce the pretty-boy actor? Dante's mouth tightened. He had been concerned at the beginning of the party that she might feel shy when she did not know any of the other guests. But he need not have worried. It was not only her appearance that was transformed tonight. His quiet, reserved chef had turned into a confident and self-assured woman who was attracting the attention of every red-blooded male in the room.

He must have been mad to have brought her out in that dress, he thought grimly, as he changed course and headed towards the dance floor. He should have followed his first instinct and taken her to bed.

Rebekah was having the time of her life. Gaspard Clavier's praise of her cooking skills had given her self-confidence a huge boost, and she was seriously considering his job offer. If she moved to the Caribbean, surely she would forget about Dante.

Although *he* had not been impressed with her dress, she had discovered that plenty of other men were and she'd had no shortage of dance partners. Mind you, her current partner was like an octopus, she thought, as she firmly moved the hand that was sliding up to her breasts back to her waist.

'Come on, baby, let's get out of here.' Jonny Vance, who apparently was a famous actor, although Rebekah did not recognize him, stopped dancing and tugged her against him. 'My car's parked outside.'

'No!' she muttered, trying to pull away from him. 'Will you please let go of me?'

'I'd do as the lady says if I were you,' a familiar voice said dangerously. Before Rebekah realised what was happening, she was jerked away from Jonny and clamped against a broad, rock-solid chest.

Her heart lurched as Dante's arm imprisoned her and she was so surprised by his sudden appearance that her feet stumbled as he spun her round in time with the music. 'Thanks for rescuing me,' she said shakily. 'He was getting a bit over-friendly.'

'What did you expect?' Dante gave her a derisive look and Rebekah saw that he was furious. 'You were flirting with him and leading him on. Of course he thought he'd got it made with you.'

I was not leading him on.' Outraged by the accusation, she glared at him, stumbled again and would have tripped on her long skirt if it hadn't been for the fact that her body was practically welded to Dante's. 'I was just dancing with him and being friendly.'

Dante laughed. 'Do you really have no idea of the effect you were having on him and on every man here tonight?'

Rebekah was fighting the temptation to sink against Dante and enjoy the heady delight of being in his arms. She had often imagined him holding her close like this, but the reality of feeling his thighs pressed hard against her soft flesh evoked a molten heat in her pelvis.

'What do you mean?' she muttered, discovering as she lifted her head to meet his gaze that his mouth was mere inches from hers. She wished he would kiss her. She ached to feel his warm, sensual lips on hers. Unconsciously, her tongue darted out to moisten her lower lip.

'I mean that Vance, and probably every other male in this room, has been fantasising about removing your dress to reveal your delectable voluptuous, naked body,' he said harshly.

She gaped at him. 'Of course no one has been thinking that. You make me sound like a…a siren who men find irresistible—but that's just ridiculous.'

'Why is it?' Dante's voice deepened, no longer coldly angry, but rough with a sensuality that sent a quiver through Rebekah. 'I find you utterly irresistible, *mia bella*.'

Clearly he was having a joke at her expense, she thought bitterly. 'Of course you do,' she said sarcastically. 'That's why you barely spared me a glance before we left the house. If you had really thought me irresistible you would have...'

'Been lost for words,' he said softly. 'I was completely blown away when you walked into the sitting room. You look so beautiful in your dress. I had no idea that you concealed such delightful curves beneath the shapeless clothes you usually wear. And your hair—' he lifted a hand from her waist and threaded it through the rippling waves that streamed down her back '—it feels like silk.'

Dante could not control the hunger that clawed in his gut. His arousal strained uncomfortably against his trouser zip, necessitating him to shift his position. He heard Rebekah draw a sharp breath when his hardened shaft nudged her thigh.

'Don't do that!' she gasped, shocked by the realisation that he wasn't joking and unbelievably he really did seem to find her attractive.

'There's not a lot I can do to prevent it,' he said sardonically. 'Sexual desire sometimes manifests itself at the most inconvenient moments.'

'But...you don't desire me.'

'I think the evidence is pretty conclusive, don't you, *cara*?' He looked down at her, his eyes glittering when he saw her confused expression. 'Why shouldn't I desire you? You are an incredibly desirable woman.'

Dear heaven, was Dante flirting with her? Rebekah swallowed and tried to control the frantic excitement that spiralled through her.

'You shouldn't say things like that,' she muttered. 'I work for you, and it's not appropriate for you to make suggestive remarks.'

His husky laugh made the tiny hairs on her body stand on end and beneath her ribs she could feel the heavy thud of her heart.

'Are you trying to tell me you don't desire me, Rebekah?'

Her head spun. The situation felt unreal—being held in Dante's arms, their bodies pressed intimately close as they danced and his eyes gleaming with sensual heat that sent a tremor through her.

Somehow she clung on to her sanity. 'Of course I don't,' she said stiffly.

'Be honest with me.' He bent his head close to hers so that his words whispered in her ear. 'I've seen the hungry little looks you give me.'

Mortification scalded her and she felt her cheeks burn. She cringed at the knowledge that he had recognized she was attracted to him. She had felt confident that she had hidden her feelings for him. But he had known, and maybe he had been amused that his frumpy cook had fallen for him.

She did not know what to say and, to her utter relief, the music track came to an end.

'Excuse me,' she said jerkily as she pulled out of Dante's arms and almost ran across the ballroom in a bid to escape him. A waiter stopped to offer her a drink from the tray he was carrying. She took another glass of fruit punch before she stepped through the French windows that had been left ajar and walked across the terrace to rest her elbows on the stone balustrade. The night air felt cool on her hot face but her heart was still beating painfully hard. When she allowed her mind to rerun her conversation with Dante she wanted to die of embarrassment.

She could not continue to work for him now. It would be too awkward. It was bad enough that she had spent the past two months mooning over him like a lovesick teenager, but the realisation that he had known about her infatuation was so humiliating. First thing tomorrow she would hand him her resignation, she decided. And then she would phone Gaspard Clavier and discuss the possibility of working at his new restaurant in St Lucia.

Her mind was whirling as she took a long sip of her drink. Behind her, she heard the sound of footsteps striding across the terrace, and she stiffened.

'I'd go easy on the punch, if I were you. I overheard a waiter telling a guest that one of the ingredients is limoncello,' Dante murmured.

That explained why her head had started to spin when she'd come outside into the fresh air, Rebekah thought ruefully. The Italian lemon liqueur had a high alcoholic content, but she hadn't noticed it mixed into the fruit punch.

'Well, as this is my fourth glass, I'm probably tipsy and you can have a good laugh when I make a fool of myself.'

The moonlight threw his chiselled features into sharp relief and accentuated the sensual curve of his mouth. Rebekah hated herself for the physical pang of longing that made her tremble. She tore her gaze from him. 'Although, actually, I don't need alcohol to make me act stupidly,' she said miserably.

Dante frowned when he saw the faint quiver of her lower lip. 'What's the matter?' he demanded, catching hold of her shoulder to prevent her from walking away from him. 'Are you angry because I admitted I find you attractive?'

It was not what Rebekah had expected him to say. She had been certain he would taunt her about her awareness of him.

'I'm concerned it will make it difficult for me to carry on working for you,' she mumbled.

'I'm not a savage brute at the mercy of my hormones,' he said drily. 'I'm capable of controlling my libido.' He lifted his hand and brushed her hair back from her cheek, his eyes narrowing speculatively on her flushed face. 'Although it would help if you stopped looking at me like you're doing at the moment.'

Was it the sudden sensual roughness of his tone that brought Rebekah's skin out in goose-bumps or the hard glitter in his eyes that caused the ache inside her to intensify until it consumed her?

She bit her lip. 'How am I looking at you?' she whispered, and did not recognize the husky voice as her own.

'Like you want me to kiss you.' Dante gave a low laugh when she did not deny it. He stared into her incredible violet eyes, watched them darken as her pupils dilated and read the invitation she could not hide. But he also glimpsed a faint wariness that made him hesitate.

He recognized there had been an undercurrent of sexual awareness between them for weeks, long before she had taken his breath away by wearing an evening gown that revealed her hourglass figure. But he had determinedly ignored his attraction to her—partly because he preferred not to get involved with a member of his staff, but also because he had sensed a vulnerability in her that had made her off-limits. Yesterday, at the christening party, he had glimpsed an expression in her eyes that he could not forget. He suspected that she'd had her heart broken by the guy in Wales, but if she hoped he could fill an emotional void inside her she would be disappointed. Bitter experience had taught him that life was a lot simpler without emotions to screw it up.

But, as he'd watched her dancing tonight and noticed the attention she had received from other men, he had felt an unexpected surge of possessiveness that had prompted him to stride onto the dance floor and pull her into his arms. She had been on his mind all day and she had even disturbed his concentration while he had been in court representing a client. Now, as his gaze lingered on her soft pink lips, he could not control the rampant desire that surged through his veins.

She must be drunk, Rebekah thought wildly, because Dante could not be looking at her with raw sexual hunger blazing in his eyes, as if he wanted to ravish her mouth with his own. Dear heaven, how she longed to be ravished. But she must be sensible. She was always sensible.

'Of course I don't want you to kiss me… Oh!' Her tremulous denial faded away as he lowered his head and slanted his mouth over hers.

His lips were firm and demanding, ruthlessly crushing her faint resistance with a mastery that made her tremble. He traced the shape of her mouth with his tongue before teasing her lips apart to dip between them, taking the kiss to another level that made her head spin and her body tremble.

It was the most erotic experience of Rebekah's life and far exceeded the fantasies she'd had of being kissed by him. She had no thought of denying him. How could she when she was utterly captivated by the smouldering sensuality of his kiss? Instead, she responded to him helplessly, parting her lips so that he could plunder their sweetness. She heard him groan and mutter something in Italian beneath his breath. He slid his hand down to the base of her spine and pulled her hard against him, and the feel of his rock-solid arousal nudging her pelvis sent molten heat flooding through her veins.

Swept away by the sheer intensity of feelings Dante was arousing in her, she lifted her hands to his shoulders and clung to him, wishing that the magic would never end. But at last he eased the pressure of his mouth until it was a gossamer-light caress before he broke the kiss.

Rebekah stepped back from Dante and swayed unsteadily. He frowned, remembering she had been unaware that the fruit punch she'd been drinking all evening contained alcohol. He did not believe she was drunk, and he was convinced she had known what she was doing when she had responded so ardently to him. But once again he was struck by her vulnerability and he was not comfortable with the idea that he might have taken advantage of her while she was off her guard.

'I need to take you home,' he said roughly.

The sound of his voice should have brought Rebekah to her senses but she seemed to be in the grip of a wild madness that drove all sensible thoughts from her head. The fierce gleam in Dante's eyes told her that the kiss they had just shared had not assuaged his desire. He wanted her, and the knowledge was empowering, liberating. For the first time since Gareth's devastating betrayal she felt like an attractive woman instead of the grey shadow she had become.

Perhaps the full moon suspended like a huge silver

disc above them really did have mystical properties. All she knew was that tonight she wanted to take back charge of her life. For weeks she had fantasised about making love with her gorgeous, sexy boss. Why not, for one night, turn the fantasy into reality?

'When we get home, do you plan to kiss me again?' she whispered.

The moment the words were out she was shocked that she had been so bold. Dante seemed equally surprised and his gravelly voice was thick with sexual tension.

'Do you want me to?'

She stared at his hard-boned, beautiful face and her heart thundered.

'Yes.'

Dante caught his breath as desire jack-knifed through him at Rebekah's unguarded reply. He had told himself he must end this madness, but his chef, who he had thought of as prim and a little prudish, was excitingly unpredictable. She knew as well as he did that if he kissed her again the fire smouldering between them would ignite.

But, although Dante could not deny that he had earned his playboy reputation, he had a strict moral code of conduct. He always made it clear to the women he dated that sex was all he wanted, and he never slept with a woman if she did not accept his rules.

Did Rebekah even know the rules? he wondered. Before they went any further he needed to be certain she knew he would never want a long-term relationship.

'You are full of surprises tonight, *piccola*,' he murmured. 'It makes me wonder how much limoncello was in the fruit punch.'

Rebekah bit her lip. Perhaps Dante was trying to be

gentlemanly by suggesting that she was drunk and therefore not in full control of herself. His tone had been faintly condescending when he had called her *piccola*, which she knew meant 'little one' in Italian. But she was not an innocent girl. She was a mature woman who knew her own mind, and it was about time he understood that fact.

She stepped closer to him and tilted her head to meet his glittering gaze. 'I don't think the punch contained much alcohol. I'm perfectly aware of what I'm saying… and doing,' she assured him huskily, and leaned forwards to press her mouth against his.

Her heart jolted when she felt his body's immediate response. He allowed her to lead the kiss for a couple of seconds before he groaned and wrapped his arms around her, exerting his dominance by plundering her mouth with savage passion that left them both breathless.

'In that case, let's go home, *mia bella*,' he said tautly, and took his phone from his jacket to call his driver.

CHAPTER FOUR

THE Bentley was waiting outside for them with the chauffeur holding the door open. Dante slid onto the back seat and held out his hand to assist Rebekah. No doubt his sophisticated mistresses were experts at climbing elegantly into cars, she thought ruefully, but her high heels somehow got tangled in her long skirt so that she tripped and landed practically in his lap.

'Steady,' he said with a soft laugh, as though he thought she was so eager to be in his arms that she'd deliberately thrown herself on top of him.

Flushing hotly, she tried to edge away, but he pulled her against him and claimed her mouth in a sensual kiss that left her breathless and trembling when he finally lifted his head. She felt a strange sense of unreality. Dante had dominated her thoughts from the day she had met him, and she could hardly believe she was in his arms and he was trailing a line of kisses down her neck to capture the pulse beating erratically at its base.

She had imagined moments like this so often, and had indulged in erotic daydreams that Dante was running his hands over her body. But now she discovered that the reality was so much better than any daydream. As the car threaded through the busy London streets it felt as though they were cocooned in their own private world. Outside was noise and bright neon lights. But inside the car the sexually charged silence was only broken by her soft gasp when he lowered his head to her breasts.

'You have driven me mad all night,' he growled in a gravelly voice that sent a little shiver of anticipation through her. 'You were the most beautiful woman in the room tonight and every man had his eyes on you.'

Rebekah knew that was untrue and she was about to tell him that he did not need to win her over with false flattery, but she was distracted when he slid the strap of her dress over her shoulder and drew the fragile silk down until he had bared her breast. His harsh groan of feral hunger evoked a flood of heat in her pelvis. With a little spurt of shock, she realised he wasn't playing a game or teasing her. His desire for her was real and urgent, and the hard glitter in his eyes warned her that he was serious about his intention to make love to her.

Her heart leapt into her throat. She knew the driver could not see them through the privacy screen but she felt exposed when she glanced down and saw her pale breast and the darker skin of her nipple. She caught her breath when Dante cupped the soft mound of flesh in his palm and lightly flicked his thumb pad over her nipple until it felt hot and tight and she longed for him to caress her with his mouth. Never before had she felt such an intensity of need, and she could not restrain a choked cry of disappointment when he drew her dress back into place.

'We're home,' Dante told her softly. He found her eagerness such a turn-on. She looked unbelievably sexy with her long silky brown hair tumbling over her shoulders and her lips slightly parted and moistly inviting.

The ache in his groin was building to a fierce throb of sexual need that clamoured to be assuaged. If they did not get out of the car right now he was in danger of making a fool of himself, he thought derisively.

As Rebekah followed Dante up the front steps of the house her heart thudded painfully beneath her ribs. The cool night air on her heated skin had restored a little of her common sense and made her question what she was doing. She had never had a one-night stand in her life, and she had only ever slept with Gareth. Didn't that just sum up her life, she thought wryly. She was twenty-eight and had been single for two years, but she could write about her sexual experiences on the back of a postage stamp.

What if Dante found her inexperience a disappointment? Or what if he compared her curvy hips and unfashionably big breasts with the super-slim supermodels that she knew were his usual choice of women?

Maybe it would be better to stop this now, before she faced the humiliating possibility of being rejected by him. Maybe it would be safer to keep her fantasies intact and tell him she had changed her mind.

He opened the door and stood back to allow her to precede him into the hall. In front of her the stairs led to the second floor and his bedroom. She wondered how many other women had shared his bed, and she felt another pang of uncertainty.

Through an open door she could see the sitting room lamps had been activated by the timer so that the room was bathed in soft gold light. She spun round to face him, and thought with a touch of despair that he had never looked more gorgeous than he did right now. His white shirt was made of such fine silk that she could see the shadow of his dark chest hairs, and when she lowered her gaze the visible evidence of his arousal beneath his trousers evoked a fierce coiling sensation in the pit of her stomach.

She licked her dry lips. 'Dante...I...'

'Come here, *mia bellezza*,' he said roughly.

The husky Italian words shattered her fragile defences. She knew that although he had been educated in England, Italian was his first language and he often reverted to it when he was angry. But it was not anger that lent his gaze a silvery gleam. Desire blazed in his eyes. He was looking at her in a way that made her knees feel weak, and when he pulled her into his arms she clung to him and tilted her head for him to capture her mouth in a kiss that made her forget all her doubts.

She had never been kissed like this; never experienced such magic as Dante was creating as he slanted his mouth over hers and took without mercy—demanding, hungry kisses that were utterly irresistible.

She fell back against the wall and wrapped her arms around his neck as he pressed himself against her so that she was conscious of every muscle and sinew of his hard body. She felt the solid ridge of his erection nudge between her thighs, and the realisation that he was fiercely aroused increased her excitement. She might not be tall, skinny and blonde, but Dante did not seem to mind as he roamed his hands over her, exploring her contours with unashamed delight. He groaned his approval when he clasped the rounded cheeks of her bottom.

'*Dio*, you are driving me insane. I need you now, *cara*. I can't wait.'

Dante could not remember the last time he had felt so out of control. He lifted his mouth from Rebekah's and dragged oxygen into his lungs. How had he not realised how beautiful she was? he wondered as he stared at her rose-flushed face and her violet eyes fringed by long dark lashes. Her lips were reddened and slightly parted, inviting him to kiss her again and, when he did, she responded to him with such unrestrained eagerness that his last vestige of restraint shattered.

His bedroom was too far away. Without lifting his mouth from hers, he steered her into the sitting room. He slid his hand beneath her long hair and found her zip. Deftly he ran it down her spine and peeled her dress over her breasts and hips so that it slithered to the floor. The big dark pink discs of her nipples contrasted with the creamy skin of her breasts and he could not resist touching them, stroking them until they hardened into tight buds.

'Rebekah, you have a fantastic body. You are perfection, *mia bella*.'

His words, spoken in that hoarse, sexy growl, allayed the self-doubt that had swamped Rebekah when Dante had undressed her. She had felt painfully exposed when he had studied her body in the light from the table lamp that was not nearly as dim as she would have liked. It felt shockingly decadent to be practically naked in the sitting room. She had only ever made love with Gareth in his bedroom at his farm, always in the dark, and they'd had to be careful not to make any noise because his mother's bedroom was next door.

She had never felt very confident about her body. Her breasts were too voluptuous, her hips too curvy and her bottom was too big. But Dante had said she was perfection, and the hot, hungry gleam in his eyes as he caressed her told her that he meant it.

'It doesn't seem fair that you're dressed and I'm not,' she murmured. Her voice emerged as a husky whisper because her heart was pounding so hard that she couldn't breathe properly.

He gave her a wicked smile. 'Strip me, then,' he said, spreading his arms wide so that she had free access to his body. 'I'm all yours, Rebekah.'

She felt a little pang inside, knowing that he would never be hers. It would take a very special woman to persuade Dante to give up his playboy lifestyle, and perhaps no woman ever would. She knew that all he wanted from her was sex, and that was all she wanted too, she reminded herself. Dante made her feel like an attractive, sexy woman and she needed this one night with him to restore her faith in her feminine allure.

But, although she was sure of her decision, her hands shook as she tugged his shirt from the waistband of his trousers and started to undo the buttons. When she reached the top one, she slid the shirt over his shoulders and stared at his broad chest and his satiny olive skin covered in whirls of silky black hairs. He had said her body was perfection, but the hard ridges of his pectoral and abdominal muscles could have been sculpted by an artist.

Her eyes followed the mass of dark hairs lower to where they arrowed beneath his waistband. He had invited her to strip him, but did she have the nerve to slide his zip down and touch the prominent bulge that was straining against his trousers?

'Do you have any idea how much you're turning me on just by looking at me?' Dante demanded raggedly. 'For pity's sake, *cara*, touch me.'

Rebekah obeyed him, hesitantly at first, as she

skimmed her fingertips over his chest, but growing bolder as she explored each ridge of muscle with a dedication that made him groan. It was intoxicating to roam her hands freely over his naked torso. His skin was warm and golden, and he smelled of soap and sandalwood cologne and another subtly masculine scent that tantalised her senses. She had never been as intensely aware of the beauty of the male form and, acting purely on instinct, she pressed her lips to his chest, over the place where she could feel the hard thud of his heart.

He growled something in Italian as he reached for his fly and yanked it open. 'Let me help you,' he muttered, as he pulled off the rest of his clothes.

Rebekah's heart lurched as her eyes were drawn to his erection. He was indescribably beautiful, and *huge*. She was suddenly conscious that it was a long time since she had done this. Her uncertainty must have shown in her eyes, because he said harshly, 'If you've changed your mind, you have twenty seconds to get out of the room before I lose what's left of my self-control.'

She could not restrain a little shiver of feminine triumph that he was in danger of losing his control because of her. Desire throbbed hot and insistent between her legs. The notion that soon she would take his swollen length inside her made her tremble with excitement. 'I haven't…' she began, but she had no chance to request that they take things slowly because he pulled her into his arms and she was blown away by the feel of his naked body pressed hard up against hers.

'Thank God for that,' Dante muttered as he brought his mouth down on hers. Heat surged through him when she parted her lips beneath his and kissed him back with passion and an evocative sweetness that made his gut clench. He loved the softness of her body, the way her skin felt like silk beneath his fingertips and the delicate rose scent of her perfume when he pressed his mouth to the sensitive place behind her ear. Even more of a turn-on were the little moans she made when he stroked her breasts and flicked his thumbs over her nipples.

He felt as if he were going to explode. The likelihood of him making love to Rebekah with any degree of finesse was zero, he acknowledged derisively. She was too much of a temptation. This first time was going to be hard and fast and he would enjoy taking the slow route later. Right now, all he could think of was burying himself deep inside her. The sofa provided the closest flat surface and would be more comfortable than the floor. He backed her towards it and tumbled her down onto the velvet cushions.

Rebekah could not restrain a low cry when Dante bent his head to her breast and closed his mouth around her nipple. Exquisite sensation arrowed down to her pelvis and she twisted beneath him as he licked and sucked the taut peak until the pleasure was almost unbearable, before he transferred his attention to her other breast.

She had known he would be a skilled lover. No doubt his expertise had been honed by experience. The thought evoked a sharp little pain inside her, but she blanked it out. She did not want to be reminded of his playboy reputation. The way he was kissing and caressing her and murmuring soft words in a mixture of English and Italian made her feel that she really was as gorgeous and sexy as he was telling her. As if she was the only woman he would ever want.

He trailed his hand over her stomach, continued lower and hooked his fingers in her knickers.

'You are exquisite,' he murmured as he removed the fragile wisp of lace and stared at her naked body.

'Dante…?' She felt suddenly vulnerable and stupidly nervous. She wasn't a virgin, of course, but she was not one of the sophisticated and no doubt sexually experienced women he was used to. She was afraid he would be disappointed with her. It would be crushingly embarrassing if he found her relative inexperience a turn-off.

'What's wrong?' he murmured when he sensed her tension. 'Is there something you want me to do? Tell me how I can please you.'

Oh, Lord, she did not have a list of requirements. She stared at him and thought how achingly handsome he was. With a shaking hand she traced the hard line of his jaw and caught her breath when he captured her fingers and pressed his lips to them. 'Just…kiss me again,' she whispered.

'With pleasure.' His smile was unexpectedly gentle, as if he sensed she needed reassurance. He lowered his head and claimed her mouth in a deep, drugging kiss that banished her last lingering doubts.

'I want to make this good for you, *cara*,' he said softly as he slipped his hand between her thighs and gently parted her to slide a finger into the hot silken heart of her femininity.

Rebekah gasped and instinctively arched her hips. Molten heat flooded through her as he elicited an intimate caress that made her sensitive flesh quicken with excited desire. The dragging sensation in her pelvis became an urgent throb of need to feel more, to have him fill her with his steel-hard shaft that was now nudging against her opening.

Remembering how earlier he had asked her to touch

him, she tentatively closed her fingers around his erection and began to stroke the hard length. She heard his swiftly indrawn breath and felt a little thrill of delight that she was able to arouse him as he had aroused her. She grew bolder and more inventive in the way she caressed him, but after a few moments he groaned and tugged her hand away.

As Dante lowered himself onto her, Rebekah caught her breath, feeling her muscles stretch around him as he pushed deeper and deeper until he filled her. She had forgotten how beautiful lovemaking was, she thought dazedly. But she could not remember that she had ever felt this sense of completeness with Gareth.

Dante began to move and withdrew almost completely, laughed softly when she protested, and repeated the process a little faster, thrusting deep and hard so that she gave a choked cry of pleasure and begged him not to stop.

But her husky plea had the opposite effect. He stilled and, with a savage imprecation, began to withdraw again.

Disbelief turned to panic when she realised he was actually going to stop making love to her. Was he turned off by her curvaceous body after all? She felt sick with humiliation and disappointment.

Her voice shook. 'What's wrong?'

'I forgot to use a condom,' he informed her tersely. Inwardly, Dante cursed himself. He always without fail used protection. It was another of his golden rules—never get emotionally involved, and never ever risk an unwanted pregnancy. He could not believe he had been so irresponsible. What the hell was he doing having unprotected sex with Rebekah? Just because he had been blown away by her lush, curvaceous beauty was no excuse.

But even now his body was battling with his common sense. The lure of Rebekah's velvet softness made him want to keep thrusting hard and fast into her until he achieved the release he craved.

'I'm on the Pill.'

Her words were like a siren's song, and Dante could not control his body's reaction. Damn it, he could not remember ever being at the mercy of his hormones the way he was with Rebekah. He did not like the effect she had on him, but his willpower seemed to have taken a hike and he could not prevent himself from pressing forwards and sinking deeper into her sensual embrace.

'You're sure?' Stupid question, he thought grimly. She was hardly likely to admit she was lying. He either believed her or he didn't—his choice. With good reason he had vowed never to trust a woman again, but as he stared into her eyes he felt certain she was telling the truth. He relaxed, and at the same time his muscles tightened in anticipation. 'I want to reassure you that I've always used protection for health reasons as much as to prevent conception,' he told her.

Oh, God. Why did he have to make it sound so clinical? Rebekah knew she was blushing and felt angry for being so stupid. Dante was being sensible, and she should be glad that he was so realistic. When he had first started to withdraw from her the sense of disappointment had been unbearable and she had been desperate for him to continue making love to her. She was still desperate, she acknowledged, her breath quickening when she felt him stir within her. It felt as though all her nerve-endings were taut with anticipation to experience the sexual release she sensed he would give her.

'I'm...healthy too,' she mumbled. 'I've only ever had one other partner, and...and that was a while ago.'

Did she mean that the only other guy she had slept with, apart from *him*, was the ex-boyfriend she had mentioned? Or had she had an affair after she'd broken up with the Welsh guy? Why was he curious? Dante wondered impatiently. All he cared about was that with the contraception issue dealt with, there was no reason not to continue giving in to the passion between them.

He rested his weight on his elbows and circled his hips against hers, giving her a lazy smile when she drew a swift breath.

'So, there's nothing to prevent me doing this?' he murmured as he thrust forwards, drew back a little and thrust again with deep measured strokes that sent ripples of pleasure through him—and, from her wide-eyed expression, her too.

'Yes...I mean...no, *oh*...' Rebekah dug her nails into Dante's shoulders and writhed helplessly beneath him as he drove into her again and again. 'Don't stop,' she pleaded, uncaring that she sounded desperate. Each devastating thrust felt like the sweetest torture that built her excitement to an unbearable level. He was a magician, a sorcerer, who was creating mind-blowing magic that made her body tremble. She had never known sex could be like this, so intense and all-consuming that she felt as though if she died now it would be the sweetest death. She understood now why the French referred to sex as *la petite mort*—the little death.

And then she stopped thinking, as each of her senses focused on reaching the climax that she knew from experience often remained frustratingly out of reach. Dante had increased his pace and she knew from the harsh sound of his breathing that he was close to the edge.

'Please wait,' she muttered, and then tensed as she realised with agonising embarrassment that she had spoken her thoughts out loud.

Dante gave a soft laugh, but the unexpectedly gentle expression in his eyes reassured her that he was not laughing at her. 'Of course I will wait for you, *cara*. Do you think I would take my pleasure without first ensuring yours?' Was that the kind of selfish behaviour she was used to with her ex-boyfriend? he wondered. He had heard the faint desperation in her voice and he was determined to make this the best sexual experience she had ever had.

'Let me see if I can help,' he murmured as he bent his head and flicked his tongue across her nipple, teasing it and tormenting it until she whimpered and he transferred his mouth to its twin.

The sensation of Dante sucking hard on each of her nipples in turn while he continued to thrust powerfully into her drove Rebekah wild. She arched her hips and gave a little sob when he slipped his hand between their joined bodies and found her most sensitive spot. The pleasure he induced when he caressed her there was so intense that she cried out. And suddenly she was at the edge of the precipice, suspended for a few breathless seconds before she tumbled into ecstasy. The explosive orgasm was unlike anything she had ever experienced. It blew her mind and sent convulsive shudders of pleasure through her so that she threw her head back against the armrest of the sofa and could not hold back her husky cries of amazement.

It was too much for Dante. Watching Rebekah come apart so spectacularly was highly erotic. He felt the pressure build inside him until it was intolerable and, with a final thrust, he reached the exquisite moment of release and gave a savage groan.

For a long time afterwards they lay with their bodies still joined, Dante with his head pillowed on her breasts while he dragged oxygen into his lungs. That had been good, he mused. He hadn't had such intensely satisfying sex for a long while. Maybe never that good, a little voice inside his head pointed out. One thing he was certain of was that once was not going to be enough. His body was already stirring as he contemplated making love to Rebekah again. But, for now, curiously he was in no rush to move and break the languorous aftermath of physical pleasure that had left him feeling deeply relaxed.

Rebekah's pounding heart gradually resumed its normal rhythm. A sweet lassitude made her muscles feel heavy, but inside her head a voice was saying *wow!* A rueful smile curved her lips. So that was what she had been missing all these years. Her sex life with Gareth had never set the world alight. Making love with Dante had been a revelation. But there was a danger that it could become addictive, which was why she could not allow it to happen again. The pang her heart gave at the thought that this was a once-only event was a timely warning that it would be far too easy to fall for him.

She pushed against his shoulder, wondering what the protocol was now. Presumably they would spend the remainder of the night in their own rooms. Should she put her dress back on or, God forbid, saunter out of the sitting room naked? She might have enjoyed wild and abandoned sex with him, but the idea of parading her wobbly bits past him made her shudder.

Dante lifted his head and gave her a lazy smile that evoked a curious little ache inside her. 'Am I too heavy for you, *cara*?' He pressed his lips to her breast before lifting himself off her but, instead of getting up from the sofa as she had expected, he settled on his side next to her and pulled her close. 'That was amazing—*you* were amazing,' he murmured. His thick black eyelashes brushed his cheeks.

The steady rise and fall of his chest told Rebekah he had fallen asleep. For a few minutes she gave in to temptation and snuggled up to him, loving the feel of his warm skin and the faint abrasion of dark hairs beneath her cheek. It would be so easy to pretend that they were proper lovers, to imagine that what they had just shared had been special and had meant something. She was obviously not cut out for casual sex, she thought ruefully. She was finding it hard to separate her emotions from the physical act of making love with Dante, but she did not kid herself that he would suffer the same problem.

Moving carefully so that she did not disturb him, she propped herself on her elbow and studied him. His hard-boned face was all angles and planes in the lamplight. But the lock of jet-black hair that had fallen across his brow softened his features and in sleep he lost a little of his arrogance and looked relaxed and so achingly beautiful that Rebekah longed to touch him and trace the sensual curve of his mouth. But if she woke him they would undoubtedly have sex again and her emotions would become even more involved.

It was best to walk away now. But it took all her willpower to extricate herself from his arms. He gave a little grunt of protest and she held her breath, but he did not stir as she gathered up her clothes and tiptoed from the room.

CHAPTER FIVE

Soft golden light filled Dante's vision when he opened his eyes. For a few seconds he was puzzled before he remembered where he was—not in his bed, but lying on a sofa in the sitting room. He sat up when he realised that Rebekah was no longer cuddled up against him. The table lamp had been switched off and daylight was filtering through the pale curtains. Glancing down, he discovered that she had draped a cashmere throw over him. He was oddly touched by the gesture of simple kindness. A caring nature was not an attribute he sought from his mistresses. But he acknowledged that Rebekah was very different to the type of women he usually had affairs with, and in the cold light of day that fact made him question whether he had been crazy to sleep with her.

He pulled on his trousers, did not bother to don his shirt, and headed out of the room to find her. Noises from the kitchen as he walked past alerted him to her whereabouts and as he pushed open the door, the aroma of freshly brewed coffee welcomed him.

'Good morning. Coffee's ready, and I'm just about to start breakfast. How would you like your eggs?'

Dante was taken aback when she spoke in the same bright, crisp manner that she always greeted him with in the mornings. But her tone was a little too breezy, and although she quickly turned her head away he noticed the pink stain on her cheeks. He was reminded of her flushed face last night as she had writhed beneath him, her head thrown back and her lips parted as she had clearly enjoyed a shattering orgasm. But this morning her heightened colour was the only resemblance to the woman from last night. Like Cinderella, she was back in the kitchen dressed, if not in rags, then in clothes that were so unflattering they should be sent to a charity shop immediately.

He skimmed his eyes over her loose black chef's trousers and voluminous polo shirt that disguised her shapely figure. Disconcerted that she was behaving as if nothing had happened between them last night, he murmured, 'I'm not hungry, *cara*. At least not for food,' he said huskily as he walked over to where she was standing next to the worktop and slid his arms around her waist. He had expected her to feel a little awkward with him, but to his surprise she stiffened and her back became as straight as a ramrod.

He pressed his lips to the base of her neck, exposed where her hair was tied up in its usual severe style on top of her head. 'You don't need to be shy with me. Last night was enjoyable for both of us, wasn't it?'

Rebekah bit her lip. 'Enjoyable' came nowhere near to describing the incredible pleasure she had experienced when Dante had made love to her. But, although he had said he had enjoyed sex with her, she guessed that for him it hadn't been anything special. She was just another woman who had shared his bed for a night—except that they hadn't even made it to the bedroom, she thought, flushing as she recalled the wildfire passion that had exploded between them on the sitting room sofa.

She caught her breath when he trailed his lips up her neck and nipped her earlobe with his teeth. The little dart of pleasure-pain sent a quiver through her and she fought the temptation to turn in his arms so that he could kiss her properly. It would be so easy to melt into his arms and make love with him again. But she dared not risk it. Seeing him this morning, looking utterly gorgeous with his hair ruffled and his jaw shaded with dark stubble, made her realise she had been kidding herself to think she could separate her emotions from her physical response to him. There was a danger she could be hurt by him, and Lord knew she had been hurt enough in the past. It was safer to leave him now before she did something stupid like fall in love with him.

'Dante…I…' Her heartbeat quickened when he slid his hands beneath the hem of her shirt. Her skin felt super-sensitive and she caught her breath when he skimmed his fingertips over her ribcage and continued higher until he reached the undersides of her breasts.

'This is for you.' She snatched an envelope from the worktop and thrust it at him.

Dante frowned. Rebekah wasn't behaving like he had expected. He could understand if she felt a little shy, but he knew damn well she had enjoyed last night as much as he had. He glanced at the envelope with his name neatly printed on the front. 'What is it?'

'It's…my letter of resignation.'

He said nothing as he slit the envelope, withdrew its contents and read the two lines she had written, but his silence simmered with anger that was reflected in his steely grey eyes.

'I think it's best if I leave straight away,' Rebekah mumbled. She dared not spend another night under Dante's roof, not if there was a chance she might spend it in his bed. If he tried to persuade her, she was not at all sure she would be able to resist him. The problem was, she did not actually have anywhere to go. Before Dante had walked in she had been searching through the property listings on her laptop. Luckily she had saved quite a bit of money while she had worked for him and she had enough to pay a deposit on a flat, but she would have to find another job quickly so that she could afford the rent.

'Why?'

The single terse word exploded from him like a gunshot and made her jump. Dante made a slashing movement with his hand. His expression was furious, his eyes blazing, and he suddenly looked much more hot-blooded Italian than cool English lawyer. 'Why do you want to leave?'

'Last night was great,' she said stiffly. 'But it was just a…a one-night stand, and now it's time for me to move on.'

Dante stared at her, not quite able to believe what he was hearing. It was true he'd had his fair share of one-night stands but they had always been his choice. He was used to calling the shots in his relationships and he did not like the feeling that he was powerless in this situation.

He did not want to lose her. The thought slid into his head and he tensed as the implication sank in. You could not lose what you did not have, he reminded himself. Rebekah was not his and he did not want her to be. He did not want a long-term relationship—once had been enough. He simply wanted to explore the wild passion they had shared last night and he was not ready to let her go yet.

'I don't understand why you no longer want to work for me,' he said curtly. 'Why can't we just carry on as before?'

As he spoke the words Dante realised the futility of them. He could never go back to thinking of Rebekah as a member of his staff when he had seen her naked body in all its voluptuous glory.

His eyes narrowed on her flushed face, and once again he was struck by how lovely she was. The way she scraped her hair back in a severe style only emphasised the perfect symmetry of her face and the porcelain smoothness of her complexion. Few women could get away without wearing make-up, but Rebekah's beauty was fresh and natural. The way she had responded to him last night had revealed an earthy sensuality that Dante found utterly addictive. Making love to her had whetted his appetite and he had been looking forward to having her fill the dual roles of his mistress and cook for—well, he had not even thought about a timescale; he'd simply assumed that she would stay with him until their passion burned out.

But apparently Rebekah was prepared to walk away from him. He could not deny a feeling of pique. It had never happened before. He wondered if she was hoping he would try to persuade her to stay, even beg her. His mouth twisted in a grim smile. She would soon learn that he did not throw himself on the mercy of anyone. One thing his marriage had taught him was that only a fool allowed his emotions to get involved.

'I think we both realise it would be impossible for

me to continue working for you,' she said quietly, voicing his thoughts.

He shrugged. 'So what are your plans?'

If she was disappointed that he made no attempt to dissuade her from leaving, she did not show it. 'I have a few things in the pipeline,' Rebekah told him. 'There's a possible opportunity for me to work for Gaspard Clavier at his new restaurant in St Lucia.'

Dante's frown deepened. 'So that's what he was talking to you about at the party. But Gaspard told me the restaurant won't be ready to open for a few months. He's a friend of mine, and in fact I represented him in his recent divorce from the young Russian wife he had ill-advisedly married. Despite the fact that the marriage only lasted for two years, Olga claimed an exorbitant settlement. Fortunately I managed to keep the bulk of Gaspard's fortune intact, for which he was extremely grateful.'

Rebekah hated his coldly cynical tone. In his profession Dante saw some of the worst examples of human behaviour, which probably explained his attitude towards marriage and relationships, she acknowledged ruefully.

'Presumably you haven't found anywhere to live yet?' he continued, glancing at the laptop screen which displayed properties to rent.

'I'm going to ring an estate agent and hopefully view a place this afternoon.' Rebekah spoke with a confidence she did not feel. Even if she found a flat it was unlikely she would be able to move in today. She prayed that her friend Charlie, who she had met when she had worked for the catering company, would allow her to stay with him for a few nights.

Dante folded the letter and slipped it into his trouser pocket. 'I accept your resignation—but you seem to have forgotten something. Under the terms of the contract you signed when you accepted the job as my chef you are required to give one month's notice before you can leave.'

Rebekah gave him a startled glance. 'Well, yes, technically I suppose that's true. But surely, under the circumstances...'

'I have no problem with the circumstances,' he said coolly. 'It will be impossible for me to find a replacement cook in a few days and I demand you will work your full amount of notice—or I will sue you for breach of contract. Not only that,' he continued, ignoring her shocked gasp, 'but I will refuse to give you a reference. I know you left your previous job without a reference and I imagine it will be difficult for you to find another job when neither of your previous employers will vouch for you.'

He paused to allow all this to sink in and then delivered the final blow. 'If you walk out on me I will advise Gaspard Clavier that you are an unreliable employee, and he may well reconsider his job offer.'

Rebekah felt sick. She guessed it was possible Dante could sue her if she did not fulfil the terms of her contract. He knew far more about the law than she did. But more worrying than the legal implications if she left her job without working her notice was the realisation that he could ruin her career. He was a hugely influential figure and if he spread the word among his rich friends, including Gaspard Clavier, that she was unreliable, she would struggle to find anyone to employ her. An unreliable chef was a restaurant owner's worst nightmare and no one would risk taking her on without references.

'I thought you would be glad for me to leave without any fuss,' she said slowly, puzzled by his determination that she should stay.

'Why would I want you to go when you're a superb cook *and* an exciting lover?'

His arrogant drawl brought a flush of angry colour to her cheeks. 'If you insist on me working my notice, cooking is the only thing I'll do for you. Sleeping with you was a one-off event, and to be honest it was a mistake I now regret. I must have been more affected by the alcohol in the fruit punch than I realised last night.'

'You could be very bad for my ego if I believed that was true,' Dante said in an amused voice. 'But you weren't drunk; you knew exactly what you were doing. And, what's more, you want to do it again.'

'The *devil* I do!' Furiously Rebekah attempted to push past him, but to her shame she felt a flare of excitement when he snaked an arm around her waist and jerked her against him. 'Dante, let go of me—I mean it...'

He stilled her angry words by bringing his mouth down on hers and kissing her with barely suppressed savagery, grinding his lips hard against the tremulous softness of hers until she gave a low moan. Sensing her capitulation, Dante slid his hand down to her bottom and forced her pelvis into sizzling contact with his fiercely aroused body. His other hand moved to her hair and he pulled the pins from it so that it fell in a curtain of rich brown silk around her shoulders.

The evocative sensation of Dante running his fingers through her hair was too much—*he* was too much—and, although Rebekah hated herself for her weakness, she could not fight him. Helpless in the face of his passionate onslaught, she parted her lips and he deepened the kiss so that it became intensely erotic. Her body recognized its master. He had given her the most pleasurable experience of her life the previous night and revealed a level of sensuality she had not known she possessed. Her breasts felt heavy and ached for his touch, and the flood of moist heat between her legs was a damning indictment of the sexual desire coursing through her veins.

When he finally released her, she swayed on legs that felt as if they would not support her and stared at him wordlessly as she explored the swollen softness of her lips with the tip of her tongue.

'That certainly proved something, didn't it?' Dante taunted her ruthlessly, ignoring the curious tug in his gut when he saw her stricken expression. 'A word of advice—if you don't want to be kissed, say it like you mean it. Otherwise the coming month that we're going to be spending together in Tuscany could get very tedious.'

'Tuscany?' Rebekah queried shakily.

'It's written in your contract that I might occasionally want you to accompany me to Italy and carry out your duties as my cook at my home near Siena. I intend to spend the whole of July in Tuscany—' he paused and gave her a glittering look '—and I will require your services.'

He made her sound like a hooker, Rebekah thought furiously. She welcomed her spurt of temper. Anything was better than the numb sense of shame she had felt after the way she had responded to him.

'I don't want to go with you. You can't make me.'

He shrugged. 'No. But if you refuse, I can, as I have already mentioned, make it difficult for you to find another job.'

How on earth had she fooled herself into thinking he had a softer side? She must have imagined the element of tenderness she'd thought she had sensed when he had made love to her last night. Had sex with her, she amended. There had been nothing loving about it. She was infuriated by his arrogance and more than anything she wished she could tell him to go to hell.

But the stark truth was that she had no choice but to honour the terms of her contract. She would have to accompany him to Tuscany if she was to have any hope of finding a job in the future, Rebekah acknowledged heavily. She did not want to risk Dante ruining her chance of working for Gaspard Clavier.

She lifted her chin and said with cool dignity, 'Very well, I will work out my month's notice in Tuscany. But I want to make it clear that I will go there on a strictly professional basis as your chef.'

'Is that so?' Dante reached out and idly wound a strand of her long hair around his finger, but his indolent air was deceptive and the feral gleam in his eyes sent a frisson of nervous excitement down her spine.

Before she could guess his intention, he gripped the hem of her shirt and whipped it over her head.

'How *dare* you?' Breathing hard, her temper boiling over, Rebekah's hand flew to his face. But he caught her wrist before she could strike him and held her firmly while he moved his other hand behind her and deftly unfastened her bra so that her breasts spilled free.

'You are gorgeous.'

Dante's voice dropped to a husky growl that caused the tiny hairs on Rebekah's body to stand on end. She realised as she watched the sudden flare of colour on his cheekbones that he was no more in control of the situation than she was. And somehow that made her feel better, made her less ashamed of her attraction to him, because although she hated herself for her weakness she could not deny her longing for him to make love to her again.

He stroked her nipples and rolled them between his fingers until they hardened and tingled. 'Stop fighting me, *mia bellezza*, and let me make love to you,' he murmured, his breath warm on her skin, his tongue darting out to lick one tight bud so that it swelled in urgent response.

A quiver of anticipation ran through Rebekah. But, as Dante trailed a line of kisses along her collarbone, she was conscious of a different, altogether more unpleasant sensation in the pit of her stomach. She knew the headache she'd woken with was her body's reaction to the alcohol she had unwittingly consumed at the party, and now a feeling of nausea swept over her.

'Dante…' she muttered, turning her head away as he was about to claim her mouth.

'No more games, *cara*.' He did not try to hide his impatience.

'I'm not playing games,' she gasped, fighting the churning sensation inside her. 'I'm going to be sick.'

With a strength born of desperation, she pulled out of his arms and flew out of the kitchen and down the stairs to her apartment on the basement level.

Ten minutes later, she emerged from her bathroom to find Dante sitting on the end of her bed.

'That's not the reaction I usually get from women,' he said drily.

'Please go away.' A glance in the mirror told her she looked even worse than she felt and the knowledge compounded her humiliation. She was just thankful she had pulled her dressing gown around her half-naked body.

Dante stood up from the bed as she sank weakly onto it, but he remained in the room, looking unfairly gorgeous with a shadow of dark stubble shading his jaw and his hair falling onto his brow. His eyes narrowed on her white face and there was a faint note of concern in his voice.

'Are you ill?'

Rebekah shook her head wearily. 'No, I just react badly to alcohol, even small amounts. I wasn't drunk last night.' She flushed as she recalled how Dante had insisted she had known exactly what she was doing when she had slept with him. 'But my body sometimes reacts badly to alcohol, and I'll continue being sick until all traces of it have gone.'

She had barely finished speaking when another wave of nausea sent her running back into the en suite bathroom. It was so unglamorous—she couldn't imagine what Dante must think of her. On the plus side, she thought as the sickness finally passed and she splashed her face with cold water, she had probably killed his desire for her stone-dead. Surely he wasn't seriously expecting her to go to Tuscany with him?

When she staggered back to the bedroom she saw that he had placed a jug of water by the bed and drawn back the covers.

'You had better try and sleep it off. How long do you think it will be before the sickness passes and you can travel?'

'I expect I'll be fine in twenty-four hours,' she admitted wearily.

Dante unearthed her nightdress from beneath her

pillow and handed it to her. 'Come on, get into bed,' he urged, frowning when she simply stood there.

'I'll get changed once you've gone,' she muttered, faint colour stealing into her white face.

'It's a bit late now for modesty,' he said drily, but he turned around and she quickly slipped off her dressing gown and trousers and pulled the nightgown over her head.

'Can I get you anything? Something to eat, perhaps?' he asked, walking back over to the bed.

Rebekah grimaced as the queasy sensation returned when she lay down. 'Not in this lifetime,' she said with feeling.

'Poor *cara*.'

She tensed as Dante drew the bedcovers over her. The unexpected note of tenderness in his voice was the last straw. She hadn't expected him to be kind. She felt weak and wobbly and silly tears filled her eyes. The prospect of spending a month in Tuscany with him filled her with foreboding. How would she cope with her infatuation with him, especially now that she knew he was every bit the dream lover of her fantasies? Of course she did not have to sleep with him, her common sense pointed out. He couldn't force her to. But the shameful truth was that he would not need to. He only had to kiss her and she turned to putty in his arms.

'Please don't insist on me working out my notice,' she said tensely. 'There must be hundreds of women who would be willing to go to Tuscany with you. I'll forgo my last month's wages if you agree to let me go now. I really want to concentrate on finishing the cookery book of my grandmother's recipes, and I need to find a photographer who will take pictures for it.'

'That's not a problem. A friend of mine who lives in Siena is a photographer. I'm sure Nicole will be happy to work on the book with you.'

Was Nicole one of his mistresses? Angrily, Rebekah pushed the thought away. She could not see a way out of spending the next month in Italy with Dante and, with a heavy sigh, she flopped back against the pillows.

'What are you afraid of?' he asked gently.

Startled, her eyes flew open. 'I'm not afraid of anything,' she lied.

'I think you are. I think you're terrified of lowering your guard and allowing anyone to get close to you.' He recognized the barriers she put up because for years he had put up his own, and he had no intention of taking them down, Dante brooded.

Rebekah refused to admit that Dante's words were too close to the truth for comfort. Instead she turned onto her side and burrowed under the covers. 'I'm really very tired,' she muttered. He continued to stand by the bed for a few moments, but then he moved, and only when she heard the click of her door being closed did she realise she had been holding her breath.

CHAPTER SIX

THEY flew to Tuscany two days later. Rebekah's stomach still felt delicate and she had been dreading hanging around at the airport waiting for a commercial flight. The discovery that they were to travel by private jet was a shock but not an unwelcome one.

'I can't believe you own a plane,' she said as she followed Dante up the steps of his jet and looked around the cabin at the plush leather sofas, widescreen television and polished walnut drinks cabinet. The plane's interior looked more like a small but expensively furnished sitting room. This was the first time she had really appreciated that he was immensely wealthy. He came from a different world to a Welsh farmer's daughter, she thought wryly.

'It's the family plane,' he explained as he sat down next to her. 'My father uses it mainly to fly between the Jarrell estate in Norfolk and his chateau in southern France. He keeps a mistress at both places and shares his time between them.'

It wasn't hard to see where Dante's attitude towards relationships stemmed from. 'How old were you when your parents' marriage ended?'

'I was nine when they divorced, but I'd never known

them happy together. They have very different personalities and argued constantly. I never understood how they got together in the first place,' he said drily. 'Fortunately I was packed off to boarding school and escaped the tense atmosphere at home most of the time.'

Rebekah thought of the chaotic, noisy, happy home where she had grown up with her brothers. Her parents were devoted to one another, and their strong relationship was the lynchpin of the family.

'Did either of your parents marry again?'

'My father had two more attempts, but with each subsequent divorce he had to sell a chunk of the estate to pay the alimony bill and he finally realised that marriage is a mug's game. I've taken steps to ensure that his mistresses, Barbara and Elise, will be provided for if he dies before them, but they can't make a claim on the Jarrell estate's remaining assets.'

'What about your mother?' Rebekah asked curiously.

'She's halfway through her fourth marriage. They last on average about six years,' he said sardonically.

She did not miss the cynical tone in Dante's voice. 'I suppose it's not surprising you have such a warped view of marriage when your parents both had bad experiences.'

'I wouldn't say I have a warped view,' he argued, 'just a realistic one.'

Nor was his attitude towards marriage based entirely on the hash his parents had made of relationships, Dante brooded. Inexplicably, he found himself tempted to tell Rebekah about Lara. Maybe she would lose that judgemental tone in her voice if he explained how his wife had betrayed him and deceived him and played him for a fool.

But what was the point? He did not care what she thought of him, did he? He was only taking her to Tuscany with him for one reason—two, he amended—she was a fantastic cook and an exciting lover. He was looking forward to spending the coming month with her, but after that, when he had become bored with her, as he inevitably did with his mistresses, they would go their separate ways.

'Your mother still sings, doesn't she?' Rebekah said. 'I read that Isabella Lombardi is regarded as one of the greatest sopranos of all time. Will she be at your house in Tuscany?'

'No. She lives in Rome, but I think she might be on tour at the moment.' Dante shrugged. 'To be honest, I don't see her very often.'

'What about your father—are you close to him?'

'Not at all. We meet for lunch three or four times a year, but really from the age of eight I lived pretty independently from both my parents. I was at school, my mother was always travelling the world for performances and my father was busy with his own life.'

'I can't imagine not being part of a close-knit, loving family.' Rebekah pictured her parents at their remote farm and felt a sharp pang of homesickness. 'I love knowing that, whatever happens, if ever I have difficulties, I can rely on my family to help me.' She glanced at Dante. 'Who do you turn to when you have problems?'

He gave her a quizzical look. 'I don't have problems, and if I did I would deal with them on my own. I'm a big boy of thirty-six,' he said mockingly.

'Everyone needs to have someone they can rely on,' she said stubbornly.

The image of his grandmother flashed into Dante's

mind, and he felt a dull ache beneath his ribs. Nonna
Perlita had helped him through his darkest days after
Lara had left him and all he had wanted to do was drink
himself into oblivion. But that had been a long time ago,
and he would never put himself in a position where he
could be hurt again.

'I don't need anyone, so stop trying to analyse me.'
He lifted his hand and undid the clip that secured her
hair on top of her head, grinning when she gave him an
angry glare. 'Leave it loose,' he said, when she began
to bundle the long silky mass back up into a knot. 'You
look very sexy with your hair down.'

She was so lovely, he mused, feeling a curious tug
on his insides as he studied her face. There was something about her, a gentleness that touched him in some
way he did not understand. She was surprisingly easy
to talk to. He had revealed things about himself and his
childhood that he had never mentioned to anyone else.
But the kind of women he tended to be associated with
only showed a superficial interest in him and were far
more interested in his wealth and social status, Dante
thought with a flash of cynicism.

Unable to stop himself, he leaned towards her and
captured her mouth in a long, slow kiss that heated his
blood. He was conscious of the laboured thud of his
heart when after a few seconds her lips parted beneath
his.

She should not be responding to him, Rebekah
thought frantically, as Dante brushed his warm lips over
hers and probed his tongue between them to explore the
moist interior of her mouth. She had told herself that she
would keep him at arm's length; that she would be coolly
polite and professional so that he would quickly lose

interest in her—which she assured herself she hoped he would do. He might even allow her to leave her job without completing her notice and she would be able to return to England and get on with her life.

The sweet seduction of his kiss and the ache of longing he evoked inside her made a mockery of her intentions. But when he had told her about his unhappy childhood she had glimpsed a hint of vulnerability in him that he kept hidden beneath his self-assured, sometimes arrogant persona, and she had not been able to resist him.

'Tell me about your grandparents,' she said huskily when he eventually ended the kiss and she drew a ragged breath. 'It was lovely that your grandmother finished renovating the house she and your grandfather had planned together. She must have loved him very much.'

'They adored each other,' Dante agreed. 'They met during the war and were married for many years.'

'So, not all marriages in your family are doomed to failure. Doesn't the fact that your grandparents were happily married for so long make you think you should reassess your attitude towards marriage?'

He laughed, but his eyes were hard as he said, 'If that's a roundabout way of asking whether there's any possibility of our affair leading to a permanent relationship then let me make it crystal-clear there's absolutely no chance.'

Rebekah ruthlessly quashed the sharp little pain his words induced. 'I hope one day to meet the right man, and we'll fall in love and decide to spend the rest of our lives together,' she told him, wondering if she would ever really have the courage to risk her heart again. 'But he won't be anything like you.'

Why not? What the hell was wrong with him? Dante wondered, feeling an inexplicable surge of annoyance at her casual dismissal of him as prospective husband material. Not that he had any ideas on that score, of course. But he wouldn't make a bad husband. In fact he had been a damn good one. He had done his best to make Lara happy, but the bitter reality was that his best hadn't been good enough.

He stared moodily out of the plane window and was glad when the flight attendant came to serve them coffee and his conversation with Rebekah ended.

'It was once a Benedictine monastery,' Dante explained as the car rounded a bend and a huge house built of pale pink brick and darker terracotta roof tiles came into view. 'Parts of the original building date back to the eleventh century. It was renovated at various times over the years, but my grandparents—well, my grandmother mainly—turned it into the beautiful house it is now.'

'It looks amazing.' Rebekah was stunned by the size of the building and impressed by its history. The monastery stood on a hill overlooking rolling green fields and others filled with golden sunflowers and scarlet poppies. In the distance was the distinctive semi-desert landscape of the area known as the Crete Senesi. A narrow road wound past olive groves and tall cypress trees up to the Casa di Colombe—The House of Doves.

A few minutes later Dante drove through the gates into the courtyard, where it was easier to appreciate the huge amount of restoration work that had been done on the ancient monastery. On three sides of the courtyard the cloister had been fitted with arched glass windows which gleamed in the bright sunlight. In one corner was an ancient well, and all around the courtyard stood terracotta tubs planted with lavender, lemon and bay trees and a profusion of different herbs.

The splash of a fountain was the only sound to disturb the silence. As Rebekah climbed out of the car she was struck by the serene atmosphere. It was not difficult to imagine the Benedictine monks who had once lived here going about their daily lives with quiet devotion to their religious beliefs.

'Nonna Perlita was a keen gardener,' Dante told her when she admired the plants. 'The knot garden on the other side of the house was her pride and joy. There is also a swimming pool, and in the grounds of the estate there's a lake, although I wouldn't recommend you swim in it. I used to catch newts in it when I was a boy.'

'Who looks after the place now that your grandmother is no longer here?'

'I employ staff from the village—a couple of groundsmen tend to the gardens and carry out any maintenance work, and two women come regularly to clean the house.'

Dante opened the heavy oak front door and gave a deep sigh of pleasure as he ushered Rebekah into the cool stone-floored hall. 'For me this is home. One day I intend to move back here permanently.'

Rebekah gave him a surprised look. 'Did you used to live here? I thought you grew up in England.'

'I was born here—much to my father's displeasure. He wanted his heir to be born in England, at the Jarrell estate. But my mother went into labour early while she was visiting my grandparents, and so this house is my birthplace.' He gave a wry laugh. 'Apparently my father accused my mother of giving birth early on purpose because she wanted me to be born in Italy. It was just one of many things they could not agree on—as was the language I should be brought up to speak. My father only spoke English to me and my mother taught me Italian, so I grew up bilingual.

'I went to school in England, but spent most of the holidays here with my grandmother,' he continued. He shrugged. 'I enjoy living in London, but I think of myself as Italian rather than English.'

His Italian heritage was obvious in his dark olive skin tone and his jet-black hair, Rebekah mused. At his house in London she mostly saw him dressed in one of the superbly tailored suits he wore for work. He always looked gorgeous, but today he was wearing black jeans, matching shirt and designer shades and was so impossibly good-looking that she felt a fierce ache of longing whenever she looked at him. In fact she was so intent on not looking at him that she walked across the entrance hall to inspect a large framed photograph hanging on the wall.

The woman in the photo was clearly very elderly. Her hair was white and her face lined, but despite the marks of old age she was startlingly beautiful and bore an aura of serenity that was reflected in her bright silvery-grey eyes.

'Is this lady your grandmother?' She spun round and her heart lurched when she discovered that Dante had moved silently to stand beside her.

His eyes were focused on the picture. 'Yes, that was Perlita a few months before she died.'

Unexpectedly, raw emotion clogged Dante's throat. Usually when he'd arrived at the house he'd gone straight to see his grandmother. He wished she was still here, and curiously, because he had never brought any of his mistresses to the Casa di Colombe, he wished that Rebekah could have met her. In many ways the two women were very alike, he realised. Like Nonna, Rebekah was independent and, he suspected, fiercely loyal to the people she cared about. He had heard the love in her voice when she spoke about her family.

He glanced down at her and for the first time it struck him how petite she was compared to his tall frame. He hadn't noticed when he had danced with her at the party because she had been wearing high heels, but now she was wearing flat shoes and he was surprised by a feeling of protectiveness. He ran his finger lightly down her cheek. 'How are you feeling? You still look pale.'

'I'm fine now that the sickness has stopped,' she assured him.

'I want you to take things easy for the next couple of days.' Dante's eyes glinted wickedly. 'In fact I think you need to spend most of the time lying down.'

Rebekah's common sense told her to move away from him, but her heart refused to listen and her senses were swamped by his virile masculinity. The scent of his aftershave was tantalisingly sensual, as was the warmth that emanated from his body as he stepped closer and slid an arm around her waist.

'Naturally, I will lie down with you to keep you company,' he murmured in his rich as molten syrup voice.

A shiver of excitement ran through her. Common sense urged her to pull herself out of his arms, but she was trapped by the feral gleam in his eyes so that when he lowered his head she sank against him and parted her lips in readiness for his kiss.

Remembering his hot, hungry kisses when he had made love to her after the party, she was unprepared for the soft brush of his mouth on hers. As light as gossamer, he teased her lips apart in a slow, sweet kiss that was utterly beguiling. Rebekah melted into it, her whole being attuned to the exquisite sensations he aroused in her and the thudding drumbeat of desire that pounded in her blood and made her ache for his possession.

This was not keeping him at arm's length, taunted a voice inside her head. She had promised herself she would not be swayed by his sexy charm. But she had glimpsed the flare of pain in his eyes when he had looked at the photo of his grandmother and her heart had ached for him. He had told her that this was his first visit to Tuscany since his grandmother's death and she sensed he was still grieving for Perlita.

When she had slept with him two nights ago she had thought she could indulge in a passionate fling with him that would mean nothing to either of them, even though she was scared of her emotions becoming involved. But the discovery that there were depths to Dante she had been unaware of made her afraid that he could pose even more of a threat to her emotions. She could not risk falling for him, and so, calling on all her willpower, she tore her mouth from his and stepped away from him.

'I guess I should start dinner. It's getting late,' she mumbled, flushing beneath his quizzical stare. 'Although I've heard that it is usual in Mediterranean countries for people to have dinner late in the evening,' she added rather desperately as he continued to regard her with an intentness she found unsettling. 'But you're probably hungry,' she finished lamely.

'I'm ravenous, but I have a feeling we're talking about different appetites,' he said drily.

Dante did not understand why Rebekah had backed

off, but the curious half-wary, half-defensive expression in her eyes forced him to control his frustration. She clearly carried a lot of emotional baggage—which meant that she was exactly the sort of woman he usually avoided. So why wasn't he heading for the hills to get away from her? Why had he brought her to the Casa di Colombe, which was his private sanctuary and a haven of peace? He felt anything but peaceful at the moment, he thought grimly. And, strangely, his frustration was not only on a sexual level. He wanted to know who had put the shadows in her eyes, and conversely he was annoyed with himself for his curiosity when all he wanted was a temporary affair with her.

With an effort he controlled his impatience. 'I have a few things to do, so why don't you go and explore the house? The maids should have made up the beds and stocked the kitchen with basic provisions. We can pick up fresh fruit and vegetables at the market in Montalcino tomorrow.' He pointed down the hallway. 'You'll find the kitchen that way.'

From the outside, the house did not look very different from how it must have looked when it had been built and used as a monastery centuries ago. But, inside, the Casa di Colombe had been expertly renovated and turned into a charming, comfortable home. Much love had gone into the interior design of the house, Rebekah thought as she strolled through the airy, sunlit rooms on the ground floor where the old stone floors blended perfectly with the pale walls and elegant furnishings. She remembered the serene face of Dante's grandmother in the photograph hanging in the hall. Nonna Perlita had left her mark on this house, she mused.

She continued her exploration and fell in love with the kitchen the minute she walked through the door. The terracotta tiled floor, stone walls and pale oak cupboards gave it a rustic charm, but at the same time it was fitted with every piece of modern equipment she could want. It was a perfect setting to take photographs of the recipes she had now perfected for the cookery book, and she was keen to start work. She discovered that the pantry and fridge had been well stocked and she was debating what to cook for dinner when the sound of voices from outside the kitchen window made her glance towards the garden.

Dante was standing with a tall, slim blonde-haired woman wearing very short shorts that revealed her long tanned legs. The woman turned her head and Rebekah saw that she was stunningly beautiful. A tight knot formed in her stomach as she watched the woman laughing with Dante. It was clear they shared a close relationship. Was the blonde his mistress? If so, then why had he insisted on *her* coming to Tuscany with him? And why on earth did she feel jealous?

Feeling angry with herself, she went to investigate the upper floors of the house. Her suitcase had been left in the hall and she carried it upstairs. There were five bedrooms on the first floor, one of which was obviously the master suite. Next door to Dante's room, the guest bedroom had been prepared, she assumed, for her. It was a pretty room, with the same neutral-toned walls as the rest of the house and a lemon-yellow bedspread.

The blinds at the window shaded the room from the hot sunshine of a Tuscan summer's afternoon, but Rebekah still felt too warm in her skirt and jacket. A cool shower was tempting. Taking a shower cap from her case, she walked into the en suite bathroom and emerged ten minutes later to slip into a lightweight floral cotton skirt and T-shirt that she had packed for the trip. She was pulling a comb through her hair when there was a knock on her door, and she spun round to find the woman she had seen in the garden standing in the doorway.

Close up, she was a few years older than Rebekah had thought, perhaps in her early thirties. But, if anything, she was even more stunning than she had looked from a distance, with a model's slim build, perfect hair, perfect tan—perfect everything, in fact.

'Hi! You must be Rebekah?' the woman said in a distinctive American accent. 'I'm Nicole Sayer...duh...' she tutted impatiently '...*Castelli!* I've only been married for two months and I keep forgetting to use my new name. My husband Vito and I are old friends of Dante's.' She finally paused for breath and held out her hand to Rebekah. 'It's great to meet you. I was so surprised when Dante phoned and said he was bringing someone to Tuscany with him. He never has before.' She gave Rebekah a speculative look. 'I guess the two of you must be good friends.'

Rebekah felt herself blush. 'Actually, I'm his cook.' She suddenly remembered why the woman's name was familiar. 'You're a photographer, aren't you? I'm writing a cookery book based on my grandmother's recipes, and Dante mentioned that you might take photographs for me.'

Nicole's smile held genuine warmth. 'I'd love to. I used to work as a freelance photographer in New York, but now Vito and I have settled in Italy. I'm going to head back to my home in Siena,' Nicole explained as she turned to walk out of the room, 'but I'll be in touch in the next couple of days to arrange a photo shoot.

'By the way—' she paused in the doorway '—I've hung the clothes that Dante ordered for you in the wardrobe.'

Rebekah gave her a puzzled look. 'What clothes?'

Nicole crossed the room and pulled open the wardrobe door. 'These,' she said, indicating the array of outfits hanging from the rail. She took out a beautiful jade-green silk dress and gave Rebekah a teasing smile. 'You must be a very special cook for Dante to buy you designer clothes.'

Rebekah took a pale pink silk blouse from the rail. All the clothes were classical and elegant, in an array of pretty pastel colours. They were the sort of things she would love to wear if she could afford them.

'There's obviously been a mistake,' she told Nicole. 'I don't know why Dante ordered these clothes, but they can't be for me.'

Nicole looked amused. 'Maybe he wanted to surprise you.'

Or maybe Dante had bought her dozens of new outfits for another reason, Rebekah thought grimly after Nicole had left and she went in search of him. His bedroom door was open, and as she looked into the room he strolled out of his bathroom wearing nothing more than a towel sitting low on his hips. His damp hair was slicked back from his brow and beads of moisture clung to his chest hairs.

She tapped on the door to alert him to her presence and tried to ignore the tug on her insides when he smiled at her.

'Did you meet Nicole? She came up to introduce herself.'

'Yes, I met her. She seemed to think the clothes hanging in my wardrobe belong to me—paid for by you.'

'That's right. Do you like them?'

Rebekah took a deep breath. Her heart was beating very fast and she felt confused and angry, and shaken by a memory that was still painfully raw.

'I can't accept them. I can't allow you to buy me gifts.'

Dante picked up a towel from the bed and rubbed his wet hair. 'Why not?'

'Because you can't buy me,' she told him fiercely.

He stilled, and gave her a searching look. His smile faded and his eyes were cool and assessing. 'What do you mean—*buy you*?'

'Don't think that because you've spent a fortune on me I'll do what you want.'

For a few seconds the atmosphere in the room trembled with an ominous silence.

'And what do you think I want?' he asked in a dangerous voice that sent a shiver down Rebekah's spine.

She crossed her arms over her chest in an unconsciously defensive gesture as she said, 'For me to be your mistress while we are in Tuscany.'

'You think I bought you the clothes in payment for sex? What kind of man do you think I am?' He gave a savage laugh. 'On second thoughts, don't answer that question—you've made your opinion of me quite clear.'

Dante could not have sounded hurt, Rebekah told herself. But what if she had misjudged him? She bit her lip. 'Are you saying you didn't buy them for that reason?' she asked uncertainly.

He threw the towel on the bed and strode towards her. Rebekah had never seen him so furious. His face looked as though it had been carved from granite and his eyes glittered with rage and bitter contempt. Too late, she feared she had made a terrible mistake.

'How dare you insult my integrity?' he said in a blisteringly angry tone. 'The only reason I bought clothes for you is because I felt bad that I had sprung the trip to Tuscany on you at short notice. I thought it was unlikely you would own summer clothes suitable for the temperatures here in Italy. But you were too unwell to spend a day shopping in London, so I phoned a boutique in Siena and ordered some things for you.'

His hands shot out to grip her arms and he jerked her against him. 'I wasn't trying to buy your favours,' he grated. 'I don't need to, *mia bella.*'

Realising his intention, Rebekah tried to twist her head away from him, but he captured her jaw and held her prisoner while he brought his mouth down on hers. It was a kiss of anger and wounded pride. He ground her lips beneath his in fierce, furious possession, tangling his fingers in her hair so that she could not escape the onslaught.

But within seconds his anger turned to fiery passion that was far more dangerous. She gasped as he thrust his tongue into her mouth. Dante deepened the kiss so that it became a slow, drugging assault on her senses. She knew there was no point in trying to fight him when he was so much bigger and stronger than her, but suddenly his lips were no longer hard and demanding but softer as he coaxed a response from her. Rebekah did not realise he had steered her over to the bed until she felt the edge of the mattress behind her and, before she could protest, he tumbled her down and immediately covered her body with his own.

She caught her breath when he shoved her T-shirt up. She hadn't bothered with a bra when she had changed after her shower and she blushed as he stared at her bare breasts and the betraying hard peaks of her nipples.

'You don't need much persuading,' he taunted. 'I could take you right now, *cara*, and you wouldn't stop me.' His voice roughened. 'How could you think I would treat you so disrespectfully?'

'I'm sorry,' Rebekah said thickly. She knew she owed him an explanation, but she had never told anyone what Gareth had done, not even her mum. She closed her eyes to prevent her tears from escaping, unaware that Dante had glimpsed the sparkle of moisture clinging to her lashes and that his anger had been replaced by a curious ache in his chest.

She'd had no reason to think Dante would behave so crassly, Rebekah acknowledged heavily. He might be a playboy but he had a code of morals and he had always treated her with the utmost respect.

'Someone once tried to pay me to do something that I couldn't do—something that was terribly wrong,' she choked, aware from Dante's confused expression that she wasn't making a lot of sense.

'You mean a guy offered to pay you for sex?'

'No…it wasn't like that.'

When Rebekah did not continue Dante felt a surge of frustration. He wanted to demand that she tell him what it had been like—what had she meant? Why had she jumped to conclusions and thought the worst of him?

'It has something to do with the guy in Wales, doesn't it?' he guessed. He sighed as he lowered her T-shirt and smoothed her hair back from her face. 'But I take it from your silence that you don't want to talk about it.'

'Sometimes it's best to leave the past alone.' She gave him a wobbly smile. 'Dante, I am truly sorry. The clothes are beautiful, and it was such a kind gesture, but…' Rebekah gave him an awkward, apologetic glance. 'I would prefer to pay for them myself.'

He lifted himself off her and stood up. 'We'll discuss it later. Did you find the kitchen?'

'Yes.' She took a shaky breath when she realised he was not going to pursue the reason why she had accused him so unfairly. 'It's fantastic—and the fridge is well stocked. We won't need to go shopping for a few days.'

'Good. So what time is dinner?' Dante kept his tone deliberately light and was relieved to see her relax a little.

'Oh, heavens! I forgot to put the chicken in the oven.' Rebekah scrambled off the bed. 'I'd better go and do it now.'

She hurried across the room but hesitated in the doorway and turned to look at Dante. She felt terrible about the awful way she had treated him and she felt angry and upset with herself that she was still allowing Gareth and the past to affect her. She needed to forget about him, but some things could never be forgotten, she thought painfully.

'I don't object to you being in my room—' Dante's deep voice dragged her from her thoughts '—but I'm about to get dressed—which means this towel is coming off.'

As he spoke he moved his hands to the towel draped around his hips. Rebekah swallowed as she traced her eyes over the dark hairs that arrowed down his flat abdomen and disappeared beneath the towel which she noticed was totally inadequate to hide the fact that he was aroused.

For a moment she was desperately tempted to re-trace her steps across the room and remove the towel for him. But if she made love with him again wouldn't it just complicate their relationship even more? Her eyes flew to his face and she caught her breath when she saw the sensual heat in his silvery gaze.

'You have thirty seconds to leave, *cara*, or we won't be eating that chicken until midnight,' he said roughly.

Rebekah did not need a second warning, and fled!

CHAPTER SEVEN

THEY had dinner that evening on the terrace which overlooked lush green farmland and fields of tall ripe corn that rippled like a golden lake. In the distance the mountains towered majestically, their jagged outline softened by the mellow light as the sun sank slowly beneath the horizon.

The panoramic view was breathtaking. 'It's like a painting by one of the Old Masters,' Rebekah commented as she sat with her chin propped on her hand and drank in the beauty of the Tuscan landscape. 'How can you ever bear to leave this place?'

'I enjoy a busy life in London, a demanding career and good social life, but I must admit I miss the tranquillity of the Casa di Colombe.' Dante took a sip of the particularly good red wine that was made from grapes grown on his estate. 'One day I'll move here permanently and learn to make wine and press olives—' he slanted a smile at her '—perhaps even learn how to cook as well as you do. The dinner you made tonight was divine.'

'I'm glad you enjoyed it.' Rebekah gave a contented sigh as she drained her glass of pomegranate juice. Her fear that things would be strained between her and Dante after she had reacted so badly about the clothes he had bought her had been unfounded. During dinner he had been a charming and entertaining companion and had made her laugh with his dry humour. She had slowly started to feel relaxed and been fascinated when he had told her more of the history of the house and when it had been a monastery hundreds of years ago.

'Where I come from in North Wales is beautiful too, and we have mountains. You can see Snowdon from my parents' farm,' she told him. Her expression grew wistful. 'I think home is where the heart is—where the people you love are.'

'I guess there's some truth in that,' Dante agreed. His grandmother had lived here in Tuscany, and perhaps that was why he loved this house so much. But Lara hadn't liked it here. She had found the quiet, remote location boring and on the couple of occasions she had visited Nonna with him she had been impatient to get back to the city. He should have realised they were too different for their relationship to have succeeded, he thought heavily.

He glanced at Rebekah, noting how the last golden rays of the sun burnished her hair so that it looked like a stream of shimmering silk, and he felt a peculiar sensation, as if his insides had twisted.

'Tell me about your family. How many brothers did you say you have?'

'Seven—there's Owen, Aled, Cai, Bryn, Huw, Morgan and Rhys, who is the baby, only he's twenty-two now. My mother is from a big family too and I am the seventh child of a seventh child, which, according to my grandmother, means I have the sixth sense. But I don't believe in superstition. If I possessed psychic powers I would surely have known about Gareth,' Rebekah said unthinkingly. She flushed when Dante shot her an intent look.

'Gareth, I take it, is the Welsh ex-boyfriend. What would you have known about him?'

Strangely, Rebekah discovered that she wanted to talk to Dante about what had happened.

'That he was having an affair with my best friend and chief bridesmaid.'

'You mean you were engaged?' Dante did not know why he was so surprised. Presumably, if she had been hoping to marry her boyfriend she had been in love with him. Was she still? he wondered.

'For five years. But we had been dating for longer than that. We met at school, Gareth lived on the farm close to my home and we grew up together. I thought I knew him. I thought we would always be together and have a long and happy marriage like my parents—' she swallowed '—but it turned out that I never knew him at all.'

'It must have been a shock when you discovered your fiancé had been unfaithful.' Dante frowned. Had Rebekah felt the same gut-wrenching sense of betrayal that had ripped through him when Lara had confessed she had been sleeping with another man? He had heard the lingering hurt in her voice. Irrationally, he wished he could meet the Welsh farmer and connect his fist with the guy's jaw. 'So what happened—how did you find out?'

'He confessed that he didn't want to marry me two weeks before the wedding.' She could not bring herself to tell Dante of the painful event that had prompted Gareth to admit he did not love her, she thought bleakly.

She sighed. 'I had no idea that Gareth had secretly

been seeing Claire for months. In retrospect, things hadn't been right between us for a while, but I was so busy with the wedding preparations and I assumed that once we were married our relationship would go back to how it had been. I couldn't believe it when he admitted that he and Claire were having an affair. But it explained a lot,' she said wryly.

'What do you mean?'

She shrugged. 'Before we split up Gareth had lost interest in…well—' she flushed '—the physical side of our relationship. I knew he was working hard, and all relationships go through flat patches. I felt he didn't find me attractive any more and I put it down to the fact that I'd put on a few pounds. Being around food all day tends to be bad for your waistline,' she said ruefully, remembering how confused and humiliated she had felt when Gareth had regularly fallen asleep in front of the television when she had been desperate for him to take her to bed. 'I should have guessed that he didn't want to have sex with me because he was having it with someone else.'

Dante nodded, as if he understood, which puzzled her because she did not see how he could know how it felt to be rejected. It was not something a handsome millionaire was likely to experience, she thought.

'Infidelity and the betrayal of trust can be devastating,' he said harshly.

Rebekah stared at him, taken aback by his statement and the bitterness she had heard in his voice. How could a self-confessed playboy understand the pain caused by hearing that someone you loved had been unfaithful?

'Are you saying that from the point of view of the betrayer or the betrayed?'

He did not reply, and his shuttered expression gave no clue to his thoughts. But then he said tautly, 'Let's just say I learned the hard way that men and women are drawn together by lust but our so-called civilised society insists on romanticising what is essentially just a physical need and calling it love.'

'So you don't believe in the concept of everlasting love?'

'Do you, after the man you loved and were expecting to marry turned out to be a liar and a cheat?'

She turned away from Dante and watched the dying rays of the sun streak the sky with fiery flames of pink and orange. The beauty of it touched her soul and with a little flare of pain she thought how heartbreaking it was that her child had never seen a sunset.

She was shocked by the realisation that Dante must have been hurt in the past. She had believed him to be a womaniser who had no interest in meaningful relationships—a perception he promoted because it was what he wanted people to believe, she thought with a flash of insight. She was curious about the identity of the woman who had hurt him, and wondered if he had loved her. For some reason the idea evoked a needle-dart of pain inside her.

'I do believe in love,' she said quietly. 'I see it in my parents' eyes when they look at each other. They haven't had an easy life; the farm has never earned much money. But Mum and Dad have weathered the storms together and they're devoted to each other. I had a bad experience with Gareth, and I admit that for a while I thought I would never want to risk being hurt again. But I don't want to be alone all my life, and one day I hope

I'll have a relationship with someone that leads to marriage and a family.'

She glanced at him. In the rapidly fading light he looked so stern and remote that it was hard to believe he had ever allowed anyone into his heart, and she sensed that he would not do so again.

'Can you really be happy having one meaningless affair after another?' she murmured.

Perfectly happy, Dante assured himself, refusing to acknowledge the traitorous thought that for the past couple of months he had felt a growing sense of restlessness and discontentment with his life. It was pure coincidence that this feeling had begun soon after he had employed his new chef.

'Absolutely,' he drawled. His chair scraped on the patio stones and he stood up and walked around the table to Rebekah. She was wearing a simple white sundress and, with her long hair falling around her shoulders, she looked achingly beautiful and innocent. But she had proved two nights ago that she was no inexperienced virgin. The wild abandonment with which she had made love with him had been exciting and strangely humbling. She had held nothing back and the sweet honesty of her response to him had made sex with her a mind-blowing experience that he was impatient to repeat.

'While we're here in Tuscany I will prove to you how satisfying sex without emotional involvement can be,' he told her as he pulled her to her feet and stared down at her flushed face. His eyes blazed with a feral hunger that caused Rebekah's heart to miss a beat.

'Dante…' The word *don't* trembled on her lips and was muffled as he slanted his mouth over hers and kissed her. It was a hot, passionate kiss that demanded her response. She would be a fool to succumb to him warned a voice in her head, but she could already feel heat spreading through her body and a melting sensation in the pit of her stomach.

'You want me, *mia bella*,' he muttered when he finally broke the kiss to allow them to drag oxygen into their lungs. 'And my hunger for you is patently obvious,' he added sardonically as he cupped her bottom and pulled her up against him so that the hard length of his arousal pushed insistently into the cradle of her pelvis. 'Why not enjoy what we have for as long as either of us wants it to last?'

What they had was sex, pure and simple. Although pure was not how she would have described the tumultuous passion that had blazed between them when he had made love to her after the party, Rebekah thought, blushing at the memory of how he had taken her to the pinnacle of pleasure with his hands and mouth and his powerful, muscular body. She sensed the inherent danger of an affair with Dante. The discovery that, beneath his playboy image, he was a man of complex emotions had left her feeling confused. Her brain told her to resist him but her heart was softening and her body was completely in his thrall, she thought ruefully as he claimed her mouth once more. Excitement shot through her when he closed his hand possessively around her breast and stroked her nipple through her thin cotton dress.

She was shaking, or was it him? She was unaware that he had undone the buttons at the front of her dress until he pushed the material aside and she felt him caress her naked flesh. It was too much, her desire for him was too overwhelming to be denied and she melted into his hard body and kissed him back with an eagerness that caused him to groan.

Suddenly the world tilted as he swept her up into his arms. 'Put me down,' she gasped, struggling against the temptation to rest her head on his shoulder. She loved being held in his arms, loved the feeling of being safe and cared for. But she was far from safe, she realised when she saw the sensual gleam in his eyes. 'I'm too heavy. You'll injure your back carrying me,' she muttered as he strode through the quiet house and up the stairs with a purposeful intent that made her heart thud.

'Don't be ridiculous. Why do you have a problem with your body image?' he demanded as he shouldered the door to his bedroom and set her down by the bed. 'You have a gorgeous, voluptuous, sexy shape that I find such a turn-on.'

'Do you?' Rebekah murmured weakly, trying to dismiss the image of his whippet-thin ex-mistress Alicia Benson.

'Believe me, *cara*, no other woman has ever made me feel so out of control,' Dante admitted roughly. His hands shook as he peeled off her dress and cupped her breasts in his palms. He delighted in the weight of them and the creamy softness of her skin. His body tightened with anticipation as he bent his head to each of her nipples. The feel of them hardening beneath his tongue drove him to the edge and when she made a high, keening sound of need he quickly stripped off her panties, pulled off his own clothes and drew her down onto the bed.

Rebekah sensed Dante's urgency, and shared it. His olive skin felt like satin beneath her fingertips and the faint abrasion of his chest hairs against her palms was innately sensual as she trailed a path over his flat stomach. He gave a low growl of encouragement when she curled her fingers around his erection. He was already fiercely aroused and the knowledge that in a few moments he would be inside her evoked a flood of heat between her legs.

Dante slipped his hand between her thighs and made a hoarse sound when he discovered the drenching sweetness of her arousal. But, instead of lowering himself onto her as she was impatient for him to do, he trailed a line of kisses over her breasts and stomach. Rebekah's heart lurched when he moved lower still. This was new to her and she stiffened when he gently eased her legs wider and ran his tongue over her so that he could access the heart of her femininity.

'I'm not sure...' she began in a startled voice, her faint protest turning to a gasp of pleasure.

'Relax,' he murmured, 'and let me pleasure you, *mia bella*.'

Dear heaven, Rebekah thought shakily, as Dante continued his intimate exploration. She was on fire, so hot down there that she twisted her hips restlessly, not wanting him to stop, but afraid that if he didn't she would not be able to hold back the orgasm that she could feel building deep in her pelvis.

'Please...' It was unbearable torture, and she clawed at the silky bedspread beneath her as the first spasms of her climax made her body tremble. Pausing briefly to take a condom from the bedside drawer and slide it on, Dante positioned himself over her and entered her with a fierce thrust that elicited a ragged groan from his throat as he felt her relax to accept him.

Rebekah closed her eyes for a few seconds—her body

and her soul, she would swear, utterly enraptured by the feel of Dante inside her, filling her, completing her. He began to move, slowly at first so that each thrust seemed to fill her even more as he slid his hands beneath her bottom and angled her for maximum effect. Then he set a rhythm that echoed the drumbeat of her blood, faster, faster, while she clung to his sweat-slicked shoulders and hurtled towards the peak. He kept her there for time-less moments, laughing softly when she implored him to grant her the release she craved, until with a final devastating thrust they climaxed simultaneously, their bodies shuddering as waves of ecstasy pounded them.

For a long while afterwards they lay replete in each other's arms while the serene silence of the house closed around them and the outside world seemed far away. But at last Dante lifted his head and dropped a light kiss on her mouth, surprised by how reluctant he felt to disen-gage from Rebekah.

Her ex-fiancé was an idiot, he mused, as he shifted onto his side and trailed his fingers over her body. Rebekah was everything a man could want in a wife. It was almost a pity that he had absolutely no desire to try wedded bliss again, because she would be a strong candidate for the role of his wife.

Frowning at the disconcerting train of his thoughts, he rolled onto his back and curled his arms behind his head.

'You know I'm not going to let you go,' he murmured, watching her long hair spill around her shoulders as she sat up.

Rebekah tried to control the way her heart leapt at his surprising statement, and it was lucky she did because reality quickly doused her excitement as he continued,

'I don't know what Gaspard Clavier said he would pay you to work at his new restaurant, but I'll better his offer. The Caribbean's not all it's cracked up to be, anyway.' He reached out and touched one of her nipples, smiling when it instantly hardened and she drew a shaky breath. 'If you carry on working for me I can promise there will be lots of perks,' he drawled.

'Mmm, but none that will further my career as a chef, I suspect,' Rebekah said drily.

Not for the world would she allow Dante to see how much he affected her. He had made love to her with fierce passion but there had been an unexpected tenderness in the way he had kissed and caressed her and it would be easy to pretend that what they had just shared had meant something to him. Fortunately, her common sense reminded her that it had just been great sex, and probably for him it had been no different to sex with any of his previous mistresses.

Reclining indolently on the pillows with a satisfied smile on his lips, he looked like a sultan who had just been pleasured by his favourite concubine. His chiselled, masculine beauty made her heart ache, but his arrogant, faintly calculating expression sent alarm bells ringing inside her head. Dante was used to being adored by women and no doubt he expected that because she had fallen into his bed she found him irresistible and would agree to his every demand—including withdrawing her resignation. It was vital she showed him that their affair was on her terms.

'One day I hope to open my own restaurant and my ambition is to gain the highest awards,' she told him. 'The chance to work for Gaspard will be an invaluable experience that I simply can't turn down.'

He could count himself lucky that Rebekah was clearly not going to turn into a clinging vine, Dante told himself. It was good she understood he did not want a long-term relationship, and from the sound of it neither did she. He respected that her career was important to her. So why did he feel irritated and strangely let down by her casual attitude? He was tempted to pull her back into his arms and see how cool she remained when he kissed every inch of her body. The memory of how she had writhed beneath him a few moments ago when he had dipped his tongue into the honeyed sweetness of her womanhood had a predictable effect on his body.

But when he rolled towards her and saw her long eyelashes fanned out on her cheeks, a different feeling swept through him. Recounting how her fiancé had dumped her shortly before their wedding and gone off with her best friend must have been emotionally draining and it was no wonder she had fallen asleep. He had a whole month in which to sate himself with her beautiful body, he mused, as he settled her comfortably against his chest. No doubt he would have broken free from the spell she seemed to have cast on him by then.

Rebekah found that she was alone when she opened her eyes. Alone, but in Dante's bed, and the indentation on the pillow beside her was a clue that she had not been dreaming and she had really spent all night in his arms. But where was he now? Had he left to give her privacy to get up, and would he expect her to be gone when he returned to his room? She wished she was more experienced in the rules of having an affair.

She was about to slide out of bed when the door opened and he strode into the room. Dressed in faded jeans that clung to his lean hips and a cream polo shirt, he looked heart-stoppingly sexy and disgustingly wide awake, which made her painfully conscious that she had just woken up, even though it was—she glanced at the clock—*nine-thirty*, and sunshine was streaming through the half-open blinds.

'I can't believe I slept so late. You should have woken me. If you give me a minute to get dressed, I'll go and make your breakfast.'

'Stay where you are,' he ordered. 'I've made you breakfast for a change.'

She had been so focused on his handsome face that she hadn't registered the tray he was holding. Her eyes widened when he set it down on her knees. On it was a pot of coffee, a plate of toast, butter and jam, and a plate covered with a lid. Lying on the napkin was a single pale pink rosebud, just unfurling and so exquisite that Rebekah felt a lump form in her throat.

'I've never been served breakfast in bed before,' she said huskily.

Dante's smile stole her breath. 'It was my fault you were so tired,' he murmured with a wicked gleam in his eyes that made her blush. 'I thought it was only fair to let you sleep in.' He lifted up the lid covering the plate with the air of a magician pulling a rabbit from a hat. 'I cooked scrambled eggs. I hope they're done.'

To death, she thought as she stared at the congealed greyish mass on the plate.

'The toast might be a little crisper than the way you make it.'

And considerably blacker, Rebekah discovered when she picked up a piece and saw the charred underside. 'Everything looks wonderful,' she assured him. She was touched that he had gone to so much effort, especially when she noticed that his thumb was bleeding. 'What happened to your hand?'

'The rose put up a fight,' he said ruefully. To tell the truth, Dante was faintly embarrassed by the moment of impulsiveness that had made him pick a rose from the garden for her. It was not the sort of thing he ever did. When he wanted to give flowers to a woman he instructed his PA to phone a florist and arrange for a bouquet to be delivered. It was a far less painful method, he mused, glancing at the tear on his thumb inflicted by a thorn. But Rebekah's smile had made it worth it. He lowered his gaze to the creamy upper slopes of her breasts and wished she would finish eating so that he could push the sheet she'd wrapped around her aside.

'How are the eggs?'

'Excellent.' Rebekah took a gulp of coffee to help the rubbery eggs slide down her throat. She picked up the rose and inhaled its delicate fragrance. 'Thank you,' she murmured shyly. Her heart skipped a beat when he leaned forward and dropped a light kiss on her mouth. The gentle caress wasn't nearly enough. Greedily, she wanted more, and parted her mouth beneath his.

The sound of a car horn from outside made him reluctantly draw back and he stood and walked over to the window which overlooked the courtyard.

'Nicole's here. She phoned earlier to say she was coming over to discuss taking photos for your cookery book.' Dante glanced at his watch. 'I have a few things to see to this morning. But you can thank me properly later, *cara*,' he drawled, his eyes gleaming with sensual promise and something else that surely could not have been tenderness, Rebekah told herself as she watched

him stroll out of the door. Don't look for things that
don't exist, she warned herself, and went in search of a
vase for the rose.

CHAPTER EIGHT

'DANTE must be very popular,' Rebekah remarked to Nicole later that morning as she looked out of the kitchen window and watched another visitor to the Casa di Colombe walk up the driveway. 'At least six people have paid him a visit today.'

'They're coming to his clinic,' the American told her. She adjusted the angle of the camera on a tripod and checked the viewfinder. 'That's better; I can get a close up shot of the food.'

Rebekah wrinkled her brow. 'What kind of clinic?'

'Local people come to him for legal advice. Dante is a hero to many of the villagers. Some years ago they faced the threat of losing the land that they had farmed, in some cases, for generations,' Nicole explained. 'The company that owned the deeds to the land wanted to sell a huge area to a development company who intended to build a vast holiday complex here. Dante fought a legal battle to help the villagers win the right to buy their farms. He gave his services for free, and put up a lot of his own money to pay the legal costs. Not only that, but he lent many people the money they needed to buy their land without them having to pay any interest on the loans.' She smiled. 'So you see he's highly respected by everyone around here. The villagers know they can come to him with their problems and he will do his best to help them—and he charges them nothing for his advice.'

Nicole resumed adjusting the settings on her camera, and Rebekah returned to slicing up vegetables to put in a salad for lunch. The more she learned about Dante, the more it became clear that there was another side to the cynical divorce lawyer and heartless womaniser she had believed him to be. He was a man who clearly cared about other people, and who had cared about a woman in his past. What had happened to make him turn his back on relationships? she wondered.

She was still thinking about him when he walked into the kitchen a little while later.

'Something smells good,' he murmured, giving her a smile that made her heart flip. 'I hope we're going to eat the food after you've photographed it.'

'Your timing's perfect,' she told him. 'We're almost ready to have lunch. It's chicken breasts stuffed with wild mushrooms and mozzarella. I just need to add some onion to the salad.'

'Oh…the smell of onion is revolting,' Nicole muttered. She had suddenly turned pale, and dropped down onto a chair. 'Don't worry, I haven't gone mad,' she said when Rebekah and Dante stared at her. She grinned at them. 'I can't keep it a secret any longer. I'm pregnant.'

Dante reacted instantly, pulling Nicole into his arms and giving her a hug. 'That's fantastic news! When is the baby due?'

'In just over five months. I'm thrilled to bits, but the only down side is that I seem to get morning sickness at all times of the day, and I can't bear the smell of certain foods, especially onions.' She glanced apologetically at Rebekah and gave a shocked cry. 'Heck—what have you done to your hand?'

'I wasn't concentrating and the knife slipped. I'm sure the bleeding will stop in a minute,' Rebekah mumbled as she wrapped a paper towel around the deep cut. She bit her lip as Dante strode over to her and caught hold of her hand to inspect the wound.

'I think you're going to need to have that stitched,' he growled, his voice rough with concern.

'It's fine,' she insisted tautly. 'Just put a dressing on it for me.' She managed to smile at Nicole. 'I'm so pleased to hear about the baby,' she said in a fiercely bright tone. 'You must be over the moon. Try nibbling on a plain biscuit when you feel sick. It should help settle your stomach.'

Dante would not allow Rebekah to cook dinner that evening, insisting that she needed to give her hand time to heal. Instead, he took her to a charming little restaurant in the nearby town of Montalcino, where they ate bruschetta topped with roasted red peppers and olive oil, followed by a creamy risotto that was the best Rebekah had ever tasted.

Afterwards they strolled around the medieval walled town and explored the quaint narrow streets and the charming piazza. 'It's such a picturesque place,' Rebekah said as they walked back to where Dante had parked the car. 'We must be so high up. The view across the valley is spectacular.'

'You'll get a better view when we come back in the daytime.'

Dante glanced at her, relieved that she seemed more

relaxed this evening. His eyes fell to her bandaged hand and his jaw tightened. He had no idea what had upset her earlier, when Nicole had announced that she was pregnant. For some reason he recalled the strange way she had reacted at the christening party for James and Susanna Portman's baby son. He was certain there was something in her past she had not told him. But there was no reason why she would choose to confide in him, he acknowledged. They were lovers, but at the end of the month they would leave Tuscany and go their separate ways.

It was what he wanted, he assured himself. He wasn't interested in a long-term relationship and he'd already broken one of his rules and become more involved with Rebekah than he had intended. Experience had taught him that a woman with emotional baggage spelled trouble and his common sense told him to end his affair with her. So why didn't he? he asked himself impatiently. Why was the idea of sending her back to England so unappealing?

When they got back to the house Dante discovered a message on the answerphone from his office in London. 'I'll have to check some information and send a couple of emails,' he told Rebekah. 'Why don't you go up to bed and I'll join you as soon as I can?'

She nodded and went upstairs. Pausing outside her bedroom, she briefly debated whether to sleep on her own tonight. She knew it was silly, but hearing about Nicole's pregnancy had stirred up emotions that she had tried hard to bury and she didn't feel confident that she could make love with Dante and pretend that he did not mean anything to her.

Why not enjoy what we have for as long as either of

us wants it to last? he had said. But what if she wanted it to last for ever? Tonight, when her heart ached for everything she had lost, she did not want to face the truth that in a few short weeks she would lose him too.

Fifteen minutes later Dante entered his dark bedroom and paused to switch on a bedside lamp before he crossed to the balcony where he could see Rebekah's outline through the voile curtain.

He came up behind her and slid his arms around her waist, drawing her against his chest. 'Why are you out here?' he murmured, pushing her long silky hair aside so that he could press his lips to the base of her neck. When she made no reply he turned her to face him and felt a cramping sensation in his gut when he saw tears shimmering in her eyes.

'*Cara*, what's wrong?' he said urgently. He lifted up her bandaged hand. 'Are you in pain? I knew I should have taken you to the hospital to have the cut attended to properly.'

She shook her head. 'It doesn't hurt. It was my own stupid fault anyway. I should have been more careful.'

Dante stared intently at her. 'How come you know what to do to cope with morning sickness?'

She immediately stiffened and attempted to pull away from him, but he held her tight. The sight of a single tear slipping down her cheek touched something deep inside him.

Rebekah knew she was falling apart. A few days ago she would have been horrified to break down in front of Dante. But now… She thought about the breakfast he had made for her, and the rose he had picked and placed on her tray. It had been a kind gesture, nothing more, but she felt instinctively that she could talk to him, that she could trust him.

'I had a baby,' she said in a low voice. She swallowed. 'He…he died.'

Dante struggled to hide his shock. 'I'm sorry.' He knew the words were inadequate and he felt helpless. With an instinctive desire to try and comfort her, he stroked her hair and waited for her to continue.

Rebekah took a ragged breath. 'I had awful morning sickness for the first few months. That's how I knew how to advise Nicole.'

'What happened?' Dante asked gently.

'My baby was stillborn when I was twenty weeks into the pregnancy. A routine scan revealed that there was no heartbeat.' Her voice was carefully devoid of emotion, but Dante sensed how hard she was finding it to talk about the child she had lost and he drew her closer. 'The doctors didn't know why he had died, but I had been under a lot of stress and I read afterwards that that could have been a reason.

'After the scan showed that the pregnancy wasn't viable—' she stumbled over the coldly clinical terminology that had been used by the obstetrician '—I had to go through an induced labour.' She squeezed her eyes shut and felt the hot tears seep beneath her lashes. 'The baby was perfectly formed. He was tiny, of course, so tiny, but absolutely beautiful. I held him and prayed that there had been a mistake, that he would take a breath.'

She couldn't go on, and buried her face in Dante's shirt as painful sobs tore her chest. 'It shouldn't hurt so much after all this time—' she wept '—but it does. I would give my life to hold my little boy again, to see him open his eyes and smile at me.'

'Dio, cara,' he said roughly, 'who says it shouldn't hurt? Who says you shouldn't cry for your son?'

Dante's voice caught in his throat. He had thought he knew all about pain and loss, but Rebekah's raw grief made him ache for her. He sank down onto a chair and pulled her into his lap, rocking her as though she were a small child while she cried out the storm.

A long time later, when she was calmer and the tremors that had racked her frame had subsided a little, he asked the question burning in his brain. 'Was Gareth the baby's father?'

'Yes, but he didn't want our child.' Rebekah pushed her hair back from her tear-streaked face. 'I found out I was pregnant two weeks before we were due to get married. Although we hadn't planned to start a family straight away, I assumed Gareth would be pleased. But he was horrified, and that's when he told me he had been having an affair with Claire for months and wanted to marry her, not me.'

Dante frowned. 'Surely he offered to go ahead with the wedding once he knew you were expecting his child?'

She shook her head. 'I'm not sure what I would have done if he had. I felt utterly betrayed by his relationship with Claire, but I suppose for the sake of the baby I would still have married him. But there was no question of that. Gareth didn't want me or the baby and he...' She broke off, still struggling to accept how the man she had believed she loved had treated her.

'He asked me to have an abortion. When I refused he got angry and said I had no right to go ahead with the pregnancy when he didn't want the child. It turned out that he had told Claire he had stopped sleeping with me, which was almost true,' she said heavily. 'I'd thought we were both stressed about the wedding and that was why he had been avoiding having sex with me. But there was one night when he'd had a few drinks and we ended up in bed, and that's when I conceived.

'All Gareth was concerned about was that Claire would be furious if she found out that he had lied to her. He was desperate for me to get rid of the baby—' her voice shook '—so desperate that he offered to pay me to have a termination.'

Rebekah gave a bitter laugh. 'He had inherited a large sum of money from his father. He knew I'd dreamed of opening my own restaurant, and he said that if I ended the pregnancy he would buy a place and set me up in business.'

'That's why you were so upset about the clothes I bought for you,' Dante said, understanding now why she had reacted the way she had done. 'You leapt to the assumption that I was trying to persuade you to be my mistress.' He shook his head. 'In my job I'm often appalled by the way clients treat people they supposedly once cared for, but I'm stunned that your fiancé tried to bribe you to get rid of your baby.' He felt a surge of angry disgust for the Welshman. 'What a bastard!'

'I couldn't believe Gareth could be so heartless,' she admitted painfully. 'I thought I knew him. I thought he was an honest, honourable man who would make a good husband and father, and discovering that I had been so wrong about him made me question my judgement.

'The following months were awful,' she continued dully. 'I didn't tell anyone what Gareth had done but, as news of my pregnancy became public, he put more pressure on me to have an abortion and pretend I had miscarried. We had some terrible rows and I'm convinced the baby must have been affected by my tension and the stress I was under.' She twisted her fingers together, her voice shaking. 'After I had lost the baby, Gareth came to visit me in the hospital, and he said he was sorry our child had been stillborn. But I knew he wasn't sad. I knew he was relieved and I couldn't bear to talk to him or be anywhere near him. That's why I went to London—to get away from all the memories.' She dashed her hand across her eyes. 'But memories are inside you and you can't leave them behind,' she whispered. 'I'll never forget my baby.'

'Of course you won't,' Dante said softly.

Rebekah gave him a surprised look, taken aback by the compassion in his voice. She had expected him to tell her she should put the past behind her, which was the advice she had been given by the few close friends who knew what had happened.

'Your child was a part of you, and losing him must have been agonising. But he lives on in your heart, *cara*. As for the excuse of a man you were once engaged to—' his face hardened '—all I can say is that you deserve so much better than him, and he did not deserve you.'

'Gareth and Claire are married, and now they have a baby,' Rebekah said dully. 'I feel as though I lost everything, and I don't know how I will ever be able to trust someone enough to have a proper relationship.'

'I'm not surprised you feel like that.' It was exactly how he had felt after Lara had ripped his world apart, Dante thought to himself.

Rebekah sighed. 'But I've got to try. I want a long-lasting marriage like my parents have and I hope one day to have another baby.' She gave Dante a ghost of a smile. 'It's tempting to lock my heart away and never risk getting hurt again, but that's cowardly, isn't it?'

Cowardly! Dante stiffened. It seemed eminently sensible of Rebekah to want to protect herself from emotional injury. After his marriage had ended he had made the decision never to put his faith and trust in a woman ever again. But that wasn't the action of a coward, he assured himself. He was a realist, possibly a cynic, but he had good reason to be.

Yet although Rebekah had been treated so cruelly by her fiancé, she was still prepared to risk being hurt again in her search for love. It would be easy to label her a romantic fool, he brooded. But he felt admiration and respect for her, coupled with the uneasy feeling that his chosen lifestyle of flitting from one meaningless affair to the next without any emotional involvement on his part was not in any way admirable.

'Come on, *mia bella*,' he murmured when he saw her eyelashes brush against her cheeks. 'You need some rest.' He was sure she must be feeling drained and she made no protest when he stood and carried her into the bedroom. He helped her slip out of her robe and get into bed before he undressed and slid in beside her. He had assumed she would fall straight to sleep, but when she snuggled up close and ran her fingers over his chest, following the path of hairs that arrowed down his stomach, he struggled to control the heated desire that swept through him.

He turned his head towards her and felt a curious tug on his insides when he looked into her beautiful violet eyes. 'Are you sure you want this?' he said thickly.

Rebekah nodded. She could not explain why confiding to Dante about Gareth's terrible betrayal had been such a relief. It was as if something dark and festering had been exposed and she felt as though she could finally let go of the bitterness that had eaten away at her. She did not forgive Gareth—some things were unforgivable. And she would never ever forget her stillborn baby. But it was time to move forwards, time to allow the hurt to heal and embrace life once more. Dante made her feel alive, and his desire for her that she could see burning in his eyes gave her a sense of self-confidence that had been missing since she had fled from Wales two years ago.

'I want you to make love to me,' she whispered, and her heart leapt when, without another word, he bent his head and claimed her mouth in a slow, drugging kiss that quickly turned to fiery passion.

He trailed his lips over her throat, her breasts, and teased her nipples with his tongue until she shivered with delight. She curled her fingers in his silky black hair as he moved down and gently pushed her thighs apart so that he could arouse her with his fingers and mouth. And finally, when she was trembling on the brink, he lifted himself above her, groaning as her molten warmth welcomed him and urged him to fill her completely.

Afterwards she fell asleep with her head pillowed on his shoulder. But Dante lay awake long into the night, wondering what was happening to him, why making love to Rebekah had left him not only physically fulfilled but relaxed and content in a way he had never felt before. It begged the question—what the hell was happening to him? And more disturbing still was that he did not have an answer.

* * *

The hot Tuscan summer days slipped past inexorably, causing Rebekah a little pang when she thought about how many days and nights she had left with Dante. It was easier not to think, easier simply to enjoy his company and the friendship that had grown between them. His desire for her had shown no sign of abating and they made love every night with a passionate intensity that she found utterly irresistible.

'Okay, I've got enough shots.' Nicole's voice drew Rebekah from her thoughts. 'Can we eat now? The sight and smell of the food is making me feel ravenous.'

Rebekah laughed. 'We'll hang on for Dante and Vito to finish playing tennis and then we'll have lunch. Knowing how competitively those two play, I think they'll have worked up an appetite for Welsh Cawl.'

'What is it, exactly?' Nicole asked as she packed away her camera and tripod.

'It's a stew made with lamb and leeks and other root vegetables. Traditionally it was cooked in an iron pot over an open fire, but it works just as well cooking it in a casserole dish in the oven.

'Shall we eat on the terrace?' Rebekah asked as she collected plates and cutlery. 'The pergola gives plenty of shade.' She followed Nicole outside. The courtyard garden was baking, but beneath the pergola covered in grapevines and bright pink bougainvillea, it was slightly cooler.

'You know, I can't believe there are only two more recipes to make and photograph before the book is finished,' she said as she flopped down onto a chair. 'I'm amazed we've done so much in three weeks.'

'And it's great that the publishers offered a contract

after you sent them the first few pages of recipes.' Nicole smiled. 'I can't wait to see the book in the shops.'

'I'm looking forward to showing it to my grand-mother.' Rebekah fell silent, her mind turning to Nana, who, according to her mother, was growing increasingly frail.

In one more week she would finish working her period of notice and be able to leave Tuscany and go home to Wales to visit her family. She felt a familiar dull ache in her chest when she contemplated leaving the Casa di Colombe, which she loved, and Dante, who, despite her best intentions, had become a serious threat to her heart.

It was his fault that she was becoming obsessed with him, she thought ruefully, her heart-rate quickening when she caught sight of him strolling back from the tennis courts with Nicole's husband Vito. Both men were darkly tanned and good-looking but Dante's height and easy grace and the chiselled perfection of his features made him especially eye-catching—something Rebekah was made aware of whenever they visited the nearby town of Montalcino and he was a magnet for female attention.

Nicole followed the direction of Rebekah's gaze towards the men and gave her a speculative look. 'So, what is your relationship with Dante? You can't kid me any longer that you're simply his cook.' She grinned when Rebekah blushed. 'Don't get me wrong—I think it's great if the two of you are involved. I was worried that Lara had scarred him for ever.'

Rebekah stiffened. 'Who is Lara?' she asked in a carefully casual voice.

'Oh—I assumed he had told you...' The American woman suddenly became evasive. 'He knew Lara years ago when he was living in New York. That's where I met him. He was friends with Vito, and then when I started dating Vito we all hung around together.' In an obvious attempt to change the subject, Nicole said, 'Why don't you and Dante come to dinner with us at the weekend? It's about time I cooked for you for a change.'

'We can't this weekend, I'm afraid.' Dante's deep voice sounded from behind Rebekah's shoulder. He dropped into the seat next to her and gave her one of his sexy smiles that made her toes curl. 'I'm taking Rebekah to Florence for a couple of days.'

'You are?' She flashed him a surprised look.

'Uh-huh. We'll be staying at a five-star hotel in the heart of the city within walking distance of the Duomo, the Campanile and the Uffizi Gallery, and we'll eat at some of the best restaurants in the city. I think you deserve a break from cooking.' His voice dropped to a husky drawl intended for Rebekah only. 'Our room has a four-poster bed and I can't promise we'll do a lot of sightseeing, *mia bella*.'

She blushed and jumped up to begin serving the lunch. But she could not help darting Dante another glance and discovered he was watching her with a feral gleam in his eyes that filled her with excitement. On most days she worked on her recipes in the mornings and Nicole arrived to take photos for the cookery book while Dante played tennis or golf with Vito. They would all eat lunch together and in the afternoons, after the other couple had left, Dante would lead her upstairs and make love to her in his cool bedroom, where the sunlight filtered through the blinds and gilded their naked, entwined limbs.

They were lazy, golden days, and she was dreading

the day when they would leave the Casa di Colombe and go their separate ways.

'Why are you taking me to Florence?' she asked him late that same afternoon, when they lay sprawled on his bed, breathing hard in the aftermath of a particularly wild sex session that had left her feeling astonished that her body could experience such intense pleasure.

'Because you said you would like to visit the city.' He could have made up an excuse, Dante mused. But what was the point? He had given up trying to rationalise why he enjoyed spending time with Rebekah—and not only in bed.

She had got under his skin. Sex with her was more fulfilling than with any of his previous mistresses, but he had also discovered that he liked talking to her and being in her company. She was interesting and her dry wit made him laugh. She also drove him mad at times because she could be sharp-tongued and prickly if she felt he was threatening her independence. Only yesterday, when they had driven into Montalcino, they'd had a fight over her refusal to allow him to pay for the traditional Tuscan clay cooking pots she'd picked up in the market.

She was a refreshing change from the usual women he dated who treated his wallet as their own personal bank, he mused. He was starting to wonder when his interest in her would fade. When they had arrived in Tuscany he had confidently expected that he would have got over his fascination with her by now. But instead he was contemplating asking her to come back to London with him at the end of the month, not to work as his chef, nor to be his mistress. If he was going to stand any chance of persuading her to give up the opportunity of working for Gaspard Clavier in St Lucia he realised he would have to offer her something more than a brief affair. The trouble was, he did not know what he wanted, and that unsettled him more than he cared to admit.

CHAPTER NINE

FLORENCE lived up to its reputation as the most beautiful city in Italy. After three days of sightseeing, Rebekah was blown away by the exquisite architecture of many of the buildings and fascinated by the city's rich history, particularly that of the powerful Medici family, whose influence had contributed to making Florence the jewel of the Renaissance.

On their last evening Dante took her to dinner at an exclusive restaurant close to the famous bridge, the Ponte Vecchio, and they sat at a table overlooking the River Arno. The fading sun set the sky ablaze and turned the river to molten gold.

'The view is breathtaking,' she murmured.

'It certainly is,' Dante agreed. Something in his voice drew Rebekah's attention to his face, and she was startled to find that his eyes were focused on her rather than the view of the river. 'And you're breathtaking too. You look stunning in that dress, *cara.*'

She flushed with pleasure at his compliment and glanced down at the jade silk gown that had been among the clothes he had bought for her. She had decided to wear the clothes, but had insisted that he should not pay her any wages for the month and instead reimburse the money he had spent on her. 'It's a matter of pride,' she'd explained when he had tried to argue. Dante had clearly been reluctant but he had agreed to do as she had asked.

'The dress is beautiful, but it's a bit too low-cut and I'm scared I'm going to fall out of it.'

'I can hope,' he said softly. The wicked glint in his eyes sent a quiver of anticipation through her and she wished they could finish dinner quickly and return to the hotel. Their luxury suite included a hot tub, and the memory of how he had made love to her in the water last night had lingered in her mind all day.

'Thank you for bringing me here,' she said softly. 'Florence is a wonderful city, and I'll always remember this trip.'

'I'm glad you've enjoyed it. Maybe we'll come back another time,' he said casually. 'I often spend a week or two in Tuscany in the autumn.'

Rebekah did not remind him that she would no longer be working for him then.

'You've gone very quiet.' Dante's voice interrupted her bleak thoughts. 'Is anything wrong?'

'I'm worried about my grandmother,' she replied, not entirely untruthfully. When she had phoned home the previous day her mother had told her that Nana had suffered a fall. Fortunately, she hadn't been seriously hurt, but her increasing frailty was a concern. 'When we leave Tuscany at the end of the week I intend to go straight to Wales to spend some time with her.'

'I'll arrange for you to fly there on the jet as soon as we arrive in England. I imagine you will want to stay with your family for a few days.' His grey eyes sought hers across the table. 'After that, why don't you come back to London?'

Rebekah stared at him, wishing she could read his mind. Was he asking her to continue working for him, or was there another reason for his invitation? If he asked her to carry on their affair she would have to refuse, she told herself firmly. His interest in her would last for a few months at most. But while he would simply move on to another affair, she feared she would be left with a broken heart.

'We made an agreement that I would leave you when I had served my notice, and nothing has changed.'

'Of course it has,' he replied imperturbably. 'We're good together, *mia bella*.' He gave a laconic shrug. 'Why change what is good?'

Because, for Dante, what they had amounted to great sex, while for her... Rebekah swallowed when he reached across the table and captured her hand, lifted it to his mouth and grazed his lips across her fingers.

'Let's go back to the hotel and I'll show you how you make me feel,' he murmured huskily.

There had been no point in continuing the argument, she thought when they left the restaurant and strolled hand in hand through the quaint narrow streets of Florence. They arrived at their hotel and, as soon as they stepped into the lift and the doors closed, Dante pulled her into his arms and kissed her so thoroughly that she stopped worrying about the future and focused on the sensuous anticipation of knowing that they would soon be enjoying the pleasure of making love once more.

In the bedroom he undressed her by the light of the silver moon and the diamond-bright stars that were visible through the open curtains.

'*Sei così bella,*' he whispered as he drew the jade silk dress down and cradled her voluptuous breasts in his palms. He kissed her mouth, her throat and breasts before he sank to his knees and explored the heart of her femininity with his tongue.

Then he stood and she stripped him with trembling hands. Dropping to her knees, she gifted him the same pleasure he had given her, caressing him with her tongue until he groaned and pulled her to her feet.

'Wrap your legs around me,' he bade as he lifted her and held her against his hips. When she complied, he entered her and she cried out with the joy of his possession. The world disappeared and only she and Dante existed. He made love to her with a passion and an exquisite tenderness that captivated her soul and brought tears to her eyes.

As for Dante, lying with Rebekah in the sweet aftermath of their mutual pleasure, he wondered why she was insisting that she intended to leave him when it was quite clear she did not want to go. Surely she realised how much he desired her? Perhaps she was afraid that if she continued their relationship she could end up getting hurt, he brooded. Knowing how her ex-fiancé had betrayed her, he could not blame her for being wary.

Turning his head, he saw that she had fallen asleep and he felt a curious little tug on his insides as he studied her rose-flushed face and long dark eyelashes that curled on her cheeks. She was so beautiful—a beguiling mix of sex kitten and gut-wrenchingly generous lover.

He did not want to lose her, he acknowledged. So did that mean he was prepared to make some sort of commitment to her? He gave a sigh of frustration. If only they could remain in Tuscany in the private little world they had created. There would be no reason for them to discuss their relationship and he could simply enjoy being with her. But that, he realised heavily, was a coward's attitude. At some point he was going to have to come to terms with his past because he understood now that holding on to his bitter memories was preventing him from moving on with his life.

The storm broke two days after they returned to the Casa di Colombe. Ominous clouds had gathered over the distant hills and the air prickled with static electricity.

The strange tension seemed to reflect Dante's mood, Rebekah thought as she pegged the washing on the line, hoping it would dry before the rain fell. He had been behaving oddly ever since she had mentioned on the drive back from Florence that Nicole had told her he had once lived in New York. For some reason he had stiffened and muttered that it had been years ago.

She should have let the matter drop, but her curiosity to know as many details about him as she could had prompted her to ask him about Lara.

'She was someone I met in the States,' Dante had said tersely. 'I don't know why Nicole had to drag up the past.'

'Was she a girlfriend?' Rebekah could not help asking.

'What does it matter who she was? I told you, I knew her years ago.' He had given a careless shrug, but Rebekah had wondered why he had tightened his hands on the steering wheel until his knuckles had turned white. Realising that her prying had annoyed him, she had tried to make light conversation for the rest of the journey, but his responses had been monosyllabic. And that night, for the first time since they had been in Tuscany, he had not made love to her, but rolled onto his side, saying coolly that she was no doubt tired after their trip and she should get some sleep.

Maybe he was becoming bored of her, she thought bleakly as she walked back into the house. Maybe he was glad that they would be leaving Tuscany in a few short days, while she was dreading saying goodbye to him for ever. She was almost glad he had asked her to sort out his grandmother's room. At least being busy stopped her from thinking about next Saturday, when they were due to leave.

Perlita's personal belongings had not been touched since her death and Dante had requested Rebekah to empty the wardrobes and pack up his grandmother's clothes so that they could be sent to a charity shop.

He walked in while she was pulling out boxes from beneath the bed. One storage chest contained old curtains but the contents of the second box were puzzling.

'Children's clothes,' she said in surprise, 'for a baby or toddler, I should think, from the size of them. And I guess, as they're mainly blue, that they belong to a little boy. Oh, there's a photo of a child…' She reached into the box, but Dante leaned over her and snatched the picture out of her hand before she could study it properly.

'Don't touch anything in the box,' he ordered curtly. 'Shut the lid and leave it alone. In fact, you can leave the room. I'll take over packing up my grandmother's things.'

'All right—keep your hair on!' Rebekah sprang to her feet, but her irritation at being spoken to in such a peremptory tone faded when she saw Dante's unguarded expression. It was the same agonised look she'd glimpsed in his eyes when he had shown her the photograph of his grandmother the day they had arrived at the house, nearly a month ago. She had sensed his grief at Perlita's death was still raw. But why did he look devastated as he dropped to his knees in front of the box and lifted out a child's teddy bear?

'Boppa Bear,' he murmured, as if he had forgotten Rebekah was there. 'I had no idea Nonna had kept some of Ben's things.'

She felt she should slip quietly from the room and leave Dante alone. He had told her once that he did not need anyone, but she did not believe it. The haunted look in his eyes evoked an ache in her heart and, without conscious thought, she placed her hand gently on his shoulder.

'Who...who is Ben?'

'It doesn't matter.' Shrugging off her hand, he dropped the toy bear into the box and closed the lid with a sharp thud before standing up. 'It's not your concern.' He stared at her, his eyes no longer full of pain, but hard and unfathomable. 'I came to tell you I heard your phone ringing somewhere in the house. You'd better go and find it.'

It was possible Dante had made up that he had heard her phone, but Rebekah had more sense than to ignore his strong hint that he wanted to be left alone. 'I left it in the kitchen,' she muttered as she walked out of the room. She could not help feeling hurt by his refusal to confide in her about the identity of the mystery child. Clearly the toys and other items in the box had held a sentimental meaning for his grandmother. Perhaps, many years ago, Perlita had lost a son, she mused. But the baby clothes were made of modern material and the bear looked much too new to have been fifty or more years old.

She heard her phone ringing. As she hurried along

the glass-covered cloister and into the kitchen, the rain started to fall, smashing against the windows with awesome force that almost drowned out the low rumble of thunder.

The caller's number on the screen was instantly recognizable and, with a sense of foreboding, she picked up her phone. 'Mum?'

Ten minutes later, Dante swung round from the window, where he had been staring out unseeingly at the rain and frowned as Rebekah entered his grandmother's room. 'I told you I would take care of things in here,' he said harshly. He controlled his impatience when he noticed her ashen face. 'What's the matter? Did you find out who was calling you?'

'It was my mother. My grandmother is in hospital.' Rebekah strove to keep the emotion from her voice but failed. 'She…she's not expected to last much longer. I must go home.'

'Yes, of course.' As he was speaking, Dante pulled his phone from his pocket to contact his pilot. In a strange way it was a relief to focus on something else rather than dwell on the fact that his grandmother had kept some of Ben's things.

He glanced at Rebekah and his gut clenched when he saw the way she was biting her lip to prevent the tears glistening in her eyes from falling. For a moment he was tempted to take her in his arms and offer her whatever comfort he could. But a chasm seemed to have opened up between them. He could almost see her barriers going up and it was hardly surprising after the way he had snapped at her, he thought heavily.

He wished he had explained things to her. Perhaps if she knew about his past she would understand why he found it hard to open up and reveal his emotions. But now was not the time. She had problems of her own to deal with and his priority was to arrange her immediate return to Wales.

'The pilot will have the plane ready in an hour,' he told her. 'Go and pack whatever you need, and I'll arrange for the rest of your things to be sent on to you.'

'Thank you.' Rebekah blinked hard and willed her tears not to fall. So this was the end. It was possible that after today she would never see Dante again. It was better this way, she told herself, better that he had no idea she had fallen in love with him. At least she still had her pride. But it seemed a cold comfort and, as she turned in the doorway for one last look at him, she felt as though a little part of her had died.

Nana Glenys passed away peacefully a week after Rebekah returned home. The book of her recipes was still with the publishers, but Rebekah had taken copies of Nicole's photos to the hospital. Nana had seemed more like her old self that day, and she had squeezed Rebekah's hand and whispered how proud she felt that both their names were going to be on the front of the book. It was the last conversation Rebekah had with her but her grief at Nana's death was eased a little by the knowledge that she had made her beloved grandmother happy.

The funeral was attended by the whole village, and in the days afterwards Rebekah helped her parents with the task of clearing out Nana's cottage. Dante phoned when she had been in Wales for three weeks and asked if she would be returning to London. She had secretly hoped he would try to make her change her mind when she told him she wouldn't be going back to him. But he merely wished her well in a cool, faintly bored voice which told her clearly that if she had not ended their affair he would undoubtedly have done so.

She hung on to her dignity long enough to say an equally cool goodbye, but as soon as she put the phone down she had a good cry and told herself how stupid she had been for falling for a playboy. Then she blew her nose and reminded herself that she could not remain at her parents' farm indefinitely. She needed to find a job and get on with her life. Gaspard Clavier was still keen for her to work for him when she contacted him and suggested she meet him at his London restaurant to discuss plans for his new restaurant in St Lucia.

It was while she was studying her diary to pick a date to visit Gaspard that she realised she was late. It was now early September and when she flicked back through the diary's pages she saw that her last period had been in the middle of July, while she had been in Tuscany. With all the upset over Nana's death, it hadn't occurred to her that she had missed a period in August. At first she tried to reassure herself that it was just a blip in her cycle. She couldn't be pregnant. For one thing, she was on the Pill, and most of the time Dante had used a condom. But, as the days passed with no sign that would put her mind at rest, she did the only sensible thing and bought a pregnancy test.

As she sat on the edge of the bath, waiting as the minutes ticked past agonisingly slowly, she could hardly believe she was in this situation again. On the one previous occasion that she had done a test she had been looking forward to marrying the man she loved and had excitedly hoped the result would be positive. She had been overjoyed when she'd discovered she was expecting Gareth's baby, but her dreams of a family had been shattered by his terrible behaviour, which she was convinced had caused her to lose the child.

Now, as she stared at the two lines in the little window of the test kit, she was swamped by a host of conflicting emotions. A new life was developing inside her. Dante's baby! The child would not replace the one she had lost, but she felt an overwhelming sense of joy and fierce protectiveness. She would do everything possible to ensure this baby was born safe and well. And she would love it—dear God, she loved it already. But what would Dante's reaction be? She felt sick as memories of Gareth's angry rejection of her first baby haunted her. Would a notorious playboy react any differently to the news that he was to be a father?

Her GP had a further surprise in store when he said she could potentially already be ten weeks into the pregnancy. The unusually light period she'd had in Tuscany might have been what was known as spotting that sometimes occurred in the first month after conception.

'It's vital with the type of mini-pill you are on that you take it at exactly the same time every day,' the doctor explained when she pointed out that she used oral contraceptives. 'Also, sickness or a stomach upset can stop the Pill from being effective.'

Rebekah recalled the night Dante had taken her to the theatre—the first time she'd had sex with him. At the party she had unwittingly drunk alcohol in the fruit punch and the next morning her body had reacted badly and she had been sick for most of the day. She must have conceived Dante's child that first time. He had almost stopped making love to her until she had assured him she was protected, she remembered.

'I can't believe I didn't have any sign that I was pregnant,' she said to the GP, who knew her history. 'With my first pregnancy I had dreadful morning sickness, but this time I've had nothing, apart from feeling a bit more tired than usual.' She had put her lack of energy and her uncharacteristic weepiness down to the fact that she missed Dante unbearably.

'Every pregnancy is different,' the doctor told her. He gave her a kindly smile. 'You're fit and healthy, and there is no reason why you shouldn't give birth to a healthy baby in seven months' time.'

Reassured by the doctor's words, Rebekah walked out of his surgery feeling that her heart would burst with happiness as she imagined being a mother. Of course the situation wasn't ideal. She had always assumed she would be married before she started a family. Her heart jerked painfully against her ribs at the prospect of telling Dante her news. But he would have to be told that he was going to be a father, she decided. The baby developing inside her had been created by two people, and she and Dante both had a responsibility towards their child.

Dante stared unenthusiastically at the cod in white sauce on his plate. A sample mouthful had revealed that it tasted as bland as it looked. But he could not put all the blame for his lack of appetite on his new cook, he acknowledged. Mrs Hall did her best and the meals she provided were edible, if unexciting.

A memory came into his head of Rebekah's fish pie—succulent pieces of cod, smoked salmon and prawns in a creamy parsley sauce, with a crunchy rosti and grated cheese topping. Her wonderful food was the first thing that had impressed him about her. It had taken him a little longer to appreciate all her other qualities, he mused. But she had kept her fabulous figure hidden beneath shapeless clothes until the night he had taken her to the theatre and she had blown his mind when she had worn a stunning evening gown that had shown off her voluptuous curves.

He hadn't been able to keep his hands off her that night, or all the nights during the month they had spent in Tuscany. An image of her slid into his mind and Dante felt a predictable stirring in his loins, followed by the dull ache of frustration that had been responsible for his foul mood over the past few months.

He still found it hard to believe she had rejected him. She had given every impression of being happy with him when they had been in Tuscany. They had spent practically every moment together and had made love every night with a wild passion that he was convinced she had enjoyed as much as he had.

But the stilted conversation they'd had when he had phoned her in Wales had put an end to his pleasurable anticipation of continuing their affair in London. He had felt a curious hollow sensation in his stomach when she had told him she would not be coming back to him. It had crossed his mind briefly to try and persuade her, but he'd dismissed the idea. She had made her choice and he certainly wasn't going to let her know he was disappointed. He'd assured himself he did not care and that he could find a replacement mistress any time he liked. He had even dated a couple of women but, although they had both been beautiful, elegant blondes, he had realised halfway through dinner that they completely bored him and he had not asked either of them out a second time.

Giving up on dinner, he carried his plate into the kitchen and tipped away the uneaten meal. It was fortunate that Mrs Hall did not live in the staff apartment. She had no idea that most of the dinners she cooked for him ended up in the recycling bin. He wandered listlessly into the sitting room and poured himself a straight Scotch, his second since he'd got home from work an hour ago. He snapped his teeth together impatiently. Not only had Rebekah unmanned him and caused his current worrying lack of libido, but he could also blame her for the damage he was doing to his liver!

His frown deepened at the sound of the doorbell. He wasn't expecting visitors and was half-inclined not to answer, but a second strident peal suggested that whoever was standing on his doorstep was not going to go away any time soon.

Muttering an oath, he strode down the hall, flung open the door—and froze.

'Hello, Dante.'

Rebekah had to force the greeting past the sudden tightness in her throat and her voice sounded annoyingly husky rather than bright and brisk, as she had been aiming for. She hadn't forgotten how good-looking Dante was, but seeing him in the flesh made her catch her breath. Dark trousers hugged his lean hips and his pale blue shirt was open at the throat so that she could see a few black chest hairs. Lifting her eyes to his face, she was struck by the masculine beauty of his features. His cheekbones looked more defined than she remembered and his olive skin was stretched taut over them. The firm line of his jaw was hard and uncompromising but his mouth evoked memories of him kissing her, and she wished with all her heart that he would sweep her into his arms and claim her lips with hungry passion.

For a split second Dante wondered if his mind was playing tricks on him. It seemed an incredible coincidence that just as he had been thinking about Rebekah she appeared, like the fairy godmother in a children's story book. But he would bet no fairy godmother ever looked as gorgeous as the woman who was hovering—somewhat nervously, he noted—in front of him. She looked achingly beautiful, with her long chocolate-brown hair falling around her shoulders and her incredible violet eyes staring at him from beneath the sweep of her long lashes.

Dragging his gaze from her face, he saw that she was wearing a cherry-red wool coat that brightened the gloom of the misty October evening. She looked wholesome and sexy and he was unbearably tempted to pull her into his arms and crush her soft mouth beneath his until she returned his kiss with sensual passion, the memory of which kept him awake at nights. Pride stopped him from reaching for her, and that same damnable pride demanded that he should not make it too easy for her. Did she think she could simply walk back into his life?

'Rebekah—this is a surprise,' he said coolly. 'I didn't know you were in London. Have you moved down from Wales, or are you visiting?'

'I…' Rebekah was completely thrown by Dante's nonchalant greeting. This was the man who had been a passionate lover and someone she had thought of as a friend when she had spent a month with him at his home in Tuscany. From his careless tone, anyone would think they had been no more than casual acquaintances. But that was probably how he regarded her, she thought bleakly. He had enjoyed a brief sexual fling with her but now she was just another ex-mistress and it was likely that her replacement was waiting for him in his bed.

Feeling sick at the idea, she almost lost her nerve and half-turned to walk away from him.

'So, how are you?' He pulled the door open a little wider, and Rebekah glanced into the hall, half-expecting to see some gorgeous leggy blonde.

'I…' Running away wasn't an option, she reminded herself. She needed to tell Dante he was the father of her child, but so far she hadn't managed to string more than two words together. 'I'm fine, but I need to talk to you— if you're not…entertaining anyone tonight,' she choked.

He gave her a quizzical look. 'No, I happen to be free tonight. You'd better come in.'

The house was achingly familiar. Glancing round the elegant sitting room, she noticed that the potted ferns she had bought to give the room a more homely feel were thriving, as if someone had been taking care of them.

It was warm inside. She unbuttoned her coat but kept it on when she realised he might notice her slightly rounded stomach—which was silly when she was about to tell him about the baby, she thought wryly. Her mouth felt uncomfortably dry and she licked her lips nervously. His reaction to the news she was about to give him couldn't be worse than Gareth's had been. She suddenly realised how much she wanted him to be pleased about the baby. Was she being a fool to hope he would want his child?

'I suppose you're wondering why I'm here,' she said in a rush.

Dante shrugged. 'Actually, I can guess your reason.'

She was flummoxed. 'You…you can?'

'Sure.' He put down the glass he was holding and strolled over to her but, although he moved with his usual easy grace, the predatory gleam in his eyes caused Rebekah's heart to miss a beat. 'You miss what we had in Tuscany and you're hoping I'll take you back. And you know what, *cara*?' he murmured as he halted in front of her and dipped his head so that his mouth was tantalisingly close to hers. 'You're in luck. I still want you too.'

In the flesh, Rebekah was even more gorgeous than his memory of her, Dante thought. He had missed her. He finally acknowledged the truth that he had tried to deny to himself for the past weeks. It was not just her gorgeous body and the passion they had shared that he had missed; it was her lovely smile and her beautiful eyes, the soft, lilting way she spoke, the sound of her laughter and just the pleasure of her company. Unable to resist the lure of her soft lips, he slanted his mouth over hers and kissed her.

Rebekah was so surprised that she responded to him unthinkingly. Oh, she'd missed him, she thought, as he deepened the kiss to something so deeply sensual that she began to tremble, and when he pulled her close she melted in his arms.

'I recall the sofa was a very comfortable place to make love,' he murmured. 'Or shall we attempt to make it to my bedroom this time?'

'No…I mean…neither. I'm not here for that,' Rebekah gasped. The sound of Dante's voice shattered the sensual web he had woven around her and, with a little cry of despair that she had succumbed to him so weakly, she pulled out of his arms.

'You could have fooled me,' he said drily. Why was she playing hard to get? Dante wondered impatiently. He grabbed his glass and strode over to the bar. 'Do you want a drink?' he asked roughly, pouring himself another Scotch. 'I forgot—you can't drink alcohol. I can offer you a soft drink.'

'No, thanks.' Rebekah took a deep breath. 'Actually, my strange allergy to alcohol is sort of the reason why I'm here.'

Dante lifted his brows but made no comment. On the train journey from Wales Rebekah had rehearsed what she was going to say to him, but the kiss had thrown her. She hadn't expected him to still desire her. Perhaps it was a good thing, she thought shakily. It gave her hope that they might be able to make something of their relationship. But first she had to tell him, and the longer she hesitated the harder it was becoming.

'I…I'm going to have a baby,' she blurted out.

He went very still and for a second his shock showed on his face. His silence simmered with tension. Lifting his glass, he took a swig of his drink.

'Congratulations. I assume that's what you want me to say?' His jaw tightened. 'You didn't waste much time, did you? I assume the father is someone you met when you went back to Wales.'

CHAPTER TEN

REBEKAH had tried a hundred times over the past weeks to imagine what Dante's reaction would be, but it had never occurred to her that he would jump to the conclusion that she was pregnant with another man's child.

'The baby is yours,' she said quietly. 'I conceived the first night we slept together after the party.'

For what seemed like a lifetime he made no response. 'You assured me you were on the Pill,' he said eventually. His expression was unreadable. 'I trusted you.'

His words seemed to echo around the silent room. Dante felt as though a lump of ice had formed inside him and his blood ran cold as he remembered the other occasion when he had been told by a woman that she was pregnant with his child. Like a fool, he had believed Lara. This time he would not be so gullible or so trusting, he thought grimly.

How could Dante's eyes that a few moments ago had blazed with fiery passion have turned to hard steel? She hadn't expected him to be thrilled to learn of his impending fatherhood, Rebekah acknowledged, but his coldness felt like a knife in her heart.

'I certainly didn't lie to you,' she told him with quiet dignity. 'I *was* on the Pill but, because there is a history of high blood pressure in my family, I was taking the mini-pill, which isn't quite as effective as the more common type. I didn't know there was alcohol in the fruit punch at the ball, and if I had I wouldn't have touched it. When I was sick after we spent the night together I didn't realise I wasn't protected against falling pregnant.'

He stared at her speculatively. 'You must admit it sounds convenient,' he said at last, in a curiously emotionless voice. 'If the child you are carrying is really mine, why did you wait so long to tell me? It's the end of October, yet you say you conceived at the end of June. That's *four* months.'

He strode back over to her and jerked the edges of her coat open, seeing the slight but distinct mound of her belly, and shock jolted through him. There was no doubt she was pregnant, but he was struggling with the idea that it could be his child.

'My dad was seriously injured in an accident on the farm. The tractor he was driving rolled over and he was crushed beneath it.' Rebekah's voice shook at the memory of seeing her father's body trapped beneath the tractor's wheels. Her mother, usually so calm, had looked terrified, and her older brother Owen had been grim-faced as he had called the emergency services. Ifan Evans was a giant of a man who had never suffered a day's illness in his life. His near-fatal accident had shaken the whole family, and for several weeks while he remained in intensive care Rebekah had simply pushed her pregnancy to the back of her mind and concentrated on supporting her parents through their ordeal. It was only now her father was back home at the farm and making a good recovery that she was able to focus on the new life growing inside her.

'I understand you must be shocked about the baby,' she told Dante. 'I was too at first. But we're both intelligent adults and we have to accept that no form of contraception is one hundred per cent safe.'

'I'll want proof that the child is mine.'

She bit her lip and tasted blood. 'And once you have your proof, will you demand I have an abortion?' Her voice shook as she fought to control her emotions. 'If so, you'll waste your breath because I am going to have this child, with or without your support.'

He was visibly shocked. 'Of course I would not want you to…' He couldn't bring himself to finish the sentence and he cursed himself for his insensitivity when he remembered how her ex-fiancé had reacted when she had told him she was pregnant. Had Rebekah hoped he would be pleased to hear she was expecting his child? If so, then he had cruelly disappointed her, he accepted, gripped by guilt as he stared at her tense face. She deserved so much more than he had given her. But he was reeling from shock and all he could think of was how he'd felt as if his heart had been ripped out when Lara had taken Ben.

When Rebekah had told him she was pregnant he had experienced a feeling of déjà vu. It seemed unbelievable that history was repeating itself. The hurt expression in her violet eyes made him wince.

'How do you feel about the pregnancy?' he asked her gruffly.

'Happy,' she said instantly. Her voice wobbled. 'And scared.'

Dante turned away from her and sloshed more whisky into his glass, vaguely surprised to find that his hands were shaking. It was his fault that Rebekah was in this situation, he thought grimly. She had suffered the agony of her first child being stillborn and understandably this second pregnancy must bring back terrible memories and make her afraid of what lay ahead. She needed his reassurance and support, not his anger. But he could not reach out to her. It shamed him to admit that he was scared too, afraid of being hurt like he had been once before.

Rebekah felt sick with despair. Once again she was carrying a child inside her who was not wanted by its father. Blazing anger replaced her misery. Fatherhood might not appeal to Dante but he had a responsibility to his baby. How dared he try and wriggle out of that responsibility by suggesting that the baby wasn't his?

'I am carrying your child, no one else's.' She placed a hand on her stomach and her eyes blazed with maternal pride and protectiveness. 'In five months' time we are going to be parents, so you'd better get used to the idea.'

She took a steadying breath, afraid that her thudding heartbeat couldn't be good for the baby. And the baby was all that mattered. The welfare of the tiny scrap of life inside her was her only concern and it should be Dante's too. 'If you insist on proof, I'm willing for a paternity test to be done.' She closed her eyes to hold back the tears that suddenly blinded her. 'How could you think I would try and con you into fatherhood if I knew the child wasn't yours?'

Dante gulped down the rest of the whisky in his glass, aware that he owed Rebekah an explanation. In fact the explanation was long overdue, he thought heavily, when he saw the shimmer of tears in her eyes.

'Because it has happened to me once before,' he said harshly.

'I...I don't understand.' For some reason, a memory slid into Rebekah's mind of the box she had found in Dante's grandmother's bedroom at the house in Tuscany. She recalled his strange reaction when she had opened the box and found a child's clothes and toys. 'It has something to do with Ben, doesn't it?' she said slowly. '*Who* is he?'

'I believed he was my son. And for that reason I married his mother.'

That wasn't completely true, Dante acknowledged silently. He had been in love with Lara and when she had told him she was pregnant with his baby he had seized the opportunity to make her his wife.

Rebekah's legs suddenly felt as though they wouldn't support her. 'You were *married*?' She was staggered to think that Dante—the anti-marriage, anti-commitment divorce lawyer had once been married. She wondered if he had loved his wife. Something in his voice told her that he had, and she felt an agonising stab of jealousy. She frowned as she recalled his curious statement that he had *believed* Ben was his son. 'I don't understand,' she said wearily.

Dante saw Rebekah sway unsteadily. Her face was deathly pale and he feared she was about to faint. He cursed himself. She was pregnant but, instead of taking care of her, he had not even invited her to take her coat off.

'Sit down,' he commanded roughly, his frown deepening when she did not protest as he tugged her coat from her shoulders and pushed her gently down into an armchair. She rested her head against the cushions and closed her eyes so that her long lashes fanned her cheeks. While she was off her guard he studied her, roaming his eyes greedily over her firm breasts and coming to a juddering halt when he reached the rounded swell of her stomach. For the first time since she had told him she was pregnant he thought about what that actually meant. There was a strong likelihood that the child inside her was his. A strange feeling that he could not even begin to assimilate unfurled inside him. He stretched out a hand to her, compelled to touch her stomach, but snatched it back as she opened her eyes.

'Are you keeping well? Eating properly and everything?' he demanded awkwardly.

'Like a horse,' she said drily, 'which is why I'm showing already. I'm afraid I'm not going to be one of those women who sail through pregnancy with hardly any visible sign and snap back into their skinny jeans half an hour after giving birth.'

'What does it matter?' It occurred to Dante that Rebekah had never looked more beautiful than she did now. He found her curvaceous figure incredibly sexy, but there was something else about her that he couldn't explain, an air of serenity and contentment that softened her face and made her lovelier than ever.

Abruptly he moved away from her, strode over to the bar and refilled his glass. 'You said you don't understand about Ben, so I'll tell you.

'Six years ago I worked for a law firm in New York and had an affair with another lawyer at the company. Lara was a couple of years older than me. She'd been a top catwalk model but had given up modelling to concentrate on her legal career.'

So the mysterious Lara, who Nicole had mentioned in Tuscany, was beautiful and brainy, Rebekah thought dismally. She realised Dante had continued speaking, and forced herself to concentrate on what he was saying.

'I knew she had been seeing another guy before I met her, but she assured me the relationship was over.' Dante grimaced. 'I admit I was blown away by her. She was stunningly attractive, ambitious, sophisticated—everything I most admired. My parents' marital problems had made me wary of marriage, but when Lara said she was expecting my baby I was keen to marry her, and although the pregnancy was unplanned I was excited at the prospect of being a father.

'I watched our son being born and held him in my arms when he was a few minutes old. Ben stole my heart,' he said gruffly. 'I was besotted with him, and I took care of him a lot of the time because Lara wanted to pursue her career. Several times I even took him to visit my grandmother at the Casa di Colombe while Lara remained in New York.

'Perlita adored him as much as I did. But during a trip to Tuscany when Ben was two years old, Lara arrived unexpectedly and announced that our marriage was over. It was a bolt from the blue. I'd had no reason to think she was unhappy with our relationship. But she admitted she had been having an affair with her ex-boyfriend for several months and intended to divorce me and marry him.'

Dante took a long swig of whisky and relished its fiery heat as it hit the back of his throat.

'I was angry that she had cheated on me, but my main concern was for Ben and I tried to persuade her to give our marriage another try.' His jaw clenched. 'She then dropped the bombshell that I wasn't Ben's father. At the same time that she had begun an affair with me, she had slept with her ex a couple of times. When she'd realised she was pregnant she knew the other guy was the father. But he had ended his relationship with her and moved away—and he didn't have any money. I, on the other hand, had good career prospects and a ton of money, and so she deliberately led me to believe Ben was my son—until his real father showed up again, complete with a sizeable inheritance fund and a willingness to take responsibility for his child.'

'Oh, Dante.'

It was incredible how two words could hold such a depth of compassion, Dante thought, feeling that strange sensation of something unfurling inside him again when he saw the gentle expression in Rebekah's eyes.

She stood up and walked over to him, and unbelievably she reached out and touched his arm, as if she hoped the physical contact would show that she understood how devastated he had been by Lara's deception. He swallowed, thinking that he had treated her shamefully, yet she had not hesitated to show her sympathy for him.

The bleak expression in Dante's eyes told Rebekah that he had not come to terms with his wife's terrible deception or the pain of losing the child he had loved. She sensed that even after he had learned that Ben was not his son he had still cared for the little boy.

'What happened to Ben?' she asked quietly.

'Lara took him and I never saw him again. I understand she married Ben's father, and as far as I know they're still together.'

Rebekah did not know what to say that wouldn't sound trite. 'What happened to you was terrible,' she murmured. 'But this situation is different. I swear the baby is yours and I've agreed to a paternity test.'

Perhaps when he'd had a chance to get over his shock about her pregnancy he would see that his baby needed its father. She suddenly felt bone-weary, probably the result of anti-climax and a surfeit of emotions, she told herself. She felt a desperate need to be alone while she assimilated everything Dante had told her about his past. It was little wonder he had reacted with such suspicion to her claim that she was expecting his baby after the way his wife had lied to him.

'How soon can we have the paternity test?' she asked flatly.

'I'll arrange for us to give blood samples tomorrow. It usually takes a week to ten days before the results come back.' He had dealt with enough paternity issues during his clients' divorce cases to be sure of his facts. Dante's eyes narrowed as he watched Rebekah slip on her coat. 'Where are you going?'

'I'm staying at my friend Charlie's overnight. Where shall I meet you for the blood test?'

'I think you should stay here tonight.' He was surprised at how strongly he hated the idea of her leaving. It was slowly sinking in that if the baby was his they would have to discuss what they were going to do, how they were both going to bring up their child.

Dio, was he being a fool to believe the baby was his? His instincts told him he could trust Rebekah. He would swear she was honest and truthful. But he had trusted Lara once, taunted a bitter voice inside his head. After his divorce, he had vowed he would never trust a woman again.

'You can stay in your old room,' he told her. 'The

clothes you left behind are still there. In the morning I'll drive you to the clinic in Harley Street.'

'No, thanks.' Rebekah could not face the idea of sleeping in the same house as Dante. Not because she was worried he would try to persuade her into his bed, but because she knew he wouldn't. Seeing him again had made her realise just how much she had missed him. She must be even more of a fool than she'd thought because even though he was demanding proof that the baby was his she still ached for him to take her in his arms and stroke her hair, as he had often done during their heartbreakingly brief affair.

'Charlie is expecting me. If you wouldn't mind calling me a taxi, I'd like to go now.'

'Don't be ridiculous,' Dante said roughly when he realised he could not force her to stay. 'I'll take you to your friend's.'

'You can't; you've been drinking.'

She was right—the amount of whisky he'd downed meant that he could not get behind the wheel of a car. He controlled his impatience and fought the urge to pull her into his arms and tell her he believed the baby was his. His brain told him to wait for proof, and so he ignored what his heart was telling him.

'My chauffeur will drive you to where you are staying,' he said curtly, 'and I'll collect you in the morning.'

Rebekah's parents' farm was in Snowdonia National Park. If Dante had not had other things on his mind he would no doubt have admired the dramatic landscape of lush green valleys and rugged mountain peaks, the highest of which bore the first snowfall of the winter. But he was concentrating on driving along the tortuously twisting lanes and whenever his mind wandered it returned inevitably to Rebekah and the baby she was carrying.

Was it only two days since she had turned up at his house in London and told him she was pregnant? It felt like a lifetime ago. He frowned at the memory of how pale and fragile she had looked when he had collected her from her friend's house where she had spent the night, and driven her to the clinic for the prenatal paternity test to be done.

He had felt worried about her, especially as the dark circles beneath her eyes had been evidence that she had not slept.

'Come and stay at the house for a few days while we wait for the results,' he had urged her. But she had shaken her head.

'I bought a return train ticket to Wales. I want to go home,' she'd told him when he had started to argue. 'I need to be with people who care about me. My family have been brilliant and I know that whatever happens I can count on their love and support.'

Had she been making a dig at him for his lack of support? She had been perfectly within her rights to, Dante acknowledged grimly. For the past two days he had thought about her constantly and he'd come to the conclusion that he should be shot for the appalling way he had treated her.

Yesterday he had phoned her, not really knowing what he wanted to say but aware that he needed to apologise. She had answered his queries about how she was feeling with a coolness that had been infuriating and worrying.

'Obviously we will have to decide what will happen if the test proves the baby is mine,' he had said and had frowned when he realised how stilted he sounded. Her silence had rattled him. 'There will be things to discuss—financial matters and so on.' Once again his words hadn't reflected what he really wanted to say. And he'd realised as he wiped beads of sweat from his brow that he was the biggest fool on the planet.

He forced himself to concentrate as the road narrowed to a muddy track, and a few moments later he swung the car through some iron gates and came to a halt outside a rather tired-looking grey stone farmhouse. The farmyard appeared deserted apart from a few chickens pecking in the mud. As he approached the house a dog began to bark. The front door looked as though it hadn't been opened for years, but at the side of the house a door stood ajar and led into the kitchen.

No one came when he knocked, but he could hear voices talking in a language he had never heard before, which he presumed was Welsh. He supposed he should have phoned Rebekah to tell her he was coming, but he hadn't because he wanted to catch her off guard, before she had a chance to erect the barriers he had sensed she'd put in place when he had spoken to her yesterday.

A cat wound through his legs as he walked across the kitchen. He hesitated for a second and then pushed open the door in front of him and stepped into a crowded room. At least a dozen people were sitting at a long dining table, and numerous children were seated around a smaller table. At the head of the main table sat a giant of a man, grey-haired with a weathered face, who he guessed was Rebekah's father. Dante glanced at her brothers, all as huge as their father, but his eyes moved swiftly to Rebekah and he felt a sudden pain in his chest, as if an arrow had pierced between his ribs.

She was smiling, and for some reason that hurt him. He hadn't felt like smiling since…since Tuscany, when she had made him laugh with her dry wit and atrociously bad jokes.

The sound of chatter slowly died as the people in the room became aware of a stranger in their midst. The suspicious stares from the army of Welshmen and their wives emphasised that he was an outsider.

Dante had a sudden flashback to when he had been ten years old, at boarding school. It had been the end of term and most of the boys were gathered in the quadrangle, waiting for their parents to collect them to take them home for the holidays. But his parents weren't coming. His father had arranged for him to stay with the headmaster and his family for the Easter break. Staring out of a classroom window, he had felt detached from the other boys' excitement. All his life he had never felt that he belonged anywhere.

He certainly did not belong here in this Welsh farmhouse. But Rebekah did. He could almost sense the invisible bonds that tied her closely to her family—a family that at this moment were unified in protecting her.

Her father made to stand up, but the younger man sitting beside him got to his feet first, saying, 'I'll deal with this, *Tada.*'

Rebekah's smile had died on her lips and she was staring at him as if he had two heads. She scraped back her chair and, as she stood up, Dante felt a surge of emotion as his eyes were drawn to her rounded stomach. His child was growing inside her, his flesh and blood. He looked around the sea of faces all gazing warily at him and he no longer cared if they regarded him as an outsider. Rebekah was carrying his baby and he was determined to convince her that he wanted to be a father.

CHAPTER ELEVEN

'SIT down, Beka,' her brother ordered.

She threw him a sharp glance, her eyes flashing fire. 'It's my problem, Owen, and I'll deal with it.' Turning back to face Dante, she lifted her head proudly and shook back her long silky hair. 'Why are you here?'

Since when had she viewed him as a *problem*? He felt a sudden fierce blaze of anger. How dared she speak to him in that coolly polite voice, as if he were a casual acquaintance rather than the man whose child's heart beat within her? With great effort he swallowed his temper and said quietly, 'We need to talk.'

One of the women seated at the table stood up. Rebekah's mother was short and plump, her dark hair was threaded with silver strands but her violet-coloured eyes were sharp and bright. It occurred to Dante that the Evans women were formidable and he suspected that, for all their huge size, the men of the family would think twice about arguing with them.

'You must be Mr Jarrell. I am Rowena Evans. This is my husband, Ifan—' she waved a hand towards the other end of the table '—and our sons and their families. Our daughter you already know, of course,' she said calmly. 'Rebekah will take you into the parlour so that you can talk in private.'

Rebekah knew better than to argue with her mother but her legs felt unsteady as she walked out of the room, and she was desperately conscious of Dante following closely behind her. He was the second shock she had received today, but not the worst, she thought, feeling a stab of fear as she remembered her hospital appointment earlier in the day. She ushered him into the parlour and closed the door, taking a deep breath before she turned to face him.

He was wearing a soft oatmeal-coloured sweater and faded jeans that hugged his lean hips. His dark Mediterranean looks seemed even more exotic here in Wales. He would certainly attract attention in the village, she thought wryly. But it was unlikely he had come to sample the delights of Rhoslaenau, which boasted a population of four hundred, a post office and a pub.

'Would you like to sit down?' She offered him the armchair by the fire, but when he shook his head she crossed her arms defensively in front of her. 'Why are you here? I wasn't expecting you.' A thought occurred to her. 'Have you had the results of the paternity test already? I thought we wouldn't hear for a week.'

'No, I haven't had the results.' Dante hesitated, uncharacteristically struggling to find the right words. 'But I don't need a test to confirm I am the baby's father.'

Rebekah stared at him warily. 'What do you mean?'

'I mean I believe you, *cara*. I know the child you are carrying is mine.'

She bit her lip. 'I understand why you would want proof. Anyone who had been deceived as you were by your wife would feel the same way. I know you must find it hard to trust.'

He held her gaze steadily. 'I trust you, Rebekah, and I'm here to discuss what we're going to do now. How we can do the best for our child.'

His child—Dante felt a weird feeling inside: disbelief that he was going to be a father, but as the realisation sank in he felt awed and excited.

Rebekah's words sent a chill down his spine.

'You mentioned on the phone that you wanted to discuss financial matters. Please don't feel obliged to give me money,' she said with excruciating politeness. 'My parents have been wonderful and have offered to support me and the baby until I can move to St Lucia to work at Gaspard Clavier's new restaurant.'

Dante could not hide his shock. 'You intend to take the baby to live in the Caribbean?'

'Not immediately after it's born. But Gaspard assures me it's a wonderful place to live and bring up a child.'

On the way to Rebekah's parents' farm he had rehearsed what he planned to say to her but now he was groping for a response. He felt as if a rug had been pulled from beneath his feet. 'And where do I feature in this wonderful new life you're planning?' he said harshly. 'Do you expect me to allow you to take my child to the other side of the world where I can have no part in its life?'

'Allow?' She gave an angry laugh. 'You have no right to tell me where I can or can't live. To be frank, I hadn't anticipated you would want anything to do with our child. That's the impression you gave when I told you of my pregnancy. But if you insist on some sort of contact I imagine you know more about access rights than I do.'

Contact and access rights were surely the ugliest words in the English vocabulary, Dante thought bleakly. He could not think rationally and his words were torn from his heart. 'I'll be damned if I'll let you take my baby away from me to St Lucia.'

Rebekah was startled by the raw emotion in Dante's voice. He spoke about the baby as if he cared about the new life inside her, as if it was a real little person to him, as it was to her. She swallowed the lump in her throat. Maybe he did care for their child even if he did not care about her.

'It's a boy,' she told him huskily. 'They asked me at my ultrasound scan if I wanted to know the sex of the baby.'

Originally she had intended not to find out, but when the scan had revealed a possible problem she had wanted every scrap of information she could get.

He was going to have a son! Fierce joy surged through Dante. 'If you had told me the date of your appointment I would have made sure I was here,' he said curtly, unable to hide his disappointment that he had missed the special moment of seeing his baby for the first time.

'I didn't realise you would want to.' Rebekah bit her lip. 'You are under no obligation to be part of this. I'll manage perfectly well if you decide to have nothing to do with the baby. He will be born into a big, loving family.' A tremor shook her voice as she offered a silent prayer that her son *would* be born safe and well in a few months' time. 'My parents will adore him, he'll have cousins to play with and as I have seven brothers, he'll have plenty of male influence.'

In other words, *he* wasn't needed, Dante thought grimly. He was the father of Rebekah's child but she did not consider it necessary for him to play a role in his son's life.

He recalled how he had looked around the table at all her relatives and sensed the close bond between them. Something hardened inside him as he had a sudden stark image of the future and him arriving at the farmhouse to visit his son. Would his little boy stare at him warily and regard him as an outsider who did not belong to the tight-knit Welsh family?

Pain burned in his chest. *No*, he would not let it happen. His son belonged with him, as well as with his mother.

'There's no chance I will simply walk away and allow my child to be brought up here with your family, however well meaning they are. I want my son, and I will go to any lengths to claim my role as his father.'

He exhaled heavily. 'When you came to see me in London I was shocked about your pregnancy and I reacted badly. I'm sorry,' he said gruffly. 'I accept the baby is mine and I want to take care of you and our child.' He took a swift breath, conscious that his heart was beating painfully hard. He had barely slept for the past two nights as he had debated what to do, and he had concluded that only one solution made sense. 'I want to marry you, Rebekah.'

If only he did truly want her, Rebekah thought emotionally. Fool that she was, his words had evoked a fierce longing to accept his proposal. But she was not so naïve that she did not understand why he had suddenly decided that marrying her was a good idea.

'The only reason you want to marry me is because of the legal implications regarding the baby. Let's face it, you specialise in Family Law and you know you will have equal parental rights if we are married,' she said curtly.

He did not deny it, but the flare of colour along his cheekbones told her she had guessed right. She stared at the flickering flames in the grate and willed the tears blurring her eyes not to fall.

'I realise we will have to make arrangements about how we can share bringing up our son—if you are certain you want to be part of his life. But I can't think about that now. There…there's something you should know.' She hugged her arms tighter around her. 'The scan revealed there might be a problem with the baby's heart.'

Dante felt his own heart drop like a stone. 'What kind of problem?'

'I don't know—something to do with a possible defect with a heart valve. The consultant at my local hospital is trying to organise for me to have a more detailed scan at a better equipped hospital in Cardiff, but it probably won't be until the middle of next week.

'Oh, Dante!' Rebekah's voice shook, the nameless dread that had swamped her since her hospital visit suddenly shattering her determination to remain calm. 'I'm so worried.'

Dante's stomach clenched when he saw the strain etched onto her face. He knew she was thinking of the child she had lost, who had died inside her and been stillborn. He strode towards her and pulled her into his arms, holding her tight as he felt her tremble uncontrollably. 'You should have called me the minute you knew. I would have come immediately.'

'I only found out this morning. I haven't told my family. My parents have been through enough with my father's accident.' She stared at Dante as he pulled out his phone. 'What are you doing?'

'I have a friend in London who is a cardiologist. I'll call him and tell him we need an urgent appointment. The sooner we find out if there is a problem, the better—don't you agree?'

'Yes, but it's Friday afternoon. He won't be able to see us before Monday.' It was only two days, Rebekah reminded herself. But the thought of waiting and worrying all over the weekend was unbearable.

'James will see you as soon as we reach London.' Dante's voice softened when he saw the tears in her eyes. 'Try to keep calm. I'll take care of everything, *cara*.'

Dante was as good as his word. His jet was waiting at Manchester Airport and within a few hours they were in London. They had an appointment at the hospital, where his friend James Burton was a consultant cardiologist, first thing the following morning. It was strange to be back in the staff apartment she had occupied when she had been Dante's cook, Rebekah thought as she climbed into bed. It had been equally strange that Dante had cooked her dinner.

'You're dead on your feet,' he'd said when she had offered to cook. 'Go and sit down while I make you something to eat. Just don't expect miracles,' he'd added with a wry smile that for some reason had made her want to burst into tears.

In fact the herb omelette he served was delicious, and after they'd eaten they watched a couple of TV programmes, which helped to occupy her mind for a while. To her surprise, they slipped into their old companionship that reminded her of the month they had spent in Tuscany, and she wished they could turn back the clock to those golden days when they had been friends as well as lovers.

Worrying about the baby meant that Rebekah barely slept that night and she was pale and tense the next morning when she lay on the couch in the hospital room while a more detailed scan was carried out. James Burton's calm manner was reassuring, but as the minutes ticked by and he continued to study the baby's heart on the screen, Rebekah could not hide her fear.

She remembered when she'd had a scan during her first pregnancy, the nurse had grown quiet and had called for a doctor, who had broken the news to her that her baby was dead.

Panic surged through her. 'There's something wrong, isn't there?'

'Yes, I'm afraid there is,' James said gently.

Terrified, she gripped Dante's hand and felt him squeeze her fingers. His expression was shuttered, but she sensed his grim tension.

'What exactly is the problem?' he asked.

'Your son has a partial atrial septal defect, which is sometimes known as a hole in the heart. It is a treatable condition, but the baby will require heart surgery, probably when he is a few months old—' the consultant hesitated '—but possibly sooner after birth, depending on his condition.'

Rebekah swallowed hard. 'Could…could he die?'

'My medical team will do everything possible to help him.' James's expression was gravely sympathetic. 'But I would be lying if I said there was no risk.' He studied Rebekah's ashen face and glanced at Dante. 'While Rebekah gets dressed, why don't we go into my office and I'll give you as much information as I can?'

Dante felt numb. He moved like an automaton, and once inside James's office he sank onto a chair and dropped his head into his hands. In his mind he could see the scan image of his son. Although the image had been grainy, he'd seen that the baby was already fully formed, right down to ten tiny fingers and toes, and Dante had wanted to touch the screen, as if he could somehow make contact with his unborn child. *Dio*, he had been so concerned with demanding his paternal rights. But now there was no certainty that he would have a child. He felt an agonising pain like a red-hot knife skewering his stomach as the realisation sunk in that his son's life was in danger and there was nothing he could do to help him.

He swallowed the shot of brandy James handed him and concentrated hard on the medical information regarding the baby's heart problem so that he could explain it all to Rebekah later. What must she be thinking? He recalled the stark fear in her eyes as the cardiologist had broken the news of the baby's heart condition. Slamming his glass down on the desk, he jerked to his feet.

'I have to see Rebekah,' he said raggedly. 'I need to be with her.'

'Take it easy, old man.' James put a hand on his shoulder and steered him over to a door at the back of the office that led to a small private garden. 'Have five minutes to calm down. You're going to need to be strong for her.'

Rebekah still had a door key to Dante's house, which she used to let herself in. He wasn't at home, but she hadn't really expected him to be. When she had walked out of the changing cubicle after the scan she'd walked up and down the corridor, searching for him. Eventually she had gone back and asked James Burton's secretary if she knew where he had gone.

'I saw him go out about ten minutes ago,' the woman had informed her.

He had left the hospital! Still dazed with shock at the diagnosis of the baby's heart condition, Rebekah had reeled at this further blow. Dante had disappeared without even leaving a message to say where he had gone. There was only one explanation she could think of. He must have been deeply shocked to learn that his son's chance of being born safely was uncertain. Maybe he had decided that he could not cope with the possibility of losing another child, she thought bleakly. She knew he had been devastated when he had discovered that the little boy Ben, who he had believed was his son, was another man's child. Now, having been told of the baby's prognosis, perhaps he intended to walk away rather than risk being hurt again.

She'd caught a cab back to his house and immediately started to pack the few clothes she had left behind when they had gone to Tuscany—a lifetime ago, it seemed. Suddenly her fragile control of her emotions cracked and she sank down onto the bed, harsh, painful sobs tearing her chest. She felt so scared for her baby and so desperately alone. She knew she must try to be strong. Her son was totally dependent on her—poor little scrap. It seemed so unbearably cruel that not only would he have to fight for his life, but his father had abandoned him.

When Dante walked through the front door, the sound of weeping directed him down to the basement level.

The raw, heartrending cries ripped him apart, but he felt relieved that at least he had found Rebekah.

'Why did you leave the hospital without me?' he demanded raggedly as he strode into her bedroom. 'I was waiting for you, but then James said he had seen you get into a taxi, and I thought...' He closed his eyes briefly as he recalled his shock and confusion when he'd realised Rebekah had left the hospital. 'I didn't know what to think,' he admitted thickly.

He opened his eyes and felt something snap inside him as he stared at her ravaged, tear-stained face. Rebekah did not cry prettily. Her face was blotchy and strands of hair were stuck to her wet cheeks.

'Tesoro...' Dante's voice shook and he tasted his own tears at the back of his throat. The sight of his strong, wonderful Rebekah so utterly distraught affected him more than anything had ever done in his life. 'Oh, my angel,' he said hoarsely, 'we'll get through this.'

Rebekah cried harder, her shoulders heaving. After the strain of the previous twenty-four hours and the devastating news that her baby's life was at risk, Dante's appearance was one shock too many. 'I thought you'd gone,' she choked. 'I thought you'd left me and the baby, be...because you couldn't cope with his heart problem.'

'Sweetheart, I will *never* leave you.' Dante dashed a hand across his eyes and dropped to his knees beside the bed, drawing her shuddering body into his arms. She smelled of roses and, despite the fact that his emotions felt as if they had been put through a mangle, he knew with sudden startling clarity that he belonged with Rebekah and she was who he had been searching for all his life.

'I'm going to take care of you and our son.' He

stroked her hair back from her face with an unsteady hand. Everything was falling into place and he was desperate to convince her that he did not care about parental rights or duty. The only important thing was how he felt about her and how, he prayed, she felt about him.

'Please, *cara*,' he said in a voice shaking with emotion, 'will you marry me so that I can be your protector and provider and everything that a husband who is devoted to his wife and child should be?'

Rebekah shook her head, tears still streaming down her cheeks. 'There's no reason for you to marry me. We might not have a baby...' The thought was so unbearable that she felt a tearing pain inside her. 'And then you would be trapped in a pointless marriage,' she whispered, 'with a wife you never really wanted.'

'But I do want you, my angel—to be my wife, my lover, my best friend—always and for ever.' The lump in Dante's throat made it hard for him to speak. 'I love you, Rebekah,' he said huskily. 'That's the only reason I want to marry you—not to gain rights over our child, or because it would be convenient.'

He felt his tears spill from his eyes, but he could not hold them back. He had stifled his emotions for so long and pretended to himself that he did not care if he never found love. But he saw now that he had been lonely for all those years, and he was terrified that this precious, profound love he had found would slip through his fingers.

'I know you're scared for the baby,' he said gently. 'But James believes his chances are good. The scan showed that he's developing as he should be, and he's already a good weight. I know our son is a fighter— how could he not be when he has such a strong and determined mother? He'll have the best care before and after he's born, and James says there is every reason to believe the surgery to repair his heart will be completely successful.'

He looked into Rebekah's eyes and glimpsed something in their depths that gave him hope. 'Whatever the future holds, I want to share it with you, to celebrate the joyous moments, and comfort and support each other through sad times that are an inevitable part of life. You are my world, the love of my life, and without you—' his voice cracked with emotion '—I have nothing.'

Stunned and incredibly moved by Dante's words, Rebekah touched his face and brushed away the trails of moisture from his cheeks. Hearing that her baby's life was threatened had put other things into perspective. She owed it to Dante and to herself to be honest about her feelings for him.

'I love you too,' she said softly. 'I know it sounds silly, but I took one look at you and felt like I'd been shot through the heart by an arrow.' Faint colour stained her white face and some of the terrible tension left her. She could not help but worry about the baby, but she was comforted by the cardiologist's assurances. 'I knew of your playboy reputation and I told myself it would be very stupid to fall in love with you.' She gave him a tremulous smile. 'But my heart refused to listen.'

'*Tesoro mio cuore*—my darling heart.' Dante's words were a jumble of Italian and English, but their meaning was the same. '*Ti amo*—for eternity,' he whispered against her lips, before he claimed her mouth in a tender kiss that brought more tears to her eyes.

'I look like a frog when I cry,' she muttered, burying her head against his shoulder, knowing that her face must be puffy and her eyes red-rimmed.

'I love frogs,' he assured her gravely. His heart turned over as he kissed away the tears clinging to her lashes. He wanted to wrap her in cotton wool and protect her from all harm and hurt. 'Will you marry me, and let me love you for the rest of my life?' he asked with fierce urgency.

'Yes,' Rebekah said shakily, 'on the condition that you'll let me love you with all my heart.'

Dante swallowed when he saw the unguarded emotion in her eyes. He also noted the signs of intense weariness and strain. 'You need to rest, my angel,' he told her as he stood up and scooped her into his arms.

'You'll injure your back,' Rebekah warned him anxiously. 'I weigh a ton.'

'I'm strong enough to carry both of you,' he promised, and carried her up two flights of stairs as if she were as light as a feather. When he reached his bedroom he set her down by the bed and undressed her and then himself before pulling back the covers and drawing her into his arms.

He reacquainted himself with her lush curves and stroked the firm mound of her stomach, his breath catching in his throat when he felt a fluttering sensation beneath his fingers. 'Was that...'

'Your son is saying hello,' she told him gently. 'I've just started to feel him kicking. That's a good sign, isn't it?' Her voice trembled. 'It must mean he's strong.'

'He needs a name. How about calling our little lion cub Leo?' Dante suggested.

'That's perfect.' Rebekah laid her hand next to

Dante's and their eyes met as they felt their son give another kick.

He bent his head and kissed her softly, and then made love to her with such exquisite care and told her he loved her in a voice that shook with the intensity of his feelings. This was what had been missing from his life. Rebekah filled a void inside him and he knew his life would be empty without her.

'When did you know you loved me?' she asked him as she emerged dazedly from the waves of pleasure induced by the most beautiful lovemaking she had ever experienced.

'I don't know,' he admitted honestly. 'I saw you at some business dinner in the City and seized the chance to offer you a job as my chef. I tried to ignore my awareness of you, but I started making excuses to leave the office early because I liked knowing you were waiting at home for me—although I told myself it was because I appreciated your wonderful cooking. But I found myself thinking about you a lot, and after we slept together I was determined to make you my mistress. When we were in Tuscany I couldn't imagine a time when I wouldn't want you and when you left and refused to come back to me...' His voice deepened and he said raggedly, 'I missed you like hell.'

'I went because I was fathoms deep in love with you, and I was afraid that if I stayed you would break my heart.' Rebekah gave a contented sigh as she snuggled close to him and felt his lips brush hers.

'I will always love you,' Dante promised her. 'I never felt I truly belonged anywhere, but I belong with you, my darling. And you belong with me. For ever.'

EPILOGUE

MELLOW September sunshine bathed the Casa di Colombe in golden light. In the courtyard Rebekah was collecting herbs to use in the new recipe she was planning to make for dinner. Her first cookery book had been such a success that she had been commissioned to write another one, and this time her recipes were influenced by traditional Tuscan dishes.

She glanced up at the sound of excited laughter and smiled at the sight of her son, held in his father's arms, trying to catch the spray from the fountain in his chubby hands.

'Easy, tiger,' Dante murmured as he held the wriggling baby a little tighter. 'He's so strong,' he said proudly. 'And so determined to get into the water,' he added ruefully as he moved away from the ornamental pool and Leo gave a loud yell of protest.

'He likes to have his own way—just like his father,' Rebekah said drily. She had experienced Dante's forceful personality ten months ago, when in the space of a week he had arranged their wedding and booked a honeymoon in the Seychelles. They had married in the tiny chapel in Wales close to her parents' farm. Her father had given her away, and her seven brothers and their families had packed the pews. Rebekah had worn an exquisite white silk and lace dress and carried a bouquet of pink roses, and her five little nieces had acted as bridesmaids.

She recalled how her heart had leapt when she had walked towards Dante and seen his love for her blazing in his silver-grey eyes. He had looked breathtakingly handsome in a tuxedo. But he looked just as gorgeous now, she thought as she skimmed her gaze over his denim shorts and bare chest. His skin was dark olive after the month they had spent in Tuscany and she could not resist running her fingers through the whorls of black hairs that arrowed down over his flat abdomen.

'If our son would deign to take a nap, I would take you upstairs to bed and make love to you,' he murmured, his eyes glinting with sensual promise that sent a quiver of longing through Rebekah.

'He doesn't look very tired,' she said doubtfully as she lifted Leo into her arms and her heart melted when he gave her a wide smile that revealed his solitary tooth. She hugged the baby tightly and felt a fierce surge of emotion. 'He's amazing, isn't he? It's hard to believe he had heart surgery three months ago.'

There had been no complications with Leo's birth, and he had fed and thrived so well that when he was three months old the doctors had decided he was strong enough to undergo the operation to repair his heart defect. The few days he had spent in intensive care had been the most nerve-racking ordeal of Rebekah's life, but the worrying time had brought her and Dante even closer and she did not know how she would have coped without his support. Fortunately Leo's quick recovery had been nothing short of miraculous and now, at six months old, he was healthy, full of energy and seemed to require remarkably little sleep.

'I think he'll drop off,' Dante said, watching the baby nestle against Rebekah's neck and give a yawn. 'And when he does I'll have my wicked way with you.'

'Is that a promise?' she said teasingly.

Her soft smile stole Dante's breath. He hadn't known he could feel this happy, he reflected, swallowing the lump that had formed in his throat. For the first time in his life he felt utterly content and secure in the knowledge that his wife loved him as much as he adored her.

'Oh, yes,' he assured her huskily as he pulled her and their son into the circle of his arms. 'I promise I will never stop loving you.'

* * * * *

HIS UNKNOWN
HEIR

For my mother-in-law Julia, my other mum.
Thank you for all your encouragement.

PROLOGUE

RAMON VELAQUEZ'S private jet touched down at London City Airport exactly on schedule. He swiftly cleared customs, and as he walked out of the airport building to his waiting limousine his chauffeur sprang forward to take his suitcase.

'Welcome back, Mr Velaquez. I hope you had a good trip.'

'*Gracias*, Paul.' Ramon climbed into the rear of the car and rested his dark head against the plush leather upholstery. A sense of well-being swept through him when he lifted the glass of whisky and soda that had been prepared for him from the drinks cabinet. 'It's good to be home.'

As the car pulled smoothly away he dwelled on his unconscious use of the word home. Because of course England was *not* his home; he was Spanish, and immensely proud of his country and his long and noble ancestry. His true home was the Castillo del Toro, and one day—he feared in the not too distant future, when he considered his father's health problems—he would be the new Duque de Velaquez and would live permanently at the castle, surrounded by an army of servants.

He knew from his childhood that it would be a life dictated by formality and protocol—so different from the relaxed atmosphere of his London penthouse apartment, where he employed the minimum of staff and enjoyed a sense of freedom away from the avid gaze of the Spanish media.

He felt a faint pang of guilt that he had chosen to fly from his business meeting in New York to England rather than to Spain. He cared deeply for his parents, but he had been reluctant to face another lecture about the necessity for him to marry a highborn Spanish woman and provide an heir to ensure the continuation of the illustrious family name. So he had made the excuse that he needed to be in London to deal with an urgent business matter.

Ramon knew his father, the Duque, was pleased with his dedication to Velaquez Conglomerates, but it was doubtful he would be so impressed if he knew that Ramon's real reason for racing back to London was because he was impatient to see his English mistress.

Lauren was at her desk, reading through a complicated lease agreement, when her mobile phone rang. Her heart gave a jolt, and she scrabbled in her handbag, a smile curving her lips when she saw that the caller was Ramon. She had been on tenterhooks all day, waiting for him to call. Like a lovesick teenager in the throes of her first romance, she thought ruefully.

Of course today there was a special reason why she was anxious to speak to him, she acknowledged, feeling once again the curious sensation that she was plummeting downwards in a fast-moving lift and had left her stomach behind. She was still reeling from the shock she had received a week ago—still couldn't quite believe it was true. It had made her desperate to hear Ramon's voice and to feel reassured that their relationship had developed into something deeper than a casual sexual liaison.

The closeness that she sensed had grown between them

over the past months was not simply her imagination or wishful thinking, she assured herself. When she had first met the enigmatic Spaniard in a nightclub six months ago her journalist friend Amy had told her that Ramon Velaquez had a reputation as a playboy—but he conducted his affairs discreetly, and his love-life was rarely reported by the English media.

Lauren had been unable to deny the fierce chemistry that had blazed between her and Ramon, but mindful of Amy's warning, she had embarked on an affair with him accepting that he would not want a serious relationship any more than she did. She was busy with her career and sceptical of love. And yet somehow, against all the odds, a relationship had developed between them that she felt was more than simply mind-blowing sex.

Admittedly Ramon discouraged discussions about his personal life. All she really knew about him was that his family owned a famous winery in the Rioja region of Northern Spain. But in every other way they were a couple who shared a life together: companionship, laughter, a mutual appreciation of art galleries and the theatre, and frequently, of late, Ramon's London apartment. For whenever he was in town Lauren always stayed with him.

One important lesson she had learned during their affair was that he disliked displays of emotion, and an instinctive sense of self-protection had made her keep to herself the fact that she had fallen in love with him. But now she forgot her resolve to act cool with him, and quickly answered her phone.

The sound of his gravelly, sexy accent sent a little shiver of pleasure down her spine. '*Buenas tardes*, Lauren.'

'Ramon.' Her voice sounded annoyingly breathless, but she had never been able to control the effect he had on her. 'How was your trip?'

'Successful. You must know me well enough by now, *querida*, to understand that I would not settle for anything less.'

Ramon had smiled at the sound of Lauren's voice. It was good to be back in London, and even better to know that soon he would be making love to his beautiful English rose, whose demure smile hid a delightfully passionate nature.

Business had kept him in the States for two weeks, and he was impatient to relieve the ache of sexual frustration that had grown more intense with every day that he had been away. Lauren had been in his mind more often than he was comfortable with, but now was not the time to question why she had such an effect on him. He wanted her with an urgency he had never felt for any of his previous lovers, and he knew that tonight she would be gratifyingly impatient for him to take her to bed.

He almost gave in to the temptation to instruct her meet him at his apartment when she finished work, but he resisted. A leisurely meal in an exclusive restaurant would heighten his anticipation of the delights to follow, and on a practical level he had refused the bland in-flight meals served on the plane so it was not only his sexual appetite that demanded appeasement.

'I've booked a table at the Vine for seven-thirty,' he said. It was satisfying to reflect on his business trip, which had gone just the way he had planned it. As usual he had left nothing to chance, and the take-over bid had been completed with a brutal swiftness that had taken his competitors by surprise. 'We're celebrating.'

Lauren's heart missed a beat, and for a few seconds her brain went into freefall before her common sense returned. She was the only person in the world who knew the result of the pregnancy test she had done a week ago. There was no way Ramon could be suggesting that they were celebrating the fact that she was expecting his baby, which must mean—Lauren's heart gave another little flip— he had remembered it was the six-month anniversary of when they had first met.

She stared at the silk tie she had bought him after spending her entire lunch-break agonising over whether she should give him an anniversary gift. Clearly she had made the right decision. Ramon had remembered the special significance of today, and tonight, over dinner, she would tell him about the baby.

'Wonderful,' she murmured, unable to disguise the little tremor in her voice. Trying to hide her feelings for Ramon was always a struggle, and the knowledge that she was carrying his child made it even harder to mask her emotions.

Ramon glanced at his watch. 'I'll meet you at the restaurant in three hours.'

A little shiver of pleasure ran through Lauren at the thought of seeing him again, but she could not help feeling anxious at the prospect of telling him about the baby. 'I can't wait to see you,' she said. 'My afternoon meeting is going to drag intolerably.'

He had missed her, Ramon acknowledged. The thought caused his dark brows to draw together. No woman had ever been important enough in his life for him to miss being with her, and he was startled to realise just how often he had thought about Lauren while he had been away. But he did not intend to share that information with her. He did not want her to think she could ever be more to him than his mistress.

His frown deepened as his thoughts turned once more to the news that his father's cancer had returned after a brief period of remission. This time it was incurable. Now he understood why lately the Duque had been more insistent than ever that he should choose a suitable bride—with emphasis on the word *suitable*, Ramon thought grimly, recalling how his father had raked up the old story of Catalina during their last conversation.

Catalina Cortez was a mistake from his past of whom he did not like to be reminded, he brooded irritably. *Dios*, he had been a testosterone-fuelled eighteen-year-old when he had lost his heart and his head to the gorgeous glamour model whose bountiful curves had been regularly displayed on the pages of certain top-shelf magazines. But almost two decades later his father still would not allow him to forget that he had been utterly determined to marry Catalina.

Ramon did not suppose he was the first man to have been made a fool of by love, but he had learned his lesson well and he would not be a fool again. The memory of discovering Catalina with her lover and realising that she was a slut who had only been so flatteringly eager to marry him to get her greedy hands on the Velaquez fortune still touched a raw nerve—but no more than the humiliation he had felt that his father had been proved right.

Far worse than Catalina's treachery had been the knowledge that he had disappointed his family. But it had been a long time ago, Ramon thought impatiently. Since then he had assured his father that he was prepared to do his duty by marrying a woman suitable to be a *duquesa* and to beget an heir. Now it seemed that assurances were no longer enough. His father was dying and wanted to see his only son married. Duty was calling him in an ever louder voice, and the freedom to take his pleasure with mistresses was drawing to an end—for when he did marry he intended to be a faithful husband to his as yet unknown bride.

'Ramon, are you still there?' Lauren's voice dragged him from his thoughts. 'It must be a bad signal. I thought I'd lost you for a moment.'

'I am still here,' Ramon replied smoothly. 'I'll see you tonight.' He ended the call and stared out at the London traffic, conscious that his earlier feeling of contentment had evaporated.

Lauren arrived at the restaurant ten minutes early, and went to the bar to wait. Butterflies were leaping in her stomach at the prospect of seeing Ramon again. She had missed him badly while he had been away, and wondering how he would react to the life-changing news she was about to tell him exacerbated her tension.

Even though her back was to the door she knew the exact moment he walked into the restaurant by the startled silence that fell, followed by a ripple of curiosity in the voices of the diners and those, like her, at the bar. She turned her head and her knees felt weak.

Six foot four, with heart-stopping good-looks and a simmering sensual magnetism, he drew interested glances wherever he went. Mainly from women, Lauren thought ruefully as she noticed an attractive brunette who was sitting at the bar attempt to gain his attention by crossing her legs so that her skirt rode up her thigh.

But who could blame the woman? Ramon was utterly gorgeous, she thought helplessly, her heart-rate quickening when he strode towards her. His dark eyes focused on her face, seemingly oblivious to every other female in the room. His superbly tailored suit drew attention to his broad shoulders and lean, hard body, while the bright lights of the restaurant danced over his bronzed, chiselled features and made his black hair gleam like raw silk. As he came nearer his sensual mouth curved into a smile that touched her soul—a smile that was just for her and made her feel as if she was special to him.

She hadn't planned to fall in love with him. Until Ramon

had swept into her life she had been scornful of love, and although she had had other relationships they had been conducted on her terms and had left her emotions untouched. But Ramon was different. From the very beginning she had felt at ease with him; he was witty and intelligent, with a wicked sense of humour, and she enjoyed his company.

The fact that he was an incredible lover who had given her the confidence to explore her intensely passionate nature was just one reason why he had captured her heart—although at this moment it was a very pressing reason, she acknowledged, conscious that her nipples had hardened and now felt acutely sensitive as they rubbed against the silk bustier she was wearing beneath her jacket.

He was so close now that she could inhale the familiar spicy scent of his cologne, and the urge to fling her arms around his neck and press her lips feverishly over his face, his mouth, was almost irresistible. But she did resist, knowing that he would be appalled by such a public display. Ramon guarded his privacy fiercely, and only ever kissed her when they were alone. But when he halted in front of her and she saw the genuine warmth in his smile she gave up trying to act cool and beamed at him.

'You look gorgeous, *querida*,' Ramon greeted her, heat flaring inside him as he raked his eyes over Lauren's tight-fitting, pillar-box-red skirt, and settled on the tantalising confection of silk and lace visible beneath her jacket. 'And very sexy. I'm amazed the male lawyers at your firm can concentrate on their work when you are such a delicious distraction.'

'I wore a high-necked, very prim blouse to the office,' Lauren assured him. 'But I thought you would appreciate it if I changed into something more decorative.' The low-cut black silk bustier which revealed a daring amount of cleavage had cost a fortune, but the flare of dull colour that winged along Ramon's cheekbones told her it was worth every penny.

'I will demonstrate my appreciation all night long,' he promised her huskily.

The heat inside him was now a burning throb of need that was centred in his groin and caused his blood to pound through his veins. Lauren was a delectable package of honey-blonde hair and voluptuous curves, and it was not surprising he had missed her, Ramon assured himself. He was sorely tempted to pull her into his arms and plunder her pouting scarlet lips in a searing kiss until she clung to him, trembling and eager, but with an enormous effort of will he controlled himself.

It was not only the Spanish paparazzi who were fascinated by the son of one of the nation's most prominent and wealthy families. The English media had labelled him the most eligible bachelor in Europe, and a picture of him kissing a blonde in a bar would make the kind of headlines he was determined to avoid. And so, nostrils flaring as he breathed in the floral fragrance of Lauren's perfume, he placed his hand lightly on her waist and propelled her out of the bar.

'I believe our table is ready.' He dipped his head towards her as they followed a waiter, and murmured, 'Let's hope service is quick tonight, *querida*, because I am *very* hungry.'

The gleam in his eyes left Lauren in no doubt of his meaning, and a quiver of excitement ran the length of her spine. After two weeks apart she ached for him to make love to her. Soon they would go back to his apartment. But first—her heart skittered—first she must tell him that she was expecting his baby.

She simply did not know how he was going to react to her accidental pregnancy. For unquestionably it *was* an accident—caused by one forgetful moment when they had shared a shower, she remembered ruefully. She had not planned to have a baby at this stage of her life, and had spent the past week veering between panic and disbelief. But, strangely, the moment she had seen Ramon tonight the baby had become real to her—no longer simply a blue line on the pregnancy test, but a new life growing inside her, created by her and the man she loved.

She caught her bottom lip with her teeth. Would Ramon feel the same way? He had never made any reference to the future, and although he was a wonderful lover who treated her with consideration and respect she did not know how he really felt about her. But he *had* invited her to dinner tonight to celebrate their six-month anniversary, Lauren reminded herself. Surely that meant something?

The waiter took their drinks order. Ramon made no comment when she requested fruit juice, because she had told him when they had first met that she disliked alcohol—although not her reasons for being strictly teetotal. The memory of how her mother had regularly drowned her sorrows in gin after her father had left them was something Lauren never spoke about to anyone.

With impressive speed the waiter returned with their drinks, and Ramon lifted his glass of champagne. 'I'd like to make a toast—to another successful take-over bid by Velaquez Conglomerates.'

Lauren froze—until the lengthening silence became awkward, and then she hurriedly snatched up her glass of juice. 'Oh…yes—to Velaquez Conglomerates.' She touched her glass to Ramon's and gave him a tentative smile, which faltered when he made no mention of the other reason they were celebrating.

'So, tell me what you've been doing while I was away,' Ramon said comfortably.

It was not a question he had been prone to asking his previous lovers, he mused. Usually he was bored to death by the details of shopping and celebrity gossip that most women seemed to find so fascinating, but Lauren was a highly intelligent corporate lawyer, and he enjoyed discussing their respective careers, or the latest political thriller by an author they both admired.

Lauren could recall little of the past two weeks other than the mind-numbing panic that had swamped her after she had discovered she was pregnant. She could think of nothing to say, and instead fumbled in her handbag and handed Ramon a small gift-wrapped package.

'It's a present,' she told him when he viewed the package suspiciously, as if he expected it to blow up in his face. 'It's nothing, really.' She could feel hot colour flooding her cheeks. 'Just a little token…to celebrate our anniversary.'

Ramon stiffened, and the sense of impending disaster he had felt when he had spoken to Lauren earlier in the day settled over him like a black cloud. 'Anniversary?' he queried coolly.

'It's six months since we met. I thought that was what we were celebrating—the reason you'd arranged for us to have dinner at the restaurant where you brought me on our first date…' Lauren's voice trailed away. She stared at Ramon's shocked expression and cringed with embarrassment as it became apparent that she had got things very wrong. 'I thought you had remembered,' she muttered, wishing that a hole would open in the floor beneath her chair and swallow her up.

Ramon regarded her in a taut silence. 'I must admit I did not,' he said bluntly, frowning as the implication of her words sank in. Six months! How had so much time passed without him noticing it? And how had Lauren insinuated herself into his life so subtly that he had grown used to her being there? Ordinarily he never dated women for more than a few weeks before he reached his boredom threshold. But even though she had been his mistress for half a year Lauren never bored him—either in bed or out—he acknowledged grimly. He hadn't even been tempted to look at another woman.

His frown deepened. *Dios!* He had been faithful to her without realising the longevity of their affair, but now that she had made him aware of it he was shocked that he had allowed what had started off as just another casual fling to continue for so long. He felt as though it was Lauren's fault. If she had started to irritate him—or, as so often happened with his mistresses, shown possessive tendencies— he would have ended the affair months ago. But she had been the perfect mistress: undemanding, and happy to take a discreet role in his life. Her desire to celebrate an anniversary was like a bolt from the blue. It had overstepped a line in their relationship, Ramon brooded, annoyance replacing his contentment of a few minutes ago.

'I do not set great store by anniversaries,' he told her curtly.

Impeccable manners forced him to untie the gold ribbon on top of the package, and he parted the wrapping paper to reveal a striped silk tie in muted shades of blue and grey. It was exactly the sort of thing he would have chosen for himself, but the realisation that Lauren knew his tastes so well did not improve his temper.

He looked up to find her watching him anxiously, and it struck him that she had seemed unusually tense since he had greeted her at the bar.

'It's charming,' he said, forcing a smile as he lifted the tie from its wrapping. 'An excellent choice. *Gracias.*'

'I told you it was only a small gift,' she mumbled, sounding defensive.

But it was not the size or the value of the present that was a problem. It was the reason *why* she had given it to him that disturbed him, Ramon mused. Lauren had never seemed the type who indulged in sentimental gestures, and it was disconcerting to think that he might not know her quite as well as he had believed.

Thankfully the waiter arrived with their first course, and while they ate he steered the conversation away from the contentious topic of their so-called anniversary to a discussion about the mixed reviews for a new play that had opened in the West End.

The food at the Vine was always superb, but afterwards Lauren had no recollection of what she had eaten. She ordered a camomile tea to end the meal, and sipped it frantically to try and counteract her queasiness induced by the aroma of Ramon's coffee. Usually she loved coffee, but for the past week just the smell of it had been enough to send her running to the bathroom.

Morning sickness—which seemed to strike at any time during the day—was a physical indication that her pregnancy was real, and if she was honest she felt scared and uncertain of the future. *Tell Ramon about the baby now*, her brain insisted. But she could not forget his harsh tone when he had announced that he did not set much store by anniversaries, and the words *I'm pregnant* remained trapped in her throat.

Ramon's reaction to her innocuous gift had been bad enough. He had made her feel like a criminal for wanting to celebrate the fact that their relationship was special to her. Clearly it was not special to him, she thought miserably. But the stark fact remained that she was expecting his baby, and sooner or later he was going to have to know.

During dinner she'd managed to smile and chat to him

as if her humiliating discovery that their anniversary meant nothing to him had never happened. Ramon certainly seemed to have put it out of his mind. But when he draped his arm around her shoulders in the back of his limousine and instructed the chauffeur to take them to his apartment overlooking Hyde Park, anger slowly replaced the hurt inside her. If they did not have a relationship that was worth celebrating, what *did* they have? she wondered bitterly.

The car purred into the underground car park beneath his apartment block. Moments later they entered the lift and he pulled her into his arms.

'Alone, finally,' Ramon murmured in a satisfied voice. Lauren's perfume tantalised his senses, and his breathing quickened when he took the clip from her chignon and ran his fingers though the mass of silky blonde hair that tumbled to her shoulders. *Dios*, he was hungry for her. She was like a fever in his blood. With a muttered oath he covered her mouth with his and teased her lips apart with his tongue to plunder her moist warmth.

The unsettled feeling that had dogged him throughout dinner faded when he felt her instant response. For a few moments he had wondered if he was going to have to end their affair, and he was surprised by his reluctance to do so.

But once a mistress started to mention anniversaries it was time she became an ex-mistress—because how could you celebrate what was essentially a casual sexual relationship? He had thought Lauren understood the rules, and he was relieved that it seemed now, after all, that she did. She had made no further reference to the amount of time they had been together, and when she pressed her soft, curvaceous body against him his doubts were swept away by the thunderous intensity of his desire.

He steered her out of the lift and through the front door of his apartment without lifting his lips from hers. His hands deftly tugged off her jacket and set to work unlacing the front of the sexy bustier while he backed her along the hall towards his bedroom.

How could she resist him? Lauren thought despairingly, her body trembling with anticipation. Soon he would be caressing her naked flesh. With his dark hair falling over his brow, his jacket and tie flung carelessly to the floor and his shirt now open to the waist, to reveal a muscular, bronzed chest covered with a mass of wiry dark hairs, he was lethally sexy—but, more than that, he was her world.

But she wasn't *his*. The thought forced its way into her head, and her mouth quivered beneath the demanding pressure of his kiss. Her legs hit the end of the bed at the same time as he loosened the bustier and her breasts spilled into his hands.

'I missed you, *querida*,' Ramon groaned hoarsely.

But instead of his words soothing her battered pride they caused her to stiffen and draw back from him.

'Did you miss *me*—or sex with me?' she asked him tremulously, watching him with wary grey eyes when he frowned.

'Don't play games,' he said impatiently. 'It's one and the same thing. Of course I missed having sex with you. After all, you *are* my mistress.'

The blood drained from Lauren's face, and she could have sworn she actually heard the ripping sound of her heart being slashed by sharp knives as her pathetic hopes crumbled to dust.

'I am *not* your mistress,' she said tightly, gritting her teeth to stop herself from wailing like a distraught child—because that was how she felt.

Just as she had as a little girl, when she had witnessed

her pony bolt out of the field into the path of a lorry, or as a teenager when she had watched her adored father walk down the garden path and out of her life for ever.

She stepped away from Ramon and clutched the edges of the bustier together, her hands shaking. 'A mistress is a kept woman, and you do *not* keep me. I have my own flat, a job, and I pay my own way.'

'You virtually live at my apartment when I am in London,' Ramon reminded her tersely. He was frustrated that Lauren was wasting time arguing when all he could think about was thrusting his throbbing erection between her soft thighs.

'True. But I keep the fridge stocked with your favourite foods—including caviar and champagne—and I take your suits to the cleaners. They are only little things, I know, but I try to balance out our living costs fairly.'

Irritated beyond measure, Ramon raked a hand through his hair. How on earth had he allowed his affair with Lauren to evolve into such cosy domesticity that she dealt with his dry-cleaning? That was the sort of thing a wife did, not a mistress. And how were they even having this conversation when seconds ago they had been on the verge of making love?

Having sex, he corrected himself. Love was certainly not a factor of their relationship. Yes, she had become important to him, he admitted. More so than he had realised until he'd spent the past couple of weeks missing her like hell. But, whether she agreed or not, she *was* his mistress. The course of his life had been determined from birth, and the responsibilities that came with being a member of the Spanish nobility meant that she could never be anything else.

Tension thrummed between them, and the unedifying label of *mistress* drummed in Lauren's brain. She had thought they were lovers who shared an equal relationship, but clearly Ramon did not view her in that way. Her voice sounded rusty when she forced herself to speak. 'I...need to know where we're going,' she said baldly.

Dark eyebrows winged upwards in an expression of arrogant amusement, and sherry-brown eyes rested insolently on the unlaced bustier that she was clutching across her breasts. 'I had thought we were going to bed,' Ramon drawled.

The flare of hurt in her eyes tugged on his conscience, and he cursed his quick temper. But, *Dios mio*, she had started this ridiculous conversation. He was tempted to snatch her back into his arms and kiss her until she melted into submission, but she looked as fragile as spun glass tonight—something he had only just noticed, he thought grimly. He wondered if she was ill. She was certainly upset. But why was she insisting on defining the nature of their affair when it worked perfectly well for both of them without the need for explanation?

'I mean where our relationship is going,' Lauren said with quiet dignity.

Sick fear churned in her stomach. Under ordinary circumstances Ramon's forbidding expression would have warned her not to proceed with a conversation that felt horribly as if it was going to smash full-pelt into a brick wall. But these were not ordinary circumstances. She was pregnant with his child, and her instinct to do the best for her baby was more important than her pride.

'Tell me honestly: do you envisage us having any kind of future together?' she asked quietly. 'Or am I just another blonde to temporarily share your bed?'

His silence confirmed what her heart already knew.

Ramon's eyes narrowed. 'I have never made false promises, or led you to believe that I wanted more than an affair.

You never hid the fact that your career plays a major part in your life, and I thought you were content with a relationship that did not put the pressure of unrealistic expectations on either of us.'

She had never had expectations, Lauren thought sadly. But she had hoped that she was beginning to mean something to him. How could she have been such a fool? she asked herself angrily. She had been blinded by her love for Ramon, and had kidded herself that the companionship they shared was proof that he cared for her. Now she knew that he had only ever regarded her as a convenient mistress—who provided sex and entertaining conversation on demand, but never made demands of her own.

As for her career... Her hand moved instinctively to her stomach. She had worked hard to become a lawyer, and undoubtedly her job was important to her. But in eight months time she was going to take on the most important role a woman could fulfil—and it looked increasingly as though she was going to be bringing up her baby on her own.

She stared at Ramon's perfectly sculpted features and her heart clenched. 'Things change,' she said huskily. 'Life can't stay the same or we would stagnate. How do you see *your* future, Ramon? I mean...' her voice shook slightly '...do you ever want to marry?'

This was not how he had envisaged spending his first night back in London, Ramon thought furiously. Up until now he had been clinging to the hope that this new Lauren, who had broken the unwritten rules of their liaison by demanding to discuss it, would suddenly metamorphose back into the familiar, delightfully easygoing Lauren, whose sole aim had always seemed to be to please him in bed. He was outraged that she had brought up the thorny subject of marriage, but now that she had asked he did not intend to lie to her.

'The Velaquez family are among the oldest members of the Spanish nobility, and can trace their ancestors back to the eleventh century,' he told her harshly. 'As the only son of the Duque de Velaquez it is my duty to marry a bride from another aristocratic Spanish family and provide an heir to continue the bloodline of Velaquez.'

'You're the son of a *duke*?' Lauren said faintly, stunned by the revelation. She had thought that the supreme self-confidence which sometimes revealed itself as arrogance was simply his nature. But he was a titled member of the Spanish nobility—it was small wonder he had a regal air about him.

'The title will pass to me on the death of my father,' Ramon said tersely, feeling a shaft of pain when he thought of his father's prognosis. The Duque had always been a strict, rather remote parent, and Ramon's childhood had been dominated by rules and stifling formality, but sadly lacking in displays of affection. He had always respected his father, but it was only now that he realised he also loved him, and it was for that reason more than any other that he intended to one day fulfil his duty and marry a woman suitable to fill the role of Duquesa.

He stared grimly at Lauren, and was infuriated by the hurt he could see in her grey eyes. *Dios*, he had never given her any reason to believe that their affair might lead to him offering her a permanent place in his life. They had a good routine that suited both of them, and he wished they could abandon this discussion that had no purpose and lose themselves in the fiery passion that had blazed between them from the moment they had first met.

He took a deep breath. Perhaps, if he was patient, he could salvage the evening. Now that he had explained his situation to Lauren he could see no reason why their affair should not continue. Duty beckoned him, but, his father's illness aside, he was in no hurry to sacrifice his freedom and choose a bride.

'What is the point in worrying about the future when the present is so enjoyable?' he murmured, stepping closer to her and lifting his hand to stroke her hair back from her face. She instantly shrank away from him, and his jaw hardened.

How could she do anything else *but* worry about the future? Lauren thought wildly. 'Let me get this straight. You intend to marry—not necessarily for love—you will choose a bride who is of suitably noble birth in order to have a child—presumably it will have to be a boy—who will carry on your family name,' she said slowly.

Ramon's mouth tightened at her insistence on carrying on with the conversation when he had made it clear that he wanted to drop it. 'As I have explained, it is my duty to ensure the continuation of the Velaquez line,' he said curtly. 'When my father dies I will return to Spain to live at the historic family home, the Castillo del Toro, and it is important that I have a son who will one day take my place.'

'You live in a castle!' Maybe this was all part of some horrible nightmare, Lauren thought desperately, and soon she would wake up and find that Ramon had *not* turned into an icy stranger who inhabited the rarefied world of the Spanish nobility which an ordinary English lawyer from Swindon could never belong to.

Duty was such a cold word, she thought with a shiver. Ramon did not sound as though he planned to have a child because he wanted to be a father, but because it was necessary for him to produce an heir. But would he want the baby she was carrying? Would he demand that she marry him so that his half-English child would be his legal heir? Or—and this seemed more likely—would he offer her money? Maybe buy somewhere for her and the baby to live and pay his illegitimate child the occasional duty visit, retaining his freedom to marry a woman suitable to be his *duquesa*, who could give him a child with noble Spanish blood running through its veins?

A primitive maternal instinct to protect her child swept through Lauren. She stared at Ramon and saw him for what he really was—a ruthless billionaire businessman. It struck her then that she had never known him at all. He had acted the role of charming lover, but he had never allowed her to see the real man, the son of a *duque*, whose home was a castle. And in that moment she decided that she must keep her baby a secret from him. Ramon needed an heir to continue the Velaquez name, but her baby deserved a father who would love it unconditionally. It would be better for her child to have no father at all than one who did not love it, and would perhaps make him or her feel inadequate and not worthy of the Velaquez name.

Never the most patient of men, Ramon had suddenly had enough of being grilled by Lauren. 'Is there any point to this conversation?' he demanded explosively.

She hesitated, sure that the painful thudding of her heart could not be good for the baby. 'I think there is,' she said sombrely. 'I felt it was time to establish what kind of relationship we have, and it's clear that we view things very differently. I am *not* your mistress,' she insisted fiercely, when he lifted his brows sardonically.

His eyes dropped deliberately to the sexy silk bustier that barely covered her breasts. 'Yet, like a good mistress, you dressed to please me,' he drawled, his mouth curving into a hard smile when she blushed scarlet and frantically pulled the laces together. 'A mistress is all you can ever be to me, *querida*.' He could not pretend that there were any other possibilities.

The careless endearment tore at her heart, but she refused to cry in front of him. The tears could come later, when she was alone—which was likely to be for a very long time, she thought dismally.

'In that case I would like to go home,' she whispered. 'And...and I won't be coming back.'

Incredulity ripped through Ramon, but his disbelief that Lauren appeared to be dumping him swiftly turned to outrage. Although he had ended more affairs than he cared to remember, no woman had ever broken up with *him* before.

'*Dios!* What do you expect from me?' he demanded furiously. 'Would you rather I made false promises I can never keep?' He did not want to lose her, but he was certainly not going to plead with her to change her mind. It was not as if he needed her. There were plenty more attractive blondes willing to share his bed.

He regarded her arrogantly, the noble lines of his illustrious ancestry etched onto his perfectly sculpted features. 'If you really want to leave then I will arrange for my driver to take you home,' he informed her in an icy tone. 'But once you walk out of the door our arrangement is over, and I will not have you back.'

Lauren felt numb beyond words as it hit her that this really was the end. 'I just want to go,' she said huskily. She stiffened when he caught her chin and forced her face up to meet his angry gaze. Tension throbbed between them. For a moment she thought he was going to kiss her, and she despaired that she would have the strength to resist him, but then he swore savagely and flung her from him.

'Go, then,' he said savagely. And without another word she fled.

CHAPTER ONE

EIGHTEEN months later, Lauren hurried through the open-plan office of the big City law firm where she worked, and gave a silent groan when she checked the time on her watch. The staccato tap of her stiletto heels on the tiled floor came to an abrupt halt when Guy Hadlow stepped in front of her.

'The old man has been asking for you since nine o'clock this morning. He wants to see you in his office as soon as you arrive.' Guy gave her a malicious grin. 'You're forty-five minutes late. Did you fancy a lie-in? You look like you had a heavy night.'

'Not that my being late is any of your business, but it's snowing in the North London suburbs and my train was cancelled,' Lauren told him tersely.

Like her, Guy was a lawyer at Plessy, Gambrill and Hess, working in the commercial property department. The only son of a wealthy banker, he was used to having what he wanted. Lauren's polite but consistent refusal to date him had revealed an unpleasant side to his nature. The fact that they were now in competition for the same promotion had exacerbated the hostility between them.

As for her having a lie-in! That would be the day, she thought ruefully. Her ten-month-old son, Mateo, was cutting another tooth, and Lauren couldn't remember the last time she'd had a full night's sleep. Matty had woken at five that morning, and after she had given him his early-morning bottle and changed his nappy she had showered, dressed, loaded the washing machine and unloaded the dishwasher before bundling him into his all-in-one suit and into the car.

The icy roads had caused the traffic to crawl, the usual ten-minute drive to the daycare nursery had taken double that, and when she had finally arrived she'd had no time to do more than thrust Mateo into the arms of one of the staff before dashing off to the station. The sound of his pitiful sobs had haunted her throughout her journey to work, and she was in no mood to put up with Guy's sarcastic wit.

'Do you know why Mr Gambrill wants to see me?'

Guy shrugged. 'I'm just the messenger boy. But it's a pity you chose this morning to turn up late. That won't help your chances of promotion.'

'I didn't *choose* to be late,' Lauren snapped, feeling her stomach swoop down towards her toes. Alistair Gambrill headed the commercial property department at PGH—a senior partner who did not suffer fools gladly and was a stickler for punctuality. But if he had asked to see her at nine o'clock he could not have known then that she had been delayed, so it was unlikely that he wanted to discuss her time-keeping, Lauren reasoned.

Brow furrowed in a frown as she silently debated the reason for the summons, she dumped her coat and handbag on her desk and hurried along the corridor towards her boss's office suite. His PA was speaking on the phone, and while she waited she made a lightning study of her appearance in the mirror behind the secretary's desk.

Her pillar-box-red suit was stylish and defiantly bright on yet another grey February day. Her crisp white blouse added a touch of professionalism, and thankfully there was no sign of the blob of baby sick on her shoulder, which she had scrubbed off on her way out of her flat that morning. But Guy was right. The dark circles beneath her eyes which could not be completely concealed with foundation *were* an indication of regular sleepless nights.

The joys of being a single mother, she thought heavily. Yet, given the choice, she would not change things. Her son had been unexpected and unplanned, but she loved him with a fierce intensity that was beyond anything she had ever experienced. Just thinking about Matty's darling little face, his shock of black hair and enormous sherry-brown eyes made her heart clench.

The PA put down the phone and gave Lauren a brief smile. 'Go straight in. Mr Gambrill is waiting for you.'

Had there been a tiny emphasis on the word *waiting*? As she opened the door Lauren made a frantic mental checklist of recently completed assignments, as well as the current commercial property transactions she was working on. Had she made a mistake that she was unaware of? Had a client filed a complaint about her work? The purchase of a new office block for a well-known City bank was taking longer than expected after problems had arisen with the wording of the lease.

'Ah, Lauren.'

To her surprise Alistair Gambrill sounded delighted to see her, rather than annoyed at her lateness. But she barely heard him. As she entered the office her eyes were riveted on the second man in the room, who rose to his feet and subjected her to an arrogant scrutiny that made her blood run cold.

Her steps faltered. Every muscle in her body clenched in fierce rejection and she could feel the blood drain from her face. This could not be happening, she thought dazedly.

Ramon could not be here, strolling towards her with the easy grace she remembered so well.

Alistair's attention was focused on his guest, so he was oblivious to the fact that his member of staff had whitened to the colour of the pristine blotting pad on his desk. 'Lauren, I'd like you to meet our new client, Ramon Velaquez. Ramon, may I introduce one of PGH's finest commercial property lawyers, Lauren Maitland?'

One of the company's finest lawyers! That was news to her, Lauren thought blankly. But Alistair was smiling at her as if she was his favourite niece. He was clearly keen to impress Ramon, and she sensed his impatience as he waited for her to speak.

She could feel her heart slamming against her ribs. Should she reveal to Alistair that she was already acquainted with the client? She choked back a hysterical laugh. *Acquainted* seemed such an old-fashioned word, but what else could she say—that she and Ramon had once been lovers? Would *he* explain that they knew each other?

Somehow she forced her throat to work. 'Mr Velaquez.'

'Ramon, please. Let us dispense with formality.'

His voice was just as Lauren remembered it: deep, melodious, with a faint huskiness that was spine-tinglingly sexy. It tugged on her soul like a siren's song, drawing her gaze inexorably to his face.

Matty had his father's eyes, she thought faintly. The likeness between them was almost uncanny. When her son had been born and the midwife had placed him in her arms she had stared in awe at his tiny face and been reminded of Ramon. But her joy had been tinged with an aching sadness that he was not with her to welcome their child into the world. She had never expected to see him again, but now, unbelievably, he was here in Alistair Gambrill's office, and she was overwhelmed by the conflicting emotions that stormed through her.

'I'm pleased to meet you, Lauren.' Only Ramon could make her name sound so sensual, his discernible accent lingering over the vowels like a lover's caress, causing the tiny hairs on her arms to stand on end.

Her face suddenly felt hot as the blood moved in her veins once more. Even worse was the instant effect Ramon had on her body, and she bit back a gasp when she felt her nipples tighten so that they strained uncomfortably against the lacy restriction of her bra.

Why was he here? she wondered fearfully, tension knotting in her stomach. Could he have found out about Mateo? She glanced desperately at Alistair. Everyone at PGH knew she had a son. Had her boss unwittingly revealed her secret by explaining to Ramon that her lateness this morning might have been due to childcare issues?

She fought the frantic urge to turn and flee from Ramon's speculative gaze. Alistair had introduced him as a new client, she reminded herself. He *couldn't* be here because of Matty. But he had known the name of the law firm she had moved to shortly before they had broken up, and she was sure his presence at PGH was not merely coincidence. Nothing Ramon ever did was unplanned.

What game was he playing? she wondered. But it was easier to go along with it in front of Alistair than to admit to a history that was well and truly in the past. Pride and professionalism were her only weapons against Ramon's lethal charm, and she called on both, forcing her lips to curve into a polite smile as she extended her hand. 'And I am delighted to meet you...' She paused infinitesimally while she steeled herself to say his name. 'Ramon.'

In the few brief seconds before his hand closed around hers she allowed her gaze to roam over him. It was only eighteen months since she had last seen him, but he looked older. Still stunningly handsome, but there were a few faint lines around his eyes, and his aristocratic features seemed harder somehow, his skin drawn tight over his slashing cheekbones. The silky black hair that had once touched his collar was now cropped short—less jet-setting playboy, more billionaire businessman, she mused.

She had read in the newspapers of his father's death a year ago. Ramon was now CEO of Velaquez Conglomerates, which included among its business interests the famous Velaquez winery, a bank, and a chain of five-star hotels around the world. He must also have assumed the title of Duque de Velaquez, she realised. But then her thoughts scattered as his hand clasped hers, his strong, tanned fingers contrasting starkly with her paler skin, and the contact of flesh on flesh sent an electrical current shooting up her arm and a quiver of reaction down her spine.

Ramon studied Lauren in a leisurely appraisal, frowning slightly as he felt his body's involuntary response to her. His arousal was instant and embarrassingly hard. He was not a testosterone-fuelled youth, he reminded himself, irritated to discover that his desire for her had not lessened in the year and a half since he had last seen her.

She was wearing the scarlet suit she had worn the night she had abruptly ended their relationship—although today she had teamed it with a demure white blouse rather than the black silk bustier that had displayed her breasts like plump velvety peaches. Her close-fitting jacket showed off her slim waist, while her pencil-skirt moulded her hips and stopped several inches above her knees to reveal long slender legs in sheer hose. Black patent stiletto heels added another three inches to her height and made her legs seem even longer—he wondered if she still liked to wear stockings.

He inhaled swiftly, and tore his eyes and his over-active imagination away from her legs. Her face was attractive, rather than pretty, oval in shape, with creamy skin, intelligent grey eyes beneath hazel brows. Her dark honey-blonde was hair swept up into a chignon.

What was it about this woman that he found such a turn-on? Ramon wondered irritably. He had dated some of the world's most beautiful women— actresses and models whose looks were their fortune. Only this graceful English rose had taken him to the edge of sexual insanity.

The passion they had shared had been mind-blowing— the best he'd ever known. Although he had refused to admit the intensity of his need for her during their affair. The last eighteen months had passed swiftly—his father's illness and subsequent death had been followed by a period of mourning, while at the same time he had taken his place at the head of the company, endeavouring to please shareholders and trying to comfort his mother and sisters. There had been little time for introspection, yet memories of Lauren—the silky softness of her hair, her taut, slender body, the soft cries she let out when he made love to her— had continued to invade his mind.

She had become a thorn in his flesh, he acknowledged grimly. A persistent ache that he had put down to sexual frustration but which, for some reason, he had been unable to assuage with other women. Now he was back in London to oversee a business project—but it was also an ideal opportunity to discover if his lingering sexual attraction to his ex-mistress was real, or a memory that he should have dismissed from his mind months ago.

'Please have a seat, Ramon. I know you have a tight schedule, and we have plenty to discuss.' Alistair Gambrill's voice sliced through the aching silence, although the man seemed unaware of the tension in the room.

Lauren tried to pull her hand free from Ramon's grasp, but he retained his hold for few more seconds, his eyes narrowing on her flushed face before he finally released her.

He already had his answer, Ramon brooded. His desire for Lauren was not imagined. In fact his imagination was enjoying a highly erotic fantasy in which they were alone in the office and she was spread across the desk, with her skirt rucked up around her waist and her long, shapely legs wrapped around him.

Eighteen months ago he had been furious when she had walked out on him, and had vowed to dismiss her from his mind. But he had been unable to forget her. There was still unfinished business between them. The flare of emotion in her eyes when she had first entered Alistair Gambrill's office, and the slight tremble of her hand when she had placed it in his were evidence that she was not as immune to him as her cool smile would have him believe.

Lauren's legs were trembling as the shock of Ramon's unexpected appearance seeped through her, and she sank weakly onto the chair next to him. She had no idea why Alistair had summoned her to meet this new client, but while she was trying to guess the reason the senior lawyer cleared his throat.

'I have studied your remit, Ramon, and it all seems straightforward. As I understand it, Velaquez Conglomerates are looking to purchase a number of suitable commercial properties in London, with the intention of applying for planning permission to run these establishments as wine bars.'

Ramon nodded. 'That's correct. I would like to open two, maybe three bars here in the capital. I already have a shortlist of potential properties suggested by estate agents, and what I require is a commercial property lawyer who will work exclusively on this project and who has additional expertise in planning and development laws.'

He turned his head and looked directly at Lauren, his predatory smile reminding her of a wolf stalking its prey. 'Put simply, I need *you*, Lauren. I understand that you have specialised particularly in Town and Country planning matters, and I believe you are best suited to advise me on any potential problems with the properties I am interested in.'

She gaped at him, her mind reeling in horror as it sank in that he seemed to be suggesting that he wanted her to work for him. 'There are several other commercial property lawyers at PGH who are more qualified and experienced than I am—and who I am sure would suit your requirements b-better,' she stammered quickly, glancing frantically at Alistair for confirmation.

Ramon's eyes narrowed on her flushed face. 'I have read the reports on your recent assignments and I am impressed by your work,' he said coolly. 'I also noted on your CV that you studied Spanish and speak it fluently, which would be additionally useful,' he added, the gleam in his eyes telling her that he had been aware before he had read her CV that she could speak his language.

He turned back to Alistair Gambrill before she could comment. 'I understand that PGH promote a service whereby Lauren could be seconded to Velaquez Conglomerates to give personalised in-house legal advice until the project is completed?'

Alistair nodded enthusiastically. 'That is certainly possible. The in-house legal practice offered by our company is fairly unique, and enables companies such as your own to access specialist lawyers without having to employ their own full-time solicitor.'

'So in effect Lauren would be working directly for

Velaquez Conglomerates until the project is finalised?'
Ramon queried. 'Can I take it you would be happy with
that, Lauren?'

This time there was no mistaking the predatory nature
of his smile; the hard gleam in his eyes told her that he
could read her mind.

Apprehension churned in the pit of her stomach. *No*, she
damned well would *not* be happy, she wanted to cry. How
could she work for him, spend hours every day with him,
and manage to keep Matty a secret from him? Once again
she felt a desperate urge to flee, to run out of the office and
keep on running. But if she did that she was highly likely
to lose her job, her only means of supporting her son, and
so she remained in her chair and knotted her trembling
fingers together as Alistair spoke.

'I have no doubt that you will find Lauren a dedicated
and hard-working employee who will do her utmost to
please you.'

'That's good to hear.' The wolfish smile widened, and
despite her tension the wicked glint in Ramon's eyes sent
heat coursing through Lauren's veins.

Utterly dismayed by her reaction to him, she did not trust
herself to speak. But inside she felt sick with panic. She
would have to speak to Alistair privately later, she decided
frantically. But what excuse could she give for not wanting
to work for an influential new client? For now at least she
would have to go along with it.

'I will certainly do my best to ensure that all transactions are completed as smoothly and quickly as possible,'
she said coolly.

'Good.' Ramon smiled, showing his white teeth, and
Lauren felt a sharp pain, as if she had been kicked in the
ribs. Missing him had become a part of her life, a persistent

ache in her chest, and she quickly compressed her lips to disguise their betraying quiver.

'I hope to open at least one wine bar this summer,' he continued, his eyes fixed intently on her, 'which is why I want you to give your exclusive attention to this project. We will need to liaise on a daily basis, and an office will be made available for you at my London headquarters.'

'Oh, but...' This time she refused to keep silent, despite Alistair's warning frown. 'I think it would be better if I remained here at PGH. I'm responsible for several other accounts—'

'I will personally allocate other members of staff to take over those accounts,' Alistair interrupted smoothly.

Lauren guessed he was very eager for her to work directly for Ramon. The in-house legal practice might save clients the expense of employing their own full-time corporate lawyer, but PGH charged high fees for the service.

'I'll have a contract drawn up immediately, and Lauren is at your disposal as of now.'

'Excellent.'

The satisfaction in Ramon's voice sparked Lauren's temper. She did not want to work for Velaquez Conglomerates, and she certainly did not want to work for Ramon. But to object would be tantamount to suicide for her career. This was a fantastic opportunity for her to prove her suitability for the upcoming promotion at PGH, and a higher position would mean a rise in her salary, which would help with Matty's exorbitant nursery fees. But she couldn't shake off the idea that Ramon had deliberately engineered the situation. The million dollar question was *why*? What did he want from her?

She was agonisingly aware of him sitting beside her. The spicy tang of his cologne assailed her senses, so achingly familiar that she felt a sudden constriction in her throat.

Her eyes were drawn to his face, searching for an answer that was not forthcoming, and instead she glimpsed a ruthless determination in his gaze that sent a prickle of unease down her spine. The moment passed, and he gave her a bland smile as he reached into his briefcase and retrieved a folder.

'These are the details of the properties I am interested in. Perhaps you could spend some time looking through them this morning, and we can discuss your opinion on their potential suitability over lunch?'

He was too much! 'How about I read through the notes and email you a résumé of my initial thoughts?' she countered, oh-so-politely. 'I don't want to interrupt your schedule.'

Sherry-brown eyes glinted gold with amusement, but the subtle nuance in his tone brooked no argument. 'One o'clock, the Vine, Covent Garden. I expect you to be there, Lauren.' He stood up and extended his hand towards Alistair Gambrill. 'Thank you for your time, Alistair.'

'It's a pleasure to do business with you, Ramon.'

'The pleasure is all mine, I assure you.' There was pure devilment in Ramon's smile as he paused in the doorway and glanced back at Lauren, satisfied to see that she looked flustered and pink-cheeked—and infinitely kissable. But the expression in her eyes made him frown. What had he ever done to cause her to look at him as if she feared him?

She had been on edge from the moment she had walked into Alistair Gambrill's office, he brooded. But perhaps she was simply surprised to see him again after their affair had ended so explosively eighteen months ago. He recalled the ridiculous argument they had had because she had objected when he had referred to her as his mistress. Notoriously hot-tempered, he had reacted to her threat to walk out by telling her that if she did, he would not have her back.

Later, when his temper had cooled and he'd had time to think rationally, he had acknowledged that he had spoken in anger, and he had wondered if Lauren had too. But by then he had returned to Spain, after a frantic call from his mother telling him that his father's health had deteriorated and that the Duque was gravely ill. Sorting out his personal life had come way down the list of his priorities as he had taken charge of his family.

It was not only business that had brought him back to England, Ramon admitted to himself. He had come because he hoped to persuade Lauren to resume their affair. She was a fiercely independent career woman, and had informed him that she did not want to be his mistress, but he was confident he would be able to convince her that they should be lovers and enjoy an affair for as long as either of them wanted it to last.

He was the Duque de Velaquez, and had a duty to choose a bride from the ranks of Spanish nobility. But he was in no hurry to marry—certainly not until he had got Lauren out of his system, he acknowledged self-derisively. But first he needed to discover why she seemed so wary of him.

CHAPTER TWO

LAUREN arrived at the restaurant at two minutes to one. From his vantage point seated at the bar Ramon watched her slip out of her coat and hand it to the waiter, who had sprung to attendance the moment she walked through the door. Her smile was a killer, he mused. He had never met anyone who could resist its warmth.

Her hair was still swept up into an elegant chignon, and her designer suit and heels were the uniform of a busy professional—a corporate lawyer with a high-flying career. But he remembered the other Lauren. The passionate and sensual woman who had responded to his lovemaking with such sweet eagerness. As she walked towards him Ramon fought the fierce urge to tug the pins from her hair, bury his fingers in the silky mass and hold her captive while he claimed her mouth until she melted against him.

'Ramon.'

He stood up as she reached his side, faintly irritated that while the waiter had received a smile he did not. 'As punctual as ever,' he murmured.

'It would be extremely unprofessional to be late for an appointment with a client,' she replied crisply.

A subtle reminder that *business* was the only reason she had agreed to have lunch with him? Ramon felt a spurt of amusement at Lauren's determination to put him in his place, but he also acknowledged a strong desire to shake her equilibrium.

'Our table is ready.' He paused, and then added softly, 'It's a pity it's not summer; we could have eaten outside as we used to. Remember, Lauren?'

Her eyes flew to his face. Of course she remembered, Lauren thought shakily. The memories of the good times they had shared during their affair were ingrained in her mind for ever. The Vine had been one of their favourite haunts, and they had frequently dined here before returning to Ramon's penthouse apartment to sate another kind of hunger. The sex had been urgent, intense, and unbelievably erotic—a sensual nirvana that was beyond anything she could ever have imagined.

But it had just been sex. Without strings or the expectation of commitment or emotion. At least it had for Ramon, she thought bleakly. For her it had become something infinitely precious, and the realisation that she had fallen in love with him was one reason why she had left him.

A waiter led them to their table. 'What would you like to drink?' Ramon enquired when they were seated.

'Iced water, please. And I'd like the Dover sole with new potatoes.' Forgoing a starter and dessert meant that, with luck, lunch should last no longer than thirty minutes.

The waiter departed with their order and she glared across the table. 'What are you playing at, Ramon?'

Dark brows rose slightly at the sharpness of her tone, but he did not immediately reply, instead surveying her flushed face with a speculative gleam in his eyes that lit a flame to her temper.

'Why did you invite me here?' she demanded.

'You know why. I wish to discuss a business venture with my new legal advisor.' He paused, and then added laconically, 'I admit I chose the Vine for purely nostalgic reasons. We shared some good times here.'

'I have no desire to take a trip down memory lane,' she said shortly. 'We've both moved on.'

Ramon stared at Lauren speculatively, aware of the surreptitious glances she had been darting at him. The chemistry was still there, simmering beneath the surface of her cool façade, but the faint tremor of her mouth warned of her determination to fight her awareness of him. For now it was enough to know that he bothered her. He controlled the urge to walk around the table and kiss her into submission, and instead turned his attention to the approaching waiter.

Lauren gave a sigh of relief when their meals were served. The fish was delicious, but she was so acutely conscious of Ramon that her appetite deserted her after a few forkfuls.

'I ran a few preliminary checks on the properties you are interested in, and I can see possible problems with two of them,' she explained, taking the folder of notes from her briefcase. 'The property in Chancery Lane is a Grade II listed building, which means it is of historic interest and you would need to apply for special building consent to do any kind of refurbishment. The property in Jermyn Street has a short lease. I've spoken to the company who own the freehold and have learned that they would consider extending the lease. But obviously that would have to be negotiated.'

Ramon speared his last forkful of steak and savoured it before replying. 'Your efficiency is commendable.'

'That, presumably, is the reason you hired me.'

'One of the reasons.' He met her glare with a bland smile. He'd forgotten how much he enjoyed their verbal sparring, and their conversations about everything from the arts to topical news items.

'Alistair Gambrill thinks highly of you,' he commented. 'Eighteen months ago I remember you had only recently moved to PGH from another law firm, and now I understand that you are being considered for promotion. You must have worked hard to make such a positive impression on the senior partners.'

Lauren threw him a sharp glance, wondering if he was being sarcastic. Her dedication to her job and her refusal to cut down on the long hours she worked had been the only source of friction between them during their affair. Ramon had made it clear that he expected her to be at his beck and call, while she had been infuriated by his chauvinistic attitude and had not held back from telling him so.

He had never understood that her single-minded focus on her career stemmed from an almost obsessive need for financial independence, and a determination never to be reliant on anyone—as her mother had been on her father. But how could he have understood, when she had never told him about her parents' bitter divorce, or that her father had abandoned his family for his mistress and left his wife and daughter virtually penniless?

'The move to PGH has certainly given me an opportunity to further my career,' she agreed. 'And I work hard at my job.'

He could not know that she felt pressurised to work harder than her contemporaries. Discovering that she was pregnant a month after she had started at PGH had meant that her career had no longer been a choice but a necessity as she faced life as a single mother.

Anxious to prove her worth to Alistair Gambrill and the other senior partners, she had continued to work long hours. Fortunately Mateo's birth had been straightforward, and three months later she had returned to work full-time, afraid that lengthy maternity leave would be detrimental to her chances of promotion in the male-dominated, highly competitive world of corporate law.

She took a sip of water, fiddled restlessly with her napkin, and then said abruptly, 'I'm sorry about your father.' Ramon had always been reluctant to discuss his personal life, and she knew little about his family, but Esteban Velaquez had been a prominent politician in the Spanish government and his death had been reported worldwide.

She did not expect him to comment, and was surprised when, after a long pause, he admitted, 'It was a shock. Cancer had been diagnosed six months earlier, but after surgery his prognosis was good. Unfortunately the disease returned in a more aggressive form and there was nothing more the doctors could do. My mother has taken his death badly,' he continued heavily. 'My parents had been married for over forty years and she is heartbroken.'

His mother's grief had been as much a shock as the loss of his father, Ramon conceded silently. He had assumed that his parents' marriage had been a union between two influential Spanish families—an arrangement that had developed into a contented relationship based on mutual friendship and respect. But after witnessing Marisol Velaquez's raw despair as she wept for her husband he had realised that it had been love that had bound his parents together for almost half a century—the kind of profound and everlasting love that poets wrote sonnets about and which he had cynically doubted existed in real life.

Lauren stared at Ramon's handsome face and felt her stomach dip. He was impossibly gorgeous, but she was not the first woman to be blown away by his sexy good-looks and she certainly would not be the last. Since Esteban Velaquez's death, the press had frequently reported on the playboy lifestyle of his only son and heir. Ramon had been photographed with a number of women—in particular a well-known catwalk model, Pilar Fernandez, who was the daughter of a Spanish aristocrat and whose impeccable pedigree was reflected in her exquisite features. The pictures of Ramon and beautiful Pilar had reinforced Lauren's belief that he would not be interested in his illegitimate child.

'I'm sorry for your mother,' she murmured. 'Perhaps the prospect of you marrying soon will help to alleviate her grief a little? There is speculation in the media that you are about to announce your engagement to Pilar Fernandez,' she added, when his dark brows lifted in silent query.

'I've no doubt my mother would be delighted at the news of my impending nuptials,' he drawled. 'Since my father's death she seems to have made it her life's mission to find me a bride. But the speculation is unfounded. Certain elements of the Spanish press are fascinated with my private life, but Pilar is simply a friend. Our families have known one another for many years. I'm afraid that even for my dear *madre's* sake I am in no hurry to find a *duquesa*.'

His eyes rested deliberately on Lauren's mouth, and the sensual gleam in his eyes sent a quiver of reaction down her spine. His message was loud and clear. Some time in the future he would select a member of the Spanish aristocracy to be his wife and provide him with blue-blooded heirs to continue the Velaquez name, but until then he would enjoy his freedom and satisfy his high sex-drive with numerous mistresses.

But she had been there, done that, Lauren brooded.

Ramon had gone to some lengths to arrange for her to work for him. She recognised the hunger in his eyes, and could feel the undercurrent of sexual tension that had simmered between them since she had walked into the restaurant. It was inconceivable that he wanted to re-ignite their affair when he had insisted eighteen months ago that if she left him he would never take her back. But if that *was* his intention—dear heaven, she thought shakily—she could only pray she had the strength to resist him.

Tension tightened its grip on her. She could not allow him to find out about Matty. He would surely not deem her son a suitable heir for a family who could trace its ancestors back to the eleventh century, when Rioja had been fought over by the ancient kingdoms of Castile and Navarre. Matty was her baby, her responsibility, and it would be better for everyone if he remained her secret.

The arrival of the waiter dragged her mind back to her surroundings. 'Would you like dessert?' Ramon asked.

'No, thanks.' Her hands were trembling as she shoved the notes on the properties back in her briefcase. 'I should go. I need to get back to the office to hand over the accounts on my file to other lawyers in the department.'

'I'm sure they can wait another fifteen minutes,' he said dryly before he turned to the waiter, 'An Americano, please, and a jasmine tea.'

Did it mean anything that he remembered she always liked to end a meal with cup of herbal tea? All it proved was that he had a good memory, Lauren told herself firmly.

The waiter returned with their beverages and she sipped her fragrant tea.

'So, what has been happening in your life since we split up?' Ramon queried in a casual tone, the intent expression in his eyes shadowed by his thick lashes. 'Is there anyone special in your life, Lauren?'

Only her son, who filled her life so completely that there was no room for anyone else—but she could not tell Ramon that, and gave a noncommittal shrug. 'I don't think that's any of your business.'

So there *was* some guy. It was hardly surprising, Ramon conceded. Lauren was a beautiful, sensual woman, and she would not have spent the past eighteen months alone. What *was* surprising was how much he disliked the idea of her with a lover.

He leaned back in his chair and studied her broodingly. 'I feel sorry for this guy, whoever he is.'

'What?' It took a few seconds for it to sink in that Ramon believed she was dating someone. Lauren frowned. 'Why?'

'Because he doesn't satisfy you.'

'Oh? You know that, do you?' She had forgotten how infuriatingly arrogant he could be.

'I can tell.' He moved so suddenly that she had no time to react as he leaned across the table and captured her chin in his hand. 'If lover-boy satisfied you, your eyes wouldn't darken to the colour of woodsmoke when you look at me.' He ran his thumb pad over her lower lip and felt its betraying tremble. 'And your mouth wouldn't soften in readiness for my kiss.'

'It doesn't… I don't…' Shaking with anger, and another emotion she refused to define, Lauren jumped to her feet so abruptly that her chair toppled over and hit the floor with a clatter that drew curious glances from around the restaurant.

The noise brought her to her senses and she snatched a breath, willing herself to act with calm dignity even though her heart was pounding.

'I don't know what game you're playing,' she said coldly, 'but perhaps I should remind you that I ended our affair a year and a half ago. You might have employed me to work for you, but I expect our relationship to be conducted on a purely professional level, with no references to my private life and no…'

'Kissing?' Ramon suggested dulcetly.

His teasing smile tugged on her heart. She had forgotten his wicked sense of humour, and how often he had made her laugh, and for some inexplicable reason tears stung her eyes.

'You are insufferable,' she hissed, suddenly aware that the waiter, who had hurried over to pick up her chair, was clearly intrigued by their conversation. 'I'm going back to work.'

'I'll take you,' Ramon handed the waiter his credit card to settle the bill. 'After I've shown you where you'll be based while you are working for me.'

Lauren knew enough about cars to recognise that Ramon's sleek silver Porsche was a top-of-the-range model. As she slid into the passenger seat she felt a little pang of regret for her beloved red sports car, which she had traded in for a family saloon big enough to fit in Mateo's baby seat and the mountain of other paraphernalia required for one small child.

Her life was so different now, she brooded. She was no longer a carefree young woman, swept up in the excitement of a passionate affair with a sexy Spanish playboy. Now she was a mother, with all the responsibilities that entailed. But she wouldn't have it any other way. Matty was her life; and the highlight of her day was when she picked him up from the daycare nursery and he wrapped his chubby arms around her neck and smothered her face in wet kisses.

Lost in her thoughts, she did not pay any attention to the route Ramon was taking through the congested London streets until they neared Marble Arch and swung into Park Lane.

'Why are we here?' she asked him with a frown when he drove through a gateway and down a ramp which led to an underground car park. She recognised the place instantly. Eighteen months ago she had often stayed at Ramon's luxurious penthouse apartment, but she could not understand why he was taking her there now.

'I have my offices here.' He parked, climbed out of the car and walked around to open her door.

Lauren followed him into the lift, her heart suddenly beating painfully fast as she remembered all the occasions when Ramon had pulled her into his arms and kissed her until they had reached the top floor, dispensing with her clothes, his, the moment they reached his apartment, sometimes making it to the bedroom, sometimes only getting as far as the sitting room sofa, before their hunger for each other overwhelmed them.

The image of his muscular naked body descending slowly onto hers, his powerful erection penetrating her inch by glorious inch, was so vivid that she closed her eyes, terrified he would guess her wayward thoughts. She could sense his intent scrutiny but refused to meet his gaze, and bit down hard on her lip when he stood aside for her to precede him out of the lift.

'Are your offices up here?' She glanced along the corridor, frowning as she searched for a door other than the one that she knew led into the penthouse.

'Uh-huh.' Ramon slotted a card into the door security system and ushered her inside. The apartment was achingly familiar—a wide hallway, with various spacious rooms leading off it, all decorated in neutral shades and furnished with contemporary pieces which provided splashes of bold colour. Through a half-open door Lauren could see the master bedroom. Memories crowded in on her and she halted abruptly, gripped by sudden panic.

'Is this is another one of your games?' she demanded sharply. 'You said you were going to show me my office.'

Ramon gave her a musing look, taking in her flushed face and the slight tremor of her mouth. This wasn't the first time she had seemed uneasy with him, and he was intrigued to know what was bothering her.

'It's in here.' He pushed open a door at the far end of the hall and led the way into a room which Lauren remembered had once been a small sitting room. It now housed a desk, computer, and other office furniture. 'I'm working from my study, adjoining this room, until I can rent a suitable office complex for the London subsidiary of Velaquez Conglomerates,' he told her. 'In fact, that will be your first task. I recently viewed a new commercial building at St Katherine's Dock, and I want you to deal with the lease contract.'

When Lauren made no reply he continued, 'My PA has remained in Spain, and I'm using secretarial staff from a temp agency until I find a permanent base. Sally comes here a couple of mornings a week so that I can dictate correspondence.'

So working from the apartment would only be a temporary arrangement, Lauren tried to reassure herself. But it could still take weeks, maybe months, before Velaquez Conglomerates took over the new offices—which meant that she would have to come here every day and re-live memories of all the times Ramon had made love to her. Dear heaven—Mateo had been conceived here!

She had walked across to the window, to stare at the view over Hyde Park, but now she swung round to face him, her body rigid with tension. 'This isn't going to work,' she said tersely. 'It's easier for me to commute from PGH's offices than here. I can be in constant communication with you by email or phone...'

Ramon shook his head. 'I'd prefer you to be here.'

'*Why?*' she cried, unable to control her emotions any longer. She had been so shocked to see him again, and coming back to the apartment where they had been lovers was sheer agony. Throughout lunch she had felt as though he was stripping away her protective shell, layer by layer, and she was terrified that if she didn't leave now he was going to guess how much he affected her.

Ramon's eyes had narrowed at her outburst, and now he strolled towards her, as silent and intent as a panther stalking its prey, and twice as deadly. The atmosphere shifted subtly, the tension between them so tangible that Lauren's skin prickled.

'What exactly are you worried about, Lauren?' he asked softly.

'I'm not worried about anything,' she denied desperately, sure he must hear her heart hammering against her ribs. He was too big, too close, and memories of his demanding mouth plundering hers hurt too much. 'I simply don't understand what all this is about, Ramon. Why you've gone to such lengths to manipulate me into working for you.'

He said nothing, just kept on coming towards her, and the stark hunger in his eyes robbed her of breath. 'What do you want from me?' she whispered, and her heart stopped when his hand shot out to cup her nape and his head slowly descended.

'I want this, *querida*,' he said harshly, and covered her mouth with his own.

CHAPTER THREE

LAUREN'S lips parted to voice her protest, but the words were lost beneath the bruising pressure of Ramon's mouth. The kiss was no gentle seduction, but a hot, hungry ravishment of her senses as he took without mercy, demanding a response she was powerless to deny.

Sexual tension had smouldered between them since he had walked into Alistair Gambrill's office, and now it exploded in a firestorm of passion. She was vaguely aware of his hand moving up from her nape, and felt him release the clip that secured her chignon so that her hair fell around her shoulders in a fragrant, silky curtain.

She should stop him, insisted the voice of reason in her head. But the bold thrust of his tongue into her mouth drove everything from her mind but her need for him to keep on kissing her and never stop. It had been so long since she had been held in his arms, and acting purely on instinct she pressed closer to him, so that her soft breasts were crushed against the solid wall of his chest.

'*Querida.*'

The gravelly sexiness of his voice made her tremble. She had placed her hands on his chest to push him away, but now they crept of their own accord to his shoulders as he freed the buttons of her jacket and pushed the material aside, so that he could cup her breast in his palm.

His hand felt deliciously warm through the fine silk of her blouse, and she caught her breath when he stroked his thumb-pad lightly over her nipple so that it tightened and strained against the sheer fabric of her bra. She wanted more, Lauren acknowledged restlessly. She wanted to feel his naked flesh on hers. Her fingers tugged urgently on his shirt buttons, her breathing fractured as she stroked her hands over the intoxicating warmth of his satiny skin and felt the faint abrasion of the crisp dark hairs that covered his chest.

It was as if she had hurtled back in time, and the months that they had been apart had never happened. When they had become lovers Ramon had unlocked her sensuality, and only he had the key. Her breasts felt heavy, and she was aware of a betraying dampness between her legs as she felt the hard ridge of his arousal nudge against her pelvis. And all the time he continued to kiss her, slow and deep now, and so incredibly sensual that a low moan rose in her throat.

Satisfaction swept through Ramon when he felt Lauren melt against him. He hadn't planned for things to get this out of hand—not yet—but it seemed that she shared his urgent need to rediscover the sexual ecstasy that he knew without doubt he would experience with her.

With deft fingers he unbuttoned her blouse, and groaned as he slipped his hand inside her bra and rolled her swollen nipple between his finger and thumb. He felt the tremor that shook her, and suddenly his patience snapped. He wanted her now—hard and fast across the desk—and with a muttered oath he thrust his other hand beneath the hem of her skirt and skimmed his fingers over her gossamer-fine hose, the wide band of lace at the top of her stocking, and finally the silky-smooth flesh of her inner thigh.

'*Dios mio, querida*—I have to have you now.'

Oh, please, yes—now, *now*. The words were like a chant in Lauren's head. She hadn't felt sexual desire for so long. It was as if those feelings had been locked away since she had ended her affair with Ramon. But now he was here, and her body was screaming for the fulfilment only he could give. The feel of his hand on her thigh was unbearably frustrating when she longed for him to move it higher and slip it beneath the edge of her knickers, to touch her where he hadn't touched her for so long.

She could sense his impatience, and the thought filtered into her mind that she hoped he would be gentle. Mateo's birth had been relatively short, but nonetheless it had been a painful experience...

Matty!

She tensed, and her eyes flew open as reality doused her in an ice-cold shower. *What in heaven's name was she doing?*

For a few seconds she was torn between the powerful drumbeat of her desire and the firm insistence of her brain, that told her she must stop this *now*—because allowing Ramon to make love to her would only make an already complicated situation even worse.

'*No!*' Her sharp denial sliced through the air, and, taking advantage of Ramon's surprise, she pulled out of his arms and stood shaking like a leaf in a storm as she frantically refastened her blouse.

'No?'

His tone was deceptively soft, but she could sense his anger. It was justified when she had responded to him with such wanton enthusiasm, she thought miserably. She had given him every reason to believe that she was happy to leap into bed with him, but thoughts of Mateo had brought her crashing back to earth. She could not make love with Ramon when she had kept his son a secret from him.

Ramon drew a harsh breath as he fought the urge to snatch Lauren back into his arms and finish what they had started. Frustration clawed in his gut and made him want to lash out.

'We both know how easily I could make you change your mind,' he taunted. He stared at her nipples, jutting so provocatively through her blouse, and cursed the throbbing ache in his groin. 'You say no, but your body says yes, *querida*.'

'Well, it's been outvoted,' Lauren bit out, barely trusting herself to speak as she struggled to regain some sense of composure. 'You…you took me by surprise, but I don't want you, Ramon.'

'Are you sure about that?' Ramon demanded disbelievingly. 'I've just proved that the fire still burns for both of us.' She had tormented his thoughts and disturbed his dreams for months, until he had given in to his need to find her again. 'I want you back, Lauren,' he admitted roughly.

His voice had softened, and when Lauren stared into his sherry-brown eyes that were so like Matty's her heart ached. His words were beguiling. Perhaps it was being back here at his apartment, where they had shared so many good times, that was undermining her defences, but Ramon had sounded serious. Did he mean that he wanted a proper, meaningful relationship with her? she wondered, clutching at the fragile green shoot of hope. And, if so, would he want Mateo too? Was there the slightest possibility that they could work things out?

'I thought you were supposed to marry a woman from the Spanish nobility who would give you an heir to continue the Velaquez name?' she said shakily. 'Are you saying the situation has changed?'

Ramon shrugged. 'No. It is still my intention to fulfil my

duty. But that is for the future. For now I want to concentrate on running Velaquez Conglomerates and the Castillo del Toro. I do not wish to have a child yet, and therefore I do not need to consider marriage for several years.' He paused, and deliberately dropped his gaze to her breasts. 'But neither do I have any wish to live like a monk, *querida*,' he drawled softly.

Lauren cursed her body's traitorous reaction to the hungry gleam in his eyes. So all he wanted was an affair. The little shoot of hope shrivelled and died. Nothing had changed, she thought painfully. She wondered if he realised how insulted she felt to be told that he only considered her good enough to be his mistress, but not his wife.

Admittedly marriage was not something *she* wanted, she thought wearily, rubbing her brow as myriad confused thoughts swirled inside her head. Having witnessed her mother's devastation after her father had walked out, she had decided that she would never give up her independence for any man.

Plenty of couples lived together without being legally bound in a relationship. But Ramon was not even suggesting a long-term commitment, she thought dully. He simply wanted her in his bed for a month or two—until he grew tired of her. Perhaps if she'd only had herself to consider she might be tempted to bury her pride and accept his offer. Eighteen months ago he had stolen her heart, and she longed to recapture the fun and laughter and the long nights of tender lovemaking that they had shared during their affair. But there was not only herself—there was Matty. And Ramon had stated that he did not want a child yet. She wasn't sure he would *ever* want a child born to his English mistress.

Her conscience prickled. She had never given Ramon the chance to show how he would react to the news that he had a son. But everything he had said a few moments ago reinforced her belief that he would not want Matty. His strong sense of duty might compel him to offer financial support for his child, but, as she knew only too well, a child needed to feel loved and cherished, and she feared that Matty would find a monthly maintenance cheque a poor substitute for a father.

She dragged her gaze from the sight of him refastening his shirt, blushing when she recalled how she had wrenched the buttons open in her feverish need to touch his naked skin.

'It would be inappropriate for me to have an affair with you,' she told him stiffly. 'You are a client of PGH, and you must see it would be highly unprofessional.' She walked over to the door, praying that she appeared more in control of herself than she felt. 'For that reason I think it would be best if you chose another lawyer from the commercial property department to work on your project. There are a number of excellent lawyers at PGH who would be delighted to work for Velaquez Conglomerates.'

Guy Hadlow would seize the chance, she thought dismally. She would have to make the excuse to Alistair Gambrill that she did not feel capable of taking on the Velaquez project because of personal commitments. It would almost certainly ruin her chances of promotion, but she could not work with Ramon now that she knew he wanted her back in his bed.

'I'll speak to Alistair.' She opened the door, and was about to step into the hallway when Ramon's voice halted her.

'How do you suppose Alistair Gambrill will take the news that I am cancelling the Velaquez contract with PGH?' he drawled.

'You're not.' Startled, Lauren swung back to face him,

imagining with horror the senior partner's reaction if he learned that the lucrative contact with Velaquez Conglomerates would not go ahead. 'I mean, there's no need for that. I've explained. There are other commercial property lawyers...'

'I want *you*.' His expression was unfathomable, but something in his voice warned Lauren that his threat to cancel the contract with PGH was deadly serious. 'I will respect your position as my legal advisor and there will be no other relationship between us—unless you wish there to be.'

'I don't,' she snapped.

He ignored her interruption and continued smoothly, 'My decision to use PGH only stands if you agree to act as my lawyer on the wine bar project. If you refuse then I will find another law firm—which I am sure that both you and Alistair Gambrill would prefer not to happen,' he added, with a gently mocking smile.

If she was deemed responsible for the loss of a highly influential client her career would suffer irreparable damage at PGH, and probably with other law firms, Lauren thought sickly. Senior lawyers were a tight clique. Doubts about her professional ability would spread, and she would find it hard to get another job in the City.

She stared at Ramon's hard face and her heart sank. 'That's blackmail.'

He lifted his shoulders laconically, utterly unconcerned by her accusation. 'You should know by now that I always get what I want.'

Oh, yes, she knew all right, Lauren brooded bitterly. Ramon's reputation as a ruthlessness businessman was legendary. She had no option but to work for him, but if he thought she was going to fall into his bed because he had decided that he wanted her back as his mistress he had better think again.

'Doesn't it bother you to know that you'll be working with someone who dislikes you intensely?' she said tightly.

'No.' His arrogant smile caused her to grind her teeth. 'But I have to say I'm surprised that someone who dislikes me as much as you say you do could have responded to me with such passion a few minutes ago. Perhaps you don't know what you want, *querida*?' he suggested softly.

While she struggled to formulate a reply, he strolled over to the desk and opened a file. 'These are the details of the office complex in St Katherine's Dock. I'd like you to start work on the lease agreement straight away. If you're staying, that is?' he added, when she continued to hover uncertainly in the doorway.

With as much dignity as she could muster Lauren marched back across the room, sat down at the desk, and immediately focused her attention on the pile of documents, her silence thrumming with fury.

Ramon resisted the urge to brush a tendril of hair off her face, and dropped her hairclip on the desk. 'I guess you want this back.'

'Thank you.' Her voice dripped ice.

He watched her scrape her hair back and clip the honey-gold mass on top of her head, and tried to ignore the sharp tug of desire in his gut. 'I have a couple of meetings booked for this afternoon, and I probably won't be back until late.'

'Then it's likely I'll have left by the time you return.' Lauren lifted her head and met his gaze steadily. 'I finish at the office at five-thirty. That's non-negotiable. But I'm happy to take work home to complete in the evenings if necessary.'

Ramon's eyes narrowed, his curiosity aroused by the

quiet determination in her voice. 'Everything is negotiable, Lauren.'

'Not this.' She collected Mateo from the day nursery at six-fifteen every evening, and not even the threat of losing her job would persuade her to work late.

'I remember that you frequently used to work until seven or eight p.m.' Ramon paused. 'Maybe there's someone you rush home to?'

He was skating dangerously near the truth. She flushed, and tore her eyes from his to stare down at the papers in front of her. 'We've already established that my personal life is not your concern.'

'Oh, we've established a number of things,' Ramon drawled in a dangerously soft voice. 'Not least that you are hot for me—much as you want to deny it.'

Lauren's face burned, and she cursed those moments of weakness when she had responded to his kiss with a hunger that had more than matched his own. 'As a matter of fact I need to leave half an hour earlier tonight. My mother is arriving from Jersey, and I've arranged to meet her at Gatwick.' She hesitated. 'I've already asked Alistair Gambrill for the time off. I hope it's all right with you.'

Ramon gave her a sardonic look. 'It will have to be, won't it?' He paused and studied her speculatively. 'Is there anything else you should tell me?'

Her heart almost leapt out of her chest, and her eyes flew to his face. Did he mean Matty? Did he know…? His expression was unfathomable. 'Wh…what do you mean?' she stammered.

'I simply wondered if you had any other engagements booked that I should know about, so that I can arrange viewings of properties around any other commitments you might have.' Ramon stared at her impatiently. 'Why are you so edgy, Lauren? And why do I get the impression that you're hiding something from me?'

Her palms felt clammy, and it took all her will-power to meet his gaze. 'I really don't know where you would get such a ridiculous idea from,' she said, managing to sound coolly dismissive. 'I'm not hiding anything.'

'Liar. You are doing your best to hide the fact that you are still attracted to me.' Ramon suddenly leaned forward, rested one hand on the desk, and placed the other on her nape. 'But you are not succeeding. Your eyes give you away, *querida*,' he drawled, before he swooped and captured her mouth in a brief, hard kiss that left her aching for more.

He smiled sardonically at the confused mixture of anger and desire in her eyes, and then released her and strolled across to the door. 'I'll see you later,' he threw over his shoulder—leaving Lauren too emotionally drained to wonder why he had said *later* rather than on Monday.

'I'm sure Mateo will be walking before he's a year old. Look how well he's balancing on his feet.'

Lauren glanced up from her laptop and smiled at the sight of her mother, kneeling on the floor playing with Matty. 'Do you think he's advanced for his age?'

'Goodness, yes.' Frances Maitland beamed at her little grandson. 'You were such a cautious baby—you didn't even crawl until you were eleven months—but he's so active. He certainly doesn't get his daring nature from you. He must have inherited it from his fa—' She stopped abruptly and looked flustered.

'From his father,' Lauren finished her mother's sentence dryly. 'You *can* say the word you know, Mum.'

'Well, it seems strange to talk about Matty's father when I don't even know his name,' Frances muttered. 'I wish you would tell me about him. I don't know why it's all so secret.'

Lauren stifled a sigh. 'I *have* told you about him. He's a playboy. We had a brief affair, but when I found out I was pregnant I knew he wouldn't want a child, so I didn't tell him. End of story.'

Frances sniffed. 'It's not right that you have to work so hard to support Matty on your own. You must be entitled to maintenance from his father.'

Lauren shook her head fiercely. 'I would never demand money for my son. Mateo is my responsibility, and I can give him everything he needs.' She watched the baby zooming around the carpet on his hands and knees and frowned. 'I still think he looks a bit flushed. And it's strange that he didn't eat his tea. Usually he loves his food. I don't think I'll go to the party tonight, in case he's coming down with something.'

Frances stood up and lifted the chuckling baby into her arms. 'He's absolutely fine. You can't miss the Valentine's Ball—I thought it was PGH's big social event of the year?'

'It is,' Lauren said heavily.

Alistair Gambrill's wife organised the ball each year, and a proportion of the ticket money was donated to charity. The law firm's most prestigious clients were invited, and every member of staff was expected to attend—particularly those who were chasing a promotion, she thought ruefully. She was still reeling from the shock of seeing Ramon again today, and felt in no mood to socialise, but she knew her absence would be noted by the senior partners.

'Well, maybe I'll go, but then come home tonight,' she muttered. The ball was held in a hotel, and the ticket included overnight accommodation so that guests could drink and not have to worry about driving.

'It's one night, for goodness' sake,' Frances said impatiently. 'Don't you trust me to look after my grandson for one night?'

'Of course I do, but—' Lauren broke off helplessly when she saw the light of battle in her mother's eyes. Mateo's flushed cheeks were probably because it was warm in the flat. He looked the picture of health, with his bright eyes and cheeky grin, and she knew Frances had been looking forward to spending some time with him. 'All right.' She gave in. 'I'll go.'

'Good.' Frances beamed. 'You never know—you might be swept off your feet by a handsome stranger.'

'God forbid!' Lauren said fervently as she pressed the 'send' button on her laptop to email the report she had been working on to Ramon. 'The expression "once bitten, twice shy" has never been more apt.'

Huge, ornate chandeliers illuminated the ballroom and sparkled down on the dozens of guests who were milling about the room. Lauren smiled her thanks to the waiter who offered her a glass of champagne, and smoothed her hand down her dress as she made her way towards the group of senior partners and their wives. Her floor-length black silk-jersey gown was simple but elegant; the diamanté shoulder straps and narrow belt around her waist broke the starkness of the dress, and matched her silver stiletto heels.

It was amazing to think that ten months ago she had looked like a barrage balloon in full flight, she mused when she caught sight of her reflection in a mirror. She was lucky that her stomach had regained its pre-pregnancy flatness, but she had eaten sensibly while she was expecting Mateo, and, thanks to her hectic life of combining work and motherhood, she was actually a few pounds lighter than before she had conceived him.

It made a change to dress up for once, she admitted, feeling a little spurt of confidence when she became aware of the admiring glances from a couple of lawyers from another department of PGH. She continued on her way over to the senior partners, but her steps faltered, and for the second time that day shock drained the blood from her face as she caught sight of a familiar tall, dark figure.

What in the devil's name was Ramon doing here?

'Ah, Lauren, delighted you could make it.' Alistair Gambrill chose that moment to turn his head in her direction, so she had no option but to carry on walking, her heart thudding painfully as she felt Ramon's intent scrutiny.

'Good evening.' She managed a brittle smile for Alistair and the other partners, and somehow forced herself to meet Ramon's glinting gaze.

'You and Ramon have met, of course.' Alistair gave her a faint frown. 'Actually, I was surprised you hadn't invited Ramon tonight. I'm sure you are aware that PGH are always delighted to welcome clients to our Valentine's Ball.'

'I…' Hot colour stormed back into Lauren's face.

'As a matter of fact, Lauren did issue an invitation,' Ramon murmured smoothly. 'I had to decline because of a prior engagement, but that engagement was cancelled just before you telephoned me, Alistair, so I was able to attend the ball after all.'

'Ah, well. Good!' Alistair's face cleared and he gave a jovial smile. 'Ramon was just saying that he is new to London and isn't acquainted with any of the other guests here tonight. I know you'll be delighted to introduce him to people, won't you, Lauren?'

'Delighted,' she assured the senior partner through gritted teeth. She knew she should be grateful to Ramon for covering up her lapse in not inviting him to the ball, but he knew of course that she had deliberately not done so, and his smug smile was infuriating.

'I will certainly appreciate your company,' Ramon assured her, pure devilment gleaming in his eyes. 'Allow me to get you another drink.'

'New to London!' she snorted, stalking furiously beside him when he took her elbow and guided her towards the bar. 'Presumably Alistair is unaware that you've slept with just about every woman in the capital between the ages of eighteen and sixty?' She glared at him when he chuckled, the sound of his sexy laugh causing a squirming sensation in the pit of her stomach. 'Would you like me to hold your hand while I introduce you around?' she queried sarcastically.

'To be honest, I would prefer you to hold another area of my anatomy, *querida*,' he said dulcetly. 'But as we are in public I will settle for your hand in mine.'

'How dare you...?' Scarlet-cheeked, Lauren tried to snatch her hand from his grasp, but with insulting ease he tugged her onto the dance floor and settled his other hand on her hip, the mocking glint in his eyes warning her that she would come off worst if she caused a scene.

'Relax,' he bade her, his breath whispering against her ear as he drew her rigid body closer against his broad chest. 'You used to enjoy dancing with me.'

But that had been back in the heady days of their affair, when she had kidded herself that he saw her as more than a convenient mistress, Lauren thought bleakly. Now she knew that she could never mean anything to him.

But trying to disguise her intense awareness of him was not her only problem. Far more seriously, most of the PHG staff knew she had a child, and it would only take one unwitting remark to alert Ramon to that fact. Panic surged through her. Perhaps it would be better if she danced with him all night, she thought wildly. At least that way he could not speak to anyone else.

Ramon inhaled the lemony scent of Lauren's hair, and could not resist sliding his hand up her back to tangle his fingers in the long honey-blonde tresses that she had left loose tonight. *Dios*, she was beautiful. And soon she would be his again, and he would slide his hands not over her dress but across her naked satin-soft skin. He moved his hand down to her *derrière*, and felt the tremor that ran through her when he drew her hard against the throbbing erection straining beneath his trousers. For a second he almost gave in to the temptation to scoop her up and stride out of the ballroom, up to his hotel room, but he forced himself to be patient and bide his time.

'How about that drink?' he murmured, a long while later.

Lauren lifted her head from Ramon's chest and stared at him dazedly, appalled that she had been so seduced by the warmth of his body that she had melted against him. She had no idea how long they had been dancing. All she had been aware of was the sensual, spicy scent of his cologne and the steady thud of his heart beneath her ear.

The heartbeat was such a poignant sound—the drumbeat of life, she thought emotively. When she had been pregnant, hearing her baby's heartbeat on the monitor at her antenatal appointments had been so exciting. It had been a link with her child—a link that Ramon had never experienced, because she had never told him that she had conceived his baby.

She bit her lip and tore her gaze from the golden-brown eyes that were so like Matty's. Had she been wrong to deny him his child? she wondered desperately. It was a question that had haunted her constantly over the past months. She had tried to do the right thing for Matty—had been so afraid that Ramon would not love her baby that she had decided to bring him up on her own. But what if that decision had been wrong? Supposing Ramon would have loved Matty even if he was not the noble heir deemed necessary for the Duque de Velaquez?

Her thoughts swirled in her head until she felt as though her skull was about to split open. Unable to meet Ramon's gaze, she glanced around the ballroom and realised that many of her work colleagues were staring at her speculatively. Their curiosity was not surprising, since she *had* been snuggled up to PGH's most prestigious client, she acknowledged grimly. Guy Hadlow was leaning against a pillar, watching her, and his knowing smirk was mortifying.

'I seem to have monopolised your attention for far too long,' she said stiffly.

'I'm not complaining, *querida*.' Ramon's confident smile held it all—satisfaction that she had succumbed to his potent charm, and the expectation that he had only to click his fingers and she would fall into his bed.

She had to get away from him before she made an even bigger fool of herself. 'Actually, I've got a headache. Please excuse me,' she mumbled, and spun away from him before he had a chance to protest.

She walked swiftly across the ballroom, needing to escape the cacophony of noise, the sound of people's voices and the music. She needed to be alone, to think, as the enormity of her decision to keep Matty a secret from Ramon evoked the nagging guilt that she had tried to push away.

She hurried into the lift and pressed the button to take her to the fifth floor. The door had started to close when a figure appeared, and she gave a silent groan when Guy Hadlow joined her.

'Off to bed so early, Lauren?' he taunted.

She ignored him, but he moved closer, trapping her

against the wall of the lift. She wrinkled her nose in distaste when she inhaled the strong smell of alcohol on his breath.

'The question is—whose bed? Are you going to bunk up with your Spanish playboy?' Guy gave a mocking laugh. 'No wonder you were picked for the Velaquez job. What did you do? Promise to drop your knickers if he gave you the contract?'

The crack of Lauren's hand on Guy's cheek resounded around the lift and he jerked his head back, his mouth thinning to an ugly line.

'You bitch. I'm only saying what everyone is thinking.'

'Well, it's not true.' Lauren felt sick with shame and misery. She heard the ping of the bell announcing that the lift had arrived at her floor and tried to push past Guy—but he gripped her arms with bruising force.

'Really? You give it away for free, do you, Lauren?' the lawyer sneered nastily.

To her horror he hit the button to prevent the lift door from opening. She could tell from his flushed face and glazed eyes that he was seriously drunk, but while she was desperately searching for something to say that would defuse the situation he grabbed one strap of her dress and wrenched it down over her shoulder.

'For God's sake, Guy, let me go.' She could hear the panic in her voice, and shuddered when he lowered his head towards her.

'I wanted you long before Velaquez,' he slurred.

Nausea swept through Lauren when he put his hand on her breast, but she quickly took advantage of the fact that he had released his grip on her arm, and somehow found the strength to push him away. The lift was still stationary.

She frantically jabbed the button to open the door, and stumbled blindly out into the corridor—straight into the solid wall of a broad, muscular chest.

CHAPTER FOUR

'LAUREN? What's going on?'

Ramon stared down at Lauren's paper-white face, and the purple bruises already appearing on her upper arms, then swung his gaze to the man still lounging against the lift wall. He had felt a faint sense of unease when he had watched the man follow her into the lift a few minutes ago, and had quickly taken the other lift up to the fifth floor. It seemed that his instincts had been right, he thought grimly.

Lauren shook her head, beyond speech. She was sure she had been in no real danger from Guy, but the memory of his sweaty hands on her skin as he had pawed her made her sway on her feet.

She could have no idea how vulnerable she looked at this moment, Ramon thought savagely, white-hot fury surging through him. He was startled by the strength of his need to protect her. He wanted to take her in his arms and simply hold her—let her know she was safe with him and that he would never allow anyone to harm her—but first he had to deal with the jerk in the lift.

'Just a moment, *querida*,' he said, as he gently moved Lauren to one side. 'Let me get rid of this trash.'

'Ramon, what are you doing?' Lauren gasped, when

Ramon grabbed Guy by the lapels of his jacket and raised his fist. '*No!* You can't hit him. He's drunk.'

'And that's his defence?' Ramon growled. 'He hurt you.'

Guy's bravado had deflated like a popped balloon, and he cowered away from the furious Spaniard. 'He was just being an idiot,' Lauren said heavily. She still felt sick when she remembered how Guy had dragged the strap of her dress down her arm, but it was obvious he had had too much to drink. 'Look at him; he can hardly stand up. Anyway, brawling with him will only make everything a hundred times worse.'

Ramon frowned, but reluctantly released Guy. 'Go and sober up,' he ordered the younger man harshly, 'and if you value your life keep away from Miss Maitland in the future.'

Guy did not argue as he stumbled out of the lift and almost ran along the corridor. Lauren hugged her arms around herself, shivering as shock set in.

'Here.' Ramon slipped off his jacket and draped it around her shoulders.

The silk lining was warm, and carried the faint scent of his cologne. Lauren hugged it to her as he guided her back into the lift. 'That was my floor,' she muttered, her brain finally clicking into gear when the lift moved smoothly upwards. 'Where are we going?'

'You need a drink, and I have a bottle of brandy in my room—unless you want to go back downstairs to the bar?' he suggested, when she looked as though she was about to argue.

Lauren shuddered at the thought of returning to the party with Ramon, knowing they would attract curious glances from the other PGH staff. But she could not risk being alone with him, she thought desperately. Not because she feared him in any way. No—it was herself, and her overwhelming awareness of him that scared the life out of her.

But when the lift halted at the top floor it was easier to follow him down the corridor than to cause a scene—especially as her legs suddenly felt as though they were about to give way beneath her. Unlike her small, functional hotel room, Ramon's suite was large and luxurious, and she sank down onto one of the leather sofas while he crossed to the bar and poured them both a drink.

'Here—drink this. It might bring some colour back to your face.'

She was about to remind him that she never drank alcohol, but the expression in his eyes warned her that his patience was dangerously thin, so she obediently took a sip of brandy and winced when it burned the back of her throat.

Ramon dropped down onto the sofa beside her, close enough that she was aware of the heat emanating from his body. He loosened his bow-tie and unfastened the top couple of shirt buttons to reveal several inches of olive-gold skin and a sprinkling of dark chest hairs. After one furtive glance at him, Lauren took another gulp of brandy.

'So what was all that about?' His eyes darkened as he inspected the bruises on her arms. 'You should have let me hit the bastard.'

'Guy was just being…Guy. He's asked me out a few times in the past, and didn't like it when I turned him down. Anyway, maybe he has a point,' Lauren said dully, feeling another wave of sick misery wash over her when she remembered Guy's remarks about the reason she had been given the Velaquez contract.

Ramon frowned. What do you mean?'

'I mean that, according to Guy, everyone at PGH thinks

you picked me to work for you for other reasons than my capabilities as a lawyer,' she said bitterly. 'There are several other commercial property lawyers who are more qualified and experienced than me, so I suppose it's not surprising that people believe I slept my way into the job.'

'As a matter of fact Alistair Gambrill recommended that you would be the best person to work on my project,' Ramon told her quietly.

The knowledge made her feel marginally better. 'But you know what office gossip is like,' she burst out, jumping to her feet in agitation. 'People will have been wondering why I was chosen for the contract above more senior lawyers, and the fact that you danced with me all evening will fuel the rumours about me.'

Anger and humiliation surged up inside her, and she spun round to face Ramon, her eyes flashing fire. 'I'll be known as the Mata Hari of the legal world,' she cried wildly, 'and it's all your fault.' Once again he had turned her world upside down. 'Why did you have to come back, Ramon?'

'Because I couldn't keep away,' he countered harshly. He stood up, his eyes fixed intently on her, and the blazing fire in their golden depths sent an answering heat coursing through her veins. 'I tried to forget you—but, *Dios*! You were always there in my mind. Even on the day of my father's funeral I found myself thinking about you,' he revealed grimly, his voice laced with self-disgust, because in the midst of his grief he had closed his eyes and imagined himself resting his head on Lauren's breasts. Of course he had not wanted to be comforted by her, he told himself angrily. He had wanted sex: the physical satisfaction that for some reason was so much more intense with her than with any other woman.

She should move, Lauren told herself as Ramon strode

towards her. She should run for the door and keep on running. But her feet seemed to be welded to the floor, and her heart was beating so fast that her breath came in sharp little gasps.

He was so close that she could see the flecks of gold in his eyes, and a rampant, undisguised sexual hunger that filled her with fear and shameful longing. 'Leave me alone,' she said shakily, putting out a hand to ward him off.

He laughed and caught hold of her, dragging her up against his hard, aroused body. 'Oh, *querida*, I would if I thought for one minute you meant it. But your body gives you away—see?' He curved his hand possessively around her breast, his smile mocking as he stroked his thumb lightly across her nipple and it instantly swelled and jutted against the sheer fabric of her dress.

Why couldn't she feel the same disgust she had felt when Guy had touched her? Lauren asked herself despairingly. But Ramon was no clumsy, drunken boor. He was a highly skilled lover, with a wealth of experience in the art of sex. More than that, he was the man who had stolen her heart, her one love, she acknowledged silently, unable to tear her eyes from his as he slowly lowered his head.

She had expected his kiss to be hard and demanding—a demonstration of his power over her. But the gossamer-soft brush of his lips across hers was so exquisitely gentle that her defences instantly crumbled. Slow and sweet, his mouth explored hers in a sensual tasting that evoked a desperate yearning inside her for him to hold her close and never let her go. He explored the shape of her mouth with his tongue, and there was no thought in her head to resist him when he probed between her lips in a caress that was so intensely erotic that she trembled with need.

And yet she recognised the restraint he had imposed on himself. She was clinging to him, pressing her slender curves eagerly against his rock-solid body, but for some reason he held back, dampening the passion between them to a slow burn rather than allowing it to blaze into a wild firestorm.

She realised that he was giving her a choice. He would not force her into his bed. But she was ashamed to admit that she wished he would sweep her into his arms and carry her into the bedroom. She did not want to think about the implications of having sex with him. She wanted him to seduce her and make love to her with all his considerable skill, so that conscious thought was obliterated and she could lose herself in the sensual mastery of his touch.

He traced his mouth over her cheeks, her eyelids, little teasing caresses that tormented her until with a soft moan she cupped his face with her hands and brought his mouth down on hers. Parting her lips beneath his, she initiated a bold exploration with her tongue.

Ramon's tenuous hold on his self-control shattered. 'Is this what you want, *querida*?' he growled, tightening his arms around her until she was welded to his hard frame and could be in no doubt of the urgency of his arousal, jabbing insistently between her thighs. She was his woman, and he kissed her with a fierce possessiveness, his hunger for her an unstoppable force that demanded appeasement.

Suddenly, explosively, the barriers shattered into pieces, releasing their mutual desire like molten lava flow from a volcanic heart. Lauren's lips were swollen when Ramon finally lifted his head and trailed burning kisses down her throat, over the smooth slopes of her upper breasts. Her nipples were tight and hot, tingling in anticipation of his touch, and she gave a shiver of pleasure when he drew the straps of her dress over her shoulders, lower and lower, until her breasts spilled into his hands.

'Your breasts were always incredibly sensitive,' he

murmured hoarsely as he rolled her nipples between his fingers, squeezing and releasing until she made a keening sound in her throat. 'I have never wanted any woman the way I want you.'

The admission was torn from him as she tugged clumsily at his shirt buttons and ran her hands over his bare chest and abdomen, her fingers stilling when she reached the waistband of his trousers. His erection was so hard that Ramon feared he would come at any second, and with an impatient growl he reached around her, unzipped her dress, and tugged it down so that it pooled at her feet.

Tiny black lace knickers covered her femininity. He hooked his fingers in the elastic and deliberately held her gaze as he slowly drew them down her legs. 'You want me, Lauren,' he told her harshly, and to prove his point he slid his hand between her thighs and discovered the slick wetness of her arousal. 'You can't deny your need is as great as mine.'

Lauren could not deny it; she did not even attempt to try. She had missed him so much, ached for him for so many nights, that she simply did not possess the will-power to resist him. Everything seemed strangely distant—Matty, the knowledge that she could never mean anything to Ramon, her colleagues and bosses downstairs. Would it be so wrong to have this one night with him? her mind argued.

Recriminations could come later—but when Ramon dropped to his knees and parted her womanhood with gentle fingers, before closing his mouth around the sensitive nub of her clitoris, she curled her fingers in his hair and sobbed his name.

He explored her with his tongue, delving into her moist heat and stretching her a little wider with his finger to intensify her pleasure. 'Oh, now—please now.' Delicious little spasms were rippling through her, building quickly to a crescendo, but she wanted more.

'Tell me what you want, *querida*,' he demanded.

For a crazy second she wondered what he would say if she revealed that she wanted him to love her. But of course he never would, and at that moment nothing mattered but that he should possess her.

'I want you...inside me.' For a few tense seconds her confession simmered between them, and then with a muttered oath he swept her into his arms and strode into the bedroom. He dropped her onto the mattress and she watched, wide-eyed, as he stripped with violent haste, his boxers hitting the floor to reveal the powerful length of his arousal.

Lauren's mouth ran dry, but when he pulled her to the edge of the bed, spread her legs and stood between them, her faint wariness disappeared beneath a tidal wave of excitement and desire. He swiftly donned protection, and then with slow deliberation rubbed the tip of his penis up and down the silken folds of her opening. She gasped, and instinctively bent her knees to allow him to penetrate her, closing her eyes blissfully when he filled her with his thick, iron-hard shaft.

'I've missed you.' The stark admission caused her lashes to fly open, and as she met his gaze she glimpsed a fleeting emotion that disappeared before she could define it, leaving his expression once more unfathomable. She wanted to tell him that she had missed him too, that her very soul had felt empty without him, but her words were lost beneath the pressure of his mouth as he crushed her lips in a hungry kiss at the same time as he began to move within her.

She was so tight, Ramon thought as he sank deeper into her warm velvet embrace. And her eagerness suggested that she hadn't had sex very often during the past eighteen months. The thought filled him with a primitive satisfaction. It was time he reminded her just how good they were together. He thrust deeper and harder, setting a rhythm that soon elicited little whimpers of delight from her.

A coiling sensation was growing low in Lauren's pelvis, tightening with every powerful thrust as Ramon drove into her again and again. The sensations he was arousing were indescribable. Her entire body was thrumming with pleasure, and when he closed his mouth around first one nipple and then its twin, sucking hard on each rosy crest, she writhed beneath him.

She stared up at him—at the bunched muscles of powerful shoulders and the beads of sweat that glistened on his chest. His face was a taut mask and she sensed that he was close to the edge. A feeling of tenderness swept over her, and the need to satisfy the frantic demands of her own body became secondary to her yearning for him to experience the pleasure of sexual release.

He gripped her hips, and she tilted her pelvis so that he could drive even deeper into her, welcoming each devastating thrust and whispering a husky plea for him to take her faster, harder. With a groan he obeyed her, the last vestiges of his restraint decimated by her fiery passion. And suddenly Lauren found that she had reached the pinnacle. She had been so intent on giving him pleasure that she was unprepared when the coiling sensation deep inside her snapped, and spasm after spasm of exquisite sensation ripped through her.

Dear heaven, it had been so long since she had experienced such intense pleasure that she had forgotten the sheer wonder of climaxing in Ramon's arms. She squeezed her eyes shut to prevent her tears from escaping. Ramon must never know that, for her, making love with him was a beautiful and emotional experience. He did not *do* emotions—for him this was just sex, she accepted, as he gave one final savage thrust and groaned as his big body shook with the power of his release.

The silence in the room was broken by the sound of ragged breathing gradually slowing. Ramon felt strangely reluctant to disengage his body from Lauren's, but after a few minutes he rolled from her and saw that she was drifting off to sleep.

'You will be more comfortable under the covers,' he murmured, settling them both on the pillows and drawing the sheet over them.

'I must go back to my room,' Lauren muttered. 'I can't keep awake.'

The shock of Guy Hadlow's assault, followed by her utter capitulation to Ramon's hungry demands had left her exhausted, and a little voice in her head taunted that it was easier to allow sleep to claim her rather than face up to what she had done.

'I know!'

His gravelly laughter held a hint of something that sounded almost like tenderness. But she must have imagined it, Lauren told herself sleepily.

'Stay here with me,' he bade her firmly.

She was too weary to argue when he drew her into his arms so that her head rested on his chest. The rhythmic thud of his heart beneath her ear seemed to echo through her body, strong and steady, and she gave a sigh as her lashes drifted down.

Ramon smoothed her hair back from her face, switched off the bedside lamp, and could not hold back a satisfied smile in the darkness. Sex with Lauren was even better than he remembered. He hadn't felt this sated in a long time. The wine bar project would keep him in England for several weeks, and then, although it would be necessary for him to return to Spain, he would keep his London apartment and visit Lauren regularly.

His life had been mapped out from birth, and he accepted the obligations and responsibilities that came with being a *duque*. But before he settled down to a life of duty he deserved a final fling with this woman who could send his temperature soaring with one look from her cool grey eyes.

With that settled, Ramon fell asleep.

It was still dark when Lauren stirred, but she was instantly awake. Shame, guilt, and a whole host of other emotions were storming through her when she turned her head and saw Ramon sprawled on his back beside her. His face looked softer in sleep, and the thick black lashes fanning his cheeks were a piercingly sweet reminder of Mateo.

What a fool she had been—a weak-willed fool who had allowed the sweet pull of sexual desire to drown out the voice of caution in her head, she thought bitterly. She had spent the night in Ramon's bed, and now he would think she was willing to be his mistress again.

It would be impossible to keep Matty hidden from him, she realised, panic making her heart pound. She would have to leave PGH, leave London, take Matty away somewhere and pray that Ramon did not try to find her...

She took a shuddering breath. What on earth was she thinking? She could not uproot Matty from his home. She stared at Ramon's beautifully sculpted face. The shadow of dark stubble on his jaw gave him a strangely vulnerable air. He was not a demon, she reminded herself. He was the man she had fallen in love with—the man who had made love to her last night with tenderness as well as passion.

When she had ended their affair he had told her he would not take her back, yet he had come to find her.

Perhaps he had only come because of the fierce sexual chemistry between them, but what mattered was that he was here. She could no longer use the excuse that she did not know where to contact him. She was through with playing God. Ramon had a right to know that he had a son, and as soon as he woke she would tell him.

The sound of her mobile phone made her jump, and she quickly slid out of bed and hurried through to the sitting room, rifling through her handbag to answer it before it disturbed Ramon. She gave a faint smile when she saw that it was her mother calling. She'd warned Frances that Mateo invariably woke at dawn, and not to expect a lie-in.

'Mum?' She kept her voice low. 'Has Matty been awake for long?'

'Oh, Lauren…' Frances's voice shook. 'Lauren, Matty's not well.'

'What do you mean—he's not well?' An icy hand of fear gripped Lauren's heart. 'What's wrong with him?'

'He…he settled fine when I put him in his cot last night, and he slept well. But this morning I woke up when I heard him make a funny noise. It wasn't a cry…' Frances's voice wavered. 'More a sort of choking sound.'

Dear God! Lauren gripped her phone so hard that her knuckles whitened.

'Of course I rushed into his room,' her mother continued. 'And, well…he seemed to be having some kind of a fit. I called an ambulance immediately, and the medics are here now. They're going to take him to the hospital.'

'I'll go straight there,' Lauren told her mother urgently, and cut the call. Her dress and underwear were scattered on the carpet—a shameful reminder of how she had become a wanton creature in Ramon's arms last night. But at this moment she could think of nothing but being with her sick child.

Heart pounding with fear, she dragged the dress over her head and tore out of Ramon's suite, into the lift. Once back in her own room she changed into jeans and a jumper, snatched up her overnight bag, and minutes later was racing across the hotel's reception area. She did not allow herself to dwell on what might be wrong with Mateo. Her brain focused exclusively on the necessity to get to the hospital as quickly as possible. Nothing and no one else mattered right now—not even Ramon. She did not spare him a thought.

She cannoned into Alistair Gambrill, who was standing on the hotel steps, holding a set of golf clubs. 'Lauren, you're up early.' He frowned when he saw her tense expression. 'Is everything all right?'

'Matty's ill. I have to go,' she called over her shoulder as she flew down the steps. There was no time to stop and talk to the senior partner. Her baby was on his way to hospital, and the devil himself would not prevent her from being with him.

Ramon gunned his Porsche along the busy North London streets. It was late on Saturday afternoon, and there was a lot of traffic as he headed in the direction of Lauren's flat.

'Lauren left early this morning because her son is unwell.'

Alistair Gambrill's words played over and over in his head. *Her son!* Lauren had a child? *Dios!* His brain could not take it in. Whose child? He wanted, *demanded* an explanation, but all day her phone had been switched off, and his anger had increased with every abortive attempt to call her.

His mind re-ran the day, from the moment he had woken at the hotel and discovered that his bed was empty. At first he had thought she was in the bathroom, but when he had found that her clothes were gone he'd felt irritated that she must have returned to her room some time during the night. But he had reminded himself that Lauren had been upset by the idea that the other lawyers at PGH were discussing her relationship with him, and he understood her reluctance to risk being seen leaving his room.

With that in mind he had eaten breakfast in his suite and visited the hotel gym. He had only later learned from a casual remark by Alistair Gambrill of Lauren's early departure—and the astonishing reason for it.

'You'd never believe Matty was rushed into hospital this morning,' Lauren said for the umpteenth time, as she watched her son crawling energetically around the sitting room. 'He looks a hundred times better than he did when I saw him on the children's ward.'

'He looks a lot better than you,' her mother commented. 'You're still as white as a ghost.'

'I was worried.' Lauren grimaced at the understatement, and tears blurred her eyes. *Worried* came nowhere near the stark fear she had felt as she had raced to the hospital. The possibility that Mateo was seriously ill had filled her with terror, as well as guilt that she had left him with her mother while she had attended the Valentine's Ball. 'I shouldn't have gone to the wretched ball last night,' she said thickly.

'The doctor said that febrile convulsions are fairly common in babies when they are running a high temperature,' Frances reminded her. 'He confirmed that Matty has a throat infection and that the antibiotics should take effect quickly. He's going to be fine, Lauren.'

'I know. I just keep thinking what if it had been worse? What if he'd had something life-threatening? I couldn't bear to lose him.' Lauren's voice wobbled and she lifted Mateo up and hugged him to her. 'I love him so much.'

Her legs suddenly felt weak, and she collapsed onto the sofa. She had been feeling unwell since they had brought Matty home from the hospital a few hours ago, but had put her pounding headache and aching limbs down to the after-effects of shock. Now she had developed a sore throat, and felt shivery. It seemed likely she had caught the virulent flu virus that had been going round the PGH offices recently. That was all she needed, she thought wearily.

The doorbell pealed. 'That's probably my taxi,' Frances murmured, getting to her feet. 'Are you sure you'll be all right if I go to Southampton tonight?'

'Of course I will,' Lauren assured her mother. 'You can't miss a world cruise—and you *must* go tonight if you're to board the ship at eight tomorrow morning.'

She rested her aching head against the back of the sofa, grateful that Matty was playing contentedly with a new toy for a few minutes. She could hear voices in the hall. Maybe her mother's taxi wasn't here yet, and a neighbour who had seen the ambulance arrive that morning had called to ask after the baby? Footsteps sounded in the hall. She glanced towards the living room door as it opened. Her mother walked in—and then Lauren gave an audible gasp at the sight of the dark and infinitely dangerous-looking man following closely behind Frances.

Ramon! A grim-faced Ramon, whose eyes were glittering with rage. Lauren instinctively tightened her grip on Mateo and swallowed when Ramon's gaze swung from her to her baby son.

CHAPTER FIVE

'LAUREN—Mr Velaquez has explained that he is one of your clients…' Frances's voice tailed to a halt as she glanced from her daughter to the darkly handsome man whom she had invited into the flat, and who was now staring grimly at Lauren and Mateo.

Silence fell in the room. A silence that simmered with an undercurrent of tension that made Lauren's skin prickle. She was barely aware of her mother. Her eyes were riveted on Ramon's face. He had paled beneath his tan, his shock palpable. She could not tear her gaze from him, and she watched as his shocked expression changed to one of bitter fury.

'So it's true—you have a child.' His voice was so harsh it was almost unrecognisable, his accent very pronounced. Silence stretched between them once more, shredding Lauren's nerves, before he spoke again. 'He is my son.'

It was a statement, not a question. The resemblance between Ramon and Matty was startling. Lauren could not have denied the truth even if she had wanted to, and she gave a tiny nod.

He swore violently, and Lauren flinched. 'You kept my son a secret from me,' he said hoarsely, disbelievingly. He stared at the baby and saw his own features in miniature. There was no doubt that Lauren was holding his child in her arms, but his brain was struggling to comprehend what his eyes were telling him.

And not just his eyes, he thought as he walked jerkily across the room, moving without his usual lithe grace. His heart, his soul recognised his own flesh and blood. He did not understand how it had happened, but that was immaterial now. Lauren had given birth to his son—and had never told him.

For the second time in his life Ramon tasted the rancid bile of betrayal in his throat. The only other occasion he had felt like this was when he had been eighteen, standing in the doorway of a hotel bedroom, fixated by the sight of the woman he loved lying naked on the bed with another man.

'*Now* do you see why you cannot marry this trollop?' his father asked from behind him. 'Catalina Cortez was never in love with you, my son. It was all a trick, devised with her lover, to seduce you into marriage so that she could claim a vast divorce settlement. You have been taken for a fool, Ramon,' Estevan Velaquez had told him harshly. 'But fortunately no damage has been done—except to your pride, perhaps,' the *Duque* had added perceptively.

The disappointment in his father's eyes had intensified Ramon's humiliation, and as he had stared at Catalina he had vowed never to trust another woman again. Over the years that decision had served him well, for he had found most women to be untrustworthy. But Lauren had been different. One of the qualities he had most admired about her had been her honesty. He had spent his life surrounded by people who fawned on him and told him what they thought he wanted to hear, and he had found Lauren's tendency to speak her mind a refreshing change.

Now he knew that she no more deserved his trust than Catalina had, Ramon thought bitterly. Lauren had not cheated on him with another man, but she had cheated him out of the first months of his son's life, and he would never forgive her for her duplicity.

'How old is he?' he ground out, forcing the words past a peculiar constriction in his throat.

'Ten months.'

Lauren bit her lip. Ramon looked shell-shocked, almost haggard, and the terrible realisation was dawning inside her that she had been wrong to keep his son a secret from him. He was a playboy Spanish *duque*, who had freely admitted that he viewed marriage as an unwelcome duty necessary to begat the next Velaquez heir, she tried to reassure herself. But the look of *devastation* in his eyes tore at her conscience.

'Ten months?' he repeated harshly. 'You have kept my son from me for almost a year.' He did a quick mental calculation. 'You knew you were pregnant the night you ended our affair, didn't you? *Dios!*' He closed his eyes briefly, trying to take it in. '*Why*, Lauren?'

'Lauren—what's going on?' Frances interrupted in a shocked voice. 'Who is this man?' She stared warily at the formidable stranger dressed in black jeans, sweater and a leather jacket. 'Shall I call the police?'

'No. It's all right, Mum.' Lauren took a shaky breath. 'Ramon is Matty's father. I…I need to talk to him, and you need to go. I think your taxi is here now. Please don't worry,' she begged her mother, who looked as though she was going to argue. 'Everything is going to be fine.'

If only she could believe that, she thought a few minutes later, as she gave Frances a wave and shut the front door. Her headache had developed into an excruciating pain, as if someone was drilling through her skull. She longed to take some painkillers and lie down on her bed for a few minutes, but instead she took a deep breath and walked back into the sitting room.

Ramon was standing by the mantelpiece, studying a photo of Mateo taken when he had been a few days old. He speared her with a savage glare. 'I don't even know his name,' he said, in a low tone that could not disguise his tightly leashed anger.

'It's Mateo.'

'Mateo.' Ramon spoke his son's name with a sense of wonder. His son—*his son*. He still couldn't take it in. Until now he had viewed fatherhood simply as a duty he would have to fulfil at some point in the future. He had never actually envisaged what it would be like to have a child. But now he was faced with his son, whose features so resembled his own that it was like looking at a miniature version of himself, and he felt awed that this perfect, beautiful child was his.

Matty was sitting on Lauren's hip, his head resting on her shoulder, but he looked up enquiringly at the sound of his name and gave Ramon a gummy smile. The baby was usually wary of strangers, especially when he was tired, but to Lauren's shock he held his arms out to his father. Ramon moved closer, his hands visibly shaking as he touched his son for the first time, and Lauren felt a sudden, irrational feeling of panic. She did not want to let Matty go, but the baby smiled happily as Ramon lifted him and held him against his chest.

'Mateo.' Ramon stroked his son's silky black hair, and as he stared down into the baby's sherry-brown eyes that were the exact same shade as his own the tidal wave of emotion that swept through him threatened to unman him. He had missed most of the first year of his son's life. Lauren had stolen those irreplaceable months from him, and the knowledge filled him with black fury.

Lauren swallowed the tears that clogged her throat. Matty looked so small in Ramon's arms, and the look of tenderness in Ramon's eyes as he studied his son evoked a host of emotions in her. 'Matty is tired,' she said quietly. 'He usually has a nap about now. I'll put him in his cot.' She held out her hands to take the baby, but Ramon shook his head.

'I'll take him. Show me where he sleeps.'

It would be childish to refuse, and she could hardly snatch Matty out of Ramon's arms, she acknowledged as she reluctantly led the way down the hall to the tiny box-room that served as a nursery.

'He's had a traumatic day,' Lauren explained a few minutes later, after Ramon had carefully laid Mateo in his cot.

'Alistair Gambrill told me this morning that you had rushed home because your son was ill.'

So that was how he had found out about Matty. And now she could not deny Ramon the answers he clearly wanted. Her head felt as though it was about to split open, but she tried to ignore the pain and led the way back into the sitting room.

'What was wrong with Mateo?' Ramon demanded. 'He seems to be perfectly well now.'

'He had a fit this morning. My mother called an ambulance and he was rushed into hospital. Apparently it was what is called a febrile convulsion, brought on by a high temperature. Tests revealed that he has a throat infection, and the doctor prescribed a course of antibiotics. There should be no lasting damage, although babies who have had febrile convulsions are slightly more at risk of having them again,' she added shakily.

Tears filled her eyes once again, although she knew it

was pathetic to cry when the doctor had assured her that Matty had been completely unharmed by the fit.

She dashed her hand across her face and glanced up, to find Ramon watching her through narrowed eyes. He had taken off his leather jacket, and suddenly he flung it forcefully onto a chair, his barely leashed violence making Lauren jump.

'Why did you do it, Lauren?' He caught hold of her shoulders in a bruising grip that made her cry out.

'Ramon! You're hurting me.'

'I could *kill* you,' he snarled. His face was a hard mask, his skin drawn taut over razor-sharp cheekbones. He glimpsed the fear in her eyes and felt infuriated that even in the midst of his anger Lauren's air of vulnerability got to him. He flung her from him, disgusted as much with himself as with her. 'You treacherous bitch. How could you deny me my own son?'

Lauren rubbed her shoulders and stared at him with huge, wary eyes. 'I didn't think you would want him.'

'*You never gave me a choice.*' Nostrils flaring, Ramon fought to control his temper. 'Why would you think that I would not want my own child?'

Lauren gave a bitter laugh. 'Because you told me that it was your duty to marry an aristocratic Spanish bride and provide a blue-blooded heir to continue the Velaquez line. I was going to tell you I was pregnant that last night, when we went to the Vine for dinner, but you made it clear that I meant nothing to you.'

She would never forget his appalled expression when she had given him an anniversary gift.

'You insisted that I could only ever be your mistress. I was afraid you would think that Matty wasn't a suitable heir—because I certainly don't have any noble ancestors,' Lauren continued in a low tone when Ramon gave her a scathing look. She bit her lip. 'From the moment I walked out of your apartment I was tormented by guilt and indecision. I didn't know what to do. I was torn between wanting to tell you that I was expecting your baby, and being afraid of your reaction. Many times—before Matty was born, and after—I brought up your number on my phone. But each time I lost my nerve and didn't put the call through,' she admitted huskily.

'I didn't want Matty to grow up feeling that he wasn't good enough to be part of the illustrious Velaquez family.' She voiced the fear that had gnawed at her. 'Children need to feel valued.' It was something she had learned when her father had left and she had realised how unimportant she was to him. 'Although you might have been willing to marry for duty, I wasn't.'

'You thought it better to bring Mateo up without a father?' Ramon accused her scathingly. 'What right did you have to deny him one of his parents? Did you ever think about what *he* might want?'

Lauren paled. She *had* felt guilty that Matty would grow up without a father, but it had seemed preferable to an uninterested father whom she had feared would regard fatherhood as an irksome duty.

'And how much more of his life were you going to steal from me?' Ramon demanded furiously. 'Would you *ever* have told me about him?' His blood ran cold. 'Or was that chance remark by Alistair Gambrill the only reason I discovered my child's existence?'

When she did not answer, he glared at her with bitter contempt.

'*Dios!* You slept with me last night, and even then you said nothing. What was all that about, anyway? Were you using me as a stud, in the hope of conceiving a sibling for Mateo?'

'*No!* Don't be ridiculous.' Lauren's temper flared at his outrageous accusation. 'You came on to *me*, if you remember. You danced with me all evening, and took me up to your room.'

'You came willingly enough.'

'Only because Guy had upset me. I never intended for things to turn out the way they did.' She looked away from him, colour flooding her cheeks—because she was lying, she admitted bleakly.

During the ball she had been intensely aware of Ramon, and deep down she had longed for him to take her to his room and make love to her. Even now she was acutely conscious of him. Her traitorous body ached for him to touch her as he had touched her last night. The memory of how he had stroked his hands over her naked flesh and brought her to the peak of arousal with his clever fingers made her limbs tremble.

Ramon raked his hand through his hair and swung away from her, pacing around the small living room like an angry caged bear. 'Who cares for Mateo while you are at work all day? You told me your mother lives in Jersey, so presumably *she* is not involved in his upbringing?'

'He is in a daycare nursery. It's an excellent nursery— the absolute best,' she continued quickly, when Ramon frowned. The nursery fees were exorbitant, but she was happy to pay them for peace of mind that Matty was happy and well cared for.

'And when did you return to work?'

'When he was three months old.'

'*Dios mio!* You dumped him in daycare when he was just three months old?' There was genuine horror in Ramon's eyes. 'My sisters did not leave their babies' sides for the first years of their lives.'

Lauren gave him a startled look. 'I didn't even know

you *had* sisters. In all the months that we were together you never spoke about your family.'

He shrugged. 'I learned long ago to guard my privacy, and that of my family, after a couple of ex-mistresses blabbed to the tabloids about my personal life. Even the colour scheme of my bathroom seems to be fascinating to some people,' he added dryly.

But there had been another reason why he had maintained a distance between himself and Lauren, Ramon admitted silently. Over the years he had learned to compartmentalise his life; in Spain he had been the son of a *duque*, who could never forget the life of duty that lay ahead of him, but in London he had enjoyed a playboy lifestyle. His relationship with Lauren had begun as just another affair with a pretty blonde, and because he had known that that was all it could ever be he had deliberately not allowed his two worlds to mix.

'You must have known that I wouldn't do something like that,' Lauren muttered, hurt by his lack of trust in her. It reinforced the fact that he had regarded her as just another casual lover, and once again she wondered how she had been stupid enough to believe he had started to care for her.

'Unlike your sisters, I live in the real world,' she said curtly. 'I had to go back to work to pay the bills. I'm not saying the situation is ideal, but I have done my very best for Matty. I even used to spend my lunch hour in the ladies' loo, expressing my breast milk so that the nursery staff could give it to him the next day.'

Her life in the first few months after she'd had Mateo had been a blur of exhaustion, worry, and guilty tears shed silently in the cloakroom at work in between meetings. Ramon would never understand what a terrible wrench she still found it to leave her baby for hours every day.

'It would have been better for him if you had held him in your arms and fed him yourself,' he said harshly. 'Breastfeeding is a crucial time, when the special bond between a mother and her child is formed.'

'I had no idea you were such an expert in childcare,' Lauren snapped, infuriated by his arrogance. 'I hate having to leave Matty, but I have no choice…'

'Yes, you do. You have always had a choice,' Ramon said bitterly. 'If you had told me you were expecting my child I would have ensured that you received the best care. My son would have been born in Spain and would have spent the past ten months at the Castillo del Toro, surrounded by his grandmother and his aunts and cousins—not here in this poky flat, farmed out to a nursery all day while you pursue your precious career.'

*Poky flat…farmed out…*Ramon's scathing indictment of the way she was bringing up Mateo rendered Lauren speechless with fury. But before she could formulate a reply he spoke again—this time in a cold, implacable voice that she found more frightening than his explosive temper.

'I want my son. And I will have him; do not doubt it, Lauren.'

The moment Ramon had laid eyes on his son he had realised he did not give a damn if the baby was not deemed to be of true Spanish noble blood because he had been born to an English mother. Mateo was his child, and he felt fiercely possessive and protective of him.

'It is obvious from Mateo's striking similarity to me that he is a Velaquez, but if you deny that I am his father I will demand a DNA test, and then I will take him to Spain, where he belongs.'

'You can't do that.' Lauren shook her head, and winced as starbursts of pain shot through her skull. She could not stop shivering, yet two minutes ago she had been burning up. Her legs must be trembling because she had a fever, but as she stared at Ramon's hard face fear swept through her, and she sank weakly onto the sofa. 'You have no right to take him,' she said shakily.

He slammed his hand down on the table, his temper exploding once again. 'Don't you *dare* talk to me about rights! What right did you have to keep my son from me? And what right did you have to deny Mateo his father? This is not about us,' Ramon said grimly. 'The only important thing is what is best for Mateo.'

'How can taking him away from me be best for him?' Lauren held her hand to her throbbing head and tried to think clearly. 'I may not have specialised in family law, but no court would separate a baby from his mother.'

'We'll see,' Ramon said coldly. 'I think it is entirely likely a judge would agree that it would be better for Mateo to live with his father, who is prepared to devote his life to him, within a huge extended family who will welcome him and love him, than with a mother who is at work all day while he is left in the care of nursery staff. A child of Mateo's age needs the security of being cared for mainly by one or two family members, and *I* will be there for him night and day.'

'Really?' Lauren said disbelievingly. 'What about when you are jet-setting around the globe for work? Or attending numerous social functions? I suppose you'll leave Matty with a nanny?'

'I intend to cut my business trips to a minimum, and to be frank I'm bored with parties. I would much rather spend my time with my son.'

He stared at Lauren's white face and hardened his heart against a faint flicker of sympathy. She had cold-bloodedly denied him his child, and she did not deserve his compassion.

'What you did was unforgivable,' he said harshly. 'You had better start praying you win that promotion Alistair Gambrill told me you are in line for, because you are going to need all the money you can get to pay for the custody battle—and for the appeal if I lose the first round, and then the next appeal. Do you get the picture, Lauren? I will never give up fighting for my son because I genuinely believe he will have a better life with me. Mateo is the Velaquez heir, and I don't understand how you could want to deny him his birthright.'

Lauren suddenly sneezed violently, and could not stifle a groan as pain tore through every muscle in her body. She still could not stop shivering, but when she pushed her hair back from her face her brow felt clammy with sweat. She rested her head against the back of the sofa, unaware of Ramon's sharp scrutiny.

He frowned when he saw that her skin was a strange grey colour. 'What's the matter with you?' he demanded tersely. 'You look terrible.'

She gave a mirthless smile. 'You don't think that might have something to do with the fact that you're threatening to take Matty from me?' Her throat felt as though she had swallowed shards of glass, and talking was agony. 'I must have picked up the flu virus that's been doing the rounds at work.' She dropped her gaze from the blazing fury in his. 'I'm sorry,' she whispered. 'I honestly believed you would want nothing to do with Matty—or, worse, consider him an obligation. But, whatever you think, I swear I have done my best to be a good mother to him.'

Dark eyes stared back at her, icy cold and unforgiving. 'Unfortunately I do not consider your best to be good enough.' He frowned when she sneezed again. '*Dios!* You are in no fit state to look after a baby. You can barely stand,' he growled as she got up from the sofa and swayed.

'I understand your mother is embarking on a cruise tomorrow and won't be around?'

Lauren gave a reluctant nod, and winced as the slight movement of her head sent more starbursts of pain through her skull.

Ramon pulled his phone from his pocket. 'I'll arrange for a private jet to collect us tonight. There is an airfield about twenty miles from here.'

'Collect us and take us where?' Lauren croaked, dismayed to find that she was losing her voice. She couldn't remember ever feeling so ill in her life, and the grim determination in Ramon's voice scared her to death.

'I'm taking my son to Spain—and you're coming too. Unlike you, I believe that Mateo needs both his parents,' he said curtly.

'Oh, no.' She shook her head, and could not prevent a moan of agony. 'I won't let you take Matty anywhere,' she said wildly.

'Don't be ridiculous. You're ill, and he needs to be cared for until you are better. The only place he should be right now is with his family. My mother will be overjoyed to meet her new grandson, and I will hire a nurse who will watch over Mateo in case he should suffer more convulsions.'

A disgruntled wail sounded from along the hall. Matty often woke up grouchy after a late nap, and when Lauren hurried into his room he was standing up in his cot, rattling the bars and yelling so loudly that she felt her head would split open.

'Come on, sweetie, I expect you want your tea,' she murmured, trying to pacify him. But the baby was beside himself with temper, and wriggled so violently when she picked him up that she almost dropped him.

'Give him to me,' Ramon said grimly from the doorway.

'You don't have the strength to hold him.' He moved towards Lauren, his eyes focused on the hysterical baby.

His son had certainly inherited the Velaquez temper, he thought ruefully. Even at less than a year old it was clear that Mateo was a strong-willed little boy, who would need guidance from his father as well as his mother as he grew up.

'Mateo.' Ramon spoke gently yet firmly, and to Lauren's chagrin Matty stopped screaming and stared in fascination at the tall man who held out his hands. 'Come to your *papito, mi precioso.*'

Come to your daddy! Lauren caught her breath when Matty suddenly grinned and leaned towards Ramon. Every instinct inside her fought against the idea of handing her baby over, but Matty wanted to go, and she felt so weak that her knees sagged when Ramon took his son from her.

'Ramon…' she called him desperately.

He paused on his way out of the tiny nursery and flicked cold eyes over her. 'Get your coat,' he ordered harshly. 'The car will be here in five minutes.'

There was a picture of a cherub above her head. Lauren opened her eyes wider and saw that the cherub was part of an exquisite mural painted on the ceiling. She frowned, puzzling over how the mural had got there, and what had happened to her plain white bedroom ceiling.

'Ah, you're awake.'

The voice came from over by the window. Lauren squinted against the sunlight filtering through the blinds to see a pleasant-faced woman walking towards the bed.

'Hello, Lauren. I'm Cathy Morris,' the woman said gently. 'I'm an English nurse, and I've been helping Señor Velaquez to look after you.'

Ramon! Snatches of memory flooded Lauren's mind—

blurred images of him carrying her up the steps of a plane. And then later she had opened her eyes briefly to find herself in a car, speeding towards a huge castle, ominous and forbidding in the moonlight, surrounded by jagged-edged mountains.

She struggled to sit up, shocked to discover that she had no strength. But Ramon had Matty. She had to get up and find him.

'I don't think you're ready to get out of bed just yet,' the nurse said, in a kind but firm tone. She eased Lauren back against the pillows and straightened the bedcovers. 'You've been very ill for the past four days, with a particularly nasty flu virus. Señor Velaquez has barely left your side. He has even been sleeping in the chair next to your bed so that he could see to you during the night. He's giving your son his breakfast at the moment, but I expect he'll be back here before long.'

When Cathy finally paused for breath Lauren mumbled weakly, 'So I'm in Spain? At Ramon's castle?'

'At the Castillo del Toro,' the nurse confirmed. 'It's a wonderful place—built in the thirteenth century, apparently, and oozing with all the history of the Velaquez family. The English translation is the Castle of the Bull—named after one Señor Velaquez's ancestors, who was renowned for his fighting skills on the battlefield as well as his prowess with the ladies.' Cathy grinned. 'I get the impression from the local villagers that the current *Duque* is as revered as his famous forefather.' She walked over to the door. 'I expect you'd like a cup of tea—and then I'll help you into the bathroom so that you can freshen up.'

In the nursery, along the hall from Lauren's room, Ramon strapped his son into a highchair and surveyed the baby's immaculate clothes, scrubbed face and shining, silky black curls with a sense of achievement. Not that bathing and dressing Mateo had been without its difficulties, he thought ruefully as he glanced down at his damp trousers and shirt. He hadn't realised that a wet, wriggling ten-month-old was as slippery as an eel, and after towelling Mateo dry and struggling to fasten the fiddly buttons of his romper suit Ramon felt he deserved a medal.

'How did your *madre* do this every day before going off to work?' he asked the baby, feeling a begrudging sense of admiration for Lauren.

His first four days of fatherhood had been an eye-opener, he admitted. Of course he could have simply handed Mateo over to the nurse, Cathy Morris, whom he had also employed as a nanny, but he was fascinated by this little human being who was his son, and he wanted to get to know him better.

All his life he had known that he had a duty to provide an heir and ensure the continuation of the Velaquez name, but he had never actually considered what it would be like to have a child, Ramon reflected. For one thing he had assumed that it would not happen for several years. He had accepted that he would eventually have to choose a suitable bride, but he had been in no hurry to sacrifice his freedom. Now the privilege of choice had been taken from him. He had a child, and he would never be free again. But as he stared into Mateo's sherry-brown eyes it struck him that his freedom to jet off around the world whenever he felt like it was a small price to pay for his son.

'Breakfast time,' he announced to Mateo, when a maid entered the nursery bearing a tray.

He picked up the bowl of milky cereal, filled a spoon, and offered it to the baby—who stubbornly refused to open his mouth.

'Come on, *chiquito*, it's good,' Ramon said persuasively.

'Try it for *Papà*, hmm?' Instead, Mateo tried to grab the spoon. 'Okay, you want to be independent and feed yourself?'

Maybe his son was a child genius? he mused as he handed the baby the spoon and set the bowl down on the highchair's tray.

'You do it, then. No, Mateo—with the spoon…' In disbelief Ramon watched Mateo pick up the bowl and upend its contents on top of his head, completely covering his mop of curls.

'Now I'll have to bath you all over again!' Ramon raked his hand through his hair.

He stared at Mateo, and the baby stared solemnly back at him, his rosebud mouth suddenly curving into an angelic smile. And in that moment Ramon fell utterly and irrevocably in love.

He threw back his head and laughed until he ached. 'You're a monster—you know that?' He lifted Mateo out of the highchair, his laughter dying as he hugged the baby to him. 'You are my son, and I will never be apart from you again,' he vowed fiercely.

A faint sound made him swing round, and he stiffened when he saw Lauren standing in the doorway. She looked pale and fragile, but it was the gleam of tears in her eyes that caused Ramon to frown.

'Why are you out of bed?' he demanded roughly. 'Cathy told me you were awake, but not strong enough to get up yet.'

Lauren swallowed, unable to tear her eyes from the sight of her son sitting contentedly in his father's arms. 'I wanted to find Matty,' she said huskily. 'The nurse said that you were giving him his breakfast.' She could not disguise her surprise that Ramon had wanted to take care of the baby rather than allow the nanny to see to him. He even looked different, she noticed. In faded jeans and a black polo shirt, rather than one of the designer suits that she was used to seeing him wear, he looked relaxed and somehow more human than the coldly arrogant, aristocratic *duque* who had stormed into her flat and threatened to fight her for their child.

Ramon glanced at the cereal plastering Matty's hair and gave a rueful grimace. 'As you can see, giving him his breakfast has not been a resounding success.'

Lauren gave him a faint smile. 'I can't count the number of times he has done that at home—usually on a morning when I've been running late for work. But he doesn't like to be fed. Even at this age he's very determined and wants to do everything for himself.'

'Rather like his mother,' Ramon commented dryly. 'It can't have been easy, caring for him on your own and holding down your job, but you never considered asking for my help—did you, Lauren?'

She heard the latent anger in his voice and bit her lip. 'I didn't know how you would feel about having a baby,' she mumbled.

Ramon made an impatient sound. 'It's a pity you didn't ask me.'

Guilt surged through Lauren once more. She could stand here all day, trying to defend her actions, but in her heart she accepted that she had been wrong not to tell Ramon he had a son. She could not look at him, and instead glanced around the nursery. Through a half open door she could see an *en suite* bathroom. 'I'll run Matty another bath,' she said hurriedly, desperate to escape Ramon's accusing gaze.

Matty loved bath-time, and was perfectly happy to spend another twenty minutes playing in the bubbles.

'He's a real water baby,' Ramon said, smiling at Matty's

squawk of displeasure when at last he lifted him out of the water and Lauren wrapped the disgruntled baby in a fluffy towel. 'In a month or so, when the weather is warmer, I'll take him in the pool. It will be good for him to learn to swim at an early age.'

His words made Lauren's heart jolt. She could not stay in Spain for *months*. She needed to get back to work. The mortgage on her flat would not pay itself. But she certainly did not intend to leave Matty here at the Castillo del Toro.

She followed Ramon back into the nursery, and her heart clenched when she watched him tenderly drying Matty. For such a big man he was amazingly gentle. Tears blurred her eyes. If only she had known this side of Ramon perhaps she would have acted differently. But when he had spoken of his duty to father an heir she had assumed from his tone that he did not relish the prospect of having a child. Clearly she had been wrong. She could see that already there was a special bond between father and son, and innate honesty forced her to acknowledge that she had no right to try and break it.

Ramon glanced at her white face and frowned. 'You look terrible. Go back to bed. I'll dress Mateo and take him downstairs to my mother,' he continued when Lauren shook her head. 'Go,' he insisted. You do not need to be here. I can take care of him fine without you.'

The words felt like a knife through her heart, and with a low cry she hurried out of the nursery, wondering despairingly what on earth she was going to do.

CHAPTER SIX

A FEW minutes after Lauren had returned to her room a maid arrived, with a pot of tea and a couple of freshly baked rolls that smelled temptingly good. She couldn't remember the last time she had eaten, although she had a vague memory of sipping water from a glass on several occasions while a strong arm supported her head and shoulders.

Had that been Ramon—who, according to the nurse, had spent the last four nights in the chair close to her bed? She frowned when she glanced down at the nightgown she was wearing, and it struck her that someone must have removed her jeans, sweatshirt and underwear. It must have been Cathy, she assured herself, her cheeks growing hot at the idea that Ramon might have undressed her.

She drank two cups of tea and managed half a roll before crossing the room to the *en suite* bathroom. The sight of her reflection in the mirror was a shock. She couldn't do much about her hollow cheeks and pale complexion, but at least she could be clean. Stripping off her nightdress, she quickly stepped into the shower, relishing the feel of the spray cleansing her body and the lemony scent of the shampoo that she worked into her hair.

'What the *hell* are you doing?'

The sound of a familiar gravelly voice coincided with

Ramon's sudden appearance as he opened the door of the shower cubicle and stood glaring at her. Face flaming, Lauren realised that she would have to reach past him to grab a towel. Instead she frantically tried to cover certain pertinent areas of her body with her hands.

'I could ask you the same question,' she snapped.

'It's a bit late for modesty now, when I have spent the past few nights sponging your body to try and bring down your fever,' he said grimly. 'But at least you've finally got some colour in your cheeks.' He took pity on her and threw her a towel. 'As to what I'm doing here—I came to check that you had gone back to bed. I might have known you would be stupid enough to try and shower without assistance.'

'I am not stupid.' Lauren gave him a furious look. 'I'm feeling much better, and I don't need help.' She refused to admit that her legs felt dangerously unsteady, but of course they chose that minute to give way, so that she would have collapsed onto the floor of the shower if Ramon had not caught her.

'Of course you don't,' he said sardonically as he swept her into his arms and strode into the bedroom. 'But it's one thing to cause harm to yourself with your obsessive independence, and quite another when it affects our son.'

'I never did anything to harm Matty,' she said sharply. 'The day nursery he attends is excellent—the staff adore him, and he seems quite happy there.' It was she who was miserable when she left her baby each morning, and she frequently spent the train journey to work trying to hold back her tears.

She clutched the towel to her when Ramon set her on her feet. He pulled open a drawer in the bedside cabinet and handed her a gossamer-fine peach silk nightgown that definitely did not belong to her.

'You were so ill when we left your flat that I had to carry you down to the car, and I forgot to pack you any clothes,' he told her. 'I've ordered new things for Mateo, and a few items for you, but you'll have to shop for more when you are feeling better.'

'That won't be necessary,' Lauren said tensely. 'Matty and I won't be staying long. You can't *make* us stay here,' she cried, when Ramon's face hardened.

'I intend to do what is best for my son,' he said ominously. 'Why do you want to uproot him from his home, separate him not just from me but from his grandmother and the extended family he has already bonded with?'

'His home is in England,' Lauren choked.

'But regrettably most of his waking hours are spent in daycare.'

Ramon strolled over to the window, and while his back was turned Lauren hurriedly donned the nightgown, dismayed to find that her hands were trembling. There was a comb on the dressing table and she tugged it through her hair's wet tangles before blasting it with a hairdryer.

She jumped when Ramon came up behind her, took the dryer and began to run his fingers through her hair to aid the drying process. It was soothing, and evocatively intimate, and she had to fight the urge to close her eyes and lean back against him.

'Does it have to be a battle?' she pleaded. 'We both want to do the best thing for Matty. Can't we come to an amicable agreement on how we should care for him?'

His eyes met hers in the mirror. 'I think that is possible—as long as we both put Mateo's needs first.' He swung her into his arms before she had time to protest, and carried her back over to the bed. 'You need to rest. You've been very ill, and it will be a few days yet before you fully regain your strength.'

'I want to be with Matty,' Lauren argued. 'Who is looking after him?'

'My mother has taken him for a walk in the gardens.' Ramon glanced at his watch. 'If he follows the pattern of the last few days he will fall asleep, and then my dear *madre* will watch over him like a hawk until he wakes. She is utterly smitten with her new grandson,' he added dryly.

It was ridiculous to feel jealous of this new woman in Matty's life, Lauren told herself, but her eyes blurred with tears all the same. 'I miss him,' she said thickly.

'He's missed you too. The only way we could settle him at night was to lie him beside you in your bed. Once he was asleep I carried him to the nursery.'

Ramon's jaw tightened. If he had needed proof that his baby son needed his mother, the sight of Mateo curled up against Lauren while his sobs gradually subsided had surely been it. The close bond between mother and son was undeniable—but Mateo needed his father too, and to Ramon's mind there was only one logical solution that would allow his baby to be brought up by both his parents.

'I'll bring Mateo up to see you after his nap.'

He paused and studied Lauren, his eyes drawn to the rounded contours of her breasts and the slightly darker skin of her nipples, visible through the sheer fabric of the nightgown. She had run such a high fever while she had been ill that it had been necessary for him to strip her and sponge her naked body on several occasions. He had done so with clinical efficiency, his libido kept firmly under control. But now she was awake, watching him with her cool grey eyes, he was unbearably tempted to join her on the bed, peel the wisp of peach silk from those creamy breasts and take each rosy nipple in his mouth.

How could he still desire her when she had callously

deprived him of his son for almost a year? he asked himself angrily, swinging away to stand by the window in the hope that she would not notice his powerful arousal. When he had first discovered that she had kept Mateo from him he had hated her, but during the days and nights that he had nursed her through her illness his anger had cooled, and he had forced himself to consider his own behaviour.

Lauren had accused him of being a playboy who had only wanted her for sex, and he could not deny the truth of that accusation. During their affair he had never considered a long-term relationship with her. His future had been mapped out: marriage—eventually—to a Spanish woman from his own elite social circle, who would provide him with the next Velaquez heir.

And yet, although he had refused to admit it, Lauren had got to him in a way that none of his numerous previous mistresses ever had.

'Who is Donny?' he asked her abruptly.

Lauren gave him a startled glance. 'He's my father,' she said after a moment. 'His name is Donald. When I was a child I used to call him Donny, instead of Dad, and his pet name for me was Laurie. It was just a silly thing between us.' She hesitated. 'Why do you ask?'

'You kept muttering his name when you were ill.'

Lauren had a vague memory of dreaming about her father. He had been walking down the garden path, holding a suitcase. It had been a dream re-enactment of the day that Donald Maitland had walked out on his wife and daughter. She had been crying and tugging on his sleeve, begging him not to leave her. She prayed she hadn't wept in her sleep. It was embarrassing to think that Ramon might have seen her crying. Impossible to glean anything from his shuttered expression.

So Donny wasn't her lover. But that wasn't to say that

Lauren did not have a lover back in England, Ramon brooded. The idea of some unknown man staying at her flat, possibly taking on the role of stepfather to Mateo, made him want to smash his fist into the wall.

'When you found out that you were pregnant you *should* have told me—for Mateo's sake,' he said harshly, unable to control his anger. 'It would have been far better for him if you had given up your job and been a full time mother. I would have looked after both of you...'

'I didn't want your money,' Lauren said sharply.

'Perhaps you didn't, but it would have been in Mateo's best interests if you had involved me,' he said inexorably. 'Because of your selfishness Mateo was denied his father for the first months of his life, and he has spent far too much time in the care of nursery staff when he could have been here with his family.'

Her selfishness! Lauren was struck dumb by Ramon's accusation. She had been self*less*. She had devoted her life to Matty. Did Ramon think she *enjoyed* leaving her baby every day?

But her conscience prickled with the knowledge that there were some grains of truth in what he had said. Ideally she would have liked to have been with Matty constantly for his first year, but one of the reasons she had not told Ramon he had a son was because of her stubborn pride. He had made it clear that she meant nothing to him, and so she had doggedly chosen to bring Matty up on her own—even though that had meant returning to work when he was only a few months old.

The guilt that had so often racked her when she dropped Mateo at the nursery churned in her stomach now. Ramon had scathingly told her that doing her best for Matty had not been good enough, and although she hated to admit it maybe he had a point?

She suddenly felt desperately tired. A legacy of the flu, she supposed. Tears filled her eyes, and she blinked frantically to dispel them. Dealing with Ramon was emotionally draining at the best of times, and they still had to discuss arrangements for sharing custody of their son.

'I have only ever wanted to do the right thing for Matty,' she told him thickly.

Ramon moved closer to the bed, and stared down at her with a hard gleam in his eyes that filled Lauren with a sudden sense of foreboding. 'In that case,' he said coolly, 'I assume you have no objection to marrying me?'

'I assume you're joking?' Lauren retorted after a lengthy stunned silence. Anger gripped her. 'You don't want to marry me, so don't try to pretend you do. I didn't even make it to girlfriend status when we were together. You only ever saw me as your mistress, and the fact that I have given birth to your child is not a good enough reason to tie us down in a relationship neither of us wants. We can both be involved in Matty's upbringing without some farcical marriage,' she insisted desperately when Ramon said nothing and simply surveyed her with his dark, unfathomable gaze.

'How?' he demanded bluntly.

'Well…' Lauren struggled to envisage how it would actually be possible for them both to care for Mateo when they lived in different countries. 'Maybe you could buy a house in England and he could stay with you when you visit,' she suggested, instantly disliking the idea that she might have to spend days, even weeks apart from Matty while he was with his father.

'I have already made it clear that Mateo will live permanently at the Castillo del Toro.'

'But it would be difficult for me to move to Spain and find a job. I speak Spanish reasonably well, but I am not familiar with the legal system over here. I would probably have to study for a Spanish law degree.'

Ramon shrugged, indicating his indifference to her concerns about her career. 'As my wife you will not need to work. I will provide you with everything you could possibly need.'

'I don't *want* you to keep me,' Lauren argued, panic surging up inside her. 'I've worked hard to have a good career, and I value my independence.' The idea of being reliant on Ramon for money and a home filled her with horror. She had first-hand experience of how those things could be snatched away.

He stared at her speculatively. 'What do you value most, Lauren? Your independence, or your son? Because you cannot have both,' he told her, in an implacable tone that made her heart plummet.

'This is ridiculous,' she said shakily, her hand trembling as she pushed her hair back from her face. 'You can't want to marry me. I'm not a blue-blooded Spanish woman, and I wouldn't know how to be a *duquesa*.'

'It's true you are not an ideal choice,' Ramon told her with brutal frankness. 'But you are the mother of my son, and for his sake I have a duty to marry you so that he can grow up in the care of both his parents.'

Lauren felt as though prison bars were closing around her, trapping her. In desperation she tried another approach. 'You must see that it would never work. For a start, how would you feel to be married to a woman you don't love?'

'Love was never on my agenda,' he said dismissively. 'I do not consider it a prerequisite for a successful marriage. We both want to be with our son while he grows up, and I believe we are adult enough to be able to work things out. We were friends once,' he reminded her. 'And we proved on the night of the Valentine's Ball that we are still sexually compatible—wouldn't you agree, *querida*?' he demanded, his voice suddenly so toe-curlingly sexy that Lauren felt a tightening sensation deep in her pelvis.

She snatched a breath when he dropped down onto the edge of the bed and slowly ran his finger down the valley between her breasts. She was instantly agonisingly aware of him—of the distinctive scent of the cologne he always wore, the way his black hair gleamed like silk in the sunlight, and the sensual curve of his mouth that was so tantalisingly close to her own.

Pride belatedly came to her rescue, and she angrily pushed his hand away. 'That night was a mistake, and I regret that it ever happened,' she said shakily.

'Really?' he drawled sardonically.

Following his gaze, Lauren saw that her nipples were jutting provocatively against the sheer silk nightdress. Blushing furiously, she yanked the sheet up to her neck. She still felt horribly weak from her illness, and she wouldn't be surprised if Ramon had been relying on that to bulldoze her into doing what he wanted. But she wasn't an immature girl, in awe of him, she was a confident career woman and it was vital she took control of the situation.

'I won't allow you to intimidate me,' she told him fiercely, 'and I am certainly not going to marry you.'

'Then I hope you are prepared for a custody battle.'

Taking her by surprise, Ramon stood up and strode across the room. He glanced back at her from the doorway.

'And I hope you are prepared to lose—because I will never give up my son,' he said grimly, leaving her staring after him, her heart pounding with fear.

After Ramon had gone Lauren leapt out of bed—and then had to steady herself for a few moments as her head swam.

The weakness in her limbs was infuriating, and made her realise how unwell she must have been. She had to get Matty away from the castle, she thought frantically. It would be necessary to borrow some of the clothes Ramon had bought her, but she would return them to him the minute she got back to England.

The dresses hanging in the wardrobe were exquisite creations, from a top design house. Lauren made a quick search for her jeans and sweatshirt, feeling reluctant to wear any of the clothes Ramon had provided, but there was no sign of any of her belongings. At last she chose a simple wrap-dress in dove-grey silk, and kitten heel shoes in a matching shade. A drawer in the dresser revealed several sets of beautiful underwear. She had a weakness for pretty knickers and bras, and she slipped them on with guilty pleasure, assuring herself that she would send Ramon a cheque to cover their cost.

Her plan was to find Matty and then call a taxi to take them to the airport. She was sure Ramon would assume that she was resting in her room, and with luck she could escape from the castle before he realised she had gone. But when she stepped out into the long corridor she had no idea which way to go. To her relief, a maid appeared around a corner.

'Where is Señor Velaquez?' she asked the young woman, thankful that she spoke Spanish reasonably well. She had picked it up as a child, when her parents had taken her on holiday to Spain every summer, and she had opted to study Spanish rather than French at school.

She had a sudden flashback to her first dinner-date with Ramon, when she had surprised him by speaking to him in his own language. Sherry-brown eyes gleaming wickedly, he had proceeded to teach her several Spanish words and phrases that had definitely *not* been part of the school curriculum. The sexual chemistry between them had sizzled, and when he had suggested going back to his apartment for a drink she had willingly agreed, knowing that he would make love to her, and impatient to experience the passion his sensual smile promised.

They had shared so many good times during their affair, she thought, her heart aching as memories flooded her mind. It hadn't just been the amazing sex; they had talked and laughed, visited art galleries, and walked for miles around the London parks. He had made love to her under a weeping willow tree in the middle of a heavy rain shower, and once they had got so carried away while out in a rowing boat on the Serpentine in Hyde Park that they had nearly capsized.

Her steps slowed. Ramon had said he believed they were adult enough to work things out for the sake of their child—but how could she possibly marry him knowing that he would never love her? It was a pathway to certain heartbreak, but so too was a legal battle over Matty—a battle she was not at all sure she would win, she thought bleakly.

'I want to find my son,' she told the maid urgently. 'Do you know where he is?'

'*Sí.*' The maid nodded. 'Follow me and I will take you to him.'

Under different circumstances Lauren would have liked to linger and study the dozens of rooms the maid took her past—rooms with stunning murals on the ceilings and exquisite tapestries on the walls, filled with beautiful antique furniture and even ancient suits of armour. And yet, despite being stuffed with historical artefacts, many of which were undoubtedly very valuable, the castle still felt like a home rather than a museum.

This was Matty's heritage, she thought as she followed

the maid down a magnificent sweeping staircase and across a vast oak-panelled hall hung with portraits of dark, proud looking men whom she guessed were Ramon's ancestors. The castle and its ancient history were her son's birthright.

At the far end of the hall stood a set of doors, one of which was slightly ajar, revealing a modern addition to the castle: a beautiful glass conservatory that overlooked the extensive gardens beyond. Sunshine streamed through the windows onto the women and children who were sitting on the sofas or, in the children's case, sprawled on the floor around a laughing baby boy.

Mateo seemed completely at home amongst all these strangers, Lauren thought bleakly. She guessed that the older, rather regal-looking woman was Ramon's mother, and the three younger women—one of whom was heavily pregnant—must be his sisters.

She stood behind the half-open door and watched Matty. He was sitting on a rug, surrounded by a group of little girls and boys. The children were teaching him to clap his hands, laughing and chattering in Spanish, and to Lauren's amazement Matty already seemed to understand them and was grinning happily.

He belonged here. The thought struck her like an arrow through her heart. With his jet black curls and light olive skin he was the image of his cousins, but he shared more than a physical resemblance with them. Matty was a Velaquez—a member of the Spanish nobility. This castle was his rightful home, and these people were his family. How could she take him away, back to her undeniably small flat, to a lifestyle that was far from ideal? She hated leaving him at the nursery all day, but she had believed that she had no choice.

Her choices now were not great, she thought dismally.

She could agree to a loveless marriage, give up her job and her independence, and be tolerated here at the castle for no reason other than that she was Matty's mother. Or she could risk a court battle with Ramon, the outcome of which would at best only give her shared custody of her son, and might conceivably result in Ramon being allowed to keep Matty in Spain while she was awarded the right to visit him only a few times a year.

There was no choice, she acknowledged dully. She would rather die than be separated from her baby.

Five minutes later Ramon found her in the great hall, standing as cold and white as if she had been carved from marble as she watched Mateo and his cousins in the conservatory beyond.

'You look like death,' he said sharply when he came up to her. 'You shouldn't have come downstairs.'

At last she turned her head to him, and the glisten of tears clinging to her lashes evoked a curious pain in his gut. 'Lauren…?'

'You win,' she said, in a voice as brittle as glass. 'I can't take Matty away from here—from his family. But I can't live without him.' She swallowed and then went on quickly, before her courage deserted her, 'And so, for him, I'll marry you.'

She made it sound as though she was offering herself as a human sacrifice, Ramon thought irritably. *Dios*, he was a billionaire *duque*, and from now on she would live a life of luxury. 'Had you considered that marriage to me might not be the ordeal you seem to think it will?' he asked curtly. 'As my wife, you will want for nothing.'

'How do you know what I want?' Lauren said quietly. His words tore at her heart, for she would always long for the one thing he could never give her.

Muttering an imprecation, Ramon steered her into his

study, strode over to his desk and took something from a drawer. 'Now that we are formally engaged you will wear this,' he told her, opening a velvet box to reveal a ring that drew a gasp from Lauren.

It was plainly an antique—an enormous ruby surrounded by a circle of diamonds and another circle of smaller rubies.

'It's a monstrosity,' she muttered, voicing the first thought that entered her head as Ramon took her cold hand and slid the ring onto her finger. It was a fraction tight over her knuckle, and felt heavy and cumbersome.

'Only *you* could describe a ring that was recently valued at a million pounds as a monstrosity,' Ramon said dryly. 'For countless generations every Velaquez bride has worn this ring, and my family will expect you to continue the tradition.'

A million pounds! 'But suppose I lose it?' Lauren argued as she stared at the huge ring in horror. 'Ramon, surely there's no need? It's not as if we are marrying for conventional reasons. We're not in *love* with each other,' she explained sharply when his dark brows rose quizzically.

'I doubt that love was a factor in many of my ancestors' choices of brides,' he replied laconically. 'For most marriage was a business arrangement, between high-born families.'

While Lauren brooded on his words he gripped her elbow and led her back out of his study and across the hall, to the doors leading to the conservatory.

'My mother, however, is under the illusion that ours is a love-match,' he told her grimly, 'and I have no intention of shattering her romantic ideals.'

'Meaning what, exactly?'

Sherry-brown eyes clashed with stormy grey ones.

'Meaning that in front of my family you will act the part of my love-struck fiancée.'

'Sorry, but I'm not that good an actress,' Lauren muttered sarcastically.

'Perhaps this will help you get into character.'

Ramon's dark head swooped before she realised his intention, and her startled gasp was lost beneath the hungry pressure of his mouth. She was unprepared for the thrust of his tongue between her lips, and to her shame white-hot, rampant desire swept through her as he explored her with a bold eroticism that left her weak and trembling and clinging to him for support.

She was scarlet-cheeked when Ramon finally broke the kiss, and her embarrassment intensified when she discovered that he had opened the door while he had been kissing her and they were in full view of everyone in the conservatory.

'Well, Ramon, I hope you are about to announce your engagement and spare all our blushes,' commented one of the young women in an amused voice.

'I am,' Ramon replied, triumph in his voice as he slid his arm around Lauren's waist and drew her forward. He led her over to the older woman, who stood up from the sofa as they approached. '*Madre*, this is Lauren—the mother of my son and, I am happy to say, soon to be my wife.'

His gentle, *loving* tone caused Lauren's steps to falter. It was pathetic to wish that his tender smile was genuine, she told herself angrily. He was only turning on the charm in front of his family. But she could not drag her eyes from his face, and her heart hammered beneath her ribs when he dropped a butterfly-soft kiss on her lips.

'Lauren—welcome.' Ramon's mother spoke in English, and to Lauren's surprise took her hands and kissed her on both cheeks. 'I am Marisol, and these are my daughters:

Alissa, Juanita and Valentina—who you might have guessed is expecting twins.'

Marisol Velaquez was tall and elegant, her beauty in no way diminished by the fact that her hair was now pure silver rather than the jet-black of her children and grandchildren. Lauren liked her instantly, and her fear that Ramon's mother would not approve of him marrying an English woman rather than a member of the Spanish nobility was allayed by the warmth of the older woman's smile.

'We are delighted to meet you, Lauren, and so sorry that you have been ill.' Ramon's sister Juanita, who had first spoken, now addressed Lauren in perfect English. 'Ramon explained that you had a high fever. It is fortunate that Mateo did not contract the virus.' She glanced down at two of the children, who were tickling Matty, making him squeal with laughter. 'As you can see,' she said with a smile, 'his cousins adore him already.'

Lauren was in no doubt that Ramon's family had taken her son into their hearts—especially his grandmother, she thought heavily, when she noted the soft expression on Marisol Velaquez's face. She knelt down in front of Matty, her heart aching with love for him. He immediately held out his arms and she hugged him to her, closing her eyes as she breathed in the delicious scent of her baby. He was her *life*, and she would do anything to be with him—even marry a man who had arrogantly stated that he did not consider love to be a prerequisite for marriage.

It took every ounce of her energy to stand up with Matty in her arms. She was sure he had grown during the past four days when she had been ill. He was certainly heavier, she thought wryly—or perhaps he only felt so because the flu had left her horribly weak.

'Allow me to take him,' Ramon's mother said gently.

'You are not strong enough yet to hold this fine big baby.'

Silly tears blurred Lauren's eyes as she handed Matty over to his grandmother. But Marisol was right. Her arms were already aching from the effort of holding him. So much for her earlier plan to snatch him and take him from the castle, she thought miserably.

'Come—it's time you were back in bed,' Ramon told her, sweeping her into his arms and ignoring her protest. 'The sooner you are fully recovered, the sooner I can make you my wife,' he added, with a mocking gleam in his eyes that made Lauren itch to slap him.

'I can walk,' she told him furiously as he strode out of the conservatory and across the hall. 'Your family can't see us now, and there's no need to act the part of loving fiancé on my account. Unlike your mother, I'm under no illusions about you.'

'Perhaps not,' he said evenly, 'but you've had the good sense to agree to marry me to keep your son, and for Mateo's sake it will be better if we end hostilities and try to be friends.'

Lauren seethed silently while he carried her up the stairs and along various corridors until they reached her room. 'How can you expect friendship from me when you have blackmailed me into marriage?' she demanded bitterly when he set her on her feet. 'You have callously used my love for Matty to get your own way.'

'I have done what is best for our son,' he countered inexorably. 'Mateo needs both of us.'

Before Lauren had time to react, he spun her round and unzipped her dress.

'What do you think you're doing?' She tried to bat his hands away but he ignored her and tugged the dress over her hips so that it slithered to the floor.

'You look even better in that underwear than I visualised when I chose it,' he drawled, the sudden heat in his gaze scorching her skin as he turned her back to face him and rested his eyes deliberately on her breasts.

To Lauren's shame her nipples instantly hardened and strained against the sheer lace bra cups, and she closed her eyes to shut out his mocking smile. 'The wedding will be *very* soon, *querida*,' he murmured. 'The best place for you to recuperate from your illness is in my bed.'

He only had to look at her and she was on fire for him, she thought despairingly. Her breasts felt heavy, and a tremor ran through her when he placed his hands on either side of her waist. She lifted her head blindly, thinking that he was going to kiss her, but her eyes flew open in shock when he drew back the covers and pushed her gently into bed.

'I'm glad you share my impatience,' he said in an amused voice, 'but you are not nearly strong enough yet for what I have in mind.'

'I hate you,' Lauren muttered grittily, burning up with mortification. She jerked her head to one side when he leaned over her, but he gripped her chin and forced her to look at him as he swooped and captured her mouth in a punishing kiss intent on proving his mastery.

She should resist him. Her brain knew it, but unfortunately her body did not agree. Molten heat coursed through her veins, and her limbs shook with need as he lowered his body onto hers. His tongue probed the tight line of her lips until with a moan she parted them so that he could delve into her moist warmth. She did not *want* to want him, and bitterly resented his power over her, but like it or not she was racked with hot, urgent desire, and with a low moan she cupped his face and kissed him with a fierce passion that she could not deny.

'I love the way you hate, *querida*,' Ramon drawled when he finally broke the kiss and they both dragged oxygen into their lungs. He got up from the bed and watched dispassionately as she dragged the sheet over her half-naked body. 'Blackmail is an ugly word. I may have coerced you into marrying me, for our son's sake, but however much I desire you I would never force you to share my bed. Fortunately I won't have to—will I, Lauren?'

She gave him a furious glare. 'Don't sulk,' he chided. 'Passion is as good a basis for marriage as any other—particularly when combined with our mutual desire to do the best for Mateo. What else is there to wish for?'

Love! Lauren wanted to cry. She wanted him to love her as she had loved him practically since the day she met him. But at this particular moment she felt so angry with him for demonstrating his power over her that she longed to throw a heavy object at his head.

'Get out,' she snapped, goaded beyond bearing by his arrogant smile.

'That's no way to talk to the man you are soon going to promise to honour with your body.'

Ramon wondered if Lauren had any idea how tempted he was to strip out of his clothes and bury his burgeoning arousal between her satin-soft thighs. Only the purple smudges beneath her eyes and the faint tremor of her mouth prevented him from joining her on the bed and making love to her until she accepted that marrying him was not just the right thing to do for their child, but for them too.

He drew the bedcovers over her as he saw that she was struggling to keep her eyes open. He had told himself that he hated her for hiding his son from him, but he had been lying, he thought bleakly. He did not understand why she had done what she had, and he was still furious with her, but she was the mother of his child and Mateo would always be a special link between them. Deep in his heart, and for reasons he chose not to define, he was *glad* he had a reason to make Lauren his wife—and he couldn't give a damn that she was not the aristocratic bride his family had expected him to choose.

'Trust me, *querida*,' he said with sudden urgency. 'I believe we can make our marriage work.'

Something in his voice brought tears to Lauren's eyes, and she turned her head slightly on the pillow so that he would not see them. 'I don't find it easy to trust,' she admitted thickly, losing the battle with the waves of sleep that were pulling her under.

Had something happened in her past which had caused her to value her independence so highly and made it hard for her to trust? Ramon brooded as he stood by the bed and looked down at her. There was so much he did not know about her, for during their affair he had deliberately not involved himself in her personal life. Maintaining that distance between them had made him feel he was in control of their relationship, but now she was to be his wife he could allow himself to lower his barriers. Perhaps, in time, he would be able to persuade her to lower hers.

CHAPTER SEVEN

THEY married two weeks later, in the private chapel in the grounds of the castle. The wedding was a low-key affair, with only close family and friends from the groom's side in attendance and no one at all from the bride's.

Ramon had asked Lauren if she wished to invite anyone from England, but she had decided against it, thinking to herself that it was going to be hard enough to fool his family that she was a joyous bride without having to maintain the charade for her friends. She *could* tell a few close colleagues from PGH the truth, she'd acknowledged. But stubborn pride made her want to hide the fact that her fairytale wedding to a handsome Spanish duke was in reality a marriage of convenience for the sake of their son.

'I don't want Mum and Alan to interrupt their cruise,' she had explained to Ramon when he had called her into his study to discuss the wedding arrangements.

'Who is Alan?' he'd queried.

'My stepfather. Mum married him two years ago, and this trip is a belated honeymoon.'

'What about your real father?' Ramon had hesitated when Lauren visibly tensed. 'Is he dead?'

Not that she was aware of, she'd thought bleakly. But she had not heard a word from her father since the day he had left, and she had no knowledge of his whereabouts.

'My parents are divorced, and I know Dad will be unable to come to Spain,' she'd told him, and had changed the subject before he could question her further.

And so, on a bright spring day, as the sun shone from a cloudless sky, Lauren arrived at the chapel alone and was escorted through the arched doorway by the chauffeur, Arturo.

Despite the warmth of the day she was icy cold, with tension cramping in the pit of her stomach as she began what seemed like an endless walk down the aisle under the curious gazes of the guests, her eyes fixed on the handsome, unsmiling man waiting at the altar. For a few seconds her nerve deserted her, and she was tempted to turn and flee. But then she caught sight of Matty, sitting on Cathy Morris's lap at the front of the church, and she took a deep breath. She would rather die than be parted from her son, and if she wanted to avoid a custody battle with Ramon she must marry him. It was as simple as that.

The skirt of her ivory silk wedding gown rustled as she walked. She had planned to wear the lilac suit she had worn to her mother's wedding two summers ago, but Ramon had insisted that the Velaquez bride must look the part, and had arranged for a top couturier to visit the castle and design her dress. The result was a deceptively simple sheath which emphasised her slender waist and the soft swell of her breasts, its neckline decorated with crystals that sparkled like teardrops in the sunlight which streamed through the chapel windows.

It was a dream dress, she had thought when she had stared at her reflection in the mirror back at the castle, while a maid had fussed around her, smoothing invisible creases from her skirt. But that was where the dream ended, and perhaps it was better this way. She wasn't going into this marriage with the weight of expectation that most brides carried, and so, she reasoned, she could not be disappointed.

She was too old to believe in fairytales anyway, she reminded herself as she halted beside Ramon and forced herself to meet his gaze. Something flared in his sherry-brown eyes as he stared down at her, but it was gone before she could define it as his thick lashes swept down and masked his expression.

Moments later the priest's voice rang out in the silent chapel.

'You're not going to faint, are you?' Ramon asked beneath his breath as they emerged from the cool church into bright sunshine and posed on the steps for photographs. 'You look very pale. Perhaps today is too much for you when you have only recently recovered your strength after the virus?' he said, frowning with concern.

She resembled a fragile wraith, he thought grimly, gripped by guilt because he knew he should have allowed her longer to recover from her illness. His impatience to make Lauren his wife was because he wanted to secure Mateo's future, he had told himself, but he knew that was not the whole truth. He wanted her with an urgency he had never felt for any other woman, and when she had walked down the aisle towards him in her bridal gown, her honey-blonde hair caught up in a loose knot so that stray tendrils framed her face, her clear grey eyes fixed steadily on him, his breath had hitched in his throat.

The pulse beating frantically at the base of her throat had been the only indication that she was nervous, and that betraying sign of her vulnerability had tugged on his emotions. He had blackmailed her into marriage by threatening to fight for custody of their son, and he'd half expected her to refuse to go through with the wedding at the last moment. But she had come to the chapel, to him, and when she had lifted her soft grey eyes to him and given him a tentative smile he had felt a curious ache around his heart.

'I'm fine,' Lauren assured him. Not for anything would she admit that the surge of emotions which had stormed through her when the priest had proclaimed them man and wife had made her feel light-headed. She glanced down at the bouquet of red roses she was holding and breathed in their exquisite fragrance.

'Thank you for the flowers,' she murmured shyly. 'They were a lovely surprise.' The butler had presented her with the bouquet as she had been about to leave the castle for the short journey to the chapel, informing her that they were from *el Duque*.

Ramon had sent her three dozen red roses the day after she had met him, with a note inviting her to dinner, she remembered. Her heart gave a little flip as she wondered if giving her roses on her wedding day held special significance for him.

'It would have looked strange if my bride had not carried flowers,' he said coolly.

Her smile did not falter. Theirs was a marriage of practicality, not a fairytale, she reminded herself, and steeled her heart to ignore the haunting regret that things could not have been different.

The church service was followed by lunch at the castle. The kitchen staff had surpassed themselves, and the meal was spectacular, its finale being a beautifully iced five-tier wedding cake, which Ramon and his new bride cut together.

Lauren guessed that there was a certain amount of gossip among the guests concerning the fact that the Duque de Velaquez was marrying the mother of his son almost a year after the child had been born, and also that his new wife was not a member of the Spanish nobility. But no one mentioned such matters—at least, not to her face—and Ramon's relatives seemed happy to welcome her into the family.

Only one guest did not seem to share the delight of everyone else that the Duque had married. Throughout the lunch Lauren had been conscious of dark eyes subjecting her to a lengthy scrutiny, and on the few occasions when she had looked across the room her gaze had collided with the icy stare of a haughtily beautiful Spanish woman.

'Pilar is stunning, isn't she?' Ramon's sister Juanita murmured as she joined Lauren by the open French doors and followed her gaze out to the terrace, where Ramon was in deep conversation with the willowy, elegant woman whose mass of silky black curls fell halfway down her back.

'You've probably heard of her, or seen pictures of her at any rate,' Juanita continued. 'Pilar Fernandez is one of the world's top models. Only someone with her fantastic figure can wear a skirt that short,' she commented, with a rueful glance at Pilar's pure white suit, which contrasted so eye-catchingly with her exotic colouring.

'I suppose she'll concentrate on her modelling career now that—' Juanita halted abruptly, and looked so uncomfortable that Lauren's curiosity was aroused.

'Now that what?'

'Now that Ramon has married you,' Juanita muttered, clearly regretting that the subject of Pilar Fernandez had come up. 'It was kind of expected that they... Well, anyway,' she hurried on when she saw Lauren's face fall, 'Pilar is adored by top designers around the world, so I don't suppose she'll visit the castle as much as she used to.'

Ramon's sister's words were not reassuring, Lauren thought dismally. When Ramon had taken her to lunch in London he had dismissed his relationship with Pilar as nothing more than friendship, but clearly it had been more than that if there had been an expectation that he would choose *her* to be his wife.

It would have made sense for him to marry her, she brooded. Pilar was an aristocratic Spanish woman, from Ramon's elite social circle, elegant, sophisticated, and ideally suited to be a *duquesa*. Added to that, she was exquisitely beautiful. Doubts swamped Lauren with the force of a tsunami, drowning her common sense in a flood of insecurity. She could not compete with Pilar on any level, she thought dully as she tore her eyes from Ramon and his gorgeous 'friend' and looked down at the white gold wedding band that he had placed on her finger, next to the ostentatious ruby engagement ring that had been worn by previous generations of Velaquez brides.

Jealousy burned in her stomach when she saw the Spanish woman place her hand on Ramon's shoulder and lean close to him to whisper something in his ear. Suddenly she was fourteen, wearing her new dress and handing around mince pies at her parents' annual Christmas party. Her mum was rushing around, in her element as the busy hostess, but there was tension behind her smile when she came up to Lauren and asked if she had seen her father.

'I'll look for him,' she had promised, unconcerned. Her mother always flapped. But she had lugged the plate of mince pies all around the house, looking for Donny, and had found him at last—in the conservatory, with a blonde woman with a big bust who was the secretary of the golf club. Jean had been leaning close to her father, whispering something in his ear. And her dad had been smiling—just as Ramon was smiling at Pilar now.

'Hello, pet. What have you got there—mince pies?'

Donny had walked towards her, laughing, blocking the view of Jean frantically pulling up the strap of her dress.

The awkward moment had passed, because Lauren hadn't understood why it was awkward, but a long time later, after her father had left his wife and daughter for an exotic dancer, she had recalled the incident and her mother had revealed that Jean had been one of Donny's many mistresses.

Lost in her memories, she stepped onto the terrace and wandered in the opposite direction from Ramon and his companion. She gave a start when someone spoke to her, and her heart sank when she looked up and met Pilar's haughty stare.

'Mateo is a charming child. Ramon is clearly very proud of him,' the Spanish woman commented in a distinctly cool tone.

'We both are,' Lauren replied politely, feeling uncomfortable beneath Pilar's intent scrutiny.

'Ramon married you to claim his son, of course.'

It was a statement rather than a question, and Lauren did not know what to say—it was the truth, after all, she thought dully.

Pilar's black eyes were as cold and hard as polished jet. 'How do you think you will cope with being a *duquesa*? I imagine that your life in England did not prepare you for joining the ranks of the Spanish nobility.'

Which, of course, was a pointed reminder that while Pilar had blue blood running through her aristocratic veins Lauren was a very ordinary English lawyer.

'I'm sure I'll manage,' she told the stunning model tightly.

Pilar shrugged her thin shoulders dismissively. 'Perhaps you will not be a *duquesa* for very long now that Ramon has his son,' she suggested softly, and walked away, leaving

Lauren staring after her, shivering suddenly as a cloud covered the sun with a grey shadow.

The castle's huge master bedroom was dominated by a four-poster bed hung with velvet drapes. It was an enormous bed for one person—but perhaps Ramon did not sleep alone in it very often? Lauren thought bleakly. Perhaps Pilar Fernandez had shared the bed with him during the eighteen months that they had been apart?

Stop it, she told herself angrily. She was making something out of nothing, just because Pilar had made that spiteful comment about Ramon not wanting her for his wife for very long.

Ramon was still downstairs, bidding farewell to the last guests, but in a few minutes he would join her. After her run-in with Pilar she had forced herself to rejoin the wedding celebrations, and had chatted and smiled until her jaw ached. But she had been conscious of his speculative glances, and when, in answer to his query, she had assured him that she was enjoying the day, his expression had been sardonic.

With a heavy sigh she walked through the connecting door into an adjoining room that he had explained was traditionally the Duquesa's bedroom. She did not know if Ramon and Pilar had once been lovers, and she did not want to know, she told herself fiercely. But she could not dismiss the sight of him standing close to the Spanish beauty. Their body language had spoken of an easy familiarity, and somehow the image of Ramon and Pilar had become muddled with the image of her father and Jean from the golf club, and she wondered if she was as blind now as she had been naïve at fourteen.

Her eyes felt scratchy, and when she caught sight of herself in the mirror she was suddenly desperate to get out of her wedding finery. The dress and the roses had all been part of an illusion, created by Ramon to fool everyone into believing that the Duque de Velaquez and his new bride were blissfully happy. But she knew the truth, and with trembling hands she tore off the dream dress and the fragile lacy bra she had worn beneath it. Searching through a drawer she dug out an oversized cotton tee shirt that had been among her things sent over from England.

She was standing in front of the dressing table, brushing her hair, when Ramon walked in.

'Not quite what I had envisaged,' he drawled, as his eyes skimmed the baggy tee shirt that had faded to an unbecoming shade of sludge in the wash. 'Your choice of nightwear leaves much to be desired, *querida*. Although even *that* shapeless garment does not dampen my desire for you,' he added self-derisively, when she spun round to face him and he noted the faint outline of her nipples beneath her thin shirt.

He had discarded his tie and unfastened the top buttons of his shirt, and Lauren glimpsed his bronzed skin beneath. Leaning nonchalantly against the doorframe, his dark hair falling across his brow and his eyes gleaming with sensual heat, he was so sexy that she felt weak with longing—and she despised herself for it.

'What *did* you envisage?' she asked sharply. 'That you would stroll in here and demand your marital rights?'

His eyes narrowed on her tense face. His instincts had been right, he brooded. Something had upset her during the wedding party, and now she was as prickly and on edge as she had been when he had first seen her again in London.

'Not demand,' he countered quietly. 'I did not think I would need to. You are my wife, and I admit I had assumed we would spend our wedding night rediscovering the passion that has always burned between us.'

'I'm only your wife because you've decided that you want Matty to be your heir,' Lauren said stubbornly.

Ramon's jaw hardened. 'He is my son, and by definition also my heir. I would always have wanted him, but you did not give me the opportunity to be his father.'

'You had made it clear that I could only ever be your mistress. In your eyes I wasn't good enough for the grand Duque de Velaquez, and I believed you would feel the same way about my child.'

And that was the root of her resentment, Lauren acknowledged. She was only good enough for Ramon now because she had given him a son. Without Matty he would only have wanted her as his mistress. She was not a sophisticated Spanish aristocrat like Pilar Fernandez, but she was certainly not going to reveal her jealousy of the beautiful model to Ramon.

'I do not think of Mateo in terms of your child or my child. He is part of you and part of me, and we have married so that we can both care for our son, who we created together,' Ramon said, his accent suddenly very strong, and his words tugging on Lauren's emotions. 'I thought that for him we were going to do our best to build a relationship.'

'By having sex?' Lauren muttered scathingly.

He did not deny it. 'Sex is a start. It is where everything began, after all. I saw you across a crowded nightclub and I wanted you more than I had ever wanted any woman.' He paused, and then added softly, 'I still do. And I think, Lauren, although you seem determined to deny it, that you want me too.'

She could not meet his gaze, and stared at the floor through blurred eyes. Maybe he was right. Sex *was* a start. It had bound them together for the six months of their affair, and if she had not fallen pregnant who could say how long they would have stayed together? Ramon's desire for her had shown no sign of lessening. And it hadn't just been a physical act. There had been closeness, companionship—and for her, of course, love.

Was it fair to hold it against Ramon because he hadn't fallen in love with her? And was it fair to push him away and deny them what they both wanted because she was afraid that he would be a serial adulterer like her father? He had asked her to trust him, she remembered. He had no idea how hard that was for her, but if she wanted their marriage to stand a chance she was going to have to try.

'I'm not a beautiful blue-blooded aristocrat,' she mumbled, unable to forget Pilar.

'You are the most beautiful woman in the world to me,' Ramon said intently. 'And your blood could be bright green for all I care. You are the mother of my son.' He gave a rueful grimace. 'And the reason I have taken enough cold showers in the past few weeks to last me a lifetime.'

Her hair streamed down her back like a river of gold. There was wariness in her eyes, but something else too, that made him ache with his need to possess her.

'I have made a commitment to you, Lauren, and I want to put our differences aside and make our marriage work,' he said steadily. 'But you have to want that too—because it takes two to make a marriage.' He trapped her gaze, and she swallowed at the latent warmth in his golden eyes. 'Do you want to make our marriage a proper one?'

She could deny it and keep her pride, or she could accept a marriage that was not perfect, but which over time might grow and develop into a deeper relationship. It was her choice.

'Yes,' she whispered. A shiver of excitement ran down her spine at the hard glitter in his eyes.

'Then come here.'

The first step was the hardest, the second a little easier. And then he moved too, and met her halfway across the room, breathing hard as he snatched her into his arms. 'You looked so beautiful today, *querida*. But I have to admit that my main thought when I saw you in your wedding dress was how soon I could rip it off you.'

His sensual smile stole her breath. 'It gives me even greater pleasure to remove *this* monstrosity,' he growled, tugging the shirt over her head in one deft movement to reveal her firm breasts and slender waist, the tiny wisp of the lace thong hiding her femininity from him.

With a groan of need he swept her up and strode into the master bedroom, where he placed her on the bed and lowered his body onto the softness of hers, crushing her breasts against his chest as he claimed her mouth in a devastatingly sensual kiss. When he lifted his head, streaks of dull colour highlighted his magnificent cheekbones, and his hand was unsteady as he smoothed her hair back from her face.

'This was always how we communicated best,' he said roughly.

She did not reply, for really it was true. When they made love there was no need for words. They were perfect together. And that was why, in the heady days of their affair, she had fooled herself into believing that he was starting to care for her. She would not make the same mistake again, but she could not deny her need for him, and she tugged impatiently at his shirt buttons.

'Then make love to me,' she invited softly.

Their eyes locked and held for infinitesimal seconds, before he made a feral sound in his throat and captured her mouth again in a kiss that plundered her soul. She loved the way he kissed her, Lauren thought dazedly. Loved the hungry pressure of his lips on hers and the bold thrust of his tongue that erotically mimicked the act of making love to her. And then her mind ceased functioning as instinct took over, and she curled her arms around his neck and hugged him so tightly to her that she could feel the erratic thud of his heart beating in unison with her own.

She shivered with anticipation when he cupped her breasts in his palms. 'Gorgeous—and all mine,' he growled with intense satisfaction as he lifted his head to stare at the creamy mounds. He stroked his thumbs over her rose-pink nipples so that they swelled and pouted provocatively at him, and smiled at her soft whimpers of delight. 'You will find me a very possessive husband, *querida*,' he warned her, before he closed his mouth around one taut peak, and then its twin, and suckled her until she writhed beneath him and begged him never, *ever* to stop.

Ramon loved the way his cool English rose discarded all her inhibitions and became a wanton creature in his arms. Sex with Lauren had blown his mind from the start. No other woman had ever made him lose control the way he did with her, and he was already dangerously close to the edge. The long, leisurely seduction he had planned would have to wait until later, he thought self-derisively. Right now all he could think of was burying his swollen shaft deep inside her.

Lauren pressed back into the mattress and closed her eyes blissfully as Ramon trailed his mouth down from her breasts to her stomach, and then lower still. Her limbs felt boneless as the dull ache deep in her pelvis became an urgent throb of need, and she lifted her hips obligingly so that he could pull her knickers down. The molten heat between her thighs was evidence of her arousal, but Ramon seemed intent on giving her the maximum pleasure, and she gasped when he pushed her legs apart and dipped his dark head.

The feel of his tongue stroking up and down before probing gently made her tremble, and she tangled her fingers in his silky hair and sobbed his name when he closed his mouth around the sensitive nub of her clitoris. Everything was happening too fast; she was spinning out of control. But as the first spasms of her orgasm began to ripple he moved swiftly over her and entered her with one hard thrust that made her cry out.

'Did I hurt you?' he demanded tensely, his chest heaving as he fought for control.

'No.' She arched beneath him and wrapped her legs around his back, desperate for him to thrust again. 'Don't stop,' she breathed.

He suddenly seemed to realise that she was close to the edge, and slid his hands beneath her bottom to angle her so he could drive deeper into her.

It was hard and fast, both of them driven by a mindless urgency as he pumped into her with thrust after powerful thrust. Lauren clung to his shoulders, her eyes closed and her lips parted as she snatched air into her lungs. It couldn't last. The coiling sensation inside her was growing tighter and tighter. Her lashes flew open when he stopped moving, but before she could beg him to continue he altered their position and pushed her legs up so that they rested on his shoulders.

'Trust me, *querida*, it will be even better for you like this,' he promised.

And it was. He slammed into her and filled her to the hilt, each thrust so deep and intense that the pleasure was indescribable, impossible to withstand.

'Ramon…' The coiling in her pelvis tightened one more notch, held for a few agonising seconds, and then snapped with explosive force, so that she bucked beneath him and clawed at his arms, utterly overwhelmed by the tidal wave of ecstasy that swept through her.

Her orgasm was mind-blowing, but a tiny part of her consciousness sensed that he was nearing his own nirvana, and she lifted her hips to meet his final savage thrust, heard the groan that was wrenched from his throat as his big body shuddered with the force of his release.

It took a long time for Lauren to come back down, and she lay contentedly beneath Ramon, loving the feel of his warm, lax body pressing her into the mattress. At last he rolled off her, but immediately curved his arm around her and pulled her close.

'Tears, *querida*?' he asked roughly, brushing his fingers over her face and tracing the twin rivulets of moisture.

She could not tell him that in those moments of intense passion she had felt as though their souls as well as their bodies had merged as one.

'I just wish things had been different,' she whispered, imagining how it would be if he loved her. Perhaps he would murmur tender endearments in her ear, and she would be free to voice her love for him instead of hiding her feelings away.

Ramon frowned. 'Is being married to me so unbearable?' he demanded, feeling as though he had been kicked in the gut.

'Of course not. I accept that it was the right thing to do for Matty's sake.'

Why was her answer not as satisfactory as it should be? Their son *was* the only reason he had insisted on marriage, he reminded himself. He was pleased Lauren shared his belief that Mateo should grow up with both his parents, and the sizzling sexual chemistry between them was a bonus he intended to enjoy to the full.

'As you say, our son's needs are paramount. But tonight I intend to satisfy all *your* needs, as well as my own,' he growled, before lowering his head and slanting his mouth over hers to initiate a deep, sensual kiss that stirred the embers of their mutual desire.

Lauren might only have married him to keep her son, but she was a highly sensual woman. Her enjoyment of sex was uninhibited, and Ramon was unable to restrain a shudder of pleasure when she wrapped her fingers around his already thickening shaft.

He curled his hand possessively around her breast and lifted his head to stare down at her, pleased to see that her eyes were glazed with desire.

'Now you are my wife,' he murmured, unable to hide his satisfaction as he slid his hand between her legs and found that she was ready for him. 'And we have just proved that passion, together with a mutual desire to do the best for our son, are key elements to making our marriage work.' His voice roughened as he positioned himself over her. 'Especially passion—don't you agree, *querida*?'

She didn't, but she did not tell him. Instead she gave herself up to the exquisite pleasure only he could arouse in her. But later, when she lay listening to the rhythmic sound of his breathing, she wondered dully if she was destined to spend her life wanting more than he could give her.

CHAPTER EIGHT

'I'VE decided that we should have a honeymoon.'

Lauren opened her eyes to find Ramon leaning over her, looking disgustingly wide awake despite the fact that they had both had very little sleep the previous night.

'All right,' she mumbled, snuggling deeper under the sheet.

'Where would you like to go?'

She glanced at the clock, and firmly closed her eyes once more. 'Do we have to decide at seven o'clock in the morning?'

Ramon studied her, noting how the early-morning sunshine slanting through the blinds had turned her hair to pure gold. Her mouth was slightly swollen from his kisses, and recalling the taste of her and the feel of her soft lips parting beneath his he felt unbearably tempted to make love to her again. But she was clearly exhausted after their energetic wedding night, he thought, a feeling of tenderness tempering his hunger. Lauren was his wife now, and they had all the time in the world.

'We need to make plans so that I can mobilise the staff,' he told her.

Lauren gave up trying to sleep and rolled onto her back, her heart missing a beat when she met Ramon's warm sherry-gold gaze. 'You make it sound like a military operation. Why would the staff need to come on our honeymoon?'

'I have a villa in Barcelona. I thought we could take Mateo to the beaches there, and there are plenty of designer shops for you in the centre of the city. But there are no permanent staff at the villa, so we will need to take a cook and a butler, and other household staff—and Cathy, of course, for Mateo.'

'It's going to be quite a crowded honeymoon, then,' Lauren murmured, her initial excitement fading a little now that it sounded as though their stay at the villa would be as formal as life at the castle. 'To be honest, I think Matty is a bit young for the beach—we'll spend all our time trying to stop him eating the sand. And I really don't need to do any more shopping,' she added ruefully.

In the two weeks prior to the wedding Ramon had insisted on taking her shopping in Madrid several times, and her wardrobes were now bursting with couture clothes from all the top design houses.

'Couldn't we go somewhere on our own—just you, me and Matty? Do you remember that weekend we spent at a lodge in Scotland?' She smiled, remembering the trip they had made to the beautiful Scottish Highlands a month or so before she had found out that she was pregnant and their relationship had been blown apart. Ramon had been so relaxed that weekend, and had made love to her so tenderly in front of a blazing log fire that she had found herself falling ever deeper in love with him. 'It would be nice to go somewhere peaceful,' she said wistfully.

In the hectic run up to the wedding she had barely spent any time with him, and as the castle had been full of his various relatives they had had no chance to be alone.

Ramon frowned. 'Scotland will be cold at this time of year. But if it's mountains you want, I know of a place that is quiet and peaceful, with just the sound of a stream outside the house to disturb us. But it's not much—just a simple lodge. And there isn't room for any of the staff.'

'It sounds perfect,' Lauren assured him.

She knew many of her friends back in London would love to have an army of staff to take care of the cooking, housework and childcare, but she found the stiff formality of the castle rather stifling, and she didn't think she would ever get used to the maids bobbing a curtsy every time they saw the new Duquesa.

Ramon dropped a kiss on her mouth. 'That's settled, then. I'll instruct the staff to pack for us, and we'll leave in a couple of hours.'

'This is spectacular,' Lauren said in an awed voice a few hours later, as she climbed out of the four-by-four Ramon had driven from the castle up into the Cantabrian mountains. Below them was a lush green valley, with farmhouses dotted here and there, and orange and almond groves in full bloom. The stream that threaded through the valley was glinting like a silver ribbon in the sunshine. All around the wooden lodge where they were to stay were tall pine trees, and rising up behind them were the higher peaks of the mountains, capped with snow that sparkled pure white against the cornflower-blue sky.

The lodge was as basic as Ramon had said, but perfectly comfortable, with a large sitting room and kitchen, a main bedroom with a bathroom leading off it, and a smaller room where they would set up a travel cot for Matty.

They unpacked the car, and then Ramon took charge of his son while Lauren spread out a rug on the grass and opened the picnic hamper the castle cook had prepared for them.

'What a heavenly place,' she murmured, her eyes

drawn to the towering mountains. 'Do you often come up here?'

Ramon carefully spooned some yogurt into Matty's mouth while the baby was distracted by playing with the car keys. 'Not as much as I would like. The responsibilities of running the company and the castle estate leave me with little free time, but when I was a boy I came up here most weekends, to hike or to fish in the mountain lakes.'

Lauren nodded. 'I can understand why. I love it here. And I love picnics. I always seem to eat twice as much when I'm out in the fresh air,' she said ruefully as she bit into another smoked salmon sandwich. 'I must admit I prefer meals like this much more than the formal dinners we have at the castle, with the butler and a dozen servants in attendance—even for just the two of us.'

Ramon frowned at her outburst. 'It has always been the tradition for the Duque and Duquesa to dine in the great hall. Even when my sisters and I were little my parents insisted that we should dress for dinner each evening, and we were expected to sit through five courses and make polite conversation without fidgeting or appearing bored.'

'Do you mean that you never ate pizza in front of the TV? Or invited a few friends round and slung steaks on the barbecue?' Lauren said in astonishment.

'Certainly not. I was brought up always to be aware of my position and to act accordingly.'

She grimaced. 'No wonder you looked shocked when you caught me eating ice-cream out of the tub at your apartment in London—and when I ordered Chinese take-away and insisted that we picnicked on the living room floor. What on earth did you think of me?' she muttered, blushing at the memory.

She doubted Pilar Fernandez would experiment with chopsticks to eat sweet-and-sour chicken balls, and dribble the sauce down her chin. It emphasised yet again that she did not belong in Ramon's world, Lauren thought dismally.

'I thought you were fun,' he told her, smiling when she stared at him in surprise. 'I'd never met anyone like you before. You liked to do crazy things, like walking in the rain, and cooking bacon sandwiches after we had made love for hours and were starving.'

'Don't remind me,' she groaned.

'I could relax with you,' Ramon said quietly.

He hadn't realised how much he had enjoyed being with her until she had ended their affair and he had returned to Spain soon after, to help care for his dying father.

'I loved my parents, but my childhood *was* restrictive,' he admitted. 'I was brought up mainly by my governess, and I only saw my father for an hour each evening, when I was summoned to his study so that he could tell me about my ancestors, and the history of the castle, and instruct me on the duties I would one day take on when I became the Duque de Velaquez.'

'Did you want to be a *duque*?' Lauren asked curiously, trying to imagine him as a little boy, perhaps not many years older than Matty, being taught the responsibilities that lay ahead of him.

Ramon hesitated. It had been impressed on him by his father that a *duque* should be strong and in control of his emotions. From a young age he had understood that he must never cry—even when he had been thrown from his horse and had broken his arm. The lessons of his childhood were deeply ingrained, and he did not find it easy to confide his thoughts and feelings. But Lauren was his wife, and he realised that for their marriage to stand a chance he must now learn to open up a little.

Ramon's sudden grin reminded Lauren of the relaxed,

carefree lover she'd had a passionate affair with eighteen—no, nineteen months ago. 'Actually, I wanted to be an astronaut,' he told her, laughing when she gave him a disbelieving look. 'I had a passion for science—especially physics, which I studied at university. After I completed my Masters degree I was offered the opportunity to study with the American Space Agency.'

Lauren's eyes widened. 'Did you take it? Why ever not?' she demanded when he shook his head.

'I couldn't,' he said with a shrug. 'I was the only son and heir of the Duque de Velaquez and I always knew that my life was to be at the castle, running the winery and the estate, and heading other Velaquez business interests.'

'So you sacrificed your dream for duty,' Lauren said slowly.

Ramon's strong sense of duty must have been ingrained in him as soon as he had been old enough to understand his family's noble heritage, she realised. And as the only son he had grown up knowing that he must marry—not necessarily for love. He must choose a woman with a similar noble pedigree to provide the next Velaquez heir.

It was small wonder he had never considered that an affair with his English mistress could ever lead to a deeper relationship. Even if he had begun to care for her, as she had hoped at the time, she understood now that he would not have put what he wanted before his duty to his family—he would never have allowed himself to fall in love with her.

'So, did you never come up here to the lodge with your father?' she asked curiously.

'No. I had various tutors. One of them enjoyed the outdoor life, and used to accompany me. I was educated at the castle because my father feared that I might make unsuitable friendships if I went to school,' Ramon explained when

Lauren gave him a puzzled look. 'I only ever socialised with young people from a similar social standing to my own. It was only when I went to university that I realised how stifling my upbringing had been,' he admitted.

'I'm surprised your father agreed to you going to uni,' Lauren commented.

'It took me a long time to persuade him.' Ramon sighed heavily. 'And then I gave him good reason to regret his decision by falling madly in love with a topless model and announcing my intention to marry her.'

Lauren gave him a startled glance, feeling a sharp stab of jealousy that Ramon, whose heart was made of granite, could ever have been 'madly in love'.

'But I thought it was your duty to marry a woman from the Spanish nobility? What did you father say?'

'Naturally he was horrified, and tried to dissuade me. But I was eighteen, enjoying my first taste of freedom, and I was hell-bent on making Catalina my bride. That's when my father took action.' Ramon's smile faded as he remembered the pain he had felt when he had learned that he had been betrayed by the woman he had loved.

'He employed a private investigator, who discovered that Catalina had a lover. The lover was a drug addict, who needed money for his habit, and so Catalina came up with a plan to seduce the wet-behind-the-ears son of a wealthy *duque*, persuade him to marry her, and then make a mint from the divorce settlement. Armed with these facts, my father dragged me along to the hotel where he knew Catalina and her lover met in secret, and presented me with the two of them naked in bed together.'

'Ow,' Lauren murmured sympathetically. 'That can't have been a good moment.'

'There were plenty of others just as bad when the press got hold of the story. My humiliation was *very* public,'

Ramon said dryly. 'I felt a fool—and, worse, I knew I had greatly disappointed my father. I soon got over Catalina, once I had seen that she was a mercenary slut, and in a way the whole sordid experience was good for me—because it taught me to be careful who I trusted. The Velaquez fortune is a powerful aphrodisiac for many women,' he drawled sardonically.

'Not for me,' Lauren told him firmly, horrified that he might have thought her to be a gold-digger when she had first met him. 'I was determined to train for a good career so that I could earn my own money and *never* be reliant on any man.'

'Your desire for independence is all very well, but you were wrong to keep my son a secret from me,' Ramon said harshly. 'You put what you wanted before the needs of our child.'

Lauren bit her lip. 'I've already explained that I didn't think you would want our baby when you'd just told me that you intended to marry an aristocratic bride. If I had known that you would love your child, regardless of his mother's social standing, I would have told you I was pregnant the night we broke up.'

The tense silence that fell between them was broken by Matty, who had grown bored with playing with the car keys and made a grab for the pot of yogurt, chuckling when yogurt flew through the air and landed on Ramon's shirt.

'You have to admit he's got a great aim,' his father commented as Lauren hastily took the yogurt pot from Matty, before he could spread its contents any further.

She glanced at Ramon, worried that he was annoyed with Matty, but Ramon laughed as he gathered him into his arms and lifted him high in the air, so that the baby squealed with delight.

'Even if you had told me, I don't think I would have

had any concept of what having a child really meant. Nor would I have known that I could feel such a strength of love for my son,' he admitted in a low tone. 'Until I saw Mateo for the first time I had viewed having a child as a duty, to ensure the Velaquez name. I had never imagined what it would be like to be a father, to feel this absolute, overwhelming love for another human being and know that I would gladly give my life for his.'

Lauren swallowed the sudden lump in her throat, startled by the raw emotion in Ramon's voice. 'I know what you mean,' she said huskily. 'The first time I held him I was swamped by the most intense love for him, and everything else, including my career, suddenly seemed unimportant.'

Her eyes locked with Ramon's in a moment of shared parental pride for their son. Matty linked them together inextricably, she realised. For the first time since the wedding she felt a sense of calm acceptance that she had done the right thing by marrying Ramon, and that giving up her career was a small sacrifice when it meant that her baby would grow up with both his parents. But hearing Ramon voice his love for Matty made her heart ache with longing that he would love her too.

'I always respected my father, but it was not until the last months of his life that I realised how much I loved him, and that he loved me,' Ramon admitted deeply. 'I was taught that men should be strong and hide their emotions. But my sisters' husbands are all excellent fathers, who do not believe it is a sign of weakness to show their love for their children. I want to be like them, but it is hard to change the habits that have been ingrained from childhood.' He hesitated. 'I need you to help me be a good father, Lauren.'

The note of uncertainty in his voice tugged on Lauren's heart. It took a strong man to admit he felt vulnerable, and she loved him even more for his honesty. Without pausing to think what he might make of her actions, she leaned towards him and pressed her mouth to his olive-skinned cheek. 'You're already doing brilliantly,' she told him softly. 'Parenting is all new to me too, but we can learn together.'

'That sounds good, *querida*,' Ramon murmured, turning his head so that his lips brushed over hers in a gentle kiss that stirred her soul.

There had been an unspoken promise in that kiss, of their unity in doing their best for their child, Lauren mused a little while later, when Matty had fallen asleep and they'd carried him back to the lodge. He did not stir when they laid him in the travel cot, and as they crept from the room and shut the door it suddenly struck her that she and Ramon were alone—and this was their honeymoon.

He must have read her mind, because he swept her up into his arms and strode into the main bedroom, the hungry gleam in his eyes causing her heart-rate to quicken. 'I think our son's idea of a siesta is an excellent idea,' he stated, as he placed her on the bed and began to unbutton his shirt.

'You're planning to go to sleep?' she asked him, her voice emerging as a husky whisper as desire flooded between her thighs.

'No. I'm planning to spend the next hour making love to you,' he promised her, feeling a gentle tug on his heart when he looked into her eyes. He smiled at her quiver of delight when he knelt above her and slid his hands beneath her tee shirt to cup her bare breasts in his palms. Her skin felt like satin beneath his fingertips, and with a groan Ramon tugged her shirt over her head and closed his mouth around one taut nipple and then its twin.

He swiftly removed the rest of their clothes, the urgency of his desire for her making him uncharacteristically clumsy. But Lauren did not mind when she heard her cotton skirt rip. Her impatience matched his. She obligingly lifted her hips so that he could tug her knickers down, sighing with pleasure when he caressed her gently with his fingers before moving over her. He made love to her with tenderness as well as passion, each deep stroke taking her higher and higher, until with a cry she reached the pinnacle and fell back down, to be held safe in his arms.

They spent a glorious week in the mountains. Away from the responsibilities of being a *duque*, and running a multi-million-pound company, Ramon relaxed and became once more the charismatic, witty and amusing lover Lauren had fallen in love with in London almost two years before. It was a chance for them to rediscover the companionship they had once shared, and to focus on being parents to their son.

Lauren privately decided that they should escape the formality of the castle and come to the lodge for a least a few days every month.

The honeymoon had been a turning point in their relationship, she thought some weeks later, as she stepped into the elegant cream silk dress she had chosen to wear to the christening of Ramon's new nephews. Two weeks after they had married his sister Valentina had given birth to twin boys. The christening service was to be held in the castle's private chapel and, knowing that Valentina was run off her feet now that she had four children, Lauren had offered to organise the reception.

Ramon emerged from the *en suite* bathroom, rubbing his hand over his newly shaven jaw. His steps slowed when he saw her, and his sensual smile evoked the familiar ache in her chest. 'You look beautiful, *mi corazón*.'

Her heart leapt at the discernible tenderness in his voice.

It was not the first time he had called her 'his heart', but she must not get her hopes too high that he meant the endearment literally, she reminded herself. And yet in the weeks since their wedding she had felt that they *were* growing closer—mainly due, it was true, to their intensely passionate sex life. In bed they were dynamite—and they were in bed a lot, she acknowledged with a smile.

Ramon worked long hours, but this gave him the excuse to insist on early nights and lazy Sunday mornings, and of course there were numerous occasions when he took a coffee break that just happened to coincide with Matty's afternoon nap!

He might not love her, but he made love to her with a dedication that bordered on the obsessive. And, while their relationship was not exactly what she longed for, Lauren told herself that she was content with what she had. Ramon did not do anything lightly, and the dedicated playboy had transformed into an equally dedicated husband and father.

'I hope I haven't forgotten anything,' she murmured, running through a checklist of preparations in her mind. 'I want the party to be perfect for Valentina.'

'It will be perfect. I know you, *querida*,' Ramon said confidently. 'I've no doubt you have planned things with military precision—just as you organised the other three parties we have hosted since we got married.'

He had been impressed with the enthusiasm with which she had organised the events: two business dinners, and a reception for local dignitaries. Lauren had taken on her role of Duquesa with the same determination with which she approached every aspect of her life—especially motherhood.

But Ramon was aware that although she was devoted to Mateo she was sometimes bored with life at the castle.

Most women would be happy to spend their time shopping with an unlimited credit card and visiting beauty parlours, but he had realised long ago that his wife was *not* most women, he thought wryly.

As he walked over to her he took a slim velvet box from his pocket. 'For you—because when I saw them they reminded me of the creaminess of your skin,' he murmured, pushing her hair over her shoulder so that he could fasten the string of pearls around her slender throat.

The necklace was exquisite, each pearl separated from the next by a tiny sparkling diamond which caught the light when Lauren turned her head. 'It's lovely, but you shouldn't keep buying me things,' she protested.

'Ah, but today is a special day,' he said, feeling the tremor that ran through her when he brushed his lips up her neck and lingered on the sensitive spot behind her ear. 'Today is the six-week anniversary of our wedding day. Did you think I had forgotten?' he queried softly, knowing that she was remembering that disastrous night in London, when she had wanted to celebrate the six-month anniversary of their affair.

'You said you didn't set great store by anniversaries,' she reminded him.

He smiled. 'But that was then, and this is now. Things have changed. I have changed, *querida*. And I think six weeks of marriage is worth celebrating, don't you?'

Her reply was lost beneath the hungry pressure of his mouth, and a long time later Lauren had to re-apply her lipstick before they hurried down to the great hall to greet the guests.

Later that afternoon the one hundred or so guests trooped back from the chapel to the castle after a beautiful christening service, to toast the birth of Valentina's newborn sons—Sancho and Tadeo.

They were adorable, Lauren mused. She had forgotten how tiny new babies were. Matty looked huge in comparison, and now that he was walking he just loved being part of the gang, getting up to mischief with his older cousins. His first birthday a few weeks ago had been a day of mixed emotions for both her and Ramon. She had shown him photos of Matty, some taken when he was a few hours old. But now, as she watched Ramon cradling one of his new nephews, she knew he was thinking of all the precious time he had missed in his own son's life.

Juanita had also been observing her brother, and now she strolled over to Lauren and Ramon. 'You're going to have to hurry up and have another baby, Lauren, if you want to catch us up,' she said cheerfully. 'Alissa has three, I have two, and now Valentina has four. It's definitely your turn next.'

There had been a lull in conversation among the guests assembled in the drawing room, and Juanita's words drew several curious glances in Lauren's direction. Conscious of Ramon's sudden intent scrutiny, she forced a smile. 'Mateo is only just over a year old, and for now I'm happy to enjoy him,' she said lightly.

The awkward moment passed, but the conversation with Juanita stuck in Lauren's mind for the rest of the afternoon. It *would* be nice to give Matty a little brother or sister, she acknowledged, and she knew, although they had not discussed the subject, that Ramon wanted more children. She sighed and wandered over to the window, watching Valentina pushing an enormous pram around the garden.

Why wasn't motherhood enough for her, as it was for Ramon's sisters? she asked herself dismally. She adored Matty, and loved being with him, but sometimes she was ashamed to admit that she longed to use her brain—and she missed her job. Perhaps when Matty was older she would be able to return to her career, she told herself. She did not want to work full-time; she loved being with her son too much to want to be away from him for any length of time. But one day she hoped to work part-time hours and regain a little of her independence.

Ramon had disappeared to take a phone call. It occurred to Lauren that he had been gone for ages, and she guessed the call was related to Velaquez Conglomerates. She hoped he would not have to rush off to the company's headquarters in Madrid, as he sometimes did, but even while she was wondering what was keeping him from the party he walked back into the drawing room and strode over to her, a forbidding expression on his face.

'Why didn't you just come out with it and tell Juanita that you are not planning on having any more children because your career is more important to you?' he demanded coldly.

One glance at his dark face warned Lauren that he was furious, but because of the presence of their guests he was fighting to control his temper.

'For that matter, why didn't you tell *me* that you're going to be working in London for one week a month—or is the welfare of our son so unimportant to you that you didn't bother to mention it?'

'Of course Matty is important to me,' she said sharply. 'He is the most important person in my life.' She frowned. 'How did you know…?'

'That you have been offered a job with a law firm in England?' Ramon finished for her. 'My mother asked to see the photo album of Mateo when he was first born, and I did not think you would mind if I took it out of your bedside drawer. But when I picked up the album I accidentally picked up this letter that was hidden beneath it.'

Lauren stared down at the letter he had thrust into her hand, and acknowledged that there was little point in denying its contents. 'I can explain—' she began, but Ramon cut her off.

'I'm sure you can,' he said sardonically. 'But it is Mateo who will want an explanation when he is a little older—as to why you have chosen to leave him for a week or more every month.'

'I have no intention of abandoning him,' she said tightly. 'And can I point out that *you* were away on business for three days last week, and you didn't worry too much about leaving Matty.'

'That's different,' he snapped. 'I am CEO of Velaquez Conglomerates, and sometimes business trips are unavoidable. But there is absolutely no need for *you* to work. You cannot deny that I give you everything you could possibly want or need.'

It was debatable whether she *needed* the numerous pieces of stunning jewellery Ramon had given her since their marriage, or the designer handbags and the wardrobe full of more beautiful clothes than she was ever likely to wear, Lauren thought heavily. She could not fault his generosity. But the fact he believed that material things mattered to her proved that he did not know her at all.

'I appreciate that it is not necessary for me to work,' she said quietly, 'but is it really so wrong to want to do the job I spent years training for? To wish for a little independence that will give me a sense of self-worth?'

'You and your damned independence,' Ramon growled impatiently. He did not understand what she wanted. He showered her with gifts in an attempt to make her happy, but hearing her bang on about wanting her independence felt like a slap in the face. 'Your place is here at the castle, as Mateo's mother and my wife. I will not allow you to leave our son for days at a time just so that you can follow some selfish whim.'

'You won't *allow*? Am I your prisoner, then, Ramon?' Lauren gave a bitter laugh, the happiness she had felt earlier in the day when he had given her the pearl necklace draining away.

A couple of guests had wandered into the drawing room, clearly intrigued by the sound of raised voices from their hosts.

'This is not a suitable time for private discussion,' Ramon ground out tensely—apparently forgetting that *he* had initiated the discussion, Lauren thought darkly.

'I think you should know—' she began, but he swung round and strode away before she could continue, leaving her staring angrily after him.

'Oh, dear! Do I sense trouble in paradise?'

Lauren stiffened at the sarcastic comment, and turned to see Pilar Fernandez step out from an alcove by the window. It was plain from her satisfied expression that the Spanish woman had overheard her spat with Ramon, but good manners prevented Lauren from accusing Pilar of eavesdropping.

'Everything is fine,' she lied, and knew from the arch of Pilar's perfectly shaped eyebrows that the beautiful model did not believe her.

There was no escaping the fact that Pilar was absolutely stunning, she thought dismally as she made a lightning inspection of the other woman's scarlet silk dress, which fitted her fabulous figure like a second skin. She already knew the Fernandez family had been close friends of the Velaquez family for several generations, and Pilar had been at school with Valentina. Ramon had explained this when

Lauren had questioned why Pilar had been included on the guest list for the christening party. Her father, Cortez, had suffered a stroke six months ago, and since then had become a recluse who never left the Fernandez home, Casa Madalena.

And so Pilar had attended the party alone—and had spent most of the day flirting with Ramon, Lauren brooded, recalling the sharp knives of jealousy that had stabbed her insides when she had watched the two of them laughing and chatting together.

'The trouble is that you do not understand a man like Ramon,' Pilar drawled.

Lauren's hold on her temper was close to snapping point. 'And I suppose you do?' she said tightly.

'Of course. We are from a similar social background. I am aware that Ramon takes his responsibilities as Duque seriously, and he requires a wife who is suited to the role of Duquesa.'

'Are you suggesting that *you* would make Ramon a better wife?' Lauren demanded, deciding that bluntness was the only way to deal with Pilar's sly insinuations.

The Spanish woman shrugged. 'Only Ramon can decide that.' She inspected her long, perfectly manicured fingernails and said obliquely, 'Do you know where he spends every Friday afternoon?'

'He drives out to inspect the vineyards with his estate manager.' Lauren frowned at the curious question. 'Why do you ask?'

'No reason.' Pilar's smile was reminiscent of a smug Cheshire cat's, but she sashayed gracefully back across the room before Lauren could ask her what she meant.

CHAPTER NINE

LAUREN was furious with Ramon, and avoided him for the rest of the party. By the time the last guests had departed she had a splitting headache, and was grateful when Cathy offered to give Matty his bath.

'Go and lie down in the quiet for a while. I always find that's the best remedy for a headache,' the nanny said kindly.

But when Lauren walked into the bedroom and found Ramon packing a suitcase her heart slammed against her ribs.

'You're going away?' she queried sharply.

'Something has come up at the Madrid office which needs my urgent attention.' Ramon glanced at her tense face and his jaw hardened.

He still felt bitterly angry with her, but seeing her looking so dejected made him want to pull her into his arms and make love to her. There were never any misunderstandings between them in bed. It was the once place they communicated perfectly.

'We'll talk when I get back,' he told her grimly.

'There's nothing to talk about,' she said flatly. 'I didn't take that job. I tried to tell you earlier, but you wouldn't listen.'

'But you were tempted to take it.'

'Yes, I *was* tempted.' She wasn't going to deny it. 'I worked for Pearson's before I went to PGH. I kept in contact with the MD there, and he emailed me out of the blue with an offer of some consultancy work. I let James Pearson know I was interested, but when he sent me more details and I realised I would have to be away from Matty I turned the offer down.'

Ramon slammed the lid of his suitcase shut. 'I don't know why you want to go back to work,' he said, his frustration tangible. 'I give you everything.'

Not the one thing she really wanted from him, Lauren thought dully. She had felt they were growing closer, but this argument proved that on an emotional level they were miles apart. She crossed her arms defensively in front of her. 'You wouldn't understand.'

'Then *make* me understand.' He caught hold of her shoulder and spun her round to face him. 'If our marriage is going to work, you have to trust me, Lauren.'

'It's not easy to trust when your trust has been broken,' she muttered. And yet if her relationship with Ramon was ever going to develop didn't she have to try?

'What happened?' he asked grimly. 'Did some guy let you down?' He raked his hand through his hair until it stood on end. 'I need some help here, because I can't work you out.'

'I told you my parents are divorced,' she said abruptly. 'They split up when I was fifteen—after my father left my mother for a twenty-year-old exotic dancer and disappeared to Brazil with her. He cut off all contact with me, and I haven't seen or heard from him since.'

Ramon heard the bitterness in her voice. Fifteen was such an impressionable age, and he sensed that she had been deeply hurt by her father's actions. 'That must have been tough,' he murmured. 'Did you have a good relationship with him before he left?'

'I adored him, and I thought he loved me—but presumably I meant nothing to him.' Lauren swallowed.

Even after all this time her father's desertion still hurt, and her sense of abandonment was as strong now as when she had been a teenager.

'The day he left was the worst day of my life,' she said bleakly. 'Dad was a barrister, and he worked long hours, but he always made time for me, and I was closer to him than to my mother. He taught me to play chess, pretended to like the music I liked, and most weekends he would drive me to gymkhanas so that I could compete on my pony.'

She stared down at her hands, ferociously blinking back her tears. 'He was my world, and I still can't believe he went away and left me. I've never even received a birthday card from him. It's as if I never existed to him—but I don't understand why. Even if he didn't want to be with Mum any more, why did he reject *me*?' She swallowed. 'I guess the truth is that he just didn't love me enough to want to keep in contact.'

'Did you have any idea that there were problems in your parents' marriage?' Ramon asked gently.

'No—they seemed perfectly happy to me. Mum was always busy with the WI and her bridge club—and, as I said, my father spent a lot of time at work. But they used to hold dinner parties and things, and people used to comment on what a strong marriage they had. I found out afterwards that it was all a façade,' she said heavily. 'Apparently Dad had been unfaithful for years, and had had dozens of affairs before he went off with his Brazilian pole-dancer. My mother put up with his infidelity because she was terrified that if she objected Dad would divorce her, and she would lose the house and the wealthy lifestyle she was used to.

In the end that's what happened anyway. Unbeknownst to Mum, Dad had remortgaged the house, and he took all the money from their joint bank accounts before he jetted off to South America.'

'It must have been hard for your mother to suddenly become a single parent and have to support a teenage daughter. How did she manage?'

'She didn't.' Lauren sighed. 'The truth is Mum had some sort of breakdown. She had never had a job or earned her own money, you see. Her parents had been well-off, and she'd married my father straight after she left finishing school. But with no income to pay the mortgage the house had to be sold, and I had to leave my private school and transfer to the local comprehensive. Most of Mum's friends from the bridge club didn't want to know her any more, and she took to drowning her unhappiness in gin and tonic.'

'*Dios!*' Ramon frowned. He had always assumed that Lauren had enjoyed a comfortable middle-class upbringing, but the truth was clearly very different. 'What happened to you? You were little more than a child.'

'I had to get a job—well, three jobs actually—that fitted around going to school. I worked in a shop and did cleaning—anything to earn a bit of money to pay the rent on our flat and buy food. Luckily I was able to keep up with my school work, and I managed to get to university. I was determined to have a good career. You wonder why I want to retain some measure of independence?' she said fiercely. 'Well, the reason is that after what happened to my mother I vowed that I would *never* be reliant on another person, as Mum was on my father. When Dad left I was forced to grow up fast. I learned to get on with things, and now when problems occur I prefer to manage on my own rather than seek help from anyone.'

'Including bringing up your child on your own,' Ramon said slowly.

He had never really understood why Lauren had kept Mateo's birth a secret from him. It seemed such a cruel and vindictive thing to do, and that had puzzled him, because he knew she was not a cruel person. Her words gave him a sudden insight into why she had behaved as she had.

'Is that the reason you did not tell me you were pregnant?' he demanded.

She nodded. 'You regarded me only as your mistress, and I honestly believed you would not want our baby. But I was afraid you would feel an obligation towards your child, and I couldn't bear the thought of Matty growing up wondering why you did not love him, as I have wondered all these years why my father did not love me. I was scared at the prospect of being a single mother,' she admitted, looking away from him so that she missed the flare of anger in his eyes. 'But I had a good job, I knew I could cope, and so I decided to just get on with it.'

'You should not have had to cope alone,' Ramon said roughly, but his anger was directed solely at himself.

If he had been more open with Lauren during their affair, instead of allowing her to believe in his playboy reputation, she might have turned to him for help when she had needed it most, and he would not have lost the first precious months of his son's life.

From Ramon's tone it was clear that he had not been able to forgive her for keeping Matty from him, Lauren thought bleakly. She saw every day how deeply he loved his son, and she bitterly regretted the decision she had made when she had discovered that she was pregnant. But she couldn't change the past. It still hung between her and Ramon, and with a flash of despair she realised that it would always define their relationship.

'I thought that if you didn't know about Matty you would be free to choose a bride better suited to being a *duquesa*.' She hesitated. 'Someone like Pilar. Juanita told me that everyone expected you to marry *her*,' she muttered when Ramon frowned.

'My sister has always allowed her tongue to run away with her,' he said tersely.

But, like a dog with a bone, Lauren found that she could not drop the subject. 'You can't deny that with her aristocratic background Pilar would have been an ideal wife and an ideal *duquesa*.'

Ramon shrugged. 'Perhaps so. But I didn't marry Pilar. I married you.'

He did not sound overjoyed by that fact, and Lauren was unaware that his mind was reeling as he tried to assimilate all that she had told him.

His jaw was tense when he picked up the suitcase and strode over to the door. 'To quote the words you used earlier—we just have to get on with it. I'll be back in a couple of days,' he told her curtly, and walked out of the room without a backward glance.

He phoned several times while he was away, but their conversations were stilted and entirely about Mateo.

'He's fearless,' Ramon said, laughing, when Lauren recounted one day how she had caught their daredevil son trying to climb out of his cot.

The mixture of pride and love in Ramon's voice tugged on her heart, and she felt a wistful longing that he would love her even half as much as he loved Matty.

He had said he would be home the following day, but when at midnight he hadn't arrived, or even called her, Lauren went to bed, made a half-hearted attempt to read a book, and finally buried her face in the pillows and wept silent tears.

He wasn't worth crying over, she told herself angrily, when she sat up to blow her nose. Her mother had cried constantly after her father had left, and she had vowed then that she would never allow any man to mean that much to her. But she had underestimated the power of love, she acknowledged wearily. She did not *want* to love Ramon, but her heart had a will of its own and it seemed hell-bent on self-destruction.

She was about to switch off the bedside lamp when the door suddenly opened and he walked in. Lauren's eyes flew to his face, and then to the bouquet of red roses he was holding. Her heart skittered in her chest.

'Thank you,' she murmured, when he silently handed the flowers to her. She buried her face in the velvety blooms and inhaled their exquisite fragrance. 'They're beautiful.'

She wished he would stop looking at her with that curious, unfathomable expression in his eyes and say something. But when he did finally speak his words evoked a feeling of dread in the pit of her stomach.

'I need to discuss something with you.'

'I see.' She had hoped the roses were a peace offering, but maybe they were a prelude to him announcing that he was no longer prepared to try and make their marriage work.

He sat down on the bed, and her senses instantly flared when she breathed in the evocative scent of his cologne.

'I've been to Bilbao.'

She frowned. 'I thought you went to Madrid?'

'I did. I flew up to Bilbao this afternoon, instead of coming straight home.' Ramon suddenly smiled, the golden warmth of his sherry-brown eyes easing a little of Lauren's tension. 'I have some information that I think you'll find interesting.' He opened his briefcase and took out a booklet. 'This is the prospectus for the university in Bilbao. As I understand it you studied a different system of law to the system we have in Spain?'

Lauren nodded, confused as to where their conversation was leading. 'The UK follows the case law system, while Spain and most other European countries follow the continental system. The two are significantly different.'

'But you could study for a Spanish law degree at the university—perhaps on a part-time basis while Mateo is a baby. Once you qualify and he starts school I thought you could join the legal department of Velaquez Conglomerates, or look for a position with a Spanish law firm—whatever you prefer,' he said quietly, when Lauren stared at him in stunned silence.

'I don't understand. You were so against me going back to work,' she said faintly, trying to suppress a little spurt of excitement as she flicked through the university brochure.

'I want you to be happy,' Ramon said simply. It had taken two miserable days and nights away from her to acknowledge that Lauren's happiness was important to him.

Lauren bit her lip. 'It's a wonderful idea, and when Matty is a bit older I'll certainly consider it. But even studying part-time would mean leaving him for two or three days a week, and although Cathy is a great nanny—

'He won't be with Cathy,' Ramon interrupted her. 'I will look after him on the days that you are at university. I've already arranged for chief executives to take over many of my responsibilities at Velaquez Conglomerates. I've decided to take a back seat role in the company while Mateo is young. I will need to continue with my duties in running the estate, but I can arrange my work around your studies.'

He paused, his brows drawing together when he saw the shimmer of tears in her eyes. 'What's the matter, *querida*? I thought a modern-thinking woman like you would welcome the idea of sharing the care of our child equally?'

'I do,' she assured him. 'It's just that you've taken me by surprise. I didn't expect you to understand how I felt,' she added huskily.

Her smile tugged on Ramon's insides. 'You *should* expect it,' he said seriously. 'You are my wife, and it is my duty to try and make you happy.'

Lauren's heart sank a little at the word *duty*. She didn't want to be another of his responsibilities. It would be so much nicer if he wanted to make her happy because she was important to him, she thought, unaware of the faintly wistful expression in her eyes.

Ramon began to undo his shirt buttons, revealing his muscular chest, the golden satiny skin covered with a mass of fine dark hairs that arrowed down over his flat abdomen. Lauren's heart-rate quickened when he leaned close to her and slid his hand beneath her chin.

'I want our marriage to work, *querida*.' He paused for a heartbeat, and then added deeply, 'Not only for Mateo's sake. And to that end I am prepared to do whatever it takes.'

The first brush of his mouth over hers was nectar after two days without him, and she responded eagerly—like someone who had been lost in the desert and had suddenly discovered an oasis. She sighed with pleasure when he wrapped his arms around her and deepened the kiss, sliding his tongue into her mouth and exploring her with a sensual mastery that made her tremble.

He grinned as he stood up and removed the rest of his

clothes with flattering speed. 'Anyway, I rather like the prospect of being a house-husband.'

Lauren's lips twitched at the idea of her macho husband transformed into a tamed pussy-cat. Her heart lifted. He might not love her, but he cared about her enough to want her to be happy, and that was more than she had ever dared hope for.

'You know that housewives are meant to be domestic goddesses in the kitchen and temptresses in the bedroom?' she murmured as she pulled him down on top of her. 'How does that work for house-husbands?'

'I've never been near a kitchen in my life,' Ramon confessed shamelessly, drawing the straps of her nightgown down her arms until her breasts spilled into his hands. 'But I'm a god in the bedroom, *querida*,' he promised, and proceeded to live up to his claim.

Was it tempting fate to think that life couldn't get more perfect? Lauren wondered a few weeks later, as she carried Matty up the steps of the swimming pool and wrapped a towel around his wet, wriggling body. Not that he needed a towel in the glorious Spanish sunshine that shone every day from a cloudless blue sky. But he *did* need sunscreen and a hat, she told him as she set him on his feet. He immediately toddled off across the grass, laughing gleefully when she gave chase.

The pool was set amid beautiful gardens, where the scent of jasmine and bougainvillaea filled the air. All around the castle stood the peaks of the Cantabrian Mountains, lush and green at their base, rising to silvery-grey bare rock towards the summits. Ramon was a keen hiker—yet another facet about him that Lauren had recently discovered—and with Matty secured in a baby carrier on his father's shoulders they went walking in the picturesque countryside most weekends.

Lauren was making the most of the summer, and treasured spending every day with Matty, but she was looking forward to starting her studies for a Spanish law degree in September. Ramon had driven her to Bilbao for her interview at the university, and afterwards they had spent a magical afternoon at the Guggenheim, world-famous for its collection of contemporary art. Then he had taken her to an exclusive five-star hotel, where they had enjoyed an even more magical night.

It was becoming harder and harder to hide her feelings for Ramon, she mused as she carried Matty back into the castle for his afternoon nap. 'At least I can tell *you* how much I love you,' she murmured to the tired little boy. He gave her a cheeky grin that as ever stole her heart, and she dropped a kiss on his cheek before tiptoeing out of the nursery.

The sound of Ramon's mobile phone greeted her when she walked into their bedroom. She frowned, realising that he must have left it behind, and after a moment's hesitation answered it. She explained to his PA that he was out in the vineyards and would not be back until early evening.

'I'll drive out to find him and give him his phone,' she assured Maria, when the PA went into a lengthy explanation about an urgent matter that required his immediate attention.

The Velaquez estate was huge, with miles of vineyards, but she guessed that Ramon would be at his estate manager's cottage. It was too far to walk in the hot afternoon sunshine, and so she slid behind the wheel of the sports car that was his latest gift to her, lowered the roof, and was soon speeding along the dusty tracks, with the warm breeze blowing through her hair.

It was a glorious feeling, and she couldn't help smiling. She hadn't thanked him properly for her car yet, but tonight she planned to wear a new sexy black negligee and show her appreciation by seducing him.

There was no sign of Ramon's Jeep outside the cottage. So he could be anywhere on the estate, she thought with a frown, as she brought her car to a halt and stared along the endless rows of vines. She sat for a few moments, wondering what to do, and was relieved when one of the estate workers ambled up the track.

'The boss not here,' the man told her in answer to her query. 'He used to come Fridays, but not now.'

Do you know where he spends every Friday afternoon?

Pilar Fernandez's curious question on the day of Valentina's twins' christening stole into Lauren's mind, and despite the hot sun beating down on her shoulderblades ice trickled down her spine.

There would be a perfectly reasonable explanation as to Ramon's whereabouts, she told herself firmly. She smiled at the worker. 'Do you know where *el Duque* is?

The man shrugged. 'Sometimes I see him drive along this track.'

'And the track leads where?' Lauren queried patiently.

'To Casa Madalena.'

All the joy went out of the day, and all the heat drained out of the sun. Lauren shivered and hugged her arms around herself, nausea churning in her stomach. So Ramon spent every Friday afternoon at the home of Pilar Fernandez, and had apparently done so for weeks—despite the fact that he had told her he visited the vineyards on Fridays. Why had he lied? she wondered, and gave a bitter laugh. It could only be because he did not want her to know about his regular visits to Pilar.

Her mother had told her that her father had pretended for years that he played squash at his sports club every Friday evening, when in fact he had been having an affair with his secretary.

Oh, God! Pain ripped through her, and she sagged against the car. She had been such a fool. When she had first met him Ramon had been a playboy who had never been faithful to any of his numerous mistresses for more than five minutes. He had married her because he wanted his son, and had bluntly admitted that she was not his ideal wife. But he had said that he wanted their marriage to work, and she had been so blinded by her love for him that she had seized on the nice things he had done for her as a sign that he was beginning to care for her.

Maybe he had encouraged her to accept a place at university in Bilbao so that she would be out of the way for a couple of days a week? Maybe he intended to invite Pilar to the castle, so that she could get to know Matty before he divorced *her* and married the aristocratic Spanish beauty who would make him a much more suitable bride?

Her overwrought imagination battled with her common sense. Ramon would have to be Superman to have the energy for an affair when he made love to *her* every night. But he had never given any indication that the wild passion they shared was anything more to him than simply good sex. He liked variety, she thought bleakly, remembering his reputation when she had first met him in London.

She climbed back into the car and stared along the track in the direction of the Fernandez home. She could go back to the castle and pretend that she did not know where Ramon really went on Fridays. Her mother had silently accepted her father's affairs for most of their marriage, and for the first time Lauren truly appreciated how much

Frances must have loved her husband to have tolerated a situation that was both humiliating and heartbreaking.

The worst thing was that she was actually tempted to do as her mother had done, she realised, wiping away her tears with shaking fingers. She loved Ramon so much that the thought of losing him lacerated her heart. But she could not live a lie. She had to know the truth.

So, heart pounding, she swung the car towards Casa Madalena.

CHAPTER TEN

THE sight of Ramon's Jeep parked in the courtyard of Pilar's home made Lauren grip the steering wheel so tightly that her knuckles whitened, and her legs felt weak as she walked up the front steps of the house.

'*Sí*, Señor Velaquez is here,' a uniformed butler confirmed when he came to the front door. 'He is in the pool house.'

It was obvious that the pool house was the new-looking glass-roofed building to one side of the main house. Lauren hurried across the courtyard, her heart racing with a mixture of anger and trepidation at the prospect of finding Ramon and Pilar together. No doubt the model would be wearing a skimpy bikini that showed off her stunning figure—or maybe she would be wearing nothing at all?

Swallowing the bile that had risen in her throat, Lauren pushed open the pool house door—and came to an abrupt halt as three startled faces stared at her.

Ramon and another man dressed in medical overalls were lifting a much older man, who could only be Cortez Fernandez, into a wheelchair.

Lauren glanced wildly around the poolside.

'Oh! I thought…Pilar…' She trailed to a halt as she met Ramon's narrowed gaze.

'Pilar is abroad on a modelling assignment. What *did*

you think, Lauren?' he queried in a hard tone—and in that moment she knew that she had made a dreadful mistake.

'I thought...' She swallowed. 'I'm so sorry for my intrusion,' she mumbled to the elderly man, who was now sitting in the wheelchair. He shook his grey head and gave her a faint smile.

'It is I who should apologise, for stealing so much of Ramon's time,' he said in Spanish. 'I should have known that a new bride would want to be with her husband.'

The nurse wheeled Cortez away, and Lauren bit her lip as she watched Ramon stride towards her. His wet swimshorts moulded his muscular thighs, and droplets of water clung to the whorls of dark hairs that covered his chest. The sight of his near naked body made Lauren feel weak for a very different reason.

He hadn't been cheating on her with Pilar. Relief overwhelmed her. But when he halted in front of her she sensed his anger and met his gaze warily.

'What did you expect to find when you rushed in here, Lauren?' he asked quietly, his voice suddenly sounding curiously bleak.

'Pilar said... Well, no, implied...' she corrected herself honestly. 'That you spent every Friday afternoon with her. I had put it out of my mind until today, when I went to the vineyard to give you your phone and discovered that you had lied about inspecting the estate, and in actual fact you came here every week.'

Ramon exhaled heavily. 'I do come every week. Cortez suffered a stroke six months ago, which left him unable to walk. His doctor suggested that he should swim regularly, to help strengthen the muscles in his legs, but the stroke left him feeling so depressed that he seemed to be giving up on life. Pilar asked for my help. I have always been good friends with Cortez, and I persuaded him to swim with me every week. But he is a proud man, who hates his disability, and when he asked me not to discuss his therapy with anyone I felt that I should respect his wish.'

Shame washed over Lauren and she dropped her gaze.

Ramon stared at her downbent head and did not know whether he wanted to kiss her or shake her. At this moment the latter seemed more tempting.

He inhaled sharply. 'How *could* you think that I was in any way involved with Pilar?' he demanded savagely. 'I have never given you any reason to doubt my commitment to our marriage.'

He hadn't, Lauren admitted, guilt gnawing at her insides. It had been her and her wretched insecurity that had driven her to think the worst of him. 'Pilar deliberately put doubts in my mind,' she muttered. 'I think she hoped to make trouble between us.'

'She seems to have succeeded,' Ramon said tersely. He swung away from her and snatched up a towel. 'I can't help feeling that you are always going to punish me for your father's sins.'

Lauren gave him a startled look. 'What do you mean?'

'You don't trust me. And I'm not sure our marriage can survive without trust. Go back to the castle,' he ordered her roughly. 'I am too angry to talk to you right now. I usually play a game of chess with Cortez—and, in case you're wondering, the only female around will be his housekeeper, who is about ninety-three,' he finished sardonically.

Ramon did not return for dinner. A member of the castle staff informed Lauren that he had phoned to say he would be dining with Cortez Fernandez. Clearly he was still angry with her, and she could not blame him, she thought miserably as eleven p.m. came and went and he still had not come home. But his explosive tempers did not usually last for long, and, hopeful that they would soon make up after this latest row, she took a bath and afterwards anointed her skin with fragrant oil, before donning the daring black negligee she had bought to please him.

She owed him an apology, she acknowledged as she sat alone on the huge four-poster bed and studied the portrait of Matty that Ramon had commissioned for her. It now hung on the wall, so that it was the first thing she saw when she woke every morning. Even if he did not love her the way she loved him, he had proved over and over that he cared about her and respected her—and she had repaid him with doubt and mistrust that threatened to undermine their marriage.

Racked with guilt, she paced around the bedroom and finally pulled on her robe, intending to wait for him downstairs so that she could greet him when he came home—if he ever did, she thought painfully.

She was shocked to see a light spilling from beneath the door of his study, and after giving a hesitant knock she entered the room. He was sprawled on the sofa, his jacket and tie discarded in a heap on the floor, a glass of whisky in his hand—not the first glass he had drunk, she guessed, glancing at the half-empty bottle on the coffee table.

'I…I didn't realise you were back,' she said shakily, when he turned his head and stared at her through blood-shot eyes.

'Where else would I be, my darling wife?' He gave a sardonic laugh. 'Don't answer that. I'm sure your fertile imagination can come up with a dozen scenarios, featuring me sleeping with one of the many mistresses that you seem to think I have stashed away.'

'I am truly sorry that I doubted you,' Lauren said in a

low tone. 'I had no reason to mistrust you. It was just…
when you weren't at the vineyards, as I had expected, I
thought about all the times my father must have lied to my
mother—all his affairs that I knew nothing about when I
was a child, but which broke her heart. For a few stupid
minutes I thought that you were like him, but I know that
you're not,' she choked, swallowing the tears that suddenly
clogged her throat.

Ramon drained his glass and stood up, moving away
from her to stand by the window that looked over the dark
castle grounds and the shadowy mountains beyond.

'I should never have forced you to marry me,' he said
abruptly. 'I can see now that it was a mistake.'

Fear greater than anything she had ever experienced
caused the blood to drain from Lauren's face, and she felt
hollow inside, as if her heart had been wrenched from her
chest. 'You didn't force me—' she began, but Ramon shook
his head.

'*Dios mio*, I threatened to fight for custody of our child.
I gave you no choice but to be my wife. And now you feel
trapped. You asked me once if you were my prisoner,' he
said harshly. 'The answer is no, Lauren. I will not keep
you here against your will any longer.'

She wished he would turn round, so that she could see
his expression, because the dark, deadly serious tone in his
voice was scaring her to death. 'I don't understand,' she
whispered.

He shrugged. 'I am setting you free. Neither of us can
be happy while you continue to be haunted by the way your
father treated your mother. You are constantly waiting for
me to let you down in some way, and ultimately that lack
of trust will destroy our relationship.'

He paused, and then continued in the same emotionless
voice. 'I will agree to a divorce, and to you taking Mateo

back to England. All I ask is that you allow me to buy a house for the two of you, and for your agreement that I can visit him often.'

She was so shocked by his stark announcement that she could not speak—couldn't think. The agonising pain, as if her heart was being crushed in a vice, made it difficult to breathe.

'I don't want a divorce,' she stammered. 'I would never take Matty away from here—from the castle, and his family, and *you*. I know how much you love him.'

She broke off when Ramon turned to face her, and the stark wretchedness in his eyes made her want to weep. She knew how much it must have cost him to offer her custody of Matty, to allow her to take his son away. He thought she wanted her freedom, but what she really wanted, *needed* to do was tell him honestly how she felt about him. She had been a coward for far too long, and had allowed her father's behaviour to colour her judgement of Ramon, but what they shared was too special to lose.

Courage was hard to find as she stared at the tall, handsome man who was her world. His jaw was tense, his skin drawn tight over his slashing cheekbones. She wished he would smile and hold her, kiss her hair as he did every night as she fell asleep in his arms.

She took a deep breath.

'I don't feel trapped. I want to remain married to you because...I love you.'

The silence was so intense that Lauren could hear the ragged sound of her breathing. There was no reaction on his hard face, and his thick lashes hid the expression in his eyes.

'Some *love*,' he said scathingly at last. 'You say the words, Lauren, but you did not show it today, when you believed that I was having an affair with Pilar.'

Feeling as though she were dying inside, Lauren stared at the floor, willing her tears not to fall until she was alone and could deal with his rejection in private. She did not see him move, and flinched when he slid his hand beneath her chin and tilted her face to his.

'True love—the kind that lasts for ever—is profound and loving, passionate and tender,' he said deeply. 'It is about trust and forgiveness, friendship, and an abiding affection that transcends all life's problems and disappointments and brings the greatest joy.' Ramon paused and stared into her grey eyes, feeling his heart contract when he saw the shimmer of her tears. 'At least that is the love I feel for you, *mi corazón.*'

It was too much to take in. He had defined the meaning of love so beautifully that she could not hold back her tears. She must have misunderstood. He could not mean that he felt that wealth of emotion for *her*, she thought desperately. But the golden gleam in his sherry-brown gaze burned into her soul, and to her amazement love blazed in his eyes.

'You...you love me?' She was a lawyer, and she always verified her facts.

'With all my heart, *mi preciosa.*'

The raw emotion in his voice touched her even more than the words, and she realised that she was not the only one who was shaking. Questions swirled in her head.

'Why didn't you say?' she whispered, still finding it impossible to believe.

He gave a rueful smile and stroked her hair back from her face with an unsteady hand. 'At first I did not know,' he admitted huskily. 'All I knew was that I fancied you like hell and wanted you in my bed. To my annoyance, I missed you when you weren't around. But I think even then, during our affair, I knew you were special,' he said slowly.

'You know what happened the one and only other time I fell in love. My heart soon mended after Catalina, but I felt ashamed that I had disappointed my father, and I was determined to one day marry a woman from my own social circle of whom he would approve. My experience with Catalina made me wary of trusting my judgement of women, so when I met you and realised I wanted more than a casual affair with you I reminded myself that I could never allow our relationship to develop.

'I was furious when I discovered that you had kept my son a secret from me, but I was secretly glad that it gave me the opportunity to make you my wife,' he admitted. 'I kidded myself that I only wanted to marry you for Mateo's sake. When you walked towards me in the church, looking like an angel, I knew that you had stolen my heart irrevocably and for ever.

'Don't cry, *mi corazón*,' he said softly, brushing his lips over her damp cheeks and tasting her tears. 'Don't you want me to love you?'

'I want it more than anything in the world, and I always have—because I fell in love with you about five minutes after I met you,' she told him fiercely. 'I'm crying because I was so unsure of you, and of the happiness that we seemed to have. I wish you had told me how you felt.'

'You wouldn't have believed me,' he said gently. 'You had to learn to trust me first. I tried to show you how much you meant to me.'

'By giving me things,' Lauren murmured, suddenly understanding that the jewellery and other presents he had showered her with had been his way of trying to teach her that he loved her. 'Oh, Ramon.' She stared at his beautiful sculpted face and ached with love for him. 'You wouldn't really have agreed to a divorce, would you?' she asked, a little tremor of uncertainty still in her voice.

'You must be joking.' He smiled suddenly, and snatched her into his arms as the restraint he had imposed on himself crumbled beneath his urgent need to hold her close. 'Even as I said it I was frantically backtracking and planning how I could persuade you to stay with me. I never want to let you go, *querida*,' he said, suddenly serious again. 'But I blackmailed you into marrying me. You have to choose whether or not you *want* to be my wife.'

Joy unfurled in Lauren's heart and radiated out, until every cell and nerve-ending in her body overflowed with happiness. 'I choose you—and I want to stay with you as your wife, friend and lover until I die.' She untied the belt of her robe and shrugged it from her shoulders, heat sizzling in her blood when Ramon studied the very daring black lace negligee with rampant appreciation in his eyes. 'But I won't object if you want to persuade me a *little*,' she invited in a sultry tone.

The sight of her creamy breasts spilling out of her sexy nightgown was too much for Ramon, and with a groan he lowered his head and captured her mouth with a sensual mastery that elicited her urgent response. She was on fire for him instantly, and curled her arms around his neck as she pressed her body up against his hard thighs.

He was breathing hard when he finally lifted his lips from hers. 'I have something for you,' he told her raggedly.

She smiled and stroked her hand over the distinct bulge beneath his trousers. 'I know.'

'Witch.' He eased away from her, strode over to his desk, and retrieved a small box from a drawer. 'I've wanted to give you this for weeks, but the time never seemed right.' He paused, and then added a shade bleakly, 'And I wasn't sure you wanted my love for you that this ring represents.'

He opened the box, and Lauren caught her breath as she

stared at the exquisite sparkling circlet of diamonds set in white gold. 'One day our son can give this "monstrosity" to *his* fiancée,' Ramon told her, his eyes glinting with amusement as he tugged the enormous ruby engagement ring that she so disliked from her finger, and replaced it with the band of diamonds. 'This ring is for eternity, *mi amor,* just like my love for you.'

There were not words to express the depth of her love for him, but he seemed to understand, and kissed away her tears before he swept her up and carried her out of the study. The speed with which he took the stairs was an indication of his fierce need to make love to her. He dropped her onto the bed and removed the wisp of tantalising black lace, his eyes burning with desire as he swiftly stripped out of his clothes and positioned himself between her satin-soft thighs.

'I can't wait, *tesoro,*' he murmured, as he caressed her with gentle fingers and found her wet and ready for him. But he forced himself to be patient, and reached into the bedside drawer for a protective sheath, giving her a puzzled look when she took it from him.

'I think it's time I caught up with your sisters,' she said softly. 'Matty needs a little brother or sister, and this time I want you to be involved from conception to birth—concentrating very much on conception,' she added with a blissful sigh, when his patience snapped and he surged into her.

'Are you sure you want another baby when you are about to start studying?'

'I can study while I'm pregnant—and one day when our children are older I'd like to resume my career. I have everything I could ever want,' she reassured him softly, 'You, Matty, and hopefully we'll be blessed with another baby. But, more important than anything, I have your love—as you have mine.'

'For ever,' Ramon vowed fervently. And there was no need for further words as he showed her with his body the love that filled his heart.

THE FRENCHMAN'S
MARRIAGE DEMAND

CHAPTER ONE

ZACHARIE DEVERELL swept along the hospital corridor, paused briefly to check the name above the door before he entered a ward and strode purposefully towards the nurse seated behind the reception desk.

'I'm here to see Freya Addison. I understand she was admitted yesterday,' he added, the hint of impatience in his voice making his accent seem more pronounced. The nurse gaped at him but Zac was used to being stared at. Women had stared at him since he was a teenager and at thirty-five his stunning looks, combined with an aura of wealth and power, meant that he was accustomed to being the centre of attention.

When it suited him he would respond to a flirtatious look with one of his devastating smiles, but today he had other things on his mind. There was only one reason why he was here, he acknowledged grimly, and the sooner he saw Freya and told her exactly what he thought of her latest stunt, the better.

'Um…Miss Addison…' Thoroughly flustered by the presence of six feet four of brooding Frenchman holding an angelic-looking child in his arms, the nurse hurriedly flicked through the pile of papers in front of her. 'Oh, yes, down the corridor, third door on the left—but you can't see her at the moment, the doctor is with her. Please, wait a minute, Mr…?'

The Frenchman was already striding along the corridor and the nurse scooted around the desk and chased after him.

'Deverell,' he murmured coolly, not slowing his steps. 'My name is Zac Deverell and it is imperative that I see Miss Addison immediately.'

Freya sat on her hospital bed and stared gloomily at her bandaged wrist. The past twenty-four hours had been hellish and she hoped that any minute now she would wake up and find that it had all been a nightmare. Instead the throbbing ache of her badly sprained wrist and a splitting headache were evidence of the force with which her car had ploughed into a fallen tree, brought down during the ferocious storm that had hit the south coast.

She had been on her way home from the yacht club where she worked as a receptionist and fortunately hadn't yet collected her little daughter from the day nursery when the accident had happened. Aimee was safe, and she was lucky to be alive, she acknowledged with a shudder, but her car was damaged beyond repair and she was going to have to take time off work, which was not going to help her ailing finances.

She had spent the night in the hospital with mild concussion and the doctor had explained that the ligaments in her wrist had been torn and she would need to wear a support bandage for several weeks. After prescribing strong painkillers he had told her she could go home, but she was worried about how she was going to manage to carry Aimee and her pushchair up and down the four flights of stairs to their attic flat when she only had the use of one hand.

She would have to ask her grandmother for help, she fretted, her thoughts turning to the woman who had brought her up after her mother had abandoned her when she was a baby. But Joyce Addison had taken on the role of parent out of a sense of duty rather than affection. Freya had endured a loveless childhood and when she had fallen pregnant and immediately been dumped by her baby's father, her grandmother had made it clear that she would not support her or her child.

She guessed Joyce had been furious when the hospital contacted her yesterday and passed on her request that she should collect Aimee from nursery. She had half expected her grandmother to turn up at the hospital last night with the toddler in tow, but there had been no word from the older woman and Freya was growing increasingly anxious. She glanced up expectantly when the door opened and felt a sharp pang of disappointment when a nurse entered the small side ward.

'Have you heard anything from my grandmother? Has she phoned? She's looking after my daughter but she's due to fly to New York any day now.'

'As far as I know, there has been no word from your grandmother, but your daughter is here at the hospital,' the nurse said cheerfully. 'Her uncle's looking after her. I'll tell him he can come in.'

'*Uncle?*' Freya stared at the nurse in bewilderment. Aimee didn't have an *uncle*.

'Yes, I asked Mr Deverell to wait in the visitor's lounge while the doctor was with you, but I know he's impatient to see you,' the nurse added wryly. The Frenchman had to be the sexiest male on the planet, but it had been evident from the haughty expression in his flashing blue eyes that patience wasn't one of his strong points.

The nurse disappeared before Freya could question her further. The world had gone mad, she decided as she ran a shaky hand through her hair. The name Deverell conjured up a face from the past that she had spent the past two years desperately trying to forget and hearing it again caused a peculiar cramping sensation in the pit of her stomach. The nurse must have made a mistake. But who was this mysterious uncle—who exactly was looking after Aimee?

'Mum-mum!'

She glanced towards the door at the sound of her daughter's gurgling laughter and focused on Aimee's cherubic face, a heady mixture of love and relief coursing through her veins. But almost instantly her gaze moved higher and clashed with the cool blue stare of the man who had haunted her dreams for the past two years.

'Zac?' she whispered disbelievingly.

Zac Deverell; billionaire businessman, renowned playboy and chief executive of the globally successful company Deverell's, which owned exclusive department stores around the world, instantly seemed to dominate the room. He was even more gorgeous than she remembered, she thought numbly as her brain struggled to assimilate the shocking reality of his presence at the end of her bed. He was tall, lean and devastatingly good-looking, his black jeans and matching sweater were effortlessly stylish and accentuated his athletic build.

Weakly Freya closed her eyes. For a few seconds the image of his bronzed, muscular torso and the covering of fine black hairs that arrowed down over his flat stomach flooded her mind. Zac was the epitome of male perfection. For a few brief, incredible months she'd enjoyed free access to his body and had revelled in the feel of his satiny skin beneath her fingertips as she'd trailed a daring path over the solid strength of his thighs. She had a vivid recall of how it had felt to lie beneath him, skin on skin, their limbs entwined so that two became one...

With a low murmur she released her breath and stared at his face, noting the male beauty of his sharp cheekbones and square chin, and the way a lock of his jet-black hair had fallen over his brow. His eyes were the deep, dense blue of a Mediterranean summer sky—the same shade as Aimee's eyes. The thought sent her crashing back to reality and she frowned at the way her daughter was sitting contentedly in his arms. It was a sight she had dreamed of frequently, but never in her wildest fantasies had she expected it to happen.

'What are *you* doing here? And since when did you become Aimee's uncle?' Shock seemed to have robbed her of her strength and to her chagrin her voice sounded pathetically weak.

Zac regarded her silently for a moment, his black brows drawn together in a harsh frown. 'It was easier to tell the hospital staff that I'm a relative—or would you rather I'd explained that I'm the man you tried to trick into believing was the father of your child?' he queried pleasantly, aware that any hint of aggression in his tone could frighten the little girl sitting on his hip.

Freya gave a bitter laugh. 'It was no trick, *Zac*—Aimee is your daughter.'

'The *hell* she is!' The denial came out as a low hiss and Zac abruptly lowered Aimee onto the bed. He smiled reassuringly at the toddler, making a Herculean effort to mask his impatience from her. It wasn't the child's fault, he reminded himself. With her halo of golden curls and enormous blue eyes, Aimee was angelic. It was her mother who was a cheat and a liar and if Freya hadn't looked so damned fragile he'd be tempted to throttle her for manipulating him into this situation.

'We went through this two years ago, Freya, when you sprang the news that you were pregnant. My response is the same now as it was then,' he told her coldly. 'You might have convinced your grandmother of my paternity but you and I both know you weren't telling the truth—don't we?'

'I've never lied to you,' Freya snapped, stung by the contempt in Zac's eyes. It was the same expression that she'd seen when she'd told him she was expecting his baby—contemptuous disbelief, followed by his devastating accusation that she had obviously cheated on him. The pain in her heart was no less intense, despite the passing of time. In a strange way it was worse. The mental wounds Zac had inflicted on her were far more painful than her injuries. Seeing him again had re-ignited her agony and she wished he would go, before she suffered the ultimate humiliation of breaking down in front of him.

'I no longer care what you think,' she told him wearily, unable to stifle a groan when Aimee scrambled over her and knocked against her sore ribs—bruised in the accident by the force of her seat belt locking against her. 'I can't imagine what you're doing here, but I think it's best if you leave.'

'Believe me, I'm not here through choice,' Zac ground out savagely. 'I was at Deverell's London office this morning to give a press conference announcing record profits made by the Oxford Street store, when your grandmother turned up with your daughter. Presumably you'd planned the timing of her visit to create maximum impact,' he added harshly. 'Her accusation, that Aimee is my child, was overheard by several journalists as well as members of my staff and rumours have already got back to the Deverell board.'

'Aimee was in *London?* I don't understand,' Freya said sharply, frowning in confusion. 'The hospital phoned my grandmother yesterday and asked her to look after Aimee. Where is Nana Joyce now?'

'Jetting off across the Atlantic for the start of her cruise, I imagine,' Zac replied. 'She went on about how she'd saved for years for a round-the-world trip and that nothing, not even the fact that you were in hospital, would induce her to miss it.'

His eyes darkened as he remembered his meeting with Joyce Addison.

'I'm sick to death of feckless fathers,' she told him when she marched into his office wheeling a pushchair in front of her and handed him an enormous holdall, which, she informed him, contained all the necessary paraphernalia for an eighteen-month-old child. 'I was left to bring up Freya after her mother got herself pregnant at sixteen by some shiftless Lothario she'd met at a funfair. Sadie soon got bored of motherhood and went off, leaving me stuck with a child I didn't want.

'I thought I'd warned Freya of the dangers of handsome men who want nothing more than a good time,' Joyce continued, trailing her eyes over him as if he were some sort of *stud,* Zac recalled furiously. 'I told her when you offered her a job on that fancy boat of yours that you were only after one thing, and evidently you both got more than you bargained for. But now it's time you took responsibility for your actions.

'I don't know how long Freya is going to be in hospital and I'm not waiting to find out. If you won't look after

Aimee, you'd better hand her over to social services, because I refuse to be landed with another baby.'

Joyce Addison's vitriolic tirade had captured the attention of everyone at the Deverell offices—although his staff had done their best to hide their curiosity, Zac conceded darkly. The whole, unbelievable scenario had been *bloody* humiliating, he thought bitterly—and there was only one person he could blame.

'You can drop the act, Freya,' he said coldly. 'It's quite obvious you told your grandmother to bring Aimee to me, and, having met Joyce, I can't even blame you,' he went on, ignoring Freya's gasp. 'I wouldn't leave a dog in your grandmother's care, let alone a young child. But if all this is a ploy to get money out of me in the form of maintenance—you can forget it.'

He glared at her, his anger increasing when he felt his body's response to Freya, with her small, heart-shaped face and mass of silky honey-blonde hair. She had intrigued him for barely three months, but two years on he could instantly recall her slender, pale limbs and small, firm breasts. The passion they had shared had been explosive, he acknowledged, aware of an uncomfortable tightening in his groin as unbidden memories surfaced. He had wanted her from the moment she'd first joined the crew of his luxury yacht, *The Isis,* and the attraction between them had been mutual.

Shy, innocent Freya had been unable to hide her awareness of him and he had wasted no time persuading her into his bed. Although it had been a shock to discover just how innocent she was, he thought grimly. He liked his women to be self-confident and experienced in bed—willing participants in the mutual exchange of sexual pleasure without the pressure of emotional ties. But the temptation of her satiny skin as she curled her legs around him and the enticement of her breathless whispers begging him to make love to her had been impossible to resist. She had proved a willing pupil and he had delighted in tutoring her. Her shyness and inexperience had been refreshing and against his better judgement he had invited her to move into his penthouse apartment as his mistress.

It was a decision he had later regretted and after discovering her to have slept with another man behind his back he had evicted her from his life with ruthless efficiency. His bed had not remained empty for very long. His vast fortune meant that there would always be a queue of willing candidates vying to be his mistress, he acknowledged cynically.

He had hardly given Freya a thought since he'd dismissed her back to England and it irritated him to realise that the chemistry between them still burned as fiercely as ever.

'I did not instruct my grandmother to bring Aimee to you,' Freya said shakily, still struggling to accept that Zac was really standing in front of her. 'Trust me; you're the *last* person I'd ever turn to for help.' She glared at him, her green eyes blazing with anger and unconcealed hurt. He was so beautiful, she thought painfully. She couldn't tear her eyes from him and the sight of his broad chest and powerful abdominal muscles, delineated by his close-fitting, fine-knit jumper, made her insides melt.

Zac was utterly gorgeous but fatally flawed, she reminded herself. His arrogance and cynicism had almost destroyed her, but her body seemed to have a short memory and was responding to his closeness with humiliating eagerness. He had treated her *diabolically*. When she had needed him most, he had let her down and demolished her pride with his foul accusations that she had been a two-timing whore. Two years ago he'd made it clear that she meant nothing to him, so why was her heart racing? And why was her brain intent on recalling every detail of his kiss, the feel of his hands on her body…?

Frantically she dragged her mind from her memories. 'I admit I once told Nana Joyce that you're Aimee's father—she kept on and on about it, and it's the truth, whatever you might think,' she stated with quiet dignity. 'You were the first and only man I've ever slept with, Zac,' she whispered sadly, 'but you had your own reasons for choosing not to believe me, didn't you?'

Zac's expression of cool disinterest did not flicker and his only reaction to her last statement was a slight quirk of his brows. 'And what was that, *chérie*?'

'You'd decided *before* I told you I was pregnant that you wanted to end our relationship. After three months together you'd grown tired of me. Don't deny it,' she said fiercely. 'I recognised the signs, the way you mentally withdrew from me during those last few weeks that we were together. The only time we were close was in bed, and even then you were…distant.'

'Not that distant,' Zac replied mockingly. 'Your voracious appetite for sex wouldn't allow any distance between us, would it, Freya? I still find it amazing that you had the energy to sleep with anyone else when you put so much effort into sleeping with me.'

His deliberate cruelty skewered Freya's heart and she blinked back the rush of tears that burned her eyelids. 'How dare you?' she whispered thickly. 'Don't try and appease your guilty conscience by blaming me. You wanted rid of me because you'd set your sights on Annalise Dubois. You were determined to make her your next mistress, but an ex who was pregnant with your baby would have seriously cramped your style.'

In her agitation she leapt off the bed and her head spun. The blood drained from her face and she swayed unsteadily before collapsing back onto the mattress.

'Enough,' Zac growled as he stepped forwards and caught Aimee who was determinedly trying to wriggle off the bed. 'You're upsetting the child.' He set Aimee down on the floor and stared speculatively at her blonde curls for a moment before glancing back at her mother.

'I don't want anything from you,' Freya stated angrily. 'Certainly not money,' she added, unable to hide the flare of contempt in her eyes. 'I just want you to accept that I'm telling the truth.'

She stared into his brilliant blue eyes, that were so like Aimee's, and gave an angry sigh. She had no intention of pursuing him through the courts for a slice of his vast fortune as her grandmother had frequently suggested. He didn't want her and he didn't want Aimee, and that was fine, she'd manage without him. She just wanted him to accept that she had never lied to him. 'Why can't you be honest with me?' she pleaded.

Zac glanced down at her and tensed. Her thin hospital nightgown had come unfastened so that he could see the curve of one small, pale breast. To his utter disgust he felt his body's involuntary reaction—a shaming surge of heat in his loins as desire corkscrewed in his gut.

She'd proved herself to be a faithless whore, damn it, who was still brazenly trying to pass off another man's child as his. It was humiliating to realise the effect she still had on him. He didn't want to want her; it dented his pride to know that he was seriously tempted to wind his hand into her hair, angle her head and plunder the softness of her moist pink lips in a kiss that would remind her of the passion they had once shared.

Instead he forced himself to move away from the bed and stared out of the window at the rain lashing against the pane. 'What would you know of honesty, Freya?' he demanded coldly, his facial muscles tightening so that his skin was stretched taut over his cheekbones. 'Did you really think I wouldn't find out about your secret assignations with that anaemic-looking street artist Simon Brooks?

'Monaco is a small place and gossip runs rife. I am—' he shrugged his shoulders in a typically Gallic gesture '—well known in the principality and the speculation that I was being cuckolded by my mistress soon reached my ears. I might even have found the situation amusing,' he drawled sardonically. 'It was certainly a novelty. But your attempts to saddle me with another man's child were not so funny, chérie.'

'I swear I never slept with Simon,' Freya said urgently. 'The bodyguard you'd assigned to protect me made a mistake that day. But at the time—when you said all those terrible things to me—I couldn't think straight.' She had been so devastated by Zac's refusal to believe that she was carrying his baby and so shocked by his accusation that she had slept with Simon that her mind had gone blank and she had simply walked out of his apartment without even trying to defend herself. 'I've had a long time to think about things since then,' she added bitterly, 'and now I believe I know what happened.' She paused for a moment and stared at Zac, faint hope bubbling in her chest when he remained silent. It was the first time since the fateful night two years ago that they had actually spoken properly. The first time he had listened.

'It's true I spent a lot of time with Simon, but he was my friend, nothing more. You were always busy working and I was lonely,' she admitted quietly, thinking of the young English art student who had befriended her during her stay in Monaco. Simon had been touring the Mediterranean coast, scraping a living selling his paintings. Unlike Zac's glamorous friends, he'd seemed refreshingly ordinary and down to earth, and she had enjoyed his company. 'We weren't lovers—he was just someone from home that I liked to talk to.'

'And I suppose Michel was lying when he told me he'd seen you and Brooks leave the beach arm in arm to return to his camper van?' Zac drawled. '*Sacré bleu!* I paid Michel to protect you, but when he saw your distinctive pink jacket hanging on the van door and glimpsed you and your floppy-haired artist rolling around inside, he didn't know what to do. He certainly didn't want to be seen as a voyeur,' he added, his lip curling in distaste. 'My wealth brings with it a very real threat of kidnap and Michel knew that, as my mistress, you were vulnerable. He didn't want to leave you without protection, but neither did he want to hang around watching your sexual gymnastics with Brooks. In the end he phoned me to ask my advice—while I was hurrying back from a business trip to take you out to dinner,' Zac finished grimly.

'Your announcement as soon as I walked through the door that you were pregnant was ill-timed to say the least, *chérie*,' he continued when it was evident that she was beyond words. 'I'd just learned from a man I trusted implicitly that you and Brooks were lovers, and I was certain that I wasn't the child's father. It wasn't difficult to work out that you were pregnant by your penniless artist and hoping to pass the baby off as mine.'

The cold fury in his eyes caused Freya to shiver but this was possibly the only chance she would ever have to defend herself and make Zac see that he was wrong about her. 'Michel didn't see me,' she insisted desperately. 'He just thought he did. I'd gone to the beach to meet Simon and a group of his friends, including his girlfriend. Kirsten was feeling cold and I lent her my jacket before I walked into the town. She has blonde hair like mine and Michel must have mistaken her for me…' She stumbled to a halt, her heart sinking at the mockery in Zac's eyes. 'I didn't go to Simon's van that day and I was never unfaithful to you, Zac,' she insisted. 'You have to believe me.'

He stared at her in silence for a few moments and then laughed unpleasantly. 'You've had two years to think of a story. Is that really the best you can do, *chérie*?' He paced the room like a caged tiger, his pent up aggression almost tangible. *'Non!'* he stated fiercely, slicing his hand through the air to emphasise his anger. 'I refuse to be manipulated by you. I want a paternity test and once I've proved conclusively that you are a liar, I never want to see you or hear from you again. Do you understand?'

'How can you be so sure that I'm lying?' Freya whispered numbly. Clearly Zac's opinion of her couldn't sink any lower and she was shocked by how much it hurt. The contempt in his tone made her want to shrivel but pride brought her head up. The silence between them vibrated with a tension that shredded her nerves and she visibly flinched when he swung round and stared at her.

His expression filled her with a curious sense of foreboding and she felt her stomach churn. She could not tear her gaze from the sculpted beauty of his face but his eyes were hard and cold and, despite the stifling warmth of the hospital ward, she shivered.

Zac paused and then said unemotionally, 'Because I had a vasectomy—years before we met. The truth is, *chérie*, that it's medically impossible for Aimee to be my daughter.'

CHAPTER TWO

ZAC watched the shock and confusion on Freya's face with clinical detachment before he glanced at Aimee. The little girl stared up at him solemnly, her pretty little face surrounded by her mass of curls and her pink cheeks glowing with health. She was not a Deverell, thank God, he thought with quiet certainty. This child would not suffer the way his twin sisters had suffered—victims of the devastating illness that had taken their lives before they were a year old.

He had been a teenager when his mother had given birth to twins. The babies had appeared normal but within a few months both had died from an incurable genetic disorder and after their deaths doctors had warned his parents there was a fifty-per-cent chance that he had also been affected. He had escaped the illness but there was no test available to show if he carried the gene.

The trauma of watching his sisters die and witnessing his parents' grief had never faded. As an adult he had made the decision that he could not risk the slightest chance of passing on the gene to his own children and had taken the necessary steps to ensure that he would never be a father. The faint regret he'd felt at the time had soon faded and he had moved on, determined to enjoy his life and take advantage of the benefits his billion-pound fortune afforded him.

He couldn't have children, but why would he want to be tied down to the responsibilities of a family when he could afford fast cars, power boats and all the trappings of his wealth? He enjoyed an endless supply of beautiful women who entertained him briefly before he grew bored and looked around for new pleasures.

Freya had intrigued him for longer than most but he had never viewed her as becoming a permanent feature in his life. It hadn't occurred to him to mention his vasectomy when she had been his mistress and he felt under no obligation to explain the reason for it now.

Freya stared wildly at Zac, feeling as though the world had actually shifted on its axis. 'The operation must have failed,' she croaked, struggling to assimilate his shocking announcement. 'I don't understand how it could have happened, but Aimee is your child,' she insisted desperately.

'Don't be ridiculous,' Zac snapped irritably. 'It's impossible.' Although that wasn't strictly true, he acknowledged silently. He'd always known that the procedure carried a one-in-two-thousand chance of reversal, but when Freya had sprung the news of her pregnancy, less than an hour after his security guard, Michel, had seen her with Simon Brooks, he had angrily assumed that she'd been having an affair with the Englishman for weeks and that the baby she was carrying couldn't possibly be his own. He was still convinced that this was the case and he felt a surge of disgust for Freya and her pathetic excuses.

He would have marginally more respect for her if she stopped lying and admitted that she'd been caught out, he brooded darkly, his lip curling in contempt. She was beautiful—more so, if anything, than she had been two years ago—but beneath her exquisite shell she was rotten to the core and once he had the proof he would have nothing more to do with her.

'The nurse informed me that you've been discharged,' he said tersely, raking his eyes over Freya's pale face as he strode towards the door. 'Hurry up and get dressed. We're flying to Monaco immediately where I'll make the necessary arrangements to carry out the DNA test and end this wild speculation once and for all.'

Half an hour later, Freya's temper was at boiling point. Zac seemed to think he could just waltz back into her life and take over. 'I am *not* going to Monaco with you,' she repeated for the twentieth time as she followed him across the hospital car park and watched him strap Aimee into the child-seat that his secretary had apparently lent him when he'd driven down from London. It was still raining hard and he had turned up the collar of his leather jacket. With his hair slicked back from his face and his black brows lowered in an ominous scowl he looked more gorgeous than ever and she groaned silently at her body's traitorous response to him.

He was mean, moody and magnificent, she thought bleakly, not to mention the most arrogant, overbearing man she had ever met. Two years ago he had swept her away on his boat and straight into his bed. She had given him her virginity but he had stolen her heart, she thought sadly. After a lifetime devoid of any emotional security she had willingly become his mistress, but his cruel rejection had almost destroyed her and she could not risk returning to the place where she had once been so happy.

'I agree that we need to do a paternity test,' she said when he made no reply. 'But why can't we do it here in England? I don't want to go anywhere with you.'

'Tough.' Zac checked Aimee was secure and then opened the driver's door and slid into the car. 'I have an urgent meeting with the Deverell board tomorrow at the Monaco office and so it's more convenient for me to have it done in my private clinic at home. Get in the car,' he snapped testily when she continued to stand outside in the rain. 'I've chartered a private jet and my pilot can't wait all day.'

Freya glowered at him as she climbed reluctantly into the passenger seat. Her heart was thumping painfully in her chest and she wished she had the nerve to snatch Aimee and run. The torrential rain, her injured wrist and the bitter knowledge that he could effortlessly outmatch her in speed and strength made her stay put, but she edged as far away as possible from him once inside the car and stared pointedly out of the window.

'You'll have to give me directions to your flat,' he said when he turned out of the hospital gates. 'Aimee's pushchair and a bag of her clothes are in the boot, courtesy of your grandmother,' he added, his voice simmering with barely concealed anger. 'You can have twenty minutes to pack, but I intend to leave within the next hour.'

Freya leaned back and closed her eyes wearily, overwhelmed by his determination. When Zac wanted his own way he invariably got it—but unless he intended to kidnap her and Aimee, he couldn't make them get on his plane.

She was acutely conscious of him sitting beside her and when she peeped at him from beneath her lashes, the sight of his strong, tanned hands on the wheel made her feel weaker than ever. Once those hands had skimmed every inch of her body and explored her so intimately that the memory made her blush. He smelled of rain and damp leather, and the subtle scent of the cologne he favoured was achingly familiar, tantalising her senses and forcing her to remember the mind-blowing passion they had once shared.

It was over, she reminded herself angrily as she tore her gaze from his stern profile. He had tried and convicted her before she'd even understood the crime she was supposed to have committed. In a strange way his revelation about his vasectomy was almost a relief. His savage anger and rejection two years ago had destroyed her, but now at least she could understand why he had been so ready to believe that she'd been having an affair with Simon.

The fact that he had never mentioned his vasectomy when she'd lived with him emphasised how little she'd meant to him. The question of children had never arisen because she'd been Zac's mistress and he hadn't wanted a permanent relationship with her.

But the operation must have reversed. She didn't know much about the procedure but presumably it hadn't worked properly because Aimee was undoubtedly his daughter, she thought on a wave of near hysteria. What other explanation could there be?

After Aimee was born she had briefly considered asking Zac for a DNA test, but had decided against it. His reaction to her pregnancy had shown that he abhorred the idea of fatherhood and she had feared he would only take a reluctant role in his daughter's upbringing.

At eighteen months old, Aimee was a happy, loving child whose confidence was built on the instinctive knowledge that she was loved unconditionally. She would not allow Zac to destroy that confidence, Freya thought fiercely, and she would do everything in her power to ensure that her child grew up with a sense of self-worth that she herself had been denied.

But now Zac had his own reasons for insisting on a paternity test. He was convinced that the results would absolve him of any responsibility for Aimee and she feared his reaction when he was finally forced to accept the truth.

After fifteen minutes, during which Zac barely contained his frustration as they crawled through the traffic, he pulled up outside the house where Freya occupied the top-floor flat and frowned at the peeling paintwork and general air of decay. 'You live here? *Mon Dieu*, I assume it's in better condition inside.'

'Don't bank on it,' she muttered, feeling a peculiar pain around her heart as she watched Aimee raise her arms for Zac to lift her out of her seat. The little girl was usually shy with strangers. Did she feel a subconscious bond with her father? Freya wondered as she led the way up the front path. Once inside she preceded him up the stairs, aware that his silence was growing more ominous by the minute.

'How were you planning to carry Aimee up and down four flights of stairs with your injured wrist?' he enquired when they finally reached her front door. 'What would you do if there was a fire? You'd never be able to evacuate quickly.'

'I'd manage somehow, just as I always have,' she replied stiffly, hovering in the narrow hallway in a vain attempt to block his way. She didn't want him here, intruding on her life, but he ignored her and stepped past her into the cramped bedsit.

The flat was a mess—it seemed a lifetime ago that she had flown out of the door to drop Aimee at the nursery and continue on to work. Yesterday's breakfast dishes were still piled up in the sink and the clothes-rack was festooned with a selection of her underwear. Zac was glancing around the room with a faint air of disbelief and she wished he would go away. She hated him seeing how she lived. 'It's not ideal, I admit,' she mumbled, 'but it's all I can afford.'

'I can't believe you're bringing a child up here,' Zac said grimly, genuinely shocked by the squalid flat. Freya had obviously done her best to make the place feel homely with brightly coloured cushions scattered on the sofa and Aimee's collection of teddies arranged on the dresser. But nothing could disguise the musty smell of damp plaster, and the bucket strategically placed to catch the rain leaking through the ceiling provided stark evidence that the old house was in a bad state of repair.

Her living conditions were none of his business, he reminded himself as he set Aimee down and she trotted over to her toy box. But now at least he could understand why she was so adamant that he was Aimee's father—perhaps she had genuinely deluded herself into believing it in the hope that he would provide for her child?

Freya shrugged listlessly. 'My living conditions have never bothered you before, Zac. Why the sudden concern?' she asked coolly. She shrugged out of her wet jacket and belatedly remembered that she'd been unable to put on her bra when she had struggled into her clothes at the hospital. Zac's eyes moved over her and to her horror she felt her breasts tighten.

The atmosphere in her tiny flat changed imperceptibly and she was aware of his sudden tension as she hastily folded her arms across her chest to hide the prominent peaks of her nipples. Now was not a good time to remember the connection they had once shared. She tore her gaze from the sensual curve of his mouth and tried to banish the memory of how it had felt when he had crushed her lips beneath his own.

'I meant what I said earlier—I'm not coming to Monaco with you,' she told him firmly, feeling more confident on her home territory. 'You can't make me, unless you intend to bind and gag me and bundle me onto your plane,' she added when he said nothing and simply stared at her as if he could read the thoughts whirling around in her head.

He seemed to dominate the small room and she swallowed when he strolled towards her. 'It's tempting,' he drawled, his blue eyes glinting dangerously. 'Don't goad me, *chérie*, or I might think you are trying to anger me on purpose.'

'Why would I do that?' Freya demanded, despising herself for the way her nerve endings sprang into urgent life at his closeness.

'We always had the most amazing sex after an argument,' he replied silkily, the sudden flare of amusement in his eyes warning her that he was aware of the effect he had on her. Freya blushed furiously and itched to slap him.

'I don't remember sex between us being anything more than mediocre,' she lied. 'Perhaps you're thinking of one of your other lovers Zac. You've had plenty, after all.'

She almost jumped out of her skin when his hand suddenly shot out and he caught hold of her chin, tilting her head so that she had no option but to meet his gaze. 'Nothing about our relationship in the bedroom was mediocre, *chérie*, and if we had more time I'd be tempted to prove that fact.' The flare of heat in his eyes scorched her skin and she focused helplessly on his mouth, her tongue darting out to trace the curve of her bottom lip in an unconscious invitation. The atmosphere was electric, she could almost feel the sparks shooting between them, but then he abruptly released her and moved away, his expression unfathomable.

'Be thankful that I am in a hurry to get back for a dinner date tonight,' he growled as he scooped her underwear from the clothes rack and dumped the pile of pretty lace knickers in her hands. 'And hurry up and pack or you'll find yourself travelling to Monaco *sans* your lingerie.'

Freya glared at him, her jaw aching with the effort of holding back her furious retort. He was so smug, and, as usual, so in control of the situation, nothing ever dented his supreme self-confidence. She hated him for every foul accusation he'd flung at her, every scathing insult that she was an unfaithful, gold-digging tramp. But even though he was looking at her as if she were something unpleasant that had crawled from beneath a stone, she could not deny the inexorable tug of desire that coiled low in her stomach.

It was devastating to realise that, despite everything he had done to her, she still wanted him. Where was her pride? she asked herself. Zac had used her body for sex and abused her fragile heart with his cruelty and contempt. But seeing him again had opened up the feelings she had tried so hard to suppress since he had ruthlessly dismissed her from his life.

She had never got over him, she acknowledged dismally. He had been the love of her life, but the molten heat surging through her veins was caused by lust, not love, she assured herself frantically. She'd learned the hard way never to waste her emotions on him because he had certainly never loved her and he never would.

The last thing she wanted to do was go to Monaco with him, but what choice did she have? she brooded as her gaze fell on her little daughter. As usual, Zac was right; she was never going to manage the stairs with Aimee and the push-chair while her wrist was so painful, and she had lain awake for most of the previous night worrying about how she would cope.

Her heart jolted in her chest as she accepted the unpalatable truth that she would have to go with him for now. She had no idea how long it would take for Zac to arrange a paternity test and await the results but it couldn't be more than a week or two, she consoled herself. And by then her wrist would be stronger and she would be able to return home.

She would go to Monaco, but this time she would be on her guard and would not give in to the undeniable sexual attraction that still smouldered between them, she vowed fiercely. She was no longer a naïve girl, she was an independent woman, and she would not be tempted by the sizzling sexual promise in Zac's bold gaze.

The bright lights of Monaco blazed against a backdrop of black velvet. As the helicopter swooped low over the coast-line Zac glanced over his shoulder. Aimee was fast asleep, sitting next to the nanny he had hired. 'We're almost there,' he murmured reassuringly to the uniformed woman. 'May I say how grateful I am that you were able to join us at such short notice, Mrs Lewis.'

Jean Lewis smiled. 'I'm glad to help. With any luck I'll be able to put Aimee straight to bed without waking her. She's worn out, poor poppet.'

With a brief nod, Zac turned back and glanced at Freya who was sitting stiffly beside him, the mutinous tilt of her chin causing him to curse irritably beneath his breath. If anyone had told him when he'd set out for Deverell's London offices that he would return to Monaco with his ex-mistress and her child in tow, he would have laughed out loud, he thought with a humourless smile.

His eyes trailed over her and he felt his body's involuntary reaction to the sight of her small breasts outlined beneath her blouse. Once again Freya had turned his life upside down. After their bitter parting two years ago, he had neither wanted nor expected to see her again, but, even knowing what she had done, he was finding it impossible to ignore her.

Freya felt Zac's eyes on her and stiffened when he shifted slightly in his seat so that his thigh brushed against hers. When they had left England aboard the private jet, he had sat at the front of the plane, his attention focused exclusively on his laptop. It had suited her fine—she had nothing to say to him that wouldn't blister his ears anyway—but when they'd arrived in Nice and boarded his helicopter for the short journey to Monaco, her heart had sunk when he had sat down next to her.

She had tried her best to ignore him but unfortunately her senses refused to fall into line and she was agonisingly aware of his closeness. The subtle tang of his cologne was tantalisingly familiar, causing her nerve endings to prickle.

She did *not* want to feel like this, she thought angrily as she edged away from him. It was humiliating to realise that he could still affect her so strongly, despite everything he had done to her. But it had always been the same; she had never been able to resist him and unfortunately just about every other woman on the planet shared her fascination.

The months she had spent with him had been the happiest but also the most nerve-racking of her life and her everpresent fear that he would tire of her had added to her deep insecurity.

Zac was one of Monaco's most eligible bachelors and at the many parties they had attended he had always been the centre of attention. Women had flocked around him and made their interest clear with a bold smile or knowing glance loaded with sensual invitation. He had responded to their blatant flirting with one of his cool, faintly sardonic smiles, and she'd felt reassured. But Annalise Dubois had been different.

The stunning glamour model had pursued Zac with relentless determination and had shamelessly flaunted her spectacular figure in clingy silks and satins that made the most of her eye-catching cleavage.

Beside her, Freya had felt pale and insipid and she hadn't been able to help but notice the way Zac's eyes had lingered appreciatively on the Frenchwoman's curves. Jealousy had been a green-eyed monster that festered in her soul, making her edgy and paranoid. She'd hated to be apart from him and had questioned his every move—every late night at the office or business trip that had taken him away for days at a time.

She'd known that her behaviour had angered him, but as he'd grown increasingly distant from her, so her terror had increased that he had been tiring of her. The only time she had felt secure was when they had been in bed. There at least his passion for her had shown no sign of diminishing, but he had shut her out of every other aspect of his life and she'd felt as though her only role had been to provide convenient sex on demand.

Choking back a cry, she dragged her mind from the past. She had spent the past two years determinedly trying to forget the life she'd shared with Zac and she must be mad to have agreed to return to Monaco with him.

'Do you still live at the penthouse?' she asked stiffly,

seizing on the faint hope that he had moved from the elegant, marble-floored apartment where she had once kidded herself that he might fall in love with her.

'*Oui*. The location suits me and I enjoy the view over the harbour,' he replied coolly.

Freya recalled the spectacular view from the penthouse over Monaco's busy port and the vast stretch of the Mediterranean beyond. 'Do you still keep *The Isis* moored there?'

Zac nodded. 'Unfortunately I don't get to spend as much time on her as I'd like. Deverell's is expanding and we're opening several outlets around the world, including the new store in Mayfair. If your grandmother had picked any other day, I would not have been in London,' he added tersely.

His frown told her that he was cursing his bad luck to have been in London on the same day that Joyce Addison had arrived with Aimee, but Freya shuddered to think what would have happened if he hadn't been there.

'I'm glad Nana Joyce found you,' she admitted quietly, forgetting for a moment that they were enemies. 'I don't know what would have happened to Aimee otherwise.'

'Your grandmother would have cared for her, surely?'

Freya's face twisted. 'I don't know. When she found out that I was going to be an unmarried mother, she was adamant that she would have nothing to do with me or my baby. She bitterly resented having to bring me up and when I was a child I lived with foster parents for a while,' she confided dully. 'My mother had married and was moving to South Africa and my grandmother assumed she would take me with her. They had a furious argument when it turned out that I wasn't included in Sadie's new life.'

Zac's mouth tightened and he was aware of a faint tug of

compassion. No wonder Freya's self-esteem was non-existent when she had been so cruelly rejected by her own mother. 'Is that when you were put into care?'

Freya nodded. 'I think my grandmother believed that once social services were involved, Sadie would finally take responsibility for me—but instead she flew out to Durban without even saying goodbye.' Now that she was a mother herself she found it impossible to understand how her own mother had been able to abandon her so easily. It was obvious that Sadie had never loved her, she acknowledged bleakly, but even after all this time, it still hurt.

'After about six months I went back to live with my grandmother...but I was always afraid that she would send me away again and I tried my hardest not to annoy her.' She thought of the years she'd spent skirting around her grandmother like a timid mouse, desperate not to bring attention to herself and pathetically grateful that Nana Joyce allowed her to live with her. It had been a dismal childhood and she was determined that her daughter would never feel so worthless or unloved.

She jerked her head round and stared at Zac. 'I love Aimee more than anything and I won't allow anyone to hurt her. I agree we should do a paternity test—it's time to set the record straight. I just hope you're prepared for the result.'

The fierceness of her tone shook Zac more than he cared to admit, but he immediately dismissed his doubts. She was bluffing, he reassured himself; or else her desperate financial situation had deluded her into believing he was Aimee's father. Either way, he was not going to be drawn into believing her lies.

'I'm prepared for the test results to confirm that you're a common tramp,' he said aggressively. 'Finally you'll have to accept the truth and move on with your life, as I intend to move on with mine.' And ignoring her furious gasp, he turned his head and stared into the dark for the remainder of the flight.

CHAPTER THREE

TEN minutes later the helicopter landed on the roof of the penthouse and Zac lifted Aimee into his arms and preceded Jean Lewis down the steps. 'Laurent, were you able to carry out my instructions?' he greeted his butler.

'Everything is as you asked, sir,' the butler replied in his usual unflappable manner. 'The nursery suppliers delivered a cot and other necessary furnishings and equipment, and the dressing room adjoining the fourth bedroom has been prepared for the child's nanny.' If Laurent was surprised by the request to prepare a room for a baby, his tone gave nothing away and his facial expression remained as bland as ever.

'*Bon,*' Zac murmured as he transferred the sleeping child back into the nanny's arms. 'Please escort Madame Lewis to the nursery and ensure she has everything she requires.'

He swung round and walked back to the helicopter just as Freya reached the bottom step. She looked pale and tired and was clearly in pain but she glared at him when he reached her side.

'There was no need for you to hire a nanny. I can look after Aimee perfectly well.'

'How exactly when you only have the use of one arm?'

he asked impatiently. 'Jean Lewis has excellent references and she'll take good care of Aimee.'

'Where has she taken her?' Freya demanded. Her whole arm was throbbing and she felt light-headed with pain but she refused to admit it to Zac—any more than she would admit to feeling jealous that Aimee had settled so happily with Jean Lewis. Her steps slowed and a feeling of panic swept over her as she followed him into the penthouse. She didn't want to be here and she didn't want to remember the past, but memories were bombarding her.

Zac travelled by helicopter as routinely as most people used a car and had regularly swept her off to parties and other glittering social functions outside Monaco, often flying along the coast to Cannes or St Tropez. The parties had always been wonderful, glamorous affairs, but Freya had only had eyes for him and even in a crowded room his slumberous stare had tormented her with the unspoken promise of sensual nirvana to follow. The hours until they could make their excuses and leave had been a slow torture and her anticipation had always been at fever pitch by the time they had climbed back on board the helicopter for the return flight.

There had been something incredibly magical about swooping low over the sea and the towering apartment blocks that lined Monaco's crowded coastline, knowing that in a few short minutes they would be home. The sensual gleam beneath Zac's heavy lids would stoke her excitement and as soon as the rotors came to a halt he would scoop her into his arms and race into the penthouse, stripping her with brisk efficiency along the way.

Sometimes they hadn't even made it to the master bedroom, she remembered as heat suffused her body. In his urgency to make love to her he had deposited her on one of the sitting room sofas, and the feel of the cool leather against her skin had added a new dimension to her pleasure when he had pushed her thighs apart and entered her with one powerful thrust. Their hunger for each other had been insatiable, a wild, primitive passion that had known no bounds as he had dispensed with her inhibitions and made love to her with an inventiveness that still brought a tide of colour to her cheeks.

Heart pounding, she forced her mind back to the present and stumbled along the hall after him. Oh, God, what was she thinking? And why had her libido chosen now to make a comeback when she had spent the last two years living like a nun?

Zac opened the door of the guest bedroom and ushered Freya inside. 'Jean has taken Aimee to the nursery,' he explained, his eyes narrowing speculatively on her hot face.

'Nursery?' Her eyebrows shot up as she frantically dragged her mind from her erotic fantasies and forced herself to concentrate on his words. She remembered Zac's chic, minimalist apartment as a confirmed bachelor pad—when on earth had he installed a nursery?

'I instructed my staff to prepare a room for Aimee since you will both be staying here for the time being. I hope it will be suitable,' he added coldly.

'I'm sure it'll be more suitable than a damp bedsit. I hope you haven't gone to too much bother, Zac—Aimee and I won't be here long,' Freya muttered, unable to disguise the sudden bitterness in her voice as she remembered how she had struggled to afford even the most basic baby equipment. With a click of his fingers Zac could provide everything Aimee needed—it was a pity he was two years too late.

His mouth tightened but he simply said, 'Laurent will

serve supper in your room and then I suggest you take your painkillers and go to bed. You look like death.'

Terrific, she really needed reminding that she looked a mess, Freya thought grimly, especially when *he* looked so gorgeous. He had removed his leather jacket and she could not help but notice the way his black sweater moulded his muscular chest. He was lean, dark and so beautiful that it hurt her to look at him, she acknowledged as desire swept through her. Zac possessed a raw sexual magnetism, and, although her mind urged caution, her body was responding to him with a reckless disregard for her emotional safety.

She was trembling; not as a result of the cool night air, she realised shamefully, but with an almost desperate longing to slide her fingers beneath his fine-knit sweater and run her hands over his olive-gold skin to feel the faint abrasion of the wiry hairs that covered his chest. The images from the past were stubbornly refusing to disappear and she felt thoroughly hot and bothered as sexual frustration spiralled in the pit of her stomach. Swallowing hard, she tore her eyes from him and stared at the carpet. 'I forgot my toothbrush. You didn't give me enough time to pack properly.'

'All the toiletries you could possibly need are in your bathroom,' Zac informed her, 'and the clothes you left behind two years ago are still in the wardrobe.'

'Really?' The surprising statement brought her head up. 'I thought you would have wasted no time getting rid of them,' she mumbled, remembering how humiliated she had felt when he'd hustled her out of the apartment. Her face burned at the memory but he merely shrugged disinterestedly.

'I didn't keep them because I was anticipating ever taking

you back, *chérie*, if that's what you're thinking,' he drawled laconically. 'I'd forgotten they were there, until the maid found them in the back of the cupboard when she was preparing your room.' He glanced at his watch and strode towards the door. 'I'm going out for the evening. Can you manage to get undressed, or do you need me to help you?'

Freya flashed him a look that told him she'd rather accept help from a self-confessed axe murderer. 'I'll be fine, thanks,' she replied in a cool voice that masked the sharp pang of dismay she felt as she wondered whom he was meeting for his dinner date. Undoubtedly the woman would be stunning and sophisticated—his current mistress? Or someone picked from his little black book? she mused sourly as she fought her irrational surge of jealousy. It was no business of hers whom he dated, she reminded herself, but the devil in her head was determined to have the last word. 'Oh, and, Zac,' she murmured as he strolled towards the door, 'I'm glad you hadn't planned on resuming our relationship because I wouldn't come back to you if you paid me a million pounds.'

His eyes narrowed on her angry face and then dropped lower, to the frantic rise and fall of her breasts. 'You're here now,' he reminded her silkily.

'Only because you forced me to come—I don't want to be here.'

'*Non, chérie,* I can see that.' The mockery in his voice taunted her long after he had stepped into the hall and closed her door, and with a yelp of impotent fury Freya spun round and stared at her reflection in the full length mirror. No wonder Zac had looked so smug, she thought dismally as she stared at her flushed face. Her pupils had dilated to the size of saucers and her lips were parted, practically begging for him to kiss her, while the hard peaks of her nipples pushing provocatively against her blouse were shameful evidence that he turned her on. Her body had turned traitor from the moment Zac had arrived at the hospital, and to make her humiliation complete it was clear that he was well aware of the effect he had on her.

Uttering a furious oath at her stupidity, she went to check on Aimee, who was sleeping soundly in one of the guest bedrooms that had now been transformed into a nursery. A temporary nursery, Freya decided firmly. Zac was going to get the shock of his life when he learned that he was Aimee's father, but she was under no illusion that he would welcome the news and she intended to return to England as soon as possible, before Aimee ever realised that he did not love her.

She didn't know what Zac would do after the test result, but she wasn't holding her breath that he would apologise for misjudging her so terribly. At best she guessed he would offer some sort of financial support for his daughter, but she would put the money in trust for when Aimee was older. She did not want a penny of his fortune for herself and once she was over the temporary setback of her injured wrist, which had partly forced her to come to Monaco with him, she hoped she would never have to set eyes on him again.

Soon after she had returned to her room the butler Laurent arrived bearing a light, fluffy omelette for her supper. He was unfailingly polite but gave no indication that he remembered her from when she had lived briefly at the penthouse. Presumably her role as Zac's mistress had been quickly filled, probably by Annalise Dubois, she brooded miserably. Was Zac with Annalise tonight? The thought was enough to ruin her appetite and she toyed with her food before heading for the bathroom where she struggled to shower while keeping her bandaged arm out of the spray. By the time she had finished she felt sick from the pain of her injured wrist and after swallowing a couple of painkillers she crawled into bed, desperate for sleep to swallow her in its comforting folds.

Zac swung his powerful sports car into the underground car park and rode the lift up to the penthouse apartment. Dinner had been an unmitigated disaster, he brooded darkly as he unfastened his tie and shoved it in the pocket of his dinner jacket. Not that it had been Nicole's fault. She had looked stunning tonight and her low-cut dress with its thigh-high split down one side had left little to his imagination.

Throughout the meal in one of Monte Carlo's finest restaurants, she had been on sparkling form and had prattled on endlessly about her life, which seemed to consist of shopping or sunbathing on Daddy's yacht, and in the rare lulls in her conversation her smile had sent the subtle signals indicating her willingness to spend the night with him.

It had been their third date, after all, he mused cynically, and the unspoken rules of the game they were both playing dictated that tonight the attractive brunette had expected their relationship to progress to a full-blown sexual affair. But somewhere between the *entrée* and dessert he had lost his appetite for both the food and his companion, and instead of envisaging Nicole's tanned, lissom limbs his mind had seemed intent on recalling every detail of Freya's slender figure.

He had never known another woman to have such pale skin. It was as if even the sun's rays had not been permitted to touch her and his hands had been the first to stroke her virginal flesh—as they had, he acknowledged, feeling an uncomfortable tightness in his groin. He had been Freya's first lover and, if he was honest, sex with her had been an amazing experience he had never come close to repeating with any other woman.

And he had tried. He'd never professed to be a monk, he conceded sardonically, but sitting in the restaurant with Nicole tonight he'd realised that he did not feel the slightest desire for her and after driving her home he had politely refused her offer of a nightcap. Clearly disappointed, Nicole had eventually accepted his rejection, but he didn't feel good about it—in fact he felt intensely irritated with himself, life in general, and, at the top of the list, the woman who had managed to disrupt his comfortable existence in less than twenty-four hours.

With a muttered oath he strode into the penthouse and headed for the lounge and the well-stocked bar, but the sight of Freya curled up on the sofa caused him to halt abruptly. The low coffee table in front of her was littered with books and papers and she was leafing through the pages of a thick folder, so engrossed that she seemed to be unaware of him.

For a few seconds Zac stood still and allowed his eyes to roam over her mass of blonde hair and perfectly defined heart-shaped face. Her grey silk robe was vaguely familiar from the past and he frowned as he focused on the way the edges had parted to reveal the wisp of silk and lace beneath.

Every item of clothing he had bought for her when she'd lived with him had been chosen with the express purpose of pleasing him, particularly her nightwear, and his mouth tightened cynically as he wondered whether she had changed into the sexy negligee set deliberately to taunt him. Freya was still absorbed in her books and his irritation upped a notch. Being ignored was a new experience for him and, giving an angry shrug of his shoulders, he stepped into the room.

Only then did she glance up. 'Zac…' She blinked at him and fire surged through his veins when he took in the image of her silky blonde hair framing her flushed face. Her skin was bare of make-up, but somehow that made her sexier, he decided as he studied her closely, noting the dusting of freckles on her nose and the fact that her long eyelashes were tipped with gold. She was staring up at him with her wide witch's eyes, casting her magic, and with a jolt he realised that he suddenly felt more alive than he had done in months.

'I wasn't expecting you to wait up for me, *chérie*,' he drawled as he crossed to the bar and poured himself a large cognac.

'Don't worry, I wasn't,' she replied shortly. 'I didn't even know you would come back tonight.' She'd lain in bed torturing herself with images of him making love to the woman he had taken to dinner, until she'd given up hoping she'd fall asleep and had dug out her college books.

Now she stumbled to her feet and clutched the front of her robe that seemed intent on parting to reveal the skimpy excuse for a nightgown underneath. In the rush to pack for the trip to Monaco, she had forgotten several essential items, including the oversized, comfortable tee shirts she usually wore in bed. The nightwear she had left behind at the penthouse had been chosen for seduction rather than sleep, and she blushed when Zac raked his eyes over her in open appreciation.

'Now that you are here, it's time I left,' she mumbled, hastily gathering up her books. In her desperation to escape him, she dropped her folder and papers flew everywhere. 'I couldn't sleep, so I thought I'd catch up on some work,' she babbled when Zac leaned down to gather up the pages and his hand briefly brushed against hers.

'What kind of work?' he asked curiously. He handed her the sheaf of papers and frowned when she quickly snatched her hand away. 'You don't have to run away from me, Freya. We may have been forced together under difficult circumstances but I'm sure we're both adult enough to manage a civil conversation.' He straightened up. 'Can I get you a drink?'

For a moment Freya was tempted to flee, unconvinced that she could manage any kind of conversation with him. It wasn't as if she'd had much practice, she thought wryly. Her time as Zac's mistress had been spent mainly in the bedroom and they hadn't wasted time on idle chit chat.

But the sight of him had inflamed her senses and sleep seemed as impossible now as it had two hours ago. Perhaps a drink would help her to relax? 'White wine, please—a small glass.' She hovered awkwardly while Zac poured her drink and mumbled her thanks when he handed her the glass, his terse, 'Sit down,' causing her to sink back into her seat. He sprawled on the opposite sofa, his white silk shirt open at the throat and his ankle balanced across his thigh in a position of indolent ease—lithe, tanned and so stomach-churningly sexy that Freya hastily tore her eyes from him and took a large gulp of wine.

'What job do you do that requires you to sit up working until midnight?' he asked again, his brow furrowing. He was regularly at his desk until the early hours, but he was the chief executive of a global business empire and a self-confessed workaholic.

'It's not my job exactly—I'm doing a home study course for an English degree,' Freya told him. 'One day I hope to train to be a teacher so that my career will fit around Aimee's schooling, but obviously I need to work and can't afford to go to college full-time. The only free time I have to study is at night, when she's in bed.' She didn't add that after a long day at work and the responsibilities of being a single mother, she often had to force herself to pull out her books, which was why she had fallen behind with the work and had several assignment deadlines looming.

Zac hid his flare of surprise. During the months that Freya had lived with him, he had never really got to know her. His workload had been particularly heavy and after a long day at the office he had simply wanted to take her to bed. He had asked about her day out of politeness rather than any real interest and had thanked his lucky stars that she wasn't one of those women who insisted on regaling him with every detail of her life.

He had found her quiet, gentle nature soothing, and, if he was honest, he had missed the calming effect she seemed to have on him after he had thrown her out. But now he realised that he knew very little about her. Perhaps it was her faint air of mystery that intrigued him, he debated as he drained his glass and stretched his arms along the back of the sofa, his eyes skimming over her and lingering on the fall of her silky hair. 'It's obvious from the state of your flat that you're struggling financially. Why don't you receive any support from Brooks?' he demanded curtly. 'Are you no longer in contact with him?'

The wine had been a bad idea, Freya decided as she carefully set her glass down on the coffee-table. It seemed to have gone straight to her head and loosened the constraints that held her anger in check. 'As a matter of fact I do see Simon occasionally,' she said with deliberate calm. 'We've remained friends, despite the fact that he now lives in Italy. I'm sure he would help me out if I asked him, but Aimee isn't his child and there's no reason for him to support her. That responsibility lies with her father, wouldn't you say?' She glared at him across the coffee-table, twin spots of colour flaring on her cheeks, but Zac held her gaze, his bland expression giving no clue to his thoughts.

'Absolutely—and I hope you find him, *chérie*,' he murmured. He raised his glass. 'What shall we drink to— absent fathers?' Beneath the mockery Freya caught the anger in his voice and indignation surged through her. What right did he have to be angry? She was the one who struggled to combine being a single mother with the necessity to work and pay the bills. He lived here in his penthouse apartment enjoying a life of unimaginable luxury, with no understanding of the real world or how many times she had felt overwhelmed by her responsibilities.

But voicing her resentment would get her nowhere. Zac was convinced that Aimee wasn't his child and, in fairness, she could understand why. But the very fact that he'd had a vasectomy meant that he did not want to be a father and his present anger was going to be nothing compared with his fury when he learned the truth.

'I guess we'll just have to wait for the results of the paternity test,' she muttered as she got to her feet. Suddenly she was bone-weary and could scarcely believe it had only been twelve hours ago that Zac had stormed into the hospital and back into her life. Returning to the penthouse and reliving the memories of the life she had shared with him was more agonising than she had anticipated and she felt the sting of tears behind her eyelids. 'I wish I hadn't come here,' she flung at him angrily. 'Aimee and I could have stayed in a hotel instead of being here with you and your horrible, suspicious mind.'

Black brows winged upwards at her outburst. 'I've already explained that I'd like the reason for your visit to Monaco to remain a private affair and I prefer to keep you here under my control. I've arranged for a nurse from the clinic to visit tomorrow to take the necessary mouth swabs,' he informed her coolly. He drained his glass and stood up, instantly dwarfing her. He was too much for her to cope with when her emotions were so precariously balanced, but when she moved to step past him, he blocked her path. 'The results should be back within ten days, and then you'll be free to leave. Until then I'm afraid we're stuck with each other. But it's possible we'll find some compensation in being forced to spend time in each other's company.'

Freya gave a disbelieving laugh. 'Such as?'

Too late she recognised the gleam in his eyes and her heart lurched as his arm shot out and snaked around her waist.

'Such as this,' he said, ignoring her punitive struggles to escape from his grip as he lowered his mouth with slow deliberation until it hovered millimetres above hers. 'You may dislike me almost as much as I dislike you, but unfortunately sexual desire seems to have no respect for our mutual loathing—does it, Freya?'

Before she could formulate a reply, he closed the gap between their mouths and kissed her, his lips moving over hers in a fierce assault that demanded her response. The mockery of his last statement rang in her ears and she pressed her lips together in a desperate attempt to deny him. How could he kiss her like this if he hated her? her brain asked numbly, but it was clear that her body did not care. It had been so long since she had been in his arms and she had missed him so much.

Weakly she tried to push against his chest but her senses flared at the scent of his cologne and the male heat emanating from him and slowly her fingers uncurled and crept up to his shoulders. His tongue probed relentlessly against her mouth until, with a little gasp, she parted her lips and he instantly thrust between them while his hand tangled in her hair and he angled her head to his satisfaction.

'Zac...' he dealt with her mumbled protest with swift efficiency, deepening the kiss until it was flagrantly possessive, his lips branding her tender flesh as his hunger escalated and he sought her total capitulation. Only when he felt her tentative response, felt the soft stroke of her tongue inside his mouth, did he ease the pressure a little as he explored her with an erotic intent that left her trembling and breathless, and with a moan of despair Freya curled her hands around his neck and clung to him shamelessly.

A quiver ran through her when she felt his hand slide up and down her body, curve possessively around her buttocks and then move up to her waist. With a deft movement he loosened the belt of her robe and pushed the material aside to reveal the wisp of lace beneath that did little to hide her breasts from his hungry gaze. His eyes darkened and with slow deliberation he pushed the strap of her nightdress over her shoulder, lower and lower until one breast was completely bared.

'No...' she whispered frantically, knowing that she should stop him but desperate to feel his hands on her sensitive flesh. She'd been starved of him for so long and she whimpered when he cupped the soft mound with his lean brown fingers and flicked his thumb pad back and forth over the taut peak of her nipple. Liquid heat coursed through her and she moaned softly and leaned into him, but he tensed and abruptly lifted his head.

'You were always completely uninhibited in the bedroom,' he stated harshly, staring down at her with undisguised contempt in his eyes. 'Don't look at me with those doe eyes and tell me you don't want to be here because I know perfectly well what you want, *chérie*, and I think I've demonstrated rather conclusively that I can provide it.'

The note of self-disgust in his voice destroyed Freya even more than his deliberate cruelty. Clearly Zac had been surprised by his desire for her and shocked by the level of his need, but he *despised* himself for it almost as much as he despised her. When he released her she swayed unsteadily and for one horrific moment she actually thought she was going to be sick.

'There's little point in denying that you can still push all the right buttons,' she said bitterly, colour storming into her pale cheeks when she remembered her wanton response to him. 'But it's just lust, Zac. I'm a normal woman and I have the usual needs, which I have no intention of indulging,' she added on a note of fierce pride. 'Don't get it into your head that it's anything more than that. You don't mean anything to me.'

She left her books on the table and flew across to the door, desperate to reach the relative sanctuary of her room, but his confident drawl followed her.

'I'm glad to hear it, *chérie*, because when I choose to take you to bed it will be on the strict understanding that your body is the only thing I desire—your conniving little mind I can do without. *Bonne nuit*,' he murmured silkily when she gave an audible gasp of fury. 'I hope you sleep well, Freya, and don't have *too* restless a night.'

It was his superior smile that did it. Freya's anger burst the tight bands of her self-control and with a choked cry she snatched up a small glass ornament from the bureau and flung it at him. He fielded it expertly—of course, she thought bleakly as she fled along the hall to her room. Was there nothing that Zac didn't excel in? Or had he had plenty of practice in avoiding missiles that irate ex-lovers hurled at his head? It was not a comforting thought and burning up with mortification, she flung herself into bed, drew the covers over her head and wished she could dismiss the sound of his cruel laughter from her ears.

CHAPTER FOUR

FREYA was running down the hall of the penthouse with Aimee in her arms, searching for Zac. She could hear his voice ahead of her but the passageway seemed to go on for ever and he remained a distant figure who taunted her desperate attempts to catch up with him. Tears filled her eyes as she struggled on. Aimee was heavy and her wrist was agony, but it was nothing compared to the pain in her heart as she faced the knowledge that she would never reach Zac and she would always be alone...

'Freya—wake up.'

A familiar, terse voice sounded loud in her ear and when she opened her eyes she discovered that she was not in the hall, but her bedroom, and Zac was standing close to her bed regarding her with undisguised impatience.

'You were dreaming,' he told her when she stared up at him warily, her eyes huge and shadowed, unwittingly revealing a degree of vulnerability that caused Zac's frown to deepen. 'I suppose you're bound to suffer flashbacks from the accident.' He glanced at his watch and his mouth tightened. He had waited for Freya to wake up and was already behind schedule, but she looked achingly fragile this morning and he was irritated by his concern. 'Do you want to talk about it?' he queried, stifling his impatience when she simply stared at him in bemusement.

The strap of her nightdress had slipped off her shoulder and he recalled with stark clarity the way he had pushed it even lower last night, to leave her pale breast exposed. The sight of her dusky pink nipple had filled him with an uncontrollable longing to bend his head and take the hard peak in his mouth, suckle her until she whimpered with pleasure, and it had taken every vestige of his will-power to stop himself from pushing her back onto the sofa and covering her body with his own. The memory was enough to make him harden until he was sure she must see the embarrassing proof of his arousal, and, inhaling sharply, he took a jerky step back from the bed.

'Talk about what?' Freya asked him in genuine confusion. Her brain seemed to be made of cotton wool this morning and her thought process wasn't aided by the sight of Zac in a superbly tailored grey suit that emphasised the width of his broad shoulders. He looked urbane and sophisticated, every inch the billionaire businessman, and she was horribly aware of her dishevelled appearance. She adjusted the strap of her nightdress, her cheeks flaming when she caught the amused gleam in his eyes. She'd hoped that last night had all been part of her nightmare, but the tenderness of her swollen lips was proof that he had kissed her and she had responded with an enthusiasm that now made her shudder.

'The accident,' he snapped, forcing her to concentrate on him. 'You were crying in your sleep and it was obviously a terrifying experience. I've heard that it helps to talk,' he added stiffly, shrugging his shoulders in a gesture that indicated he had never been afraid in his life, let alone felt the need to confide his private emotions. Zac didn't suffer from the same human frailties as normal people, Freya thought bleakly. He spent most of his waking hours at work and regarded sex as a recreational activity that occupied his nights until he could return to his office the following day.

'I'm fine, thanks,' she murmured as she dragged her gaze from him and stared down at the bedcovers. She wondered what he would say if she revealed that she had been dreaming about him, not the accident, and that he had been the cause of her tears. He would be out of her room like a rabbit out of a trap, she thought grimly. Two years ago he had made it plain that he only wanted a physical relationship with her and, if she was ever insane enough to respond to the unspoken invitation in his eyes, she would have to remember that the rules hadn't changed.

But she would not respond to him ever again, she told herself firmly, tensing when he moved closer to the bed. His eyes glittered with the flames of desire and for one terrifying moment she thought he was going to reach out and touch her, but instead he dropped a piece of paper into her lap.

'The nurse is here to perform the mouth swabs, but I require your signature before she can take a sample from Aimee,' he said bluntly. He moved away from the bed and stood with his back to her, staring out of the window while she quickly scanned the document. It seemed straightforward, but her heart was pounding as she added her signature. Now there was no going back. In ten days' time Zac would learn the truth, but how would he react when he was forced to accept that Aimee was his child?

She glanced at Zac's stern profile and bit her lip as she felt herself softening a little. He was a proud man and he was going to hate learning that he had been wrong about her.

He must have felt her silent scrutiny and swung round to

face her, his eyes narrowing. 'Having second thoughts, Freya? I thought you might when you were faced with the reality of the paternity test,' he said coolly. 'But I want this test and if you refuse to give your permission, I'll go through the courts to get it. At the moment you're a loose cannon from my past, but once I have incontrovertible proof that you are a liar I'll take out a legal injunction if necessary to prevent you from ever approaching me or repeating your fantastic claims.'

Freya waved her signature at him furiously as the soft feeling vanished and was instantly replaced by a strong desire to commit murder—his. 'Far from having second thoughts, I was wishing I'd demanded a test as soon as Aimee was born,' she retorted. 'You've vilified and insulted me once too often, Zac, and the only thing that prevents me from slapping that smug expression from your face is the knowledge that the day will soon come when you'll fall from your lofty pedestal and have to acknowledge that you're a mere mortal like the rest of us—not the superior being you think you are.'

The glinting fury in his eyes warned her that she had pushed him too far, and she shrank back against the pillows when he snatched the consent form from her fingers and leaned over her, his hands on either side of her head. 'It appears that my meek little English mouse has developed a sharp tongue. Be careful it doesn't get you into trouble, *chérie*,' he warned dangerously as he lowered his head and captured her mouth in a stinging kiss that forced her head back. He took without mercy, dominating her with insulting ease and demanding that she part her lips for him so that he could slide his tongue deep into her mouth to continue his sensual punishment.

Freya's muscles locked and her mind screamed at her to

reject him, but her body had a will of its own and she could feel its traitorous response as molten heat surged through her veins. Torn between hunger and humiliation, she groaned and he captured her despairing cry, grinding his lips on hers to prevent its escape. When he finally lifted his head she was beyond words and closed her eyes against the contempt she was sure she would see in his. She heard him swear savagely beneath his breath and tensed, waiting for the taunts that would surely follow, but there was nothing and at the slam of the bedroom door she lifted her lashes to find that he had gone.

Zac's visit had left Freya physically and emotionally drained and she lay back on the pillows, telling herself that she would get up in five minutes and go and check on Aimee. When she next woke up, sunshine was streaming into her room and she stared at the clock, horrified to see that it was mid-morning. How could she have slept for so long and not paid a single thought to her daughter? she berated herself angrily, but as she was about to get up she heard the sound of Aimee's high-pitched laughter and a moment later the nanny Zac had employed put her head round the door.

'Oh, you're awake. I've someone here who wants to see you,' Jean Lewis announced cheerfully as she opened the door wider and Aimee trotted into the room.

'Mrs Lewis, I'm so sorry, I never meant to sleep for so long,' Freya said quickly. She couldn't imagine what the nanny must think of her, but the older woman smiled reassuringly.

'It's Jean,' she said firmly, 'and of course you must sleep. Mr Deverell explained about your accident—it must have been a dreadful experience and, apart from your injuries, you're probably still in shock. Aimee's such a happy little girl and luckily she took to me straight away. I promise you, I'll take care of her as if she were my own,' she assured Freya with a friendly smile. 'If I were you, I'd spend the rest of the day in bed and I'll arrange for your meals to be brought to you.'

Freya didn't have the strength to argue. It felt strange to be mothered after the years of indifference from her grandmother, she mused after she had played with Aimee for a while before Jean Lewis had taken the little girl off to explore the roof-garden. She had warmed to Jean's kindness instantly and for the first time since Aimee's birth she felt she could relax and trust that her baby would be well cared for.

Over the next two days she began to appreciate Jean's advice. The accident had taken its toll and she was shocked at how tired and emotional she felt. The sound of laughter from the nursery indicated that Aimee was perfectly happy with the nanny, and it made a welcome change to have a temporary reprieve from her responsibilities.

To her relief she saw little of Zac. He had left for his office before she woke in the mornings and did not return until late in the evening. Some things hadn't changed, she mused wryly as she recalled the long, lonely days she had spent when she had lived with him, waiting for him to return from his office or one of his frequent business trips.

A few times he had taken her abroad with him. Deverell's owned stores in several European cities as well as New York, Rio de Janeiro and Dubai, but although the scenery was different her life had followed a similar pattern that had revolved around Zac and his hectic schedule.

She had been nothing more than a sex slave, she thought dismally, but innate honesty forced her to admit that she had taken on the role willingly. Zac had been like an addiction and at the time she had believed that she loved him. But had she confused love with lust? He had let her down so badly she could not possibly still be in love with him now, she reassured herself. The feelings he stirred in her were purely sexual. Although she hated herself, she wanted him with the same urgency that had consumed her when she had been his mistress. But she no longer believed in fairy tales, she would not mistake her physical awareness of him for a deeper emotion, and she certainly would not give in to this feverish need to allow him to make love to her.

Buoyed up by her newfound confidence that she could deal with Zac Deverell and his magnetic charm, Freya wandered through the lounge and out onto the wide balcony. Monaco was truly a billionaire's paradise, she mused as she stared down at the rows of luxury yachts and motor cruisers moored in the harbour. Zac enjoyed a glamorous lifestyle exclusive to the super-rich, but she had never felt comfortable with his wealth or fitted in with his friends.

In her heart she had always known that he was not the kind of man who would settle for a life of domestic bliss. Zac was an adventurer who lived life close to the edge with his love of extreme sports like sky-diving or power-boat racing. He got a buzz from pushing himself to the limits and playing happy families wasn't part of his game plan, as his rejection of her and their baby had demonstrated. In a few days he would learn that Aimee was his daughter, but she doubted he would sacrifice any part of his life for a child he didn't want.

With a heavy sigh she lifted her face to the sky and closed her eyes as the late-afternoon sunshine warmed her skin. After weeks of rain back in England, it felt wonderful, but her relaxed mood was shattered by a familiar voice from behind her.

'There you are. I've been looking everywhere for you,' Zac said, unable to disguise his impatience that she hadn't been instantly at his beck and call. 'I see you're keeping busy.'

Freya's eyes flew open and she glared at him indignantly. 'Aimee's having a nap and I had nothing to do for five minutes. You insisted that I should stay here,' she continued crossly when he said nothing. 'It's not my fault that there's nothing for me to do.' Her words were an eerie echo of the rows they used to have in the past, brought on by her loneliness and boredom and his refusal to cut down on his work schedule to spend time with her. Back then their arguments had ended with him sweeping her off to the bedroom to make love to her—and her capitulating at the first touch of his hands on her body, Freya thought grimly. But then she had given in too easily and now things were very different.

'Laurent informs me that you seem better today,' Zac murmured as his eyes skimmed over her in blatant appreciation of her tight-fitting jeans and tee shirt. 'You certainly look good, *chérie*, although I can see that your injured wrist still prevents you from putting on your underwear,' he added silkily.

Blushing furiously, Freya followed his gaze to the firm line of her breasts revealed beneath her thin cotton shirt and felt a tingling sensation as her nipples peaked provocatively beneath his stare. Electricity zinged between them and, despite the warmth of the sun, she shivered as each of her nerve endings flared into urgent life. With an angry murmur she swung away from him and stared out at the endless expanse of cobalt-blue sea.

'I am feeling better, and my wrist is already less painful—

so much so that there's really no reason for me to stay here any longer. I've decided to take Aimee back to England while we wait for the test results,' she said.

'I'm afraid I can't allow that,' Zac said pleasantly, but she caught the underlying note of steel in his voice and her temper flared.

'*Can't allow it?* Who do you think you are, Zac? I'm not your prisoner.'

'Certainly not.' He sounded insulted at the idea. 'You are my guest, although I admit that I took the liberty of locking your and Aimee's passports in my desk—in case you should lose them,' he added when she looked as though she were going to explode.

The breeze lifted her hair and blew the soft strands across his face, leaving behind the faint scent of lemons. Desire coiled low in his gut, but he resisted the urge to slide his fingers into her hair and carefully moved away from her. 'It suits me to keep you here until I have the results of the test,' he continued harshly, 'and then I shall personally escort you out of Monaco and out of my life, *chérie*. Until then I have a job for you, which should keep you occupied for a few hours at least.'

'You know what you can do with your damn job,' Freya choked, desperate to hide her devastation that he still had the ability to hurt her. Angry tears stung her eyes and she dashed them away with the back of her hand before swinging round to face him. 'You may have forced me to stay here, but you can't make me spend my time with you, let alone work for you.'

His mocking smile sent a frisson of alarm down her spine and she stepped back until she was jammed up against the balcony railings when he walked purposefully towards her.

'You should know by now that I can do whatever I like,' he said with breathtaking arrogance. 'And I'm not setting you to work down a salt mine. I'm having dinner tonight with an American businessman, Chester Warren, and his wife, followed by an evening at the Opera House to watch a performance by the Monte Carlo Ballet Company. My PA was supposed to be accompanying me but she's unwell. Francine is pregnant,' he told her with a grimace, 'and it seems that she suffers from morning sickness in the evenings.'

'Poor thing.' Freya nodded, forgetting her anger for a moment as she sympathised with Zac's PA. 'I was sick morning, noon and night for weeks when I was pregnant with Aimee.' She tailed to a halt beneath Zac's hard stare and a surge of bitterness flooded through her. Those first weeks after she had returned to England, pregnant, penniless and alone, had been the worst of her life as she had struggled with constant nausea and faced up to her future as a single mother. She had missed Zac desperately and begun every day hoping that he would realise he had made a mistake, and every night crying herself to sleep because he hadn't come for her. How dared he look at her with that faintly bored expression that told her he was completely disinterested in reminiscences about her pregnancy, when she had been carrying *his* child! 'I still don't understand what your PA's problems have to do with me,' she muttered stiffly.

'I need someone to take Francine's place tonight—you,' he confirmed, when she glared at him suspiciously. 'It will actually work out very well. Chester's wife Carolyn is English and I'm sure you'll be able to keep her entertained while Chester and I discuss business.'

'But…what do you expect me to talk to her about?' Freya asked, unable to hide the faint panic in her voice. She had never been good at small talk and trying to make conversation with people she'd never met before had been one of the things she'd hated when she had lived with Zac.

He shrugged his shoulders impatiently. 'I don't know. I'm sure you can swap stories about shopping in Bond Street or something.'

'Oh, yes—because I do that all the time.' She shook her head in exasperation. 'Zac, I honestly think that you and I come from different planets. I struggle to pay my bills and buy basic necessities while you live here in your gilded tower and have *no* idea of the real world.'

He didn't appear to be listening and had already swung away from her. Bristling with anger, she followed him into the lounge and stopped just inside the doorway, blinking as she stepped out of the bright sunlight on the balcony. 'I'm not coming with you. Find someone else to entertain your businessman and his wife.' She folded her arms across her chest and stared at him belligerently, frowning when he handed her a large flat box with the name of a well-known couture house on the front. 'What is this?'

'Something for you to wear tonight,' he replied blandly, seemingly unconcerned by her simmering temper or her refusal to accompany him to dinner.

Freya stared down at the box, her heart suddenly beating at twice its normal rate. 'You bought me a dress?' she said slowly, hating herself for the little thrill of pleasure she gained from the idea that he had taken time out of his busy schedule to go shopping for her.

'Actually, no, I gave Francine a rough idea of your size and she picked out a suitable outfit,' Zac instantly burst her bubble and she fell back to earth with a bump.

'Well, she wasted her time, because I'm not wearing it

and I'm not going. What made you think I would agree?' she demanded furiously, her eyes widening at the sensual gleam in his.

'I was confident of playing on your sympathy for my secretary,' he said coolly, 'but, failing that, I can think of several other methods of persuasion that we'd both enjoy—although they may well result in us being late for dinner.' His slow smile triggered alarm bells and she bit back her retort as her mind fantasised about how he would bend her to his will. With ease, that was for sure, she acknowledged on a wave of self-disgust. Just the thought of his hands and mouth caressing her was enough to send liquid heat pooling between her thighs. If he touched her, kissed her again, she seriously doubted her ability to resist him—and he knew it.

She swallowed and tore her eyes from his mocking smile, tears of shame prickling behind her eyelids. If she wanted to retain any vestige of her self-respect, she would have to agree to go to dinner with him because she could not risk him *persuading* her.

'It was kind of your PA to go to so much trouble,' she said tightly, carefully not looking at him. 'And because I know how unwell she must be feeling at the moment, I'll agree to take her place tonight.' Clutching the box he had given her, she headed for the door, her back ramrod straight as his softly spoken comment followed her.

'I hadn't expected you to give in so easily, *chérie*. What a pity,' he drawled with genuine regret in his voice. 'I was looking forward to…coaxing you round to my way of thinking.'

Hours later Freya studied her reflection in the mirror. The dress Zac's secretary had chosen for her was a deceptively simple floor-length black sheath with a lace overlay, narrow shoulder straps and a neckline that plunged lower than Freya was happy with. When she had first realised how much of her cleavage was exposed she'd seriously considered changing into something else, but challenging Zac was not a good idea and she was afraid that if he tried to *coax* her, he would almost certainly win. Instead she had piled her hair on top of her head, and slipped on a pair of high-heeled sandals. Now, deciding she was ready, she swept out to meet Zac, her pulse rate quickening at the flare of undisguised desire in his eyes when he caught sight of her.

It gave her a fierce thrill of feminine triumph to realise that she was not the only one to be suffering from sexual frustration. Zac wanted her and was fighting the same battle to control his hunger. The knowledge empowered her and, instead of slinking shyly into the lounge, she sauntered confidently across the room, aware of his eyes lingering on the creamy swell of her breasts.

He looked breathtaking in his black tuxedo and white shirt that contrasted with his olive-gold skin, but for the first time she felt almost his equal and she met his gaze steadily as faint colour briefly highlighted his sharp cheekbones. The atmosphere in the room throbbed with tension and for one wild, crazy moment she wondered how he would react if she walked over to him and kissed his mouth with all the pent-up longing she was struggling to control.

Of course she did no such thing. She wasn't completely stupid and, besides, one kiss would not have been enough for either of them. What she really wanted was to feel the hard length of him deep inside her as he drove her to the pinnacle of sexual ecstasy—and that was never going to happen again, she reminded herself firmly.

She was shaken out of her erotic fantasies by his terse

voice informing her that they had to leave, but she felt his brooding stare on her as they rode the lift down to the car park. The short journey to the hotel where they were meeting his American client was completed in silence, but once there Zac immediately exerted his usual charismatic charm as he ushered her into the bar and introduced her to Chester Warren and his wife.

From then on Freya concentrated on chatting to Carolyn Warren and struck up an instant rapport with the older woman when she discovered that she originated from a small Hampshire village, a few miles inland from Freya's home town. After cocktails at the hotel, they moved on to the wonderfully ornate Salle Garnier Opera House where the performance by the Monte Carlo Ballet Company was truly magical, and afterwards they returned to the hotel for a late dinner.

'So, Freya, do you like living here in Monaco?' Chester Warren queried when they had finished eating. 'Carolyn tells me you're from the same part of England where she was born—quaint little place, although I can never remember its name,' he added cheerfully.

Freya glanced across the dance floor to where Carolyn Warren was dancing with Zac. 'I love Monaco,' she replied, 'but I don't live here. I'm just a…friend of Zac's and I'm staying here with my daughter for a few days. I'll be going home soon,' she added, wondering why the thought caused a sick feeling in the pit of her stomach. She would be glad to get back to reality, she told herself firmly. She didn't belong here in this billionaire's playground and she had no place in Zac's life.

The bleakness in her voice caused Chester to stare at her with undisguised curiosity. 'Friends, eh,' he drawled. 'Well,

Zac's a fine man—as charming as his father was and just as ruthless in the boardroom,' he said on a note of admiration. 'I remember when Charles died a couple of years back, there were some on the Deverell board who believed Zac wasn't up to the job of Chief Executive. He was seen as a playboy—you know, fast cars, plenty of women.' Chester chuckled. 'But to give him his dues, he worked like a dog to prove he was a worthy successor to his father even though he was pretty cut up at Charles' death. Now, of course, Deverell's profits are soaring and Zac has the full support of his board, but I hear he still works all the hours God sends.' Chester winked at her conspiratorially. 'Maybe he needs to get himself a wife, although he's shown no signs yet of wanting to settle down. I guess it would take a pretty special lady to tame him.'

'She would have to have the patience of a saint for a start,' Freya agreed tightly, despising herself for the way her heart lurched at the idea of Zac getting married.

'Why, *chérie*, you make me sound as though I'm an ogre,' an amused voice sounded in her ear and she swung her head round sharply, her eyes clashing with Zac's glinting gaze. 'I'm not that unbearable, am I?'

Cheeks flaming, Freya gave him a look that warned him he did not want to know her opinion of him, but to her annoyance he gave her one of his devastating smiles and tugged her to her feet before she could think of an excuse not to dance with him.

'I obviously need to demonstrate my charming side,' he murmured smoothly as he swept her across the dance floor.

'Forget it,' Freya snapped. 'I know exactly what you are, Zac, and your famous charm does nothing for me.' She tried to ease away from him but his arms tightened around her waist and she gave a shocked gasp when she felt the rigid proof of his arousal straining against her pelvis.

'You disappoint me, *ma petite*, especially as you can be in no doubt of what you're doing to me right now,' he said mockingly. He placed his hand in the small of her back and exerted enough pressure so that she was forced up against him.

'You are disgusting,' Freya hissed as she tried to ignore the warmth that was flooding through her. The music slowed and Zac steered her around the dance floor, each subtle movement of his hips bringing his aroused body into closer contact with hers. In desperation Freya closed her eyes against the scorching heat of his gaze, but the sensations he was arousing in her only intensified and she shuddered when his hand inched lower down her back and made small, circular movements across the top of her buttocks. She stumbled and clung to him as the music faded to the periphery of her mind. Nothing existed but Zac, and the subtle, sensuous rub of his hand evoked a delicious, quivering excitement between her thighs.

Without the barrier of their clothes he would be free to take her properly and thrust deep into her, she thought dreamily, the image of him doing just that suddenly so stark in her head that her muscles clamped and to her utter shock she felt tiny spasms of pleasure radiate from her central core. She felt Zac tense, but she couldn't prevent her climax and as she shook uncontrollably he dipped his head and captured her startled cry with his mouth.

It was over almost instantly and as she came down reality intruded, bringing with it the music and hubbub of voices from the dance floor. *Oh, God, what had she done?* Had anyone seen? And was it even possible to reach a sexual climax when he hadn't even touched her intimately? Dying with shame, she could not bear to look at him, but her eyes seemed drawn to him by a magnetic force. His face was a rigid mask, his skin stretched taut over the knife-edge of his cheekbones while his eyes gleamed with sensual promise beneath his heavy lids.

She stared up at him in desperation, silently daring him to comment as his lip curled into a slow, mocking smile.

'You *are* hungry, *chérie*,' he drawled softly. 'If I'd known I would have followed my instincts when I first saw you in that dress tonight and cancelled dinner.'

Freya swallowed her retort as he led her back to their table, aware that she was not in a position to say anything when her body had behaved so abominably. To her utter relief no one else in the room seemed to have noticed her making a spectacle of herself, but Zac would never let her forget her moment of weakness, she thought on a wave of panic. He knew now she was his for the taking whenever he chose. But somehow she would have to resist him before he damaged her self-esteem permanently.

CHAPTER FIVE

IT WAS almost midnight when they bid Chester and Carolyn Warren goodnight and drove back to the penthouse. Freya wished she were tired but to her dismay she felt wide awake and filled with a wild, reckless energy. Those few moments of madness on the dance floor with Zac had inflamed her senses and left her body aching for his full possession—but it was going to be disappointed.

She intended to go straight to her room the moment they entered the apartment, but Zac's butler, Laurent, greeted them with a tray of coffee and *petits fours* that he had prepared specially for their return. 'I'd really like to go to bed,' she muttered to Zac as he ushered her into the lounge in the wake of the butler.

'And upset Laurent?' His eyebrows raised a notch. 'You're a brave woman.'

Stifling a groan, she dredged up a smile and accepted a cup of frothy cappuccino from the butler. The last thing she needed right now was the additional stimulation of caffeine, she thought gloomily as she watched Zac drain his cup in two gulps before he crossed to the bar and poured himself a cognac.

'Would you like a nightcap with your coffee?'

'No, thank you,' she replied hastily. What she needed was something to knock her senseless for the next twelve hours and prevent her disturbing fantasies about Zac, but, although getting blind drunk was tempting, she decided that her loss of control tonight had been embarrassing enough to last her a lifetime.

She stirred her coffee and glanced up at Zac, who was standing at the window staring out into the darkness. 'When did your father die?' she asked him quietly, recalling her conversation with Chester Warren. 'Chester said it was two years ago, which was when we met, but you never said anything and I had no idea you were grieving.'

Zac shrugged dismissively. 'My father died nine months before I met you and my grief was a private matter which was nothing to do with you or our relationship.'

He sounded so cold, so clinical, that Freya shivered. Zac kept his life compartmentalised into separate boxes and had clearly never considered allowing her into the box marked personal. 'But if you'd told me I might have been able to...I don't know—' she broke off helplessly '—help in some way.'

'How?' he demanded tersely. 'You couldn't have brought him back and I did not need help. I dealt with my grief.' He had neither looked for, nor wanted, sympathy, he brooded grimly, and he had been determined to deal with the loss of his father in his own way, which for the most part had been to block it out of his mind and get on with his life.

After his twin sisters had died a few months after birth, his mother had sunk into a deep depression that had lasted for most of his adolescence. He had been shocked by the power of love and had viewed it as a destructive emotion that had wreaked havoc on his parents' lives, and he had decided that he would never be held hostage to his emotions.

When his father died, his mother had been distraught and once again he had felt helpless in the face of her overwhelming grief. But Freya's soft smile and unashamedly eager sensuality had been a welcome relief from the surfeit of Yvette Deverell's emotions. He hadn't wanted to talk about grief or loss; he had wanted to forget everything and enjoy her glorious body—until he'd discovered that she hadn't been giving herself exclusively to him.

Zac's shuttered expression warned Freya that he did not welcome her intrusion into an area of his life that he had never spoken of before, but she pushed on doggedly, determined to learn more about this man who was to all intents and purposes still a stranger to her. 'Chester told me that you felt you had to work particularly hard to prove to the Deverell board that you would be a worthy successor to your father. If you had explained why you practically lived at your office, I would have understood,' she insisted.

'But instead you grew bored of waiting for me and looked elsewhere for sex.' Zac gave a harsh laugh. '*Mon Dieu*, I satisfied you every night, but it wasn't enough, was it, *chérie*? You were insatiable, you wanted me on hand morning, noon and night, and when I didn't give you enough attention you acted like a spoilt brat.'

'It wasn't like that,' Freya defended herself. 'I wanted us to have a normal life like other couples, to spend weekends together and the occasional evenings rather than you coming home at midnight and taking me to bed like I was a…a whore you paid to pleasure you.' She set down her coffee-cup with a clatter, her whole body tensing in rejection when Zac strode across the room and stood, towering over her.

'But that's exactly what you were,' he said savagely. 'I kept you as my mistress and paid for every conceivable luxury you could want, in return for your…services.' The withering contempt in his eyes as he stared down at her made her feel sick and she shook her head wildly.

'I never asked you to buy me clothes and jewellery. I never asked you for anything, apart from your time. I wanted you, Zac, not the things you could give me,' she whispered, but he snorted impatiently and dropped down onto the sofa next to her, trapping her against the cushions.

'I know exactly what you wanted, and when you decided that you weren't getting enough from me, you slept with your foppish artist.'

I did not sleep with Simon. Hurt and frustration exploded inside her and she lashed out at him, only to have him capture her hands and drag her across his lap.

'The bodyguard saw you,' he said with a steely calm that alarmed her more than if he had shouted at her. His eyes were hard and utterly implacable and she gasped in shock when he caught hold of the straps of her dress and dragged them down her arms with such force that the material ripped. The bodice of her dress instantly slipped down, leaving her breasts exposed, and when she fought manically to free herself from his hold he pushed her so that she was lying flat on her back.

'Zac, don't,' she pleaded fearfully, terrified not of him but of herself and the certainty that she would not be able to resist him. His barely leashed savagery only added to her feverish excitement and, although she hated herself, she could feel her body's treacherous response when he skimmed his hands over her ribcage and cupped her breasts in his palms.

'Don't deny that you want me, Freya,' he warned softly. 'Not after what happened on the dance floor tonight. You don't know how close I was to spreading you across the nearest table and taking you in front of a room full of on-lookers,' he growled, his voice thick and his accent heavily pronounced as he relived those few seconds when she had trembled in his arms. The shocked confusion in her green eyes had driven him to the edge and since then his arousal had been a throbbing force that he was impatient to assuage.

'That shouldn't have happened,' she muttered, her face flaming. 'It was just a horribly embarrassing physical reaction. I haven't dated anyone since we split up. Even if I'd wanted to, I couldn't when I had Aimee to care for. But I have the same urges as anyone else.' Although it seemed that only Zac could satisfy those urges, she conceded bleakly. If he could bring her to a climax simply by dancing with her, what chance did she stand if he decided to make love to her properly? she wondered despairingly. But it no longer seemed to matter; his hands were gently moulding her breasts and now his thumb pads were stroking across the tight peaks of her nipples, backwards and forwards until the pleasure was almost unbearable and she felt a sharp tug of desire.

This was dangerous territory and she should beat a retreat, her brain warned, but a curious weakness seemed to have invaded her limbs and she could do nothing but watch as he lowered his head and flicked his tongue across one sensitive crest. With a low cry she put out her hands to push him away, but her wayward fingers strayed to his shirt buttons and worked them free before she pushed the material aside and revelled in the feel of his warm golden skin beneath her fingertips.

It had been so long since she had touched him. She loved the solid strength of his chest and powerful shoulders—

loved him, whispered a tiny voice in her head. She was his, totally, and she murmured her approval when he transferred his mouth to her other breast and drew her nipple fully into his mouth. The exquisite sensation built on the need that had begun on the dance floor and was now a greedy, clamouring ache to feel him inside her.

Zac stared down at her flushed face and muttered something beneath his breath before he claimed her mouth in a kiss of pure possession, drawing a response from her that she could no longer deny. A tremor ran through his big body and he tore his mouth from hers to drag her dress over her hips. He loved watching her unguarded response to him and held her gaze as he drew her knickers down and pushed her thighs apart with deliberate intent.

Her eyes darkened to the colour of a stormy sea and she made a little half murmur of protest when he ran his hand through the soft blonde curls and then parted her and slid his fingers deep into her.

Freya held her breath, torn between the need for him to continue his wickedly intimate caresses and the dictates of her pride, which were telling her that she must stop this madness now, before it was too late. But Zac was a master of seduction and his skilful fingers continued to move inside her, while his thumb pad stroked with delicate precision over her ultra sensitive clitoris, building her excitement so that she twisted restlessly and tried to control the delicious spasms that were threatening to overwhelm her.

'Zac…' His eyes were focused on her face and there was something shockingly erotic about the way he was watching her while he pleasured her. She was going to die of shame in the cold light of day, but his fingers were moving faster in a sensual dance and with a groan she tipped her head back as wave after wave of incredible sensation tore through her. Only then did he lower his head once more to capture her mouth in a slow, drugging kiss, his tongue dipping between her lips as he mimicked the actions his fingers had performed seconds before.

'Tell me, *chérie*, am I the only man who can turn you on like that, or will anyone do when you're desperate—Brooks, for example?' Zac's coldly mocking voice shattered the sexual haze and Freya tensed as pain ripped her apart. His opinion of her hadn't changed; he still regarded her as unfaithful and his readiness to believe the worst of her was unbearable. Her desire drained away, leaving her so cold that her teeth chattered, and when his hand moved to the zip of his trousers she felt sick with misery.

'Don't,' she pleaded through numb lips, her eyes huge and overbright in her white face. 'I don't think I could bear it. You've made your point, Zac, and we both know that I'm pathetically incapable of resisting you. But if you make love to me tonight I think I might hate you almost as much as I hate myself.'

For a few mindless seconds, Zac was tempted to ignore her. He had never wanted a woman the way he wanted her, never been held at the mercy of such a gnawing hunger that caused a cramping pain in his gut. He was in agony, damn it, and he knew he could make it good for her too. But the glimmer of her tears was getting to him, even though he despised women who were able to turn on the waterworks whenever it suited them. Freya was not one of those women, he conceded grimly, and the stark vulnerability in her eyes unearthed a flare of compassion in him that he'd never known he possessed.

With a furious oath he jerked away from her, his nostrils flaring with the effort of controlling his urge to take her.

'Cover yourself and get out,' he growled, flinging her dress at her before he strode over to the bar. He'd known from the moment he stood by her hospital bed that she would be trouble and he couldn't fathom what madness had made him bring her back here. The day couldn't come too soon when he would be able to dismiss her from his life for ever, he thought savagely as he slugged back his drink and poured himself another. But when he swung round to tell her, she had gone.

Freya leaned over the cot and brushed her lips over Aimee's velvety soft cheek. The toddler's lashes were already drifting down and within seconds she was asleep, worn out from an energetic afternoon playing with Jean Lewis in the roof-garden.

Jean had become a firm friend of both mother and daughter and they would miss her warmth and kindness when they returned to England, Freya mused sadly. And that day was drawing ever closer. It was over a week since Zac had brought them to Monaco and any day now he would receive the results of the paternity test. She predicted that his reaction would not be good and had already decided that she would take Aimee home immediately.

'I thought she'd drop off quickly,' Jean said cheerfully when Freya tiptoed from the nursery. 'She loves playing outside, although she was very cross when I insisted that she wear her sunhat.'

'You're so good with her,' Freya said with a smile. 'I thought she was going to have a tantrum about the hat, but you managed to distract her.'

Jean chuckled. 'I've had years of practice dealing with toddler tantrums, and really Aimee is so well behaved. She's an adorable child.' She paused and then added, 'What a beautiful dress. You look lovely Freya.'

'Thank you.' Freya glanced down at the elegant cocktail dress that had been one of her favourites when she had lived with Zac. The green silk crêpe de Chine clung to her slender curves and the colour looked good against the light tan she had acquired while playing in the sunshine with Aimee.

Zac was hosting a dinner party tonight and had curtly informed her that, as his PA was still feeling unwell, he required her to act as his hostess. She was looking forward to the evening with as much enthusiasm as a trip to an abattoir. Relations between them had improved marginally since their last explosive confrontation, but only because she avoided him whenever possible.

It wasn't difficult; he had always left for his office before she was up and he returned late—or not at all, she thought grimly. Common sense told her he was bound to have a mistress in Monaco. He possessed a high sex drive and, although he had respected her wishes and held back from making love to her after the evening they had spent with the Warrens, she had been in no doubt of his frustration.

But there were plenty of women who would willingly satisfy his needs and all week her imagination had kept her awake at night as she had pictured him with some nubile beauty. Jealousy was a corrosive emotion. She hated herself as she lay awake each night listening for his key in the lock and hated him more when dawn brought with it the bitter realisation that he had spent the night in another woman's bed.

The results of the DNA test couldn't come soon enough, she thought miserably. Living under the same roof as Zac was destroying her self-respect. She had no idea what he would do when he discovered that she hadn't been unfaithful to him, and she no longer cared, she realised. Possibly he would offer to pay maintenance for Aimee, but it was unlikely that he would want any kind of contact with his daughter and with luck she would never have to see him again.

She found him in the lounge, staring out at the spectacular view over the bay. In a formal dinner suit he looked more gorgeous than ever. The expertly tailored jacket moulded the formidable width of his shoulders and when he swung round she noted the way his brilliant white shirt accentuated his olive-gold skin.

'Freya.' he studied her in silence for a few moments, his brows drawn into a slashing frown. '*Mon Dieu!* You have a nerve wearing *that* dress. Did you do so expressly to anger me? Because if so, you've succeeded.'

Startled by his barely leashed aggression, Freya shook her head. 'You told me to wear the clothes I'd left behind when you...' she bit down on her lip as bitter memories came hurtling back '...when you threw me out.'

'True, but I didn't expect you to parade around in the very dress you were wearing on the night you tried to seduce me into believing the child you were carrying was mine,' he hissed contemptuously.

Had she really worn this dress on the worst night of her life? Freya's brow knotted as she tried to remember, but all she could recall was Zac's savage condemnation of her. At the beginning of that fateful evening she *had* dressed to please him, but after it had all gone so spectacularly wrong she had fled to her dressing room and hastily changed into her jeans before he had ignominiously evicted her from the penthouse.

'I didn't try to seduce you,' she said, her temper flaring when she saw the acrid condemnation in his eyes.

'Non?' He gave a harsh laugh as he strolled towards her with a lithe grace that reminded her of a panther stalking its kill. 'I remember the way you flew into my arms the moment I stepped through the door. We were supposed to be going out to dinner but you clung to me. I couldn't resist you, *chérie*, and you knew it, but you overplayed your hand when you thought you could fool me into believing your lies.'

He was so close that she could *feel* the anger emanating from his body and when she tilted her head to look up at him, the stark emotion in his eyes made her tremble. Passion and fury—together they were a volatile mixture that filled her with trepidation and an undeniable excitement that had been building all week. She recognised his hunger; saw the way his eyes darkened with desire, and when his head descended she stood stock still, like a hare trapped in the headlights of a speeding car, waiting for the inevitable.

Voices from the hall shattered the haze of sexual tension and he jerked back from her, muttering a savage oath beneath his breath. 'My guests are here and it's too late for you to change now. But be aware, *chérie*, that every time I look at you tonight I'll be imagining you with Brooks.' His deliberate crudity made her wince, but when she attempted to move away from him he slid his arm around her waist and held her in a vice like grip. 'Why aren't you wearing the support bandage on your wrist?' he demanded roughly.

'I thought I'd manage without it for a couple of hours.' The butler, Laurent, was heading down the hall followed by Zac's guests and, despite feeling as though her heart had been put through a pulping machine, she forced a brittle smile. 'At least the necessity to go and put it on again will give me a reason to excuse myself from your vile company.'

From that moment on the evening became a hellish ordeal that Freya longed to end. Fortunately no one attending the dinner had known her during the few months she had lived with Zac and awkward explanations were avoided. His guests were frighteningly sophisticated but friendly—although in some cases, too friendly, she thought darkly when she caught sight of him deep in conversation with an attractive brunette. Mimi Joubert had arrived alone, but from the easy familiarity she shared with Zac it seemed likely that she would not be returning home tonight.

Freya swallowed the bile that burned her throat and forced herself to smile at the man at her side. Lucien Giraud had also arrived at the dinner party unaccompanied, but Freya was sure that had been through choice rather than because he could not find a date. He was good-looking and charming and had flirted with her outrageously throughout dinner. Fearful of appearing rude, she had called on all her acting skills to respond warmly to him, but her laughter had disguised the misery that swamped her every time she felt Zac's eyes on her. The blistering contempt in his gaze reminded her of his taunt that he was picturing her with Simon Brooks and she felt the crazy urge to jump onto the table and shout out her innocence. It would certainly be the talking point of the evening, she thought bitterly.

By midnight, she'd had enough. She was fast running out of patience with Lucien's none-too-subtle attempts to place his hand on her thigh—the man had an ego the size of Mount Everest—and she glared at him when he leaned close and whispered in her ear.

'So, Freya, what will it take to persuade you to have dinner with me?' he murmured seductively, clearly convinced that the route from the dining room to his bedroom would be completed in minimum time.

'More than you can imagine,' Freya replied sharply, trying to edge along the sofa when she felt his gaze settle on her cleavage. 'I'm afraid you'll have to excuse me,' she said as she slapped away his roaming hand and jumped to her feet. 'My arm is beginning to ache and I need to take some pain-killers. It was nice to meet you,' she lied, stifling an impatient groan when Lucien stood and captured her hand.

'It has been a pleasure for me also, Freya,' he replied, lifting her hand to his mouth with a theatrical flourish that caught the attention of everyone in the room. 'I hope very much that we will meet again.'

Not in this lifetime—if she could help it, Freya vowed silently as she repeated her excuse for leaving the party to the other guests and hurried from the room, acutely conscious of Zac's gaze burning like a laser between her shoulder blades. As his hostess she supposed she should have remained on hand until his guests departed, but watching him smile and flirt with Miss Joubert was sheer agony and she couldn't stand another five minutes of it.

Despite Freya feeling bone-weary, sleep proved elusive and two hours later she gave up her restless tossing beneath the sheets and headed for the kitchen to make a milky drink. She had heard Zac's guests depart soon after she'd left the party, but the light streaming from beneath his bedroom door and the muted sound of a woman's voice caused her to pause in the hallway. Obviously not everyone had gone home. The image of Zac and the gorgeous Mimi Joubert filled her with sick misery and she stumbled on towards the kitchen feeling as though she had been kicked in the stomach.

Oh, God! How could it hurt so much? After all this time

and all the terrible accusations he had flung at her? She wanted to cry like a baby and tears blinded her as she poured milk into a saucepan and set it on the hob to heat. Of course he had a lover. There had probably been a steady stream of sophisticated beauties in his bed during the past two years—but the stark reality that he was at this moment making love to another woman was more than she could bear.

She mopped her wet face frantically with a paper towel. It was time she toughened up and stopped being so pathetic. She had coped with rejection all her life—she should be used to it by now, she thought bleakly, recalling the years of her childhood when she had tried so hard to win her grandmother's love. But Nana Joyce hadn't wanted her any more than her mother had done, and Zac had never made any pretence that he loved her. It was her own stupid fault that she had given him her heart and it should have come as no surprise that he had treated it with callous disregard.

Too late she heard the hiss of scalding hot milk as it frothed onto the hob. With a cry she grabbed the saucepan handle as a smell of burning filled the kitchen and, to her horror, the smoke alarm activated.

'What the hell are you playing at? I thought you were in bed.'

'I couldn't sleep.' Freya jerked her gaze from Zac's furious face and ran cold water over the ruined pan while he reached up and switched off the alarm. His hair was ruffled and his robe loosely fastened, as if he had leapt up from bed and dragged it around him. He looked indecently sexy and the knowledge that he was naked beneath the black silk caused her heart to thud unevenly.

'That's no reason to wake the rest of the household,' he said tersely, his eyes narrowing as he noted the streaks of tears on her face.

'I'm sorry—I didn't mean to disturb you,' she muttered miserably, unable to dismiss the picture of him tearing himself out of Mimi Joubert's arms. 'I think the pan's salvageable if I scrub it.'

'Leave it.' He snatched the pan that she had filled with soapsuds and, infuriated by his highhandedness, she grabbed it back again.

'Let me do it. Go back to bed. You don't want to keep Miss Joubert waiting,' she hissed beneath her breath, and then gasped when he forcibly removed the saucepan from her hand and spun her round to face him.

'What?' His tone was deceptively mild, but the glinting fury in his gaze warned that he had reached the limits of his patience.

'Miss Joubert—I know she's staying with you,' Freya murmured uneasily, trying to edge away from him and finding herself jammed up against the worktop. 'I don't care,' she told him sharply, terrified that he might think she was jealous. Her cheeks burned when he continued to stare at her speculatively, as if he could see inside her head. 'We're both free agents and you can sleep with who you like.'

'*Merci, chérie,*' he murmured sardonically, 'but I have no plans to leap into bed with a business acquaintance I met for the first time a few days ago.' He paused for a heartbeat and then said softly, 'It was clear from your behaviour with Lucien Giraud this evening that you do not feel bound by the same constraints of moral propriety.'

'Meaning what, precisely?'

'Meaning that you were all over him like a rash,' he growled, his face twisting in distaste. 'You're not even fully recovered from your injuries, and yet you waste no time trying to seduce another wealthy lover. Perhaps you are already preparing for the outcome of the DNA test,' he sneered, 'and are intending to sell yourself to Giraud in return for financial security for you and your child.'

His cruel taunt pierced her heart and in an agony of hurt she brought her hand up to meet his cheek with a resounding crack. For a few seconds she stared at him in horror, and then closed her eyes as a wave of shame and nausea swept over her. She deplored physical violence, but how dared he insinuate that she was no better than a whore? The blazing fury in his eyes warned that she had pushed him too far and with a cry she shot down the hall, but had only gone a few paces before he caught hold of her and swung her into his arms.

'Take your hands off me!' She pummelled her fists against his chest and gasped when he marched determinedly towards his room. 'If you're planning a threesome, you can damn well think again.' Burning up with embarrassment, she screwed her eyes shut when he strode through the door and deposited her on the bed. Surely she had plumbed the depths of humiliation? she thought wildly, convinced that Zac and his beautiful bed-mate must be laughing at her.

But when she cautiously lifted her lashes there was only Zac staring down at her—no hint of amusement on his face, just stark, primitive hunger and an implacable determination in his eyes that sent alarm feathering down her spine.

CHAPTER SIX

'I AM a patient man,' Zac stated with a mind-boggling disregard for the truth, 'but I've had as much as I'm prepared to take from you.'

Frozen to the bed, Freya watched him activate the remote to turn off the television, before his hands moved to the belt of his robe. 'Obviously I was wrong about Miss Joubert. I'm sorry,' she muttered thickly. She watched him with wide, disbelieving eyes, her blood pounding in her veins when he loosened the belt and shrugged out of his robe to stand before her, gloriously and unashamedly naked.

'Zac!' She swallowed hard and tried to tear her gaze from the masculine perfection of his body. His skin gleamed like polished bronze in the lamplight and her eyes skittered down over the rippling muscles of his abdomen, following the path of dark hairs that arrowed down his taut stomach to his thighs. He was aroused—and it was the sight of his boldly erect manhood that finally penetrated the fog clouding her brain. 'What are you doing?'

'Taking what you were so blatantly offering to Lucien Giraud,' he replied coolly, foiling her attempt to scramble off the bed by coming down beside her and pinning her to the mattress with insulting ease.

'I was not.' Tears stung her eyes at the contempt in his, but her traitorous body recognised its soul mate and molten heat surged through her veins, leaving her weak with longing. One look was all it took to arouse her to fever pitch—what chance did she stand if he touched her, kissed her…? 'Zac, I don't want this.' She twisted her head frantically from side to side, her breath coming in shallow gasps.

'Liar.' His supreme self-confidence was mortifying, but when he captured her chin and slowly lowered his head, she shook with need and parted her lips to accept the savage mastery of his kiss.

The bold thrust of his tongue into her mouth should have appalled her, but she was drowning in sensation, her senses set aflame by his potent male heat. After the lonely years apart he was impossible to resist and with a groan she slid her arms around his neck, loving the feel of his silky hair against her fingers.

Sensing her capitulation, he eased the pressure of his mouth a little so that the kiss became a sensual, evocative tasting that brought fresh tears to her eyes. He was everything to her, the only man she had ever loved, but she meant nothing to him. It destroyed the last vestiges of her pride to accept that, even though he despised her, she wanted to make love with him one last time—a precious memory to cling to during all the bleak years ahead.

Zac trailed his lips down her throat, his fingers tugging the ribbons at the front of her negligée before he pushed the delicate peach-coloured satin aside to expose her breasts to his hungry gaze. His eyes darkened as he brushed his thumb across her nipple and watched her pupils dilate. 'I love the way you are so responsive, *chérie*,' he said roughly. 'There's no pretence with you, is there? You are the most sensual woman I have ever met and I have never been able to get you out of my blood.'

She tensed, sure that he was taunting her and expecting him to flay her with his sarcasm, but instead he lowered his head and the feel of his tongue drawing moist circles around her areola made her tremble with anticipation. He moved slowly, inexorably towards the centre until his mouth closed around the tight peak of her nipple and she gave a low cry as sensation pierced her. She arched up to him and clutched his shoulders while he teased her and tormented her, and just when she thought she could bear no more he transferred his mouth to her other breast and pleasured her until she was a limp mass of quivering need.

'You want me, Freya, and, God help me, I can't fight my hunger for you any more,' Zac growled as he tugged her negligee down over her hips and followed its path with his mouth on her skin—trailing kisses over the sensitive flesh of her stomach to the tiny triangle of peach satin that hid her femininity from his gaze.

It was purely physical, he reassured himself, his senses flaring when he caught the subtle, feminine scent of her arousal. The sexual attraction between them had always been explosive and, even though he knew she was a cold-blooded liar, he couldn't resist her. Her skin felt like silk beneath his fingertips and she was so soft and pliant that he had to restrain himself from plunging into her and taking her with primitive passion.

Drawing a sharp breath, he fought to leash his rampaging hormones as he slid his fingers beneath the lacy edge of her knickers. He pushed the material aside before he lowered his head and stroked his tongue lightly up and down the delicate folds of her femininity, coaxing and teasing until she whimpered and shifted her hips to allow him access to the moist heat within.

Freya knew she should stop him, but her limbs felt heavy and her entire body throbbed with desire. She couldn't do this again, couldn't give herself to a man whose opinion of her was rock-bottom. But Zac was the only man she had ever wanted and she couldn't deny him, not when it meant denying herself the exquisite pleasure of his possession.

His wickedly intrusive tongue seemed intent on destroying her self-control as he brought her to the brink and she gasped, part relief, part disappointment, when he suddenly lifted his head and stared down at her. 'You can't do this,' she whispered, shaken by the glittering contempt in his eyes when he removed her knickers with brisk efficiency. 'You think I'm a cheat and a liar,' she reminded him desperately, her eyes widening when he reached into the bedside drawer and took out a condom. He made no reply as he fitted it with practised ease and her heart thudded in her chest when he pushed her legs apart and moved over her. 'How can you make love to a woman you despise?' she cried jerkily, trembling with hurt and the frantic need to feel him inside her. She made one last despairing effort to halt him by beating her hands on his shoulders until he caught hold of her wrists and forced her arms above her head.

'Unfortunately you're not the only one to suffer from an embarrassing physical reaction,' he mockingly reminded her of the excuse she had made after she had climaxed in his arms on the dance floor. 'My brain tells me you're a tramp, but my body isn't so fastidious—it's just hungry,' he said grimly as he slid his hand under her bottom, lifted her and effected one deep, shockingly powerful thrust that made her gasp in awe at his potent strength.

It had been a long time since she had done this, but the ministrations of his hands and mouth had brought her to the peak of sexual arousal and she welcomed the full, rigid length of him as he slowly filled her. As her muscles stretched around him to form a tight, velvet sheath, Zac gave a low growl of satisfaction, eased back a fraction and then thrust again and again, setting a rhythm that she eagerly matched.

Each strong, deep stroke was sending Freya closer to the edge and she lost all sense of time and place as his male scent swamped her senses while the only sounds she could hear were her breathless cries for him to thrust faster and harder.

'I'll hurt you,' he muttered against her throat when she wrapped her legs around his back and urged him on.

In the dim recess of her mind she recognised the truth of his words—not that she feared he would cause her physical pain, but emotionally he had the power to destroy her. But she blanked out the thought as her whole being focused on the exquisite sensations that were unfurling deep inside her. 'You won't,' she assured him huskily as she arched her hips in mute supplication for him to loosen his hold on his self-control and take her with the primitive force she knew he was capable of. 'I want you, Zac...I want...' The rest of her words were lost beneath the pressure of his mouth as he captured her lips in a fierce, drugging kiss that drove everything but her desperate need for fulfilment from her mind.

Zac's shoulders and brow were beaded with sweat and his face was a taut mask. He was a skilful lover who knew exactly how to give pleasure, but the time for playful seduction was long past and he was driven by a basic urge to satisfy his hunger. He slid his hands down Freya's slim body and gripped her buttocks as he drove into her, his jaw clenched as he felt her muscles contract around him.

He could feel his pleasure building to a crescendo, but just when he feared he could hold back no longer, she gave a sharp cry and her whole body convulsed beneath him in a shattering climax. The sensuous pleasure-pain of her nails raking down his back tipped him over the edge and he paused for an instant before giving one last forceful thrust that annihilated his control and sent shock waves through him as his body shuddered with the power of his release.

Freya clung to Zac's sweat-damp body and revelled in the weight of him as the lingering ripples of sensation drained from her. Recriminations were already mustering in her head, taunting her with her abject stupidity, but she was determined to ignore them for a few more blissful minutes. She could feel Zac's heartbeat thudding through her and she screwed her eyes shut and breathed in his musky, male scent. Making love with him topped the list of mistakes she had made—in her life that seemed littered with them—but she couldn't regret it. Despite his mistrust and suspicion and his unshakeable opinion of her, she loved him, she acknowledged sadly, and it seemed likely that she always would.

Eventually he rolled off her to lay flat on his back, his silence growing more ominous to her ears by the second.

'I've decided that I want you back,' he said in a voice devoid of all emotion, 'to live here as my mistress the way we once were.' He turned his head on the pillows and stared at her coldly. 'You're like a drug in my veins and, although I despise myself, I seem to be addicted to you,' he grated harshly. 'I'm prepared to overlook your...indiscretion with Brooks, and if you stay I'll accept your child and provide for her as if she were my own. But if you ever look at another man the way you looked at Lucien Giraud tonight, so help me, *chérie*, I will not be responsible for my actions.'

For a few seconds Freya stared at him in stunned silence while her brain assimilated his words. Bitterness, humiliation and rage congealed her blood and she closed her eyes for a moment, shocked by the level of pain he could still inflict on her. How could she love him when he seemed determined to shred her heart into a thousand pieces? She obviously possessed a masochistic streak, she thought as agony swept through her.

'If—*overlooking my indiscretion with Brooks*—is your way of saying that you forgive me for having sex with Simon, you're wasting your breath,' she said tightly, her voice shaking with emotion. 'At a risk of repeating myself, I never slept with him or anyone else—ever.' She pushed against his chest with a force borne of desperation, terrified that she was actually going to be sick. 'How dare you! How *dare* you take that high and mighty tone with me? Your arrogance sickens me—*you* sicken me,' she flung at him.

All this time she'd struggled as a single mother, juggling work and childcare and using her few precious hours of free time while Aimee slept to study for her degree, in the hope that she could improve her financial situation. And all the while Zac had lived here in his luxury penthouse apartment, refusing to accept that he was the father of her child while he thought the worst of her. Not for much longer, she thought furiously. The results of the DNA test would force him to accept the truth and she hoped he suffered an overdose of remorse when he realised how cruelly he had misjudged her.

He was staring at her through narrowed eyes, his jaw tense, but she no longer felt overawed by him. Her pride had finally come to her rescue and, although it was way too late to salvage her self-respect, she had to try. With jerky movements she dragged her negligee over her head, ignoring the pain in her wrist. The pain in her heart was a thousand times worse and she scrambled to her feet, desperate to escape before she broke down in front of him. 'I don't need anything from you, Zac, certainly not your arrogant assertion that you'll overlook something I didn't even do,' she told him fiercely. 'But one day soon you'll come crawling to me on your hands and knees, and hear me now—I will *never* forgive you for your treatment of me.'

Freya woke with a start as sunlight filtered through the blinds and slanted across her face. Dazedly she stared at the clock on her beside table and gave a disbelieving frown—surely it couldn't really be ten a.m.? She sat up and groaned as she quickly fastened the front of her nightgown, her cheeks flaming when she recalled how Zac had stripped her last night before he had pushed her flat on her back and taken her with a savagery that had escalated her excitement to fever pitch.

What did that make her? she wondered dismally as she recalled her wanton response to him. And how could she have been so stupid and so utterly lacking in pride? He had looked down his arrogant nose at her while he'd stated that he was prepared to overlook her affair with Simon Brooks, but she was *innocent* and his lack of faith hurt as much now as it had two years ago. Every day that she spent with him he stripped away another layer of her protective shell, leaving her raw and vulnerable, and she knew she had to leave before the damage to her heart was irreparable.

A hesitant tap on the door heralded the arrival of the maid. 'Ah, you are awake,' Elise said with a smile. 'Shall I bring you breakfast in bed?'

'No, thank you, Elise.' Freya jumped to her feet. 'Where is my daughter?'

'She is in the pool with Monsieur Deverell.'

Freya snatched up her robe and paused on the way to the *en suite* to stare blankly at the maid. 'Zac has taken Aimee swimming?' she queried, her voice sounding sharp as panic and confusion mingled. To her chagrin, Aimee had developed an instant fascination with Zac and, to give him credit, he treated the little girl with a gentle patience that he never revealed to anyone else—certainly not her, Freya thought bleakly.

Elise nodded. 'Madame Lewis is with them. Monsieur Deverell said that you'd had a disturbed night, and should be left alone to sleep,' she told Freya innocently. 'I'll tell him you are awake now. He wishes to see you in his study as soon as you are dressed.'

The temptation to pass on a message to Zac telling him to go to hell was so strong that Freya had to bite her lip. It wasn't fair to involve the penthouse staff in their private war, she reminded herself, and had to be content with cursing him beneath her breath as she stormed into the bathroom.

After the quickest shower on record, she dressed in a simple skirt and blouse suitable for travelling in, although her injured wrist still made it impossible for her to fasten her bra. She packed the few belongings she had brought from England and moved into the nursery where she swiftly stowed Aimee's clothes into a holdall ready for their immediate departure. With any luck Zac was still on the roof-garden, she thought as she raced along to his study and scooted across to his desk to search for her and Aimee's passports. One thing was certain, after her humiliating capitulation in his bed she could not risk remaining in Monaco for another night.

'Looking for something?' His lazy drawl brought her head up and she blushed and jumped guiltily away from the desk to find him standing in the doorway.

'Passports,' she replied, swallowing at the sight of him in chinos and a cream shirt, open at the neck to reveal the tanned column of his throat. 'Aimee and I are leaving. I refuse to stay here and be subjected to your vile accusations any more,' she said heatedly.

'Ah.' He stepped into the room and her heart lurched when he shut the door behind him and turned the key in the lock.

She could not look at him without remembering how she had writhed beneath him in abject surrender just hours before and she gave a silent groan of despair as her body stirred into instant life. Her palms felt suddenly damp and she wiped them down her skirt. 'Elise said you wanted to see me about something,' she muttered, tension prickling her skin when he moved towards her. As he walked around his desk she edged away from him, and at his terse command to sit down she subsided into the chair facing him.

He studied her speculatively for a few moments, but his gaze did not quite meet hers and she gained the curious impression that he felt awkward.

'I owe you an apology,' he said brusquely.

Astounded, she stared at him, wondering if she had heard him correctly. Zac apologising to her had to be a first, but the fact that he felt the need to made her realise how much he obviously regretted making love to her. 'It's all right,' she mumbled as she inspected her lap with sudden fascination. 'I'm not proud of my behaviour either. We just got carried away, but obviously it's an experience neither of us wants to repeat.'

Black eyebrows winged upwards. 'I was not apologising

for last night, *chérie*,' he said silkily, his eyes glinting with amusement. 'It was an incredible experience that I have every intention of repeating. You enjoyed it too,' he added before she could comment, 'so don't play the innocent martyr with me because you're a wildcat in bed and I have the scratches on my back to prove it.'

'Oh!' Scarlet-faced, she wished a hole would open up and swallow her, and more than anything she longed to wipe his smug grin from his face.

'My only regret about last night is that I was rough with you,' he continued, his husky, accented voice sliding over her like a velvet cloak. 'I was, as you so succinctly put it, carried away, and I'm afraid that in my urgency to possess you I might have hurt you. Did I, *ma petite*?'

His words evoked a stark image in Freya's mind of how she had begged him to take her; how she had enticed him with her desperate pleas to move faster and thrust deeper into her as he took her to the heights of sexual ecstasy. Zac's regrets had nothing on hers, she thought sickly, tearing her gaze from the knowing gleam in his. 'No,' she choked thickly, 'you didn't hurt me, but last night was a mistake I regret bitterly.'

She ran a shaky hand through her hair and forced herself to look at him. 'If it wasn't…that, then what are you apologising for?'

In reply he took a folded document from the drawer and handed it to her. For a few seconds Freya's heart stopped beating and then started again at twice its normal rate. She knew instinctively that it was the results of the paternity test and she stared at him without opening it. 'I already know what it says,' she told him quietly. 'And now, so do you.'

She searched his face for some sign that would tell her

how he felt about learning that Aimee was his child, but his expression was shuttered. This should be her moment of triumph, but she felt empty inside. For two years she'd played out a stupid daydream in her head that one day he would discover he was Aimee's father and would immediately beg her to forgive him for the way he had treated her, before sweeping her into his arms and pleading for a chance for them to live together as a family—in true happy-ever-after tradition. His grim face shattered her dream and the little seed of hope she'd carried in her heart withered and died. He didn't want their child any more than he wanted her, and it was about time she accepted that fact.

'Damn you, Zac,' she burst out when his silence became intolerable. 'There's no need to look so horrified,' she muttered bitterly. 'I don't want a penny of your wretched money. All I ever wanted was for Aimee to have a daddy who would love and protect her, and that clearly isn't going to be you. But I can do those things. I'll be a mother and a father to her and right now I'm taking her home.' She glared at him, and a frisson of unease ran the length of her spine when he stood up and strode around the desk.

'No, *chérie*, you are not,' he said steadily, his eyes narrowing when she jumped up and backed away from him. He could see the hurt and confusion in her eyes and felt a flicker of remorse. But when he closed the gap between them and noted how her pulse was jerking frantically at the base of her throat, he felt a surge of quiet satisfaction. Sexual alchemy was a potent force that held her in its thrall, however much she might resent its power.

There was no point in denying that he was deeply shocked by the results of the paternity test. Aimee was his child, a Deverell who, like him, was a possible carrier of the gene that had caused the illness and deaths of his baby sisters. His one relief was that Aimee was eighteen months old and safe from the risk of developing the disease, which caused death in infants usually before they were a year old.

Discovering that he was a father was something he hadn't been prepared for, but he had felt protective of Freya's child from the moment Joyce Addison had abandoned her to his care and he knew without doubt that he would love Aimee unconditionally for the rest of his life. Aimee was adorable and, having missed the first eighteen months of her life, he was determined not to miss another day.

His feelings towards Freya were more complicated. On the few occasions that she had crept into his mind during the past two years, he had angrily dismissed her, reminding himself of her true colours. But the moment he had seen her again he'd been forced to accept that his desire for her was as fierce as it had been in the past. He had made love to her last night because he couldn't resist her, and now it seemed that he didn't have to try. She hadn't lied to him, she was the mother of his child and she wanted him with the same urgency that he wanted her. All he had to do now was persuade her to resume her place in his bed.

'It seems that I am one of the rare cases for whom the vasectomy reversed, but now I know Aimee is my child and I accept that I have a responsibility for her.' he began, but Freya interrupted him.

'No, you don't.' She shook her head fiercely, hating the fact that he felt a duty towards Aimee. Her grandmother had tolerated her out of a sense of duty, but it had been a loveless upbringing and she would do everything in her power to prevent her daughter from feeling the same sense of worthlessness that she had felt as a child. 'I hereby absolve you of all responsibility. What were you planning to do, Zac—appease your conscience by arranging regular maintenance payments and maybe send her a birthday card once a year?' she demanded sarcastically. 'Aimee's conception was the result of a freak chance, it wasn't your fault and there's no reason for you to feel obligated towards either of us.'

'It's not a question of obligation,' Zac said forcefully. 'I want to play an active role in my daughter's life.' The ring of steely determination in his voice caused Freya's heart to jerk in her chest and she stared at him, bemused by his unexpected statement.

'You mean you want to arrange visitation rights? Think carefully, Zac. A child is for life, not just for Christmas,' she said sharply. 'It's all very well for you to decide you want to see Aimee occasionally, but what happens when the novelty of fatherhood wears off? I remember how excited I used to feel when my mother promised to visit, and the crushing sense of disappointment when she let me down yet again. I won't allow you to do that to Aimee.'

'That's not how it will be,' he stated angrily. 'Aimee is my child, a Deverell, and I want her to live here in Monaco.'

'But how would that work?' Freya argued faintly, her mind reeling. 'Even if I finish my degree, I'm not sufficiently fluent in French to find a job that would pay rent on a property here. Aimee's home is in England and that's where I'm taking her. If you're serious about wanting a relationship with her, you can easily afford to visit as often as it suits you.' Her tone plainly indicated that she believed he would soon lose interest in playing daddy, and Zac's jaw hardened.

'I wasn't suggesting that we live in separate homes and pass our daughter between us like a parcel. A child needs two parents and I want you and Aimee to move into the penthouse with me.'

For the sum total of twenty seconds Freya experienced a surge of incandescent joy—quickly followed by the feeling that her heart was plummeting towards her toes with the speed of an express elevator. Of course he wanted her to move back in with him—it would be much more convenient for him than having to travel back to England to visit Aimee. She was still stunned by Zac's declaration that he intended to be a proper father. Undoubtedly Aimee would benefit from having both her parents around, but what role was he expecting *her* to play in his life?

'Won't that cramp your style?' she queried sarcastically. 'You can hardly maintain your reputation as Monaco's most eligible bachelor with an ex-lover and a baby in tow.'

His slow, sensual smile sent a tremor of awareness through her. 'Since last night, you're no longer an *ex*-lover, are you?' he murmured softly, his warm breath fanning her ear.

Freya suddenly became aware that he was too close; she could feel the heat from his body and the waves of sexual energy emanating from him triggered alarm bells in her head. She took a jerky step backwards, but his arm snaked around her waist to draw her inexorably towards him.

'You know how it was between us, Freya. Don't deny it,' he said fiercely when she opened her mouth to remonstrate. 'The passion we shared was explosive for both of us, *chérie*.'

'No.' Freya made an inarticulate sound low in her throat as she watched his head descend. Any second now his mouth would touch hers and she would be lost to the simmering, burning need that only Zac could arouse. Outrage battled with desire and won by a narrow margin. 'Do you honestly think you can click your fingers and I'll fall into your arms?' she demanded, shamefully aware that she had done exactly that the previous night. 'Yesterday I was a common slut with a predilection for wealthy lovers—'

'That was before I knew the truth,' he interrupted harshly. 'I know now that I was wrong and I am willing to accept that you didn't sleep with Brooks.'

'That's big of you,' Freya muttered bitterly, 'but you're too late, Zac. It's a pity you didn't believe me two years ago—when I needed you. Instead you almost destroyed me with your distrust, and, to be frank, I wouldn't come back to you if you were the last man on the planet.'

His slow smile disarmed her and she missed the warning gleam of battle in his eyes. 'We'll see, shall we?' he said softly, tightening his arm around her until her face was pressed against his chest.

'Let go of me, you...brute.' She hammered her fists on his shoulders, like a wild bird frantically beating its wings against the bars of a cage, but he ignored her blows and threaded his other hand through her hair, tilting her face to his. The scorching heat in his gaze sent a quiver of excitement through her and she gave a silent groan of despair. How could she fight him when this was the only place she wanted to be? Clutching the remnants of her pride, she tried to turn her head, but lean fingers held her chin as he angled her mouth to his satisfaction before claiming it with his own in a searing kiss that drove all thoughts of resistance from her mind.

His tongue explored the contours of her lips, stroking, caressing, until he judged the moment she relaxed her guard and thrust into the moist warmth of her mouth in a flagrantly erotic gesture. Freya felt the drugging sweetness of desire flood through her veins, leaving her limp and boneless with longing. Her fists unfurled and she laid her hands flat against his chest, feeling the erratic thud of his heart beneath her fingertips.

'Last night was a mistake. We can't simply take up where we left off two years ago,' she protested when he eased the pressure of his mouth and traced her swollen lips with the tip of his tongue. 'Too much has happened, Zac. You hurt me so badly,' she whispered as she relived the agony of his rejection and the countless nights when she had cried herself to sleep. She was appalled by her weakness—how could she be such a pushover? He was probably congratulating himself that he had demolished her resistance with one kiss, but when she stared into his eyes and saw the undisguised hunger flare in his blue depths she felt a heady sense of elation. He felt it too, this pagan drumbeat of desire that pounded in her veins until she was conscious of nothing but the desperate, overwhelming need to surrender her soul to passion.

'Then let me try to make amends,' he growled against her throat. 'Let me remind you of how good it was between us and show you how good it can be again. We always communicated better without words, *chérie*.' He slid his hands down and curled them possessively around her buttocks, drawing her up against him so that her pelvis was in direct contact with the throbbing force of his arousal.

Freya gasped and he captured the faint sound, grinding his lips on hers with a primitive passion that whipped her senses into a feverish state of anticipation. She was on fire for him and nothing else mattered—not the past and all the pain he'd caused her and not the future and all its uncertainties. She wanted him now, the only man she had ever loved, and when he lifted her into his arms she clung to him, her fingers tearing at his shirt buttons until she was able to part the material and run her hands over the dark hairs that covered his chest.

Zac cleared the surface of his desk with one sweep of his arm before laying her down on the polished wood and immediately covering her body with his own. He deftly removed her blouse and muttered his satisfaction that she wasn't wearing a bra, his voice hoarse as he bent his head and captured the tip of one pink nipple between his lips. The effect on Freya was electric and she arched her back so that her breasts thrust provocatively towards him, the taut, swollen peaks begging for his possession.

She was shaking—or was it him? she wondered feverishly as she pushed his shirt over his shoulders and ran her hands over his smooth, tanned skin. This was madness but they were both caught up in the conflagration that threatened to consume them in a flame of white-hot need. With a rough, almost violent movement he grabbed the hem of her skirt and jerked it up to her waist before skimming his hand over the sensitive flesh of her inner thighs.

'Zac.' His name escaped her lips as a plea rather than a protest. She lifted her hips and he dragged her knickers down before spreading her legs with a deliberate intent that made her tremble with anticipation. When he touched her she thrust against his hand and moaned when his skilful fingers slid into her and began to explore her with a thoroughness that made her clench her teeth as her pleasure built. Through heavy lids she watched his hand move to the zip of his trousers, no thought in her head other than that he should hurry before she died with the urgent need to feel the full length of him inside her.

'You see, Freya, some things never change,' he groaned as he came down on top of her, supporting his weight on his elbows so that the rigid strength of his penis pushed intimately against her eager body. He slid his hand beneath her bottom to lift her towards him, but his words penetrated the haze of sexual heat surrounding her and she bunched her hands on his shoulders to hold him back.

Was it the element of satisfaction in his voice that she had capitulated so easily—yet again? Or was it his arrogant assumption that nothing had changed and she was still a slave to his touch, despite the way he had treated her? She closed her eyes as a wave of nausea swept over her—how could she be so stupid? Zac hadn't changed—he said he believed that she hadn't had an affair with Simon Brooks, but only because the DNA test proved that Aimee was his child. Two years ago he had been so ready to believe the worst of her and if other issues arose between them in the future she had no faith that he would trust her word above all else.

'You're wrong, Zac,' she whispered fiercely. '*I've* changed. I'm not the pathetic, lovesick girl I once was. You abandoned me when I needed you most, and I had to grow up fast. I won't let you do this to me again,' she muttered, tearing her gaze from him as she fought to control the dictates of her body that *begged* for her to surrender and accept his full possession. From somewhere she found the strength to push against his chest, but the glitter in his eyes warned her that she was too late. His body was primed and ready to take her, his breath coming in harsh gasps as he fought for control.

The discreet knock on the study door shattered the tension and the butler, Laurent's, imperturbable tones sounded through the wood. 'Madame Deverell has arrived and is waiting in the salon.'

Hysterical laughter bubbled in Freya's throat. '*Madame?* You have a *wife?*'

'*Non*, I have a mother—who has impeccable timing,' Zac

replied sardonically as he rolled off her and snatched up his shirt, muttering a string of profanities beneath his breath. 'But the very fact that you believe I could be married does not say much about your opinion of me, *chérie.*'

'It's an opinion I formed during the time I've spent struggling to bring up our child,' Freya bit back sharply. She couldn't imagine what he must think of her when she was semi-naked and spread-eagled across his desk. Scarlet-cheeked, she tugged her skirt down and hopped inelegantly from foot to foot trying to pull her knickers on, praying that Zac's mother wouldn't walk in. She'd suffered enough humiliation to last her a lifetime—much of it self-induced, she thought miserably as she recalled her shameless response to him. One thing was clear: she dared not trust herself to be near him for another day. He could deal with his mother and explain why his elegant bachelor pad was littered with toys and teddies, while she collected Aimee and made her escape.

'I'll go and speak to my mother while you tidy yourself up,' he said tersely, his expression unfathomable as he inspected her dishevelled appearance and hot face. He on the other hand looked as cool as a cucumber and had obviously had no difficulty in bringing his desire under control. Any minute now and he would pop a couple of bank notes down her blouse in payment for services rendered, Freya thought furiously, shrivelling beneath his look of haughty disdain. She held her breath until he left the room, and as soon as he had gone raced around his desk and searched for the passports. Flights back to England would stretch her overdraft to its limit, she acknowledged ruefully, but it couldn't be helped, she had to get away.

Ignoring the sound of voices from the sitting room, she raced along the hall to the nursery and snatched up the holdall she'd packed with Aimee's things. With any luck she could collect her daughter from the roof-garden, bid a quick farewell to Jean Lewis and disappear before Zac realised that she had no intention of remaining at the penthouse until he grew bored of fatherhood. At the doorway she spun round and gave one final glance around the room, groaning when she spied Aimee's favourite toy rabbit at the end of the cot. With a muttered curse she dropped the holdall and flew across the carpet to retrieve the toy, her heart sinking at the sound of Zac's voice.

'There you are—I thought you were going to come and meet my mother,' Zac drawled, his eyes narrowing when Freya gasped at the sight of him.

'I...thought Aimee was here,' she said quickly, praying that he wouldn't notice the holdall behind the door.

'She's with Jean in the salon. My mother would very much like to meet you,' he added quietly.

'You never introduced me to her during the time I lived with you,' Freya muttered, remembering how hurt she'd felt when Zac had used to visit Yvette Deverell but never suggested that she accompany him. 'Why the sudden urgency?'

'The situation is different now.' He paused and then explained, 'When you lived here, my mother was still devastated at the loss of my father. She became a virtual recluse and I was the only person she wanted to see. Thankfully she is much better now and she's eager to meet you.'

The glint in Zac's eyes warned Freya that she had no option but to comply and she hastily shoved the passports behind her back and followed him down the hall. Voices were audible from the salon, Jean Lewis' calm tones and another, heavily accented voice, mingled with Aimee's gurgling laughter. 'What an adorable child—how old is she?'

'Eighteen months,' Zac answered his mother's query as

he ushered Freya into the room while Jean quietly excused herself. '*Maman,* this is Freya Addison—Aimee's mother.'

'Mademoiselle Addison.' Yvette Deverell stood and held out one elegantly manicured hand to Freya. She was tall, willowy and effortlessly chic in an exquisite dress and jacket from one of the leading fashion houses. Freya immediately felt conscious of the creases in her cheap skirt and, as had so often happened during her childhood, she was swamped by a feeling of inadequacy, not helped when Yvette continued to study her from beneath faintly arched eyebrows, in a silence that spoke volumes. 'You have a delightful little girl,' she commented at last, and Freya stiffened when Zac placed his arm around her waist and drew her forwards.

'Aimee is my daughter, *Maman.*' He spoke softly to his mother. 'You have a granddaughter.'

Freya was prepared for Yvette to look surprised, shocked even, but the expression of horrified dismay on the Frenchwoman's face filled her with cold fury. Suddenly she was eight years old, walking up the path of Nana Joyce's house clutching the hand of the social worker who had collected her from the foster family she had been staying with. There had been no look of pleasure on her grandmother's face when she had opened the door, no welcoming smile.

'You'd better go up to your room, Freya, and mind you don't make any noise. You can come down at teatime as long as you're quiet—I don't expect to be disturbed by childish chatter,' Joyce Addison had greeted her coldly.

To this day she rarely spoke unless spoken to, and even in her own flat she'd crept about on tiptoe out of habit, Freya thought bleakly. Her grandmother had crushed her spirit and destroyed her self-confidence—she would not allow Zac's mother to do the same to Aimee.

'I don't understand. How can this be?' Yvette Deverell was staring at her son, a look of blank incomprehension on her face. 'Are you certain this is your child?'

Her comments were the last straw, Freya decided furiously, her face burning with mortification as she tugged out of Zac's hold and grasped Aimee's hand. It was bad enough that Zac had doubted Aimee's paternity—how dared his mother do the same? 'There was some debate over whether Aimee belonged to the tinker, the tailor or the candlestick maker,' she snapped, her eyes flashing fire as she met Yvette Deverell's stunned glance. 'Zac is Aimee's biological parent, but that's where his involvement ends. Please don't worry, *madame*, I'm taking my daughter home to England and, I assure you, you won't see either of us again.'

'Zac! I don't understand.' Yvette bombarded her son in a torrent of rapid French while Freya spun on her heel and raced towards the door, tugging Aimee after her. But Zac beat her to it and stood blocking her path, his eyes focused intently on her face.

'Let me go,' she said in a low voice that shook as she struggled to keep her emotions in check. 'Aimee doesn't belong here. Your mother just made that abundantly clear. She's my daughter and I'm taking her home.'

'Zac, I insist you tell me what is happening,' Yvette demanded plaintively.

'Calm down, *Maman*,' he ordered impatiently as he lifted Aimee against his chest. Without giving Freya a chance to react, he captured her chin with his lean fingers and lowered his head to take her mouth in a brief, searing kiss. 'There has been a simple misunderstanding, but it's sorted now,' he said coolly, his bruising grip on her chin preventing her from speaking while his eyes burned into hers. 'Freya agrees that our daughter should grow up in Monaco with her family, and from now on she and Aimee will live permanently here in the penthouse with me. Isn't that so, *chérie*?'

CHAPTER SEVEN

'I CAN'T believe you said that to your mother.' Freya yelled at Zac as she stormed down the hall after him and followed him into his room. 'I can see we're going to have to come to some sort of arrangement so that you can see Aimee regularly—now that you're suddenly determined to win the award for Father of the Year,' she added sarcastically. 'But I'm not moving into the penthouse just for your convenience. I do have a life of my own, you know,' she said sharply, her temper rising when he ignored her. Breathing hard, she glared at him, her brain barely registering the fact that he was unbuttoning his shirt. 'Why are you doing this?' she demanded angrily. 'You don't want me living here as some sort of permanent house guest any more than you want the responsibilities of a child.

'Let me take Aimee home and I swear I'll never contact you again. I don't need you, Zac,' she said thickly, knowing that the words were a lie. She needed him in the same way that she needed oxygen to breathe, but she wouldn't allow her daughter to grow up feeling that she was an encumbrance in her father's life. Aimee was already forming an emotional attachment to Zac and Freya couldn't bear to see him hurt her with his indifference.

'Perhaps you don't, but what about Aimee's needs?' Zac

asked quietly. He deciphered the jumble of emotions on her face and felt a curious pain in his gut. After the way he had misjudged her, he supposed she had every right to mistrust his motives, but he didn't like it. 'My mother was shocked to discover that she has a granddaughter,' he said, attempting to explain Yvette Deverell's reaction to Aimee, 'understandably so when she believed I would never have a child.'

'You didn't want a child,' Freya pointed out sharply.

'*Non*, but there were reasons…'

'You mean the idea of fatherhood didn't mix with your life as a jet-setting playboy,' she agreed scathingly. 'Aimee isn't an accessory that you can pick up or set down when it suits you. She deserves to be loved.'

'And I will love her—I already do,' he vowed, his voice suddenly fierce. 'I can provide her with everything she needs. I regret missing the first eighteen months of her life more than you will ever know and I will not miss another day. I don't want to fight you, Freya—you're her mother and she needs you, but she needs me too and I'll fight through the courts if necessary to keep her here.'

The floor swayed beneath Freya's feet and all colour leached from her face. 'You can't be serious.'

'I've never been more serious in my life,' Zac assured her grimly.

Freya shook her head, feeling as though it were going to explode. She had assumed that Zac would want as little contact as possible with his daughter and she could barely comprehend that he was prepared to fight a custody battle over her. And it was a battle he would surely win, she thought sickly. He could afford the best legal representation, who would argue that Aimee would want for nothing in his care. What could she offer in comparison? she brooded miserably, thinking of the life they led in England and her daily struggle to hold down a job and look after Aimee properly. Aimee would undoubtedly have a better life here in Monaco, but Zac couldn't seriously expect her to put her life on hold and move in with him, could he?

'I can understand that you want to build a relationship with Aimee and it would be in her best interest if you decide to be a proper father to her. But what role are you expecting me to play in your life?' Freya's voice faltered as she finally registered that he had removed his shirt and was in the process of unzipping his trousers.

'I would have thought that was obvious,' he drawled, trailing his eyes over her flushed face. 'You will resume your role as my mistress. We've already proved that, on a physical level, we're made for each other,' he continued, overriding her gasp of outraged denial. 'The sexual attraction between us is as explosive now as it was two years ago. I know now that you didn't have an affair with Brooks and I can see no reason why I shouldn't take you back in my bed.' His trousers slid to the floor and he stepped out of them before strolling across the room towards her. 'Obviously providing Aimee with a secure and stable upbringing is our main concern and the fact that we can enjoy a fantastic sex life is a bonus, wouldn't you say, *chérie*?'

Despite her fury at his arrogant assumption that she would gratefully accept his offer to grace his bed once more, Freya could not prevent her eyes from straying down to his boxers and her stomach tightened at the burgeoning proof of his arousal jutting unashamedly beneath the black silk. 'You've got a nerve, Zac,' she muttered, licking her suddenly dry lips. 'Clearly, in your belief that you're God's gift, it hasn't occurred to you that I don't want to be your mistress. The idea is ridiculous. We're totally incompatible. Zac! What are you doing?' The last came out as a breathless gasp as he deftly shrugged out of his underwear.

'Taking a shower—I didn't have time earlier after my swim. Come and join me while we finish this fascinating conversation,' he invited with a wolfish smile. His eyes gleamed from beneath heavy lids and the room suddenly throbbed with sexual tension that sent Freya scooting towards the door.

'You must be joking,' she choked, but her words were muffled against his shoulder as he swept her up into his arms as if she were a rag doll and strode purposefully into the *en suite*. 'Zac, we'll talk later… What is the point in this?' she demanded when he activated the shower and stepped beneath the spray with her, still fully clothed and wriggling like an eel to escape him.

'The point, my little vixen,' he said as he trapped her flailing hands in one of his to prevent her raining blows on his chest, 'is to prove that in certain areas, at least, we are completely compatible.' His head descended and he claimed her mouth, silencing her furious words by kissing her into submission. He knew just how to please her, and he felt a jolt of satisfaction when the tight line of her lips suddenly parted and he was able to dip his tongue between them to explore the moist warmth of her mouth.

Freya gave a helpless groan of protest that was lost beneath the pressure of his lips. Her body was still agonisingly aroused from earlier, when he had laid her across his desk. It had taken all her will-power to stop him from taking her and her senses were greedily snatching this second chance for fulfilment. The powerful spray had already soaked through her clothes and, without lifting his mouth from hers, Zac stripped her of her blouse and skirt. Only then did he trail his lips down her throat to her breasts, where he paused and flicked his tongue back and forth across one tight nipple and then the other until she cried out and felt a sharp tug of desire deep in her pelvis. She clung to his shoulders when he knelt before her and drew her knickers down. Water ran down his face and made his skin glisten and the sight of his dark head moving inexorably down to the triangle of blonde curls between her thighs filled her with a frantic sense of urgency that destroyed any thoughts she'd had of denying him.

'Lift your leg,' he growled, his voice thick and slurred with sexual promise as he pushed her gently up against the tiled shower wall and hooked her ankle over his shoulder. Now she was spread before him and he tenderly parted her with his long, clever fingers before dipping his tongue between the velvet folds of her femininity.

Freya gave a muffled sob and dug her fingers into his hair as he explored her with a wicked intimacy that sent quivers of pleasure through her, building higher and higher until she was trembling with need. 'Please, Zac…' she implored him, but he ignored her and flicked his tongue over her clitoris in fierce, fast little movements that tipped her over the edge of ecstasy. She shuddered as her muscles clenched in wave after wave of exquisite sensation and in the throes of her climax he stood, lifted her into his arms and ordered her to wrap her thighs around him. Freya complied instantly, aware of nothing but the dictates of her body that still wanted more, and she closed her eyes on a shocked gasp when he penetrated her with one hard thrust.

Last night he had been so blown away by her eager response to him that he had almost lost control, but this time

Zac was determined to prove that he was her master. He cupped her bottom and drove into her with slow, steady strokes that filled her and made her arch her back as her pleasure built again. It was deeper this time, even more intense, and she clung to him, totally enslaved by his domination as he finally gave in to her desperate pleas and increased his pace, taking her hard and fast until she threw back her head and convulsed around him in an orgasm that shattered all her preconceived notions of sexual ecstasy.

Freya sobbed his name and locked her ankles tightly around his back, but, instead of taking his own pleasure, he abruptly withdrew from her and set her back on her feet, his nostrils flaring as he fought for control.

'Why…?' She tailed to a halt and looked at him with a mixture of confusion and scalding embarrassment as she recalled her shameless response to him. Once again she'd proved that she was completely in his power and she knew he would ruthlessly use that knowledge to bend her to his will.

'I don't keep condoms in the shower,' he told her bluntly, his eyes trailing over her scarlet cheeks. 'Remiss of me—I must remember in future that you enjoy sex outside the bedroom as much as in it.' His eyes glinted with amusement at her outraged glare and, before she could argue, he took the bar of soap and began to stroke it in circular movements over her breasts. 'Now I know that the vasectomy reversed I can't risk another accidental conception.'

'Aimee may have been an accident, but I don't regret having her,' Freya said heatedly, a shudder running through her when he slid the bar of soap over her stomach and lower to her thighs and buttocks. 'That'll do, I'm clean enough,' she said, bitterly resenting the way her body was quivering in anticipation of his touch once more. Clearly she was some sort of nymphomaniac, she thought grimly, because she couldn't get enough of him.

'Be honest, Zac, you never wanted children. You wouldn't have had a vasectomy if you had. You can still have a relationship with Aimee if I take her back to England,' she told him when he stepped out of the shower, wrapped a towel around her and carried her into his bedroom, 'but you don't really want to be tied down with a child living permanently here in the penthouse.' Her breath left her body on a gasp when he dropped her unceremoniously on the bed, but to her disappointment he did not join her and instead crossed to his wardrobe and selected a clean shirt and trousers.

'Aimee is my daughter and she belongs here,' he said as he slid into his clothes with his usual lithe grace. 'You know from your own childhood experiences that it's best for a child to grow up in a stable environment with two parents and, for that reason, I'm prepared to allow you back in my life.'

He slid his arms into his suit jacket and strolled over to the bed, his mouth curving into a mocking smile as he stared down at her lying sprawled on the silk bedspread. 'I have to go to the office for a couple of hours but I'll keep the image in my mind of your delectable naked body spread across my bed. This is where you belong, *chérie*, ready and willing to please me.' He leaned over her and stemmed her furious rebuttal of his arrogant statement by kissing her senseless before he straightened and traced his thumb pad over her swollen lips. 'You want me, Freya, and as my mistress you can have me, every single night. Now, be a good girl and stop arguing. Most women would be grateful for the opportunity to move in with a billionaire lover.'

Good girl! Incandescent with rage, Freya wondered if

she could beat him to death with a pillow. 'Unluckily for you, I'm not most women, and if you think I'd ever agree to be your grateful, *obedient* mistress you're going to be disappointed,' she hissed between her clenched teeth.

Zac was already at the door, but he paused and turned to give her a wicked grin. 'Good—I'd much rather have a disobedient mistress,' he drawled. 'It promises to be a lot more fun.'

Two weeks later Freya sat gloomily on a sun lounger, aware that even the beauty of her surroundings failed to lighten her mood. The penthouse roof-garden was a suntrap where scarlet geraniums grew in profusion, their bold colour vying for attention with the azure pool and the sea sparkling on the horizon. She had spent the morning watching while Aimee played with her father in the pool, but now Jean had taken the little girl to the nursery for a nap and she and Zac were alone.

'Are you hot? Come for a swim to cool off,' Zac invited, his eyes gleaming with wicked amusement when she quickly shook her head. 'I promise I won't duck you.'

'Your promises count for nothing,' Freya told him firmly, dragging her gaze from the sight of him floating on his back in the pool. His skin had darkened to bronze in the hot sun and she felt the familiar weakness in the pit of her stomach when he swam to the steps and hauled himself out. Droplets of water trickled down his chest and clung to the mass of wiry black hairs that arrowed down beneath the waistband of his swimming shorts. The muscles of his taut abdomen were clearly visible beneath his skin and when he walked over to her and picked up a towel Freya suddenly became fascinated with the view over the bay.

'You practically drowned me the last time you persuaded

me to swim with you,' she accused, recalling how he had swum up behind her and tugged her under. Taken by surprise, she'd been forced to cling to him—out of her depth in more ways than one, she acknowledged ruefully as the memory of being clamped against his muscular chest while he carried her to the edge of the pool filled her mind.

'Don't you trust me?' He grinned unrepentantly, but beneath his teasing tone she caught a hint of seriousness and she bit her lip as she silently debated the question.

Did she trust him? As far as their child was concerned, she did not doubt that he would always consider Aimee's welfare paramount. Two weeks had passed since he had received the results of the DNA test and stated his intention to be a proper father to his daughter, and in that time he had proved himself to be a devoted parent. Freya knew that the bond between father and daughter was already so strong that she could never break it.

Aimee adored her *papa* and with each day that passed Freya felt more and more trapped. She loved her daughter and wanted what was best for her, and undoubtedly Aimee was thriving here in Monaco, showered in affection from Zac, her nanny, Jean Lewis, and the other members of the penthouse staff. Even the taciturn butler, Laurent, had been won over by the baby and could often be found padding up and down the hall on his hands and knees while Aimee glee-fully balanced on his back.

Aimee was enjoying the happy family life that Freya had dreamed of as a child, but it was Zac's mother who had sur-prised her the most. Yvette Deverell seemed utterly en-tranced with her little granddaughter and was the most loving, devoted grandmother imaginable. She visited most days and Freya was still amazed by the sight of the elegant

Frenchwoman sitting cross-legged on the carpet playing tea parties with Aimee and her teddies. Aimee had formed a very special relationship with *Mamie*, which Freya would never try to destroy. Her daughter belonged here—but what about her? Where did she belong? she wondered bleakly.

Zac had told her that he wanted her to move in with him for Aimee's sake, but since then he'd made no further reference to her becoming his mistress, or how he envisaged their future together—possibly because he had now decided that they didn't have one, she brooded dismally. He had made no attempt to make love to her during the past two weeks even though he knew full well that she would not resist him. Perhaps he had found her eagerness unattractive, she thought on a wave of embarrassment, or maybe, now that he'd had her, he was already tired of her. Whatever his reasons, he had spent the past weeks being charmingly attentive each evening when he returned home from work, but conspicuously absent from her bed each night, and she felt confused and, if she was honest, incredibly frustrated.

She tried not to look at him rubbing the towel over his damp body, but she was painfully aware of the fact that his wet shorts were clinging to his thighs, leaving little to her imagination. Hopefully he would announce that he had some work to do in his study. It was Saturday, and she remembered that when she had lived with him he had spent most of his weekends either working or indulging his passion for a variety of sports, but to her dismay he did not immediately disappear into the penthouse and instead lowered himself into the chair next to hers. She instantly stiffened and her heart began to thud heavily in her chest. He was too close and her senses flared when he idly placed his arm along the back of her chair.

'What are these?' he queried, glancing at the photo albums on the table.

'You said you'd like to see some pictures of Aimee when she was first born,' she replied, grateful for the excuse to edge away from him. 'My neighbour has a key to my flat and I asked her to send these over. They're mainly snaps taken with a disposable camera and the quality isn't brilliant,' she said apologetically as he silently leafed through the album where she had faithfully recorded every milestone of Aimee's development. 'Aimee's a little poseur, don't you think?' She laughed, studying the image of her daughter on her first birthday.

'She's beautiful,' Zac murmured huskily, his accent suddenly very pronounced as he stared at the picture of a smiling Aimee proudly showing off her first tooth. He had missed so much, he acknowledged as he picked up another picture of Aimee as a newborn baby. Someone else had obviously taken the photo of Freya in the delivery room, smiling bravely despite the exhaustion in her eyes as she clutched her tiny bundle.

Freya looked young and scared as she faced the stark reality of coping with motherhood alone, but he recognised the determined set of her chin and felt a flare of admiration for her. Freya's fragile looks were deceptive; she had a backbone of steel and he found himself in awe of her strength. She had stated that she didn't need him and he had no doubts that, if it had not been for the accident, she would have brought Aimee up to be a happy, well-adjusted child without any help from him.

Now he knew Aimee was his child and he was willing to try and atone for misjudging Freya by suggesting that they become lovers once more. He knew without conceit that most women would jump at this chance—but, typically of Freya, she had reacted as though he were asking her to do something unpleasant, he thought irritably. He was offering her a life of luxury that most women would give their eye-teeth for—what more did she want, for heaven's sake?

He wanted things settled between them; he was impatient to bed her—hell, he was practically climbing the walls with sexual frustration—but, taken aback by her violent opposition to his suggestion, he had decided to play it cool and, instead of sweeping her off to bed, he had kept his distance while he waited for her to acknowledge that, on a physical level at least, they were made for each other.

He wanted a warm and willing woman in his bed, not a resentful little shrew, but unfortunately his efforts to charm her had so far been unsuccessful. For a man used to getting his own way instantly, it was hugely frustrating, and he felt curiously tense and unsettled and he was fast running out of patience. Perhaps the time had come for a change of tactics? he brooded. Perhaps he should forget his good intentions and make love to her until she was utterly compliant to the idea of resuming their relationship on his terms?

A loose photo slipped from the back of the album and he reached down to retrieve it at the same moment as Freya. Their hands briefly touched before she snatched her fingers away and she gave an incoherent murmur when he turned the photo over and stared at his own image.

She must have taken it soon after she had moved in with him, he guessed, glancing speculatively at her pink cheeks. Had she kept it because he had meant something to her even though he had done his best to destroy her with his mistrust?

'I didn't know that was in there. I'd forgotten I'd even taken it,' Freya said as she gathered up the rest of the photos and slotted them back into the album. 'I'll get rid of it. It doesn't mean anything to me.' She held out her hand for the picture, praying he wouldn't realise that the edges were furled from where she had held it so often. It would be unbearably humiliating if he should ever guess that she had mooned over his image like a lovesick teenager.

She swallowed when he leaned forwards and placed the photo in her hand, his gaze settling on her hot face. 'We had some good times, didn't we, *chérie*?' he said coolly.

'You mean the sex was good,' she muttered, striving to sound indifferent and aware that her voice was annoyingly breathless. She didn't want to remember the time she'd lived with him; it was too painful, especially now that she was back at the penthouse and Zac was suddenly being so charming. It had been easier when he'd denounced her as a cheating whore—at least then she had been able to kid herself that she hated him.

'It was more than good. There were any number of women I could have had sex with,' he said coolly, the nuance in his tone telling her that those women would have been far more experienced between the sheets than a shy virgin from a sleepy English backwater.

'Well, I don't suppose your bed was empty for very long after you threw me out of it,' Freya said bitterly. 'Annalise Dubois for one was determined to snare you.'

'Perhaps,' he agreed with a shrug. 'I admit I have never lived the life of a monk, either before you were my mistress or after we split up. But I had the best, most unforgettable sex with you, *chérie*.' He suddenly leaned forwards and placed his hands on the arms of her chair, effectively caging her in. His brilliant blue eyes glinted with a message she didn't dare decipher and for the life of her she could not help focusing on his mouth. He was so gorgeous, she thought despairingly. Would she ever be free from this ache that seemed to be a permanent feature in her chest? She could not ignore the unmistakable prickle of sexual energy between them and shrank back in her seat, fighting her body's traitorous response to him and licking her lips nervously when he leaned even closer.

'Even when I despised you, I realised that the sexual chemistry between us burns as strong as before. I know you feel it too. I've seen the way you watch me when you think I'm not looking,' he said bluntly, his gaze trapping hers as if he knew exactly what was going on inside her head.

'You obviously have a vivid imagination,' she snapped, blushing furiously. 'Let me up. I want to go and check on Aimee. She's probably woken from her nap by now.' She tried to push him away but his warm breath fanned her skin and she gave a low moan, half protest and half pleasure, when he brushed his lips lightly over hers. It felt like heaven after the past two weeks when he had made no attempt to entice her into his bed. He had treated her with polite deference, as if she were an honoured guest at the penthouse, but, rather than feeling reassured that he was obviously no longer interested in her, she had *ached* for him to take her in his arms.

Now Freya's lips parted of their own accord. She couldn't help it—he only had to look at her and she was lost, she conceded helplessly. She hated herself for her weakness, but the stroke of his tongue was sweetly beguiling, and when he delved between her lips to explore the moist inner warmth of her mouth she responded with all the pent up need that had kept her awake until dawn every night since she had arrived in Monaco.

Zac's hands remained gripping her chair, his knuckles white with the effort of restraining himself from reaching out to caress her smooth skin—no longer pale, but warmed to the colour of pale gold from the sun. She was so lovely, and he was so very hungry for her, he acknowledged grimly as he felt his body react with shaming eagerness to the feel of her deliciously soft lips parting beneath his. The time for patience was over and he wanted to reacquaint himself with every inch of her delectable body.

He knew she wanted him. He saw it in the way desire darkened her eyes to the colour of a stormy sea and felt it in her unguarded response to him when he kissed her. She belonged with him, in his bed. He had hurt her, and for that he was sorry, but he was a pragmatic man. The tension and mistrust between them was in the past and he could see no reason why they should not enjoy the explosive passion that had always existed between them. But now was not the time, he conceded with a groan.

The scent of her skin was ambrosia and he inhaled sharply, his nostrils flaring as he sought to bring his hormones under control. 'My mother has invited us over—although I believe she used the lure of lunch as an excuse to see her granddaughter,' he added dryly. 'You'd better go and put some clothes on and dress Aimee in one of the new outfits Yvette bought her.'

He moved abruptly away from her, leaving Freya with the distinct impression that she had been dismissed. But then she had served her purpose, she conceded dismally. It was obvious that Zac had wanted her to agree to take Aimee to his mother's, and kissing her into submission had seemed the simplest method of getting his own way. It was entirely her own fault that she was such a weak, pathetic fool where he

was concerned, she told herself sternly as she marched into
the penthouse, unaware that he had dived into the pool and
was slicing through the water as if his life depended on it.

CHAPTER EIGHT

YVETTE DEVERELL still lived at La Maison des Fleurs, the pretty white-walled villa where Zac had spent his childhood. She greeted Freya warmly and beamed with genuine delight when Aimee held out her arms, demanding to be picked up.

'And how is *mon petit ange* today? Have you come to play with your *mamie*?' she cooed, her elegantly made-up face breaking into a wide smile. 'Freya, Aimee looks adorable in her little dress,' she commented as she led the way outside to the terrace where lunch was to be served. 'The boutique has the same style in blue. I'll buy it for her tomorrow.'

'That's very kind, but she has so many clothes,' Freya murmured, thinking of the numerous exquisite outfits Yvette had already bought Aimee, as well as the stack of toys and teddies that now filled the nursery.

'But I love to buy her things.' Zac's mother's smile faded a little and she glanced worriedly at Freya. 'My heart was so empty after my husband died, but now my granddaughter has filled that space. Perhaps I seem too forward; too eager and you resent my intrusion? But I cannot stop myself from loving her,' she finished, her voice wavering slightly.

Freya thought of her dismal childhood with her own grandmother, whose cold indifference had been so hurtful, and she gave Yvette a smile. 'I don't resent you or your obvious affection for Aimee,' she promised softly. She glanced across the lawn, to where Zac was tickling Aimee and making her squeal with laughter and felt a flutter of fear in her chest. Did she have the right to take Aimee back to England—away from this beautiful place and the people who loved her? 'I'm glad she has a family,' she said quietly. 'She's so happy here.'

Yvette glanced at her speculatively. 'And what about you, Freya?' she enquired gently. 'I hope you are happy too. My son has not confided in me and I would never presume to ask, but I know things have not always been as they should be between you.' She smiled and tentatively touched Freya's hand. 'I would very much like us to be friends.'

Warmth stole through Freya's veins and she returned Yvette's smile. She realised that Zac's mother was probably anxious for them to have a good relationship so that she could continue to see Aimee, but she seemed to be genuinely caring, and after a lifetime of rejection Freya could not help but respond to the Frenchwoman's kindness.

'I'd like that too,' she said, swallowing the sudden lump in her throat. She was glad of the opportunity to establish a relationship with Zac's mother, but there was no escaping the fact that it was time she had a similar conversation with Zac himself. She couldn't remain in Monaco as his guest indefinitely, and she was adamant that she would not accept his outrageous offer to live with him as his mistress, but how were they going to organise parenting Aimee when they lived a thousand miles apart?

Lunch was a relaxed affair during which Yvette regaled Freya with tales of Zac's boyhood and his frequent daring exploits that she laughingly insisted had turned her hair prematurely grey. From the sound of it, Zac had enjoyed a wonderfully happy childhood in the care of his loving parents. Yvette had clearly cherished being a mother and it seemed curious that she had not had more children. Perhaps they had been content, just the three of them, Freya mused enviously. Zac must have been the centre of his parents' world and had grown up confident of their love. She wanted Aimee to grow up in the same environment of happy family life, but the reality was that she was a single mother and she still didn't know exactly how Zac saw his future role in his daughter's life.

'Now, *ma petite*,' Yvette said to Aimee after lunch, 'what shall we do this afternoon, while *Papa* takes your *maman* out on his boat? Would you like to play on your swing?'

Aimee joyfully clapped her hands and scrambled off Freya's lap. She was fascinated by the wooden swing in *Mamie*'s garden and trotted off with her grandmother without a backward glance at Freya.

'I'm not happy about leaving her,' Freya muttered, trying to hide the pang of hurt that her baby seemed perfectly happy without her. 'You go out on the boat; I'd prefer to stay here.'

'She'll be fine for a couple of hours. My mother won't allow her out of her sight for a second,' Zac reassured her. 'I thought you might enjoy a relaxing afternoon,' he added persuasively. 'You must have found it a strain being Aimee's sole carer, but now we can share the responsibility and you can spend some time off duty.'

'I've never minded looking after her,' Freya argued, refusing to admit that there had been times when she'd felt overwhelmed by the enormity of bringing up a child on her own.

'I know, and you've done an amazing job, but I don't

underestimate how hard it must have been. You're not alone any longer, Freya, and it's time you accepted that fact.' He paused fractionally and then murmured, 'Besides, it will give us an opportunity to talk. I've a suggestion I want to put to you.'

Freya couldn't help blushing when she recalled his last suggestion—that she should share his bed again. Did he think he stood a better chance of persuading her when he had her trapped on his boat? she wondered grimly. The worst of it was she wasn't at all confident she would be able to resist him if he tried to make love to her again.

But, as usual, Zac was utterly determined to have his own way, she realised bitterly as he steered her through the house and out to his car. Refusing to go with him was pointless; she didn't doubt for a second that he would fling her over his shoulder and carry her onto his boat, and she preferred to keep what little dignity she had left intact.

It was a short drive from La Maison des Fleurs to the marina and her temper at his high-handedness was still simmering when they parked, but as they walked along the quay and she smelled the sea air she could not help but relax a little. She had always loved the sea and her eyes scanned along the line of fabulous yachts and motor cruisers before straying to Zac, who was striding along next to her. In cream chinos and a navy polo shirt he was a tanned, gorgeous, billionaire playboy who turned heads and drew admiring glances wherever he went. Was she mad to have turned down his offer to be his mistress?

The Isis was a stunning looking craft from the outside and inside she was truly sumptuous. As Freya glanced around the luxuriously appointed salon with its champagne coloured leather sofas, and cherry wood fitments, she felt as though she had stepped back in time and was once again the naïve young girl who had worked briefly as Zac's stewardess, before he had enticed her into his bed with his potent, sexy charm. Stifling a sigh, she followed him up on deck and leaned against the boat rail as *The Isis*'s skipper steered smoothly out of the harbour and into the open sea.

'You said you wanted to talk,' she reminded Zac stiffly when he came to stand next to her. He was too close for comfort and she felt her senses flare into urgent life when he lifted his hand and stroked her hair back from her face.

'We need to discuss our future relationship once you've agreed to move permanently into the penthouse,' he agreed in a tone that warned Freya he intended to lay down the rules and expected her to agree.

'It's going to be a short discussion, then, as we don't have a relationship and I have no intention of moving in with you permanently,' she muttered, and caught her breath at his sudden grin.

'I'm going to have to do something about that sassy tongue of yours,' he threatened softly. He paused and stared at her as if he could not tear his eyes from the delicate beauty of her face. 'I have never felt so alive as when I'm with you, *chérie*,' he admitted, looking faintly stunned by the realisation before he lowered his head and claimed her mouth in a slow, drugging kiss that left Freya breathless and more confused than ever. She loved him and she knew he loved Aimee—wasn't that enough reason to sacrifice her pride and agree to his proposition? she thought dazedly. Shouldn't she sacrifice her own longing to be loved and settle for a life of luxury and amazing sex?

When he finally lifted his head, her lips were stinging and to her shame she realised that she didn't want to talk, she wanted him to sweep her off to his cabin, throw her down on the bed and make love to her with a fierce, primitive passion—giving her no choice in the matter and ignoring all her doubts. 'We'll talk later,' he threatened ominously, the gleam in his cobalt-blue gaze warning her that he knew exactly what he did to her. 'But first we'll swim and lie out in the sun for a while. Aimee will love staying with my mother and we have the whole afternoon to relax and unwind.'

Relax! When he was looking at her with that sensual gleam in his eyes? It seemed unlikely, Freya thought on a wave of panic. 'I didn't bring a swimming costume with me,' she muttered when he finally released her and led her over to a couple of sun loungers arranged on the deck.

'Everything you need is below deck,' Zac assured her. 'Follow me and I'll show you where you can change.'

Zac's taste in swimwear left a lot to be desired, Freya decided later as she cautiously arranged herself on a sun lounger. The minuscule green and gold bikini he'd brought for her was barely decent, just three triangles of material that left a worrying amount of her flesh on display. Not that he had voiced any objections, she mused, a tremor running through her body when he turned his head and she felt his brilliant blue gaze skim over her.

The tension was back, a prickling, tangible force, and all afternoon she had tried to ignore the sexual chemistry that simmered between them, but now, as their eyes clashed, she glimpsed his unconcealed hunger and knew that it mirrored her own.

Damn him, she thought frantically, and damn the dictates of her treacherous body. This was a man who, two years ago, had seduced her into becoming his mistress, but had considered her of so little importance that he hadn't bothered to reveal he had undergone a surgical procedure to ensure he could never father a child. When she had fallen pregnant he had adamantly refused to believe that the child was his. He had torn her heart to shreds with his vile insults, and even now he only accepted that he'd been wrong because of the results of a DNA test, not because he trusted her.

And yet, despite everything he had done to her, she still wanted him. He was like a fever in her blood and when she was around him nothing else mattered except that he assuage this burning, aching desire that was slowly sending her out of her mind.

Taking a deep breath, she sat up and faced him. All afternoon he had kept their conversation deliberately light, seducing her with his sharp wit so that she had almost kidded herself that they had gone back in time and none of the hurt and pain had ever happened. But she was no longer the impressionable young girl who had hung on his every word. She was a single mother trying to do the best for her child.

'Zac…' She paused fractionally and then said in a low voice, 'It's time I went home.'

'There's no rush,' he replied lazily. 'My mother promised to give Aimee her tea and bath.'

'No. I mean it's time I went back to England—with Aimee. I've had a letter from the yacht club, asking when I'll be returning to work,' she continued when he made no comment, 'and it's only fair that I give them a firm date. They won't keep my job open indefinitely.'

Zac stiffened and swung his legs off his sun lounger so that he was sitting facing her. 'I have never asked about your work before,' he said quietly, forcing himself to ignore his frustration that she seemed hell bent on fighting him, and trying, for the first time, to understand what was going on inside her head. 'Tell me exactly what you do at the yacht club.'

'I'm a receptionist. It's hardly a glittering career, I know,' she muttered defensively when his brows arched, 'but the wages are reasonable and the owners are nice. They've always allowed me to take time off if Aimee is ill. The nursery won't take children if they're unwell,' she explained when he said nothing.

'And this job, it means a lot to you?'

'No, it's just a job—a rather vital commodity for a single mother, wouldn't you say?' she said, feeling the first prickle of unease when he continued to study her speculatively. 'I need to work, Zac.'

'Why?' he demanded with a shrug. 'I realise that in the past it was a necessity, but now I know Aimee is my child and naturally I will support her. How can you even think about taking her away when she is clearly so happy here?' he demanded angrily. 'There's no way I will allow you to unsettle her and force her to live in that *hovel* you euphemistically call home. Apart from anything else, it would break my mother's heart if she were to be separated from her grandchild.'

The desire to point out that she had been forced to live in a *hovel* because of his utter lack of faith in her was so strong that Freya had to bite her lip. There was no point in indulging in a slanging match when what was needed was a calm, rational discussion about their daughter's future. 'I appreciate how much your mother loves Aimee and, believe me, I wouldn't want to do anything to spoil their relationship. But my life is in England.'

'Then go back to England,' Zac growled angrily, 'but

you'll go alone. Aimee's life is here now, among her family who love her.'

'Are you saying I don't?' In her agitation, Freya jumped to her feet and glared at him. 'I would lay down my life for her and I will never abandon her the way my mother abandoned me.' She spun away from him, blinded by her tears, and let out a cry when he grabbed her hand and pulled her down onto his sun lounger. 'Don't,' she pleaded when he leaned over her, his eyes glittering with an intensity that made her heart thud in her chest. 'I understand that you want to be a proper father to Aimee, but I can't leave her here with you, you must see that. We both love her,' she whispered sadly, 'but I don't know how we can ever find a solution that will allow us to both be full-time parents to her.'

'Don't you?' Zac propped himself up on one elbow and trailed his finger lightly down her cheek. 'The solution is obvious, *chérie*. We'll get married.'

'Say that again!' Freya muttered weakly as shock ricocheted through her. For a brief few seconds she was overwhelmed by a sensation of piercingly sweet joy, but already that feeling was fading as common sense kicked in. Zac had asked her to marry him, but she was under no illusion that he was about to profess his undying love for her. And as far as she was concerned, love was the only reason she would contemplate marriage.

'You asked how we could find a solution to the problem of shared parenting of Aimee and I'm simply suggesting that the most obvious answer is for us to get married,' Zac replied in a measured tone, as if he were explaining something to a small child.

'How can a marriage of convenience between two people who actively dislike each other be a solution to anything?'

Freya cried. 'I agree that the only reason for us to get married is to provide our daughter with a stable family life and it might possibly work at first, but how do you think Aimee would feel as she grew older and realised that we were only together for her sake? It wouldn't be fair on her, and it wouldn't be fair on us, either. What if you met someone and fell in love?' The idea of him loving another woman when he had never loved her was agonising, but it was a reality she had to accept. 'Or what if I did? We would have to face the agonising decision of whether to put Aimee through a divorce, or whether to sacrifice what could be our one chance of happiness.'

'If we were married I assure you I would remain faithful,' Zac bit out, his eyes glinting. He was still lying on his side, leaning over her, but she could feel the angry tension that gripped his muscles and acknowledged that now was not a good time to try and ease away from him. Instead she forced herself to lie passively on the sun lounger even though she was acutely conscious of the effect his near-naked body was having on hers.

'I cannot speak for you, of course,' he said stiffly, struggling to disguise his fury that she had obviously contemplated shopping around for another partner. Who was he? Had she already met someone back in England and was hoping that the relationship might become permanent? After the way he had rejected her two years ago, he could hardly blame her, he conceded grimly, but the idea that she could choose to marry another man who would then be Aimee's stepfather made him feel physically sick.

'I'm not saying that I have anyone in mind right now,' Freya muttered crossly, fighting the urge to reach up and stroke back the lock of dark hair that had fallen onto his brow. 'But who knows what the future holds? I might meet my soul mate tomorrow and I'd like to have the chance to experience love. My life hasn't been overflowing with it so far,' she added bleakly.

'The love you speak of is the stuff of childish fairy tales,' Zac told her impatiently. 'A successful marriage has its roots in friendship, mutual respect and common goals—in our case the desire to bring our daughter up in a happy family environment.'

'There's more to marriage than a...clinical contract,' Freya argued fiercely.

'You mean passion? I don't foresee any problems on that score, do you, *chérie*?' He moved over her with lightning speed, crushing her beneath him as he claimed her mouth in a statement of pure possession. He forced his tongue between her lips in a flagrantly erotic gesture, probing, exploring, demanding a response that she was unable to deny. One hand tangled in her hair to hold her fast while the other roamed up and down her body, traced the shape of her hip before sliding up to curve around her breast. 'The bedroom is the one place I know our marriage will work,' he growled against her throat, before he moved lower, trailing a line of kisses to the valley between her breasts.

His breath was hot on her skin. She was burning up, Freya thought feverishly, feeling her breasts swell and tighten until they ached for him to caress them. She couldn't think logically and nothing else seemed to matter except that he should continue touching her and kissing her and she made no attempt to stop him when he unfastened the halter straps of her bikini and peeled the material down to expose her breasts to his hungry gaze.

Perhaps she should stop wishing for the moon and settle

for what Zac was offering? He might not love her, but he wanted to marry her and from the sound of it he was prepared to be a faithful husband as well as a devoted father to Aimee. Freya caught her breath when he cupped her breast in his palm and lowered his head to stroke his tongue over her nipple. The sensation was so exquisite that she arched towards him, wanting, needing, more of the same and she whimpered softly when he drew the tight peak fully into his mouth.

She loved him so much. He was the only man she would ever love and for her there would never be anyone else, but what about him? What if, despite his good intentions, his desire for her faded and he met someone else? Would he embark on a discreet affair, while maintaining the façade of a happy marriage for Aimee's sake? It would be worse than suffering a slow death, she thought despairingly. She had spent her formative years knowing that she was merely tolerated by her grandmother. The prospect of spending the rest of her life trapped in a loveless marriage was unbearable.

Zac lifted his head from her breast and shifted slightly so that he could feather light kisses down over her flat stomach and a quiver of pure longing flooded through her. The urge to surrender to the desperate need for him to possess her was overwhelming, but she couldn't give in again.

'Do you honestly believe you could experience this level of passion with anyone else, Freya?' he demanded rawly, his eyes burning into hers when he lifted his head and stared down at her.

'Perhaps not, but mind-blowing sex is not a good enough reason for me to want to marry you, any more than marrying for Aimee's sake,' she said crisply, finally finding the strength to push him away. 'There has to be another way, some sort of compromise where we can both share her and also be free to get on with our own lives.'

Having spent his entire adult life avoiding commitment, Zac made the unwelcome discovery that freedom had suddenly lost its appeal and he hated the idea of Freya *getting on with life* without him. But he recognised the determined set of her chin and grimly conceded that she was the only woman he had ever met whose stubborn streak matched his own. He couldn't frogmarch her up the aisle, and for now he would have to concede a temporary defeat.

She was fumbling with her bikini, her fingers visibly shaking as she dragged the material over her breasts. The hard peaks of her nipples strained against the clingy Lycra and instinct told him that she was fighting her own internal battle. It was tempting to haul her into his arms and prove beyond doubt that the passion they shared was impossible to recreate with anyone else, but he forced himself to move away from her.

'So that's your final answer, is it? You refuse to marry me, but you agree that we need to reach a compromise whereby we can both be involved in Aimee's upbringing.' He sounded indifferent, almost bored, and faintly relieved, Freya thought miserably. In turning him down she had quite possibly made the biggest mistake of her life, but at least she had saved him from a similar fate. 'Just so long as you understand that Aimee will grow up here in Monaco,' he added coolly, a frown crossing his face when a discreet cough alerted him to the presence of the skipper who had emerged from the lower deck.

'I thought the meaning of compromise is to come to a mutual agreement, not for one person to lay down the law,' Freya muttered, but Zac was no longer listening and was already striding along the deck. Her patchy French meant that she had trouble following his conversation with his uniformed crew-member but his body language unsettled her and she quickly stood and thrust her arms into her robe.

'What is it? What's the matter?' she demanded when Zac walked back to her.

He hesitated fractionally and then said, 'My mother has sent a message via the satellite phone saying that Aimee seems unwell. I've instructed Claude to head straight back to port.'

Panic immediately coiled in Freya's stomach. 'How do you mean—unwell? Yvette must have given more details than that.'

'I'm sorry, *chérie*, that's all I know,' Zac said, his voice softening when he saw the flare of anxiety in her eyes. 'We'll be back at La Maison des Fleurs within the hour.' He paused and then murmured, 'It's quite possible that my mother is overreacting. Many years ago she lost two babies in quick succession and she is bound to be ultra-protective of Aimee.'

'How terrible for her.' Freya momentarily forgot her concern for her own baby as she contemplated Yvette Deverell's devastating losses. 'Was that before you were born?'

For a moment it seemed that Zac did not want to answer and his face was shuttered when he glanced at her. '*Non*, I was fourteen—old enough to understand my parents' grief but sadly unable to comfort them, although I did my best.'

'I'm sure you were a great comfort to them.' Freya had a dozen questions she wanted to ask, but it was clear Zac did not want to discuss the tragedy that had blighted his family. He'd said that Yvette had lost her children when they were babies—had they died as a result of cot-death? She had read somewhere that the syndrome could affect more than one sibling and certainly it must have been utterly heartbreaking for Zac and his parents. She could understand now why Yvette adored Aimee, but some maternal sixth sense warned her that Zac's mother wasn't overreacting. Something was seriously wrong.

The journey back to the port seemed to take for ever and she busied herself by going below deck to change out of her bikini. Her earlier pleasure in the boat trip had evaporated and she wished she had never allowed Zac to persuade her to leave Aimee. She felt guilt-ridden that she had abandoned her baby even for a couple of hours, especially as it had resulted in her and Zac being at loggerheads once more. Her daughter was the only important person in her life, she reminded herself fiercely, and everyone else, including Zac, took second place.

The moment the car drew up outside La Maison des Fleurs, Freya flew through the front door and skidded to a halt when Yvette hurried forwards to greet them. 'How is Aimee?' she asked urgently, fear seizing her when she stared at the Frenchwoman's worried expression.

'Not good, I'm afraid,' Yvette replied shakily, turning her gaze from Freya to Zac. 'Thank God you're here. The doctor is with Aimee now and he says she must go straight to the hospital.'

With a muffled cry Freya shot past Zac's mother, into the sitting room where Aimee was lying, pale and seemingly lifeless on the sofa.

'Aimee, Aimee! What's wrong with her?' she beseeched the doctor who was standing, grave-faced, close to the child. She could hear Zac urgently asking his mother when Aimee had first shown signs of being ill, and Yvette's explanation that the toddler had seemed tired after playing on the swing.

'I was surprised because I know she usually has a nap in the morning, but I made her a bed on the sofa and thought she would sleep for a little while. After two hours I was beginning to feel anxious,' Yvette said tearfully. 'I was relieved when she stirred, but almost immediately she was sick and when I drew back the blinds she screamed as if the light hurt her eyes. Since then she has been as you see her now. The doctor has confirmed she is running a high temperature but her symptoms could mean many things…' Yvette broke off helplessly and Freya swung round to the doctor.

'What do you think is wrong with her?'

'I can't say for sure but she is showing classic symptoms of meningitis,' he said quietly. 'It's best that she goes to the hospital where tests will confirm the diagnosis. I think the ambulance is here now.' He took one look at Freya's ashen face and patted her arm. 'Try not to worry, *madame*, your daughter will be in good hands.'

Meningitis—the word sounded over and over in Freya's head as the ambulance hurtled through the traffic. It was every parent's worst nightmare, renowned for striking without warning and with potentially fatal results. Aimee's life could not be in danger; she frantically sought to reassure herself, but when she stared at her baby's limp body her heart stood still. Please don't let me lose her, she prayed, squeezing her eyes shut to prevent her tears from falling. Crying wouldn't help, she had to be strong and help Aimee in her fight for survival.

A hand reached out and enfolded her fingers in a strong grasp. Zac was hurting too, she could see it in the tense line of his jaw, but she couldn't bring herself to meet his gaze. Sympathy briefly flared for what he must be going through, the agony he must be feeling that Aimee could be taken from him so soon after she had come into his life. But when they arrived at the hospital and the ambulance doors were flung open, she forgot everything but the need to focus on her baby. Aimee needed her and there was no room in her heart for anyone else.

CHAPTER NINE

ONE week later Freya stood in the nursery, struggling to hold back her tears as she stared into the cot. Aimee was sleeping peacefully, her long eyelashes feathering her cheeks that were now flushed with healthy colour once more.

The hours after they had arrived at the hospital had been fraught with tension as the little girl underwent a series of tests, and the eventual diagnosis that she did not have meningitis had only been a partial relief. Aimee had been suffering from a virus that had taken a hold on her young body. For the next three days she had lain in her hospital bed attached to wires and monitors and despite the efforts of the excellent medical team, had shown no signs of recovery. But on the fourth day her high temperature had gradually dropped back to normal and when she'd woken from a long nap she had sat up, demanded a drink, wolfed down a banana and only been persuaded to remain in bed because her toy rabbit was poorly and needed looking after.

Aimee's recovery had been nothing short of miraculous, and now that they were back at the penthouse Freya felt as though she had ridden an emotional roller coaster. She would not have been able to get through the past week without Zac, she admitted to herself. From the moment Aimee had been whisked away by the medical team, he had been faultlessly supportive, countering her frantic fear with quiet calm and relaying every snippet of information from the doctors in an effort to allay her anxiety.

He had been a rock and she'd clung to him unashamedly, reassured by his strength and comforted by his decision to fly in one of the world's leading paediatricians. Her pride was no longer important and she was simply grateful that he could afford the best medical care for their daughter. More than anything it had brought home to her that Aimee's future lay here in Monaco, with her father.

'Come away now, *chérie*,' Zac said softly when he entered the nursery and walked silently over to the cot. 'She's sleeping soundly and Jean insists that she will sit up all night to check on her.'

'I can't believe how well she looks,' Freya muttered past the constriction in her throat. 'Just a week ago I thought…I thought I would lose her and I was so scared.' The tears were falling, despite her determination to wait until she reached the privacy of her own room before she broke down. Overwhelmed by exhaustion and relief, she could not hold back the flood of her emotions, but as she buried her face in her hands strong arms closed around her and she was drawn up against the solid wall of Zac's chest.

'It's all right, Freya, cry it out. You can't take any more and it's no wonder after the nightmare of the past week. Aimee is completely well and she'll bounce back from this in no time,' he assured her as he lifted her into his arms and strode down the hall. 'It's you I'm worried about, *chérie*. You've barely slept for days and I can't recall the last time you ate anything. It can't go on,' he told her firmly, 'and if you won't look after yourself, then I'll have to do it for you.'

Freya was beyond arguing. Zac was arrogant and bossy and usually she would have rebelled against his authority, but the hours she'd sat at the hospital, willing her baby to recover, had left her feeling as though she had been put through a mangle.

'Bed,' he stated grimly when he reached her room and set her down, his mouth tightening at the sight of her white face and the purple bruises beneath her eyes. 'Perhaps you'll look a little less like a ghost after a good night's sleep.'

'I need a bath first,' she mumbled, almost too weary to speak, but he shook his head firmly.

'You can have a bath tomorrow. You're too tired tonight; you can barely stand up. Let me help you get changed.' He held out her nightdress and moved to unfasten her blouse.

'It's all right, I can manage.' The temptation to throw herself in his arms and beg him to hold her was so strong that she bit her lip to prevent the words from spilling out. She couldn't cope with him tonight, not when her emotions were so raw, and to her relief he stood and walked over to the door.

'Call me if you need anything. *Bonne nuit, chérie,*' Zac bade her softly before he retraced his steps back to the nursery and stood watching over his sleeping daughter. A hand seemed to curl around his heart as he absorbed the beauty of her golden curls and the tiny heart-shaped face that reminded him of Freya. He loved Aimee beyond words and the days she had spent in the hospital had been the worst of his life, but now she was home safe and well and he was struggling to assimilate exactly what he felt for her mother.

Light was still streaming from beneath Freya's bedroom door when he walked past and he hesitated momentarily before giving in to the urge to check that she was safely asleep. But her bed was empty and his mouth tightened as he crossed the room to the *en suite*, recalling her stubborn expression when he'd left her. Surely she wouldn't have risked taking a bath tonight?

'Freya!' The bathroom door was locked and he rattled the handle impatiently, his unease growing when he called again and received no reply. 'Freya—what the devil are you doing in there?'

In the distant recess of her mind, Freya recognised that someone was calling her name. She felt curiously weightless, as if she were floating, but her name sounded again and with an effort she forced her eyelids open at the same time as she swallowed a mouthful of water. Coughing and spluttering, she jerked upright just as the bathroom door splintered from its hinges and Zac burst into the room.

'*Mon Dieu!* I don't believe you! You fell asleep, didn't you? Do you have a death wish or something?' he demanded furiously. He loomed over her, hands on his hips and aggression pumping from every pore as a potent mix of fear and adrenaline coursed through his body. 'I told you not to have a bath until tomorrow. Can't you ever do as you're told? You might have drowned,' he said, his voice sharp with relief.

Freya shrivelled beneath his glowering fury and sank deeper beneath the rapidly disappearing bubbles. 'I couldn't bear feeling so dirty,' she mumbled. A spark of pride brought her chin up and she forced herself to meet his furious gaze.

'The maid could have helped you if you'd waited until tomorrow morning,' he growled, 'but instead, because of your impatience, you'll have to put up with me playing nursemaid while I rub you down.'

'I don't need you or anyone else to *rub me down*; I'm not a horse!'

'*Non,* you are the most infuriating woman I've ever met,' Zac agreed tightly as he unfolded a towel and approached her. 'You're so exhausted you can barely sit up, let alone haul yourself out of the bath. A less patient man would let you sit there all night,' he added with such supreme arrogance that Freya considered inflicting serious injury with the loofah.

'I can manage,' she muttered, but as usual Zac was right. The sheer terror she'd felt for Aimee was now taking its toll and she felt limp and utterly drained. She hadn't deliberately set out to anger Zac and the sight of his grim face brought a rush of tears to her eyes. 'I need to wash my hair,' she choked miserably.

For a moment she thought he was going to ignore her, until with a muttered oath he dropped the towel he was holding and unbuttoned his shirt cuffs before rolling the material over his forearms. 'Lie back in the water and lean against my arm,' he instructed as he knelt beside the bath and slid his arm beneath her back.

Warily, Freya did as he asked. The bubbles were dispersing fast and her cheeks burned when she felt his gaze slide over her briefly. He'd seen her naked body many times before, she reminded herself impatiently, but right now she felt acutely vulnerable. 'Zac…'

'Do you want me to help you or not?' he growled, his tone warning her that she'd already pushed him to his limits. Weakly she closed her eyes and allowed herself to be soothed by the gentle motion of his hand as he massaged shampoo into her scalp. It felt so good that her muscles gradually relaxed and even the knowledge that the bubbles had almost gone, leaving her slender limbs exposed to his gaze, failed to destroy the magic of his touch.

'There, you'll do,' he said abruptly, shattering the spell. He adjusted the water temperature and used the shower attachment to rinse her hair, his expression unfathomable as he kept his eyes fixed firmly on her face. The tension was back, a prickling, tangible force that made Freya's nerve endings quiver.

'If you could just pass me a towel, I'm sure I'll be fine,' she began, and then gasped when he scooped her out of the bath. 'Zac!' In an agony of embarrassment, she buried her face in his shirt while he wrapped a towel around her and carried her through her room and along the hall to his bedroom. 'Please—I can take care of myself,' she mumbled, but he ignored her and used the towel with brisk efficiency to rub her body until she was tingling all over.

She was going to die of embarrassment tomorrow, Freya thought sleepily, but Zac had that determined gleam in his eyes that she knew so well and it was easier to give in to him. Her eyelids felt heavy and she was barely aware of him popping her nightdress over her head. When he drew back the bedcovers she wanted to remind him that this was his room, not hers, but he ignored her small protest and tucked her between the sheets as if she were a small child.

'I know this is my bed, *chérie*,' he said with a quiet implacability in his voice that would have alarmed her had she heard it. But she was already asleep by the time he had stripped out of his clothes and slid into bed beside her. 'The time for fighting is over,' he murmured as he leaned over and brushed his lips lightly across her mouth, 'and this is where you belong.'

It was still dark when Freya awoke. Not the inky blackness of midnight, but a soft, shadowy darkness as dawn crept closer. This was Zac's room, she realised as her eyes slowly adjusted to the lack of light. She was in Zac's bed and it had been his arms holding her close throughout the night. He was still holding her, she amended when she turned her head and met a wall of warm, satin skin overlaid with a fine covering of black hairs.

The rhythmic rise and fall of his chest told her he was asleep. She shouldn't be here, and now was the ideal opportunity to slip back to her own room. But the temptation to remain close to him, cocooned in this twilight world with the man she loved, was too strong to resist. With a small sigh she closed her eyes and inhaled his clean, masculine scent. Slowly, inexorably, her senses stirred until she was conscious of each separate nerve ending tingling in illicit anticipation.

Common sense warned her to flee before he opened his eyes and saw the hunger in hers, but instead her hand curved over his heart and she felt its steady beat reverberate through her fingertips. He shifted slightly on the mattress and she held her breath, but his relaxed muscles lulled her and she could not resist allowing her hand to slide lightly down his chest and over his flat stomach. The waistband of his boxers was an unwelcome barrier that brought a halt to her exploration. But the urge to trail her fingers lower was too strong and she cautiously edged beneath the elastic, a startled cry leaving her lips when he suddenly crushed her marauding hand against his body.

'You are following a path that can only have one outcome, *chérie*,' he drawled lazily, the sensual smokiness of his voice sending a quiver of excitement down Freya's spine. 'Are you sure it's a route you want to take?'

'Yes,' she replied unequivocally, following the dictates of

her heart before her head had a chance to question her sanity. He didn't love her and maybe he never would, but he cared for her. His behaviour last night had proved that, if proof were needed after the tender consideration he had shown her during Aimee's illness. His cruel rejection two years ago had broken her heart, but since he had learned that Aimee was his child he had done everything possible to try and atone for the past. Nothing was perfect, she reminded herself, and at least he hadn't made false promises he couldn't keep. The simple truth was that she only felt half alive without him. Aimee belonged here with him, and so did she.

She heard Zac draw a sharp breath and when he turned his head the brilliant fire in his blue eyes warned her that this time there could be no going back.

'Zac.' Emotion clogged her throat and he caught her soft cry, claiming her lips in a slow, drugging kiss that coaxed and cajoled until she curled her arms around his neck and responded with all the need that had lain dormant inside her for so long.

Moments before, he had been deeply asleep but now he was wide awake and so boldly aroused that Freya suffered a tiny flutter of trepidation as the solid length of his erection straining beneath the silky material of his boxers filled her with awe and undeniable excitement. Liquid heat surged through her veins as her body recognised its mate. This was her man, the only man to know the intimate secrets of her body, and already she could feel the moist warmth between her legs as she made ready for him.

'I've missed you, Freya,' he muttered hoarsely, his lips grazing a path down her throat to settle on the pulse that beat frantically at its base. With one swift movement he drew her nightshirt over her head and stared down at her slender, naked form, tracing every dip and curve with his burning gaze. He cupped her breasts in his hands with gentle reverence and kneaded them before splaying his fingers wide, his olive-gold skin contrasting starkly against the creamy whiteness of her flesh.

'Zac, please.' She arched towards him and groaned her approval when he rolled her nipples between his thumb and forefingers until they were tight, throbbing peaks that begged for the possession of his mouth. He made her wait, teasing her with his wicked touch until she slid her hands into his hair and directed his head down to her breast. The delicate flick of his tongue across the sensitive crest was so exquisite that she tensed and moved her hips in a restless invitation. She wanted him now, this minute. She felt as if she had been waiting a lifetime and she couldn't withstand another moment of his sensual foreplay when the urgency to feel him deep inside her was driving her out of her mind.

'Slowly, *mon coeur*, I want to savour every second and taste every delectable inch of you,' he promised, putting his words into action when he moved down her body and trailed his lips over her stomach. Freya gasped when he continued lower and her fingers tightened in his hair when he gently pushed her legs apart so that he could bestow the most intimate caress of all.

It was too much, sensation piling on sensation and building to a crescendo that made her writhe beneath him. 'Please, Zac, it has to be now,' she pleaded as the first little spasms caused her muscles to clench around his probing tongue.

He finally acknowledged her urgency and for a moment his own desperate need threatened to overwhelm him so that he feared he would lose control before he had given her pleasure. Muttering an oath, he dispensed with his underwear and reached into the bedside drawer for a protective sheath.

Only then could he succumb to the demands of his desire and he groaned low in his throat when he edged forwards so that the tip of his penis was rubbing against the opening to her vagina. Slowly and with infinite care he thrust into her, and then stilled while her muscles stretched around him. She felt hot and tight and he could feel the waves of pleasure building inside him, clamouring for release. But he would die rather than hurt her and he restrained himself from plunging deep into her silken heat until he felt her relax a little.

Carefully he withdrew a fraction and then thrust into her again and again, faster now as she wrapped her legs tightly round him, her soft cries urging him on. Frantically he sought to claw back his self-control and slow his pace, possessing her with strong, hard strokes until she gave a low cry and her body convulsed around him.

'Freya...' He called her name, tried to explain that he had never known such sheer pleasure as when he made love to her, but she seemed to know, just as she had always known the effect she had on him. Her soft smile destroyed the last tenuous threads of his control and he pulsed inside her, overwhelmed by wave after wave of incredible pleasure that left him satisfied and at peace.

For a long while neither of them spoke and only the steady tick-tock of the clock broke the companionable silence. Zac had rolled onto his back, taking Freya with him, and at last she lifted her head and met his slumberous gaze. 'I need to thank you for everything you've done this last week,' she murmured huskily. 'The way you cared for Aimee—and me. I'm not sure I'd have coped without you.'

'I consider myself thanked,' he replied lightly, his eyes

glinting with teasing amusement when she blushed and tried to ease away from him. He prevented her frantic bid for escape by tightening his arms around her so that she was held prisoner against his chest. 'And from now on, *chérie*, I intend to devote as much of my time as possible to pleasing you so that you will need to thank me all through the night, and at least once during the day,' he added wickedly.

'That wasn't the reason why I—' She broke off, her face flaming and wriggled her hips in an attempt to free herself from his hold until she realised the effect she was having on certain parts of his anatomy.

'I'm sorry, *ma petite*—' he grinned unrepentantly '—but I have been patient for the last two weeks and now I am very, very hungry.'

'I'm aware of that,' she muttered, feeling the hard ridge of his arousal pushing provocatively against her belly. Her body instantly stirred into urgent life. It was too soon, surely? He couldn't...

He proved conclusively that he could by lifting her hips and gently bringing her down on top of him, filling her so completely that she groaned and clung to his shoulders while she absorbed each delicious thrust.

She was shocked that he could arouse her to such a heightened degree of need so soon after she had climaxed, but already she could feel exquisite spasms of pleasure rippling through her. His hands curved possessively around her buttocks, lifted and stroked the round globes and aided her in setting a sensual rhythm that quickly became a frantic drumbeat of desire. Within seconds they were at the edge, hovered there for infinitesimal seconds before finally tumbling over into the ecstasy of mutual release.

This time when Freya eased away from him, he rolled

onto his side and stared down at her, his face suddenly serious. 'You are so small and fragile, but you possess an inner strength that is quite incredible, *chérie*,' he said quietly. He stroked a stray tendril of hair from her face and a warm glow filled her when she caught the flare of admiration in his eyes. 'I don't doubt that you would have coped with the traumas of the past week without any help from me. You proved during the last two years that you can deal with anything life throws at you, including bringing up our daughter alone and unsupported. But, believe me, I will support you and Aimee now,' he told her fiercely.

'I do believe you, Zac,' Freya whispered softly, 'and I agree that Aimee belongs here in Monaco with both of us. If it's still what you want, then…I'll marry you.'

'Think about it for a moment,' he commanded urgently, so intent on persuading her around to his way of thinking that her words were lost on him. 'As my wife there would be no need for you to work and you could spend all your time with Aimee instead of having to leave her at a nursery. Wouldn't you like that, *chérie*? You clearly adore her and you must know from your own childhood that she would benefit from having her mother's undivided attention.'

'Absolutely,' Freya reiterated calmly, love and tenderness welling up inside her as she watched his expression change from frustration to dawning comprehension. 'The events of the last week have forced me to see that Aimee needs the love and care of both her parents and I agree that it would be best if we were married. It's the most logical solution,' she added, proud of the lack of emotion in her voice that disguised her aching heart. All her life she had dreamed of romance and roses, moonlight and the husky avowal of undying love, but she was prosaic enough to realise that fairy tales rarely came true and she was willing to accept Zac's marriage offer knowing that it was a contract based on convenience and a mutual desire to do their best for their daughter.

'And who can argue with logic?' Zac murmured in a dry tone that masked his irrational feeling of pique. Freya had accepted his marriage proposal with as much enthusiasm and excitement as if she were making a dental appointment. There was nothing wrong with assessing the situation they found themselves in logically, he reminded himself. Freya was no longer an impressionable girl, she was an independent woman who had managed quite well without him in the past and if necessary would do so again in the future. Clearly she had weighed up the pros and cons of becoming his wife and had reached a decision based on common sense rather than emotion.

He admired her determination to do the right thing for their daughter, but he couldn't deny a certain amount of wounded pride that she viewed him as a logical solution to a problem rather than the man she was eager to spend the rest of her life with.

'So, now that you've agreed to marry me, all we have to do is decide on the sort of wedding we want,' he said smoothly, settling himself comfortably against the headboard and giving her a smile that told her of his satisfaction that he had got his own way in the end.

She was cornered, but she had stepped willingly into the trap, Freya reminded herself when her heart lurched. Their marriage would be based on sexual desire and the love they shared for Aimee, but plenty of successful marriages had been built on less. Surely with a little effort on both sides they could make their relationship work?

'I assumed you would prefer a small wedding with the

minimum of fuss,' she murmured, tearing her eyes from the sight of his magnificent body sprawled on the pillows like a sultan in the midst of his harem.

'I only intend to marry once, *chérie*, and I'd like to make it a day to remember,' he surprised her by saying. 'The ceremony doesn't have to be too lavish—if that's not what you want—but I have numerous relatives and friends I would like to invite and naturally we will want to include Aimee. She'll make an adorable bridesmaid, and of course you must have a wedding dress and flowers, and a ring. I want to do this properly, Freya,' he insisted when she looked stunned by the prospect of a big celebration. 'We may not be marrying for conventional reasons, but I'm still proud that I'm making you my wife.'

He meant of course that, unlike most couples, they were not marrying for love, Freya realised, feeling her heart contract. It was stupid to feel so hurt and she gave a careless shrug, determined not to reveal that she'd be happy to marry in a barn, dressed in sackcloth, if only he loved her. 'You've obviously given the subject more thought than me so I'll leave the arrangements to you.'

She flicked back the sheets to slide out of bed, ignoring the temptation of his naked body and the sensual gleam in his eyes. Their marriage might be a convenient arrangement but they were drawn together by a fierce mutual desire. Her one fear was what would happen if Zac's passion for her died—would he still be proud to have her as his wife when he no longer wanted her in his bed? The question settled like a heavy weight in her chest and she snatched up her robe, suddenly anxious to escape him. 'Aimee's probably awake by now,' she muttered. 'I'll go and check on her.'

CHAPTER TEN

THREE weeks later Freya was still questioning her sanity at her decision to marry Zac. Undoubtedly it would be best for Aimee, but could she ever be happy, married to a man who did not love her? The only thing she was certain of was their physical compatibility, she acknowledged ruefully. The long hours of loving in his bed each night proved irrefutably that her body had been exclusively fashioned for the giving and receiving of pleasure with this one man.

When Zac reached for her she went immediately into his arms, her heart pounding with anticipation of the delight to come when he caressed every inch of her. His hands and mouth were instruments of sensual torture that he used without mercy, exploring each sensitive dip and crevasse of her body before gently parting her and stroking her until she hovered on the brink of ecstasy. Only then, when she cast her pride aside and pleaded for him to possess her, did he relent and move over her, thrusting into her with slow, sure strokes that filled her to the hilt and made her arch and writhe beneath him.

Her only consolation was that he appeared to be no less enslaved by desire. If anything, his hunger for her seemed even more fervent now than when she had agreed to marry him and his passion showed no sign of diminishing. But it was only three weeks, she reminded herself fearfully, what would their relationship be like in three months—three years?

She glanced across the crowded room, searching for his tall frame. They were to marry in a week's time and ever since he had formally announced their engagement their relationship had been the subject of frantic gossip among Monaco's social élite. Everyone was curious to meet the woman who had finally persuaded one of the principality's most enigmatic, jet-setting playboys to relinquish his freedom, and during the past weeks they had received numerous invitations to social functions.

Tonight's party being held in private rooms at Monte Carlo's famous casino was a glittering occasion—quite literally, Freya thought wryly when she studied the array of fabulous jewellery on display. Despite her designer gown and the diamond and platinum earrings that complemented the exquisite diamond solitaire engagement ring Zac had given her, she felt seriously out of place. This was not her world and she felt like an outsider amidst the other guests who inhabited the rarefied group of the super-rich.

It was a far cry from her damp attic flat in England and her life that had revolved around trying to combine motherhood, work and study while surviving on a limited budget. This was Zac's world, but it wasn't hers, and she was aware of the whispered speculation among his peers that she was a gold-digger who had used the fact that she was the mother of his child as leverage to make him marry her.

She caught sight of him standing with a group of his close friends and her heart missed a beat as she studied him, looking relaxed, tanned and toe-curlingly sexy in an impeccably tailored black dinner suit. She would never tire of looking at him, but he possessed a magnetic charm that drew admiring glances from around the room and once again she wondered what he saw in her, when other women far more beautiful than her were queuing up for his attention.

With a sigh she moved towards the group and felt a tiny surge of confidence when Zac glanced up and focused his gaze intently on her as if she was the only woman he was interested in.

'There you are, *chérie*, I've been looking for you,' he greeted her softly, sliding his arm around her waist and dipping his head to brush his mouth over hers in a brief, tingling kiss. The sensual gleam in his eyes warned her that he was planning to excuse them from the party as soon as possible and she shared his impatience. She wanted to lose herself in the private world of sensory pleasure where their loving was fierce and hard or slow and skilfully erotic, but always seemed to have an underlying tenderness that tore at her heart and let her believe, just for a little while, that she meant something to him.

'I hope you're making the most of your last week as a free man, Zac,' someone from the assembled group joked. Benoit Fournier was one of Zac's closest friends and he and his wife Camille had greeted Freya with warmth and genuine pleasure that she was soon to be Zac's wife.

'For me the next few days cannot pass quickly enough,' Zac replied with a smile that lingered on his mouth as he stared into Freya's eyes. He was either a superb actor, or he really was beginning to care for her, she thought as joy bubbled up inside her. Her brain warned her to be cautious but the expression on his face made her pulse rate quicken. Dared she hope that she could ever mean something to him?

Her heart was beating so fast that she was sure he must hear it, and when he lifted her hand and pressed his lips to her fingers she knew he would feel the tremor of excitement that ran through her.

'I know how you feel. The next few weeks can't pass fast enough for us,' Benoit laughed, patting his wife's rounded stomach.

'When is your baby due?' Freya asked Camille with a sympathetic smile. She remembered how the final weeks of her pregnancy with Aimee had dragged while her nervousness about the impending birth had increased.

'Three weeks,' Camille groaned, 'but our first child was ten days late and I'm not holding out any hope that number two will appear on time. Louis is so excited about the new baby,' she confided. 'Are you and Zac planning to have more children some day—a little brother or sister for Aimee?'

It wasn't something they had ever discussed, Freya realised silently, and, faced with the question, she wasn't sure how to reply. Aimee's conception had been an accident that had had shattering consequences. Zac hadn't wanted children, but now he was devoted to his little daughter. His vasectomy had reversed and there was no medical reason why he should not father another child.

Her eyes were drawn to Camille's belly, swollen with her unborn baby, and a warm glow filled her as she pictured herself in the same situation. She would love to have a little companion for Aimee, she mused softly, a baby whose conception was planned and the pregnancy shared with Zac. Perhaps she would give him a son, a dark-haired, blue-eyed boy who would be the image of his father.

'Aimee isn't two yet and I'd like to give her my undivided attention for a little while longer,' she murmured. 'But one day I'd like to have another baby.' She turned to Zac and froze. His smile had disappeared and the expression in his eyes turned her blood to ice. The conversation around them moved on to other topics but the buzz of words seemed distant and unintelligible. It took all her acting skills to smile and act normally, but inside she felt sick with misery. For those few unguarded seconds Zac had been unable to disguise his look of dismay at the idea of them having another child, and her little flame of hope that their marriage could work flickered and died.

The band struck up a popular tune and people began to drift onto the dance floor. Zac seemed to have regained his composure and glanced down at her. 'Would you like to dance?' His eyes gleamed wickedly. 'I have vivid memories of the last time we danced together.'

She blushed at the shaming recollection of how he had brought her to the peak of sexual pleasure simply by holding her close, and hastily shook her head. 'I need to go to the cloakroom…perhaps Camille…' Zac's eyes narrowed on her flushed face and she turned and hurried away before he could stop her, desperate to be alone for a few minutes while she dealt with the realisation that he clearly did not want another child.

Mercifully the cloakroom was empty and she splashed water on her cheeks and tried to hold back the tears that burned her eyes. Fool, she berated herself angrily. She'd known from the outset that Zac had never wanted a family and, although he adored Aimee, he had not chosen to be a father or husband. The only reason he was marrying her was to provide their daughter with a stable upbringing and, much as she might wish it, their marriage was never going to be a conventional one.

'Hello, Freya.'

A face appeared beside hers in the mirror and Freya's heart sank. 'Annalise, how are you?' she faltered, frantically trying to sound cool and collected despite the sick feeling in the pit of her stomach. Monaco was a small place and she had steeled herself to accept that she was likely to run into the stunning glamour model at some point. It was just a pity that it was tonight, when she was already feeling vulnerable and insecure, she thought miserably.

Annalise Dubois looked stunning in a black silk sheath that was split to mid-thigh and clung lovingly to her voluptuous curves while her flame-coloured hair tumbled down her back in a mass of riotous curls. Freya was suddenly glad that Zac had insisted on buying her some new clothes. She had shuddered at the price of the peach-coloured chiffon gown she was wearing tonight, but was aware that Annalise's assessing gaze had recognised the dress was from an exclusive fashion house.

'I heard you were back,' Annalise said without preamble, her eyes narrowing on the sparkling diamond on Freya's finger. 'But I admit I was surprised to hear that you've actually managed to get Zac to marry you. A baby is *such* a useful bargaining tool. I almost wish I'd tried the same trick myself. Everyone knows Zac is too much of a gentleman to allow his child to remain illegitimate, although I understand there was some question over the child's paternity,' she intoned softly. 'Presumably Zac insisted on the necessary tests before he agreed to marriage?'

Freya couldn't prevent a tide of colour from staining her cheeks and the sick feeling was so strong it threatened to choke her. 'I'm not sure that it's any of your business,' she murmured, forcing herself to remain polite even though the knives were clearly out. 'I've never made any demands of Zac, he's free to do what he wants, and he wants to marry me.'

'For the sake of his child,' Annalise stated with an air of confidence that Freya found deeply disturbing. 'I'm glad you realise he's a free agent. Zac would never be coerced into doing something unless he could see the benefits to himself. He's obviously determined to claim his child, and of course he'll stand a better chance of winning custody of her in the future if he marries you.'

'I really don't think we should be having this conversation,' Freya said sharply. Annalise was a nasty piece of work, but her vile insinuations were pooling in Freya's head like poison being drip-fed through a pipette.

'Poor Freya, you always were such an innocent.' Annalise laughed dismissively. 'Did you know that Zac and I are lovers, or has he kept that little secret from you?' She pouted prettily at the unmistakable look of shock on Freya's face. 'Don't let it worry you darling, Zac's the master of discretion when he comes to my apartment. You don't really think he works late every night?' Her brows arched in mock surprise. 'We've had an arrangement for years that suits both of us very well. A word of warning, though,' she drawled spitefully as she inspected her appearance in the mirror. 'Zac's no pussycat and I wouldn't bank on your life of domestic bliss lasting long. He lives life on the edge and thrives on adventure—he'll hate feeling tied down and he'll soon grow bored of babies.'

She swept out of the cloakroom leaving Freya feeling so shaken that she gripped the edge of the dressing table for support. Annalise was lying, she told her reflection fiercely. Zac had made love to her every night for the past few weeks; he would have to be Superman to be sleeping with the Frenchwoman as well.

Taking a deep breath, she walked out of the cloakroom to rejoin the party and watched Annalise saunter across the dance floor, heading straight towards Zac. Nausea swept over her as she saw the glamorous model kiss him on each cheek and murmur something in his ear that caused him to smile. There was an easy familiarity between them, as if they were entirely comfortable with each other—the familiarity of lovers, Freya thought on a wave of sheer agony.

It wasn't true. Please God, it wasn't true, she thought numbly. Common sense told her there was a strong possibility that Annalise had been lying. If their marriage was going to stand any chance of success, she would have to trust Zac, she told herself fiercely. He had told her he would be a faithful husband—but maybe he had just said that to persuade her to marry him.

Was this what their married life would be like? she brooded. Would she be slowly destroyed by jealousy and uncertainty, always looking around at parties and wondering if his current mistress was also present? The thought was unbearable and she choked back a sob as she watched Zac lead Annalise onto the dance floor.

She knew he didn't love her, but he wanted her in his bed, and she had kidded herself she could be content with that. Now she saw with blinding clarity that it would be a fate worse than death. He was the love of her life, the other half of her soul, and without him she was incomplete. But she was destined to spend the rest of her life with a gaping great wound in her heart, because he had never loved her and he never would.

Sheer willpower enabled Freya to keep a smile on her face for the rest of the evening, but by the time she slid into the car next to Zac for the short drive home her jaw was aching and her heart felt like a lead weight in her chest.

'What's wrong—do you have a headache, *chérie*?' Zac queried when he glanced at her drawn expression.

It was tempting to seize on the excuse. She knew it would evoke his sympathetic response and that the moment they reached the penthouse he would insist that she went straight to sleep rather than make love to her.

She needed to be alone tonight. Her mind was spinning and her run-in with Annalise had stirred up all her old insecurities. Was Zac against the idea of more children because he did not want to increase his links to her? she wondered, recalling his expression when Camille Fournier had asked if they would like more children. And was he sleeping with Annalise? If so, it gave her an insight on how he viewed their forthcoming marriage. Perhaps he was he intending to play at happy families while conducting a series of affairs behind her back.

'I feel fine,' she said shortly, refusing to admit that her emotions felt as bruised as her body had been after the accident that had brought Zac back into her life. It was strange to think that if she had been driving down that road a few minutes earlier the tree would not have fallen yet and she would not have crashed her car. It was likely she would never have seen or heard from Zac again, but in the course of a split second her life had changed for ever and now here she was, about to marry the man she loved and feeling as though her heart would break.

She was silent for the rest of the journey and as the lift whisked them up to the penthouse she was aware of Zac's sharp glances. Once inside, she headed straight for her room, but he caught up with her and swung her round to face him.

'You seem to have lost your sense of direction,' he drawled. 'My bedroom is along the hall. What's wrong with you?' he demanded tersely, when she simply stared up at him with huge, overbright eyes. 'You've looked like a ghost for most of the night. Are you ill? If you won't tell me what's wrong, I can't help you, *chérie*,' he added impatiently, the gleam of frustration in his eyes telling her that he was fast losing his patience and was tempted to shake the truth from her.

The truth—that loving him was tearing her apart—was impossible to reveal. 'Nothing's wrong,' she lied. 'I'd just rather sleep on my own tonight.' Her pride refused to allow her to confront him about Annalise's allegations. If he suspected she was jealous of the glamour model, he might realise that she was in love with him and she would rather die than have him feel sorry for her.

Zac briefly considered hauling her into his arms and kissing her until he broke through the barriers she had erected, but she looked achingly vulnerable and he accepted that, for once, making love to her was not the answer. Instead he gave an angry shrug of his shoulders. 'Fine,' he snapped, 'sleep on your own, but a week from now you will be my wife and you'll share my bed every night. There will be no separate rooms, do you understand?'

'Oh, yes,' she flung at him bitterly. 'I understand that my role in our marriage will be to provide sex whenever and wherever you want it—less of a wife, more like a glorified whore. Tell me, Zac,' she demanded, her heart fluttering fearfully at the savage anger in his eyes, 'why are you marrying me? Being tied down with a wife and child is not what you really want, is it? I saw your face tonight when Camille mentioned the possibility of us having more children,' she said quietly, 'and I realise that you'll soon feel trapped by the responsibilities of being a husband and father.'

'That's a ridiculous thing to say,' he growled, but he refused to meet her gaze and despair washed over her.

'Is it? Be honest with me, Zac. A few years from now can you see yourself as a contented family man? Can you see us having other children who will be brothers and sisters for Aimee?'

The silence was agonising, dividing them as decisively as a ravine opening up between them. 'No,' he admitted heavily, and the single word shattered her.

So now she knew. But the realisation that he viewed their marriage as a temporary contract while Aimee was growing up was unbearable and with a muffled sob she spun on her heel and raced out of the door.

'Freya!' He caught up with her just as she reached her room and she shook wildly in his grasp as if she could not bear for him to touch her. 'I will be a good father to Aimee, and a good husband.'

He sounded as though he was making a state proclamation and she could not disguise her bitterness. 'I don't doubt that you'll do your duty, Zac. I'm sure you'll take your responsibilities seriously, just as my grandmother did when she brought me up after my mother abandoned me. But I've realised that I want more than that. Is it really too much to want to be loved?' she cried. 'Is it too much to ask that one day someone will find a place for me in their heart, not because of duty or convenience, but because I'm actually special to them? Or is there something about me that fails to inspire love and affection—some genetic fault that makes me unlovable?'

Zac tensed at her words and a shutter seemed to come down over his face so that she had no idea what he was thinking. He probably thought she was a silly, hysterical mass of insecurities, she thought bleakly, and he was probably right. He had never pretended that he'd asked her to marry him for any other reason than to provide their daughter with a stable upbringing and he was looking at her now as if she had taken leave of her senses.

'You're talking nonsense,' he said quietly. 'You're tired and over-emotional. Come to bed and let me show you how good our marriage will be.'

'You mean you want sex.' Freya resisted the temptation to bury her pride and allow him to sweep her off to their special world where they communicated without the need for words. She had spent the past weeks since she'd agreed to marry him kidding herself that one day she would make him love her. It was time to face reality, but she couldn't do that while she was in his bed. 'Not tonight, Zac. I don't think I could bear it,' she whispered before she stepped into her room and shut him out.

In the morning he had gone. She was trying to persuade Aimee to eat her breakfast when Laurent informed her that Zac had been called away to deal with an urgent company matter. Freya absorbed the news silently and refrained from pointing out that it seemed unlikely he would hold a business meeting on a Sunday. She spent the day in a curiously numbed state and obligingly smiled and nodded when Yvette regaled her with the plans for their forthcoming wedding.

Zac had employed the services of a top wedding planner as well as involving his mother in organising the ceremony, which was to be held in the garden at La Maison des Fleurs. An exquisite ivory silk bridal gown was now waiting for a final fitting and Aimee was going to steal the day in a confection of pink tulle. It had all the ingredients of a fairy-tale wedding—apart from one vital fact, Freya mused bleakly. Love was missing, and, at this precise moment, so was the groom.

Sunday dragged into Monday and there was still no word from him. On Tuesday six dozen red roses were delivered to the penthouse—no accompanying note, simply a card with his name scrawled across it. Why had he sent them? she mused tearfully as she buried her face in the velvety petals and inhaled their delicate perfume. It was the first time anyone had ever sent her flowers, and she wondered if Zac had any idea how much the simple gesture meant to her. Red roses were for love but she refused to read anything into his choice of flowers. She was tired of hoping and she sternly told herself that he'd probably just instructed the florist to send a bouquet.

She missed him so much that it hurt and that night she gave up trying to sleep in her bed and moved into his, no longer caring what he might think if he returned home and found her there. The nights she'd spent without him had been purgatory, but the faint, lingering scent of him on the sheets comforted her and she fell asleep with her face pressed against his pillow.

Some time in the early hours she was woken by the faint sound of the front door closing, followed by footsteps in the hall. Zac was home and her spirits soared as she held her breath and waited for him to enter the room. She was nervous of facing him after her bout of hysteria the night before he'd left and screwed her eyes shut, hoping he would assume she was asleep. With any luck he would slide between the sheets and take her in his arms, she thought weakly as a tremor ran through her. She wouldn't reject him. Pride was a lonely bed-fellow and she couldn't fight her feelings for him any more.

But he didn't come. Minutes passed and she opened her eyes and stared at the door, willing him to open it. Maybe he had poured himself a nightcap and had fallen asleep on the sofa? Unable to stand the tension any longer, she shoved her arms into her robe and crept into the hall. Aimee and the staff were all asleep and the sitting room was deserted, but a light shone on the staircase leading to the roof-garden and after a moment's hesitation she hurried up the steps.

'Zac!'

He was sitting at the far end of the pool, slumped in a chair with his legs outstretched and a bottle of cognac on the low table in front of him. He looked…wrecked, Freya noted as her eyes skimmed over his dishevelled appearance. He had lost his tie and his shirt was open at the neck, while the full day's stubble shading his jaw only added to his raw sex appeal.

'You're home,' she said inanely. 'I heard you come in and I…thought you would come to bed.' She walked around the pool towards him and gave him a tentative, hopeful smile.

Zac's eyes narrowed and he took a gulp from the glass in his hand. 'I find it hard to believe you were waiting for me, *chérie*? And I think it's probably safer for both of us if I remain here tonight.'

'So you can get drunk?' she asked sharply, glaring at him when he poured a generous measure into the glass.

'I prefer to think of it as a necessary anaesthetic,' he drawled laconically. 'I've discovered over the last few days that life is easier to cope with if you're numb from the neck up.'

'You're not making any sense.' She took a deep breath. 'What's the matter, Zac?'

He was silent for so long that she wondered if he had

heard her, but then he suddenly got to his feet and sounded the death knell to all her foolish dreams when he coldly announced, 'I've decided to postpone the wedding.'

CHAPTER ELEVEN

FOR a few seconds the floor beneath Freya's feet seemed to sway and she inhaled sharply. 'I see,' she managed at last, past the constriction in her throat.

'I doubt it,' Zac murmured, and his light, almost casual tone opened the floodgates of sheer agonising pain.

'All right, I don't see, and I certainly don't understand.' She flew across the remaining few feet that separated them and halted in front of him, bewilderment, hurt and sheer fury blazing in her eyes. 'I thought we'd agreed that we could make our marriage work—for Aimee's sake.'

'I thought so too, but I realise that I can't go through with it right now,' he said grimly, a nerve jumping in his cheek as he stared down at her. The patio lights cast long shadows and she saw the weariness in his gaze, as if he hadn't slept for days.

Reaction was setting in, leaving her feeling numb. 'Why not?' she whispered, her voice cracking.

The silence shredded her nerves and when he finally spoke his voice was raw, as if his throat were lined with broken glass. 'Because I haven't been honest with you—and you more than anyone, Freya, deserve honesty.'

'Oh, no!' Pain tore through her and her hand flew to her

mouth as if she could somehow hold back her betraying cry. 'It's Annalise, isn't it?' She couldn't prevent the tears from sliding unchecked down her face; her world was crumbling and her heart felt as though it had splintered in two. 'You don't have to tell me, Zac, because I already know you're having an affair with her. She took great delight in revealing your little secret when I met her at the party the night before you went away.'

His head jerked up and he stared at her as if she had taken leave of her senses. 'Don't be ridiculous. Of course I'm not having an affair with Annalise—or any other woman,' he said in astonishment. '*Mon Dieu, chérie*, when would I find the time or the energy after spending my nights having the most incredible sex with you?'

He seemed so genuinely astounded by her accusation that Freya blinked at him through her tears. 'Annalise said...' she began falteringly.

'I don't care what she said, she was lying.' Seeing her abject misery, he made a huge effort to contain his impatience. 'We had a brief affair about six months after you and I split up, but that's all, and it meant as little to me as all my other relationships,' he told her bluntly.

Freya stared at him uncertainly. 'But why did she say it, if it wasn't true?'

He shrugged dismissively, as if he was bored of the subject of Annalise Dubois. 'Because she enjoys making trouble and I imagine because she's jealous of you.'

No one could lie so convincingly. He had to be telling the truth, Freya decided, but her spurt of relief quickly died. 'Well, if it's not Annalise, then in what way haven't you been honest with me?' she asked fearfully when his face became shuttered once more. 'If it concerns us, our relationship, then you don't have to worry,' she said as understanding slowly dawned. He must have guessed that she was in love with him and knew that he must be honest and tell her he would never return her feelings. 'I know you don't love me,' she whispered, 'and I accept that you never will.' She looked away from him and willed herself not to cry any more, but his next words brought her head round.

'But I do love you, Freya,' he said in a low voice that seemed to be torn from the depths of his soul. 'Although for a long time I did not know it. You lighten my day…my life, in a way that no other woman has ever done, but it was only when Aimee was ill and you were so distraught that I realised I wanted to hold you and protect you from hurt, because you are infinitely precious to me.

'I can't imagine my life without you,' he admitted huskily. 'Subconsciously I think I must have loved you for ever, and that's why I was so determined to marry you, but it was easier not to question my motives too closely. Instead I selfishly took pleasure in making love to you; took everything that you gave so generously and never offered you anything in return.

'*Je t'adore, mon ange,*' he groaned, his voice throbbing with emotions, 'but loving you beyond reason doesn't make it right.' His face twisted as if he was in pain. 'I haven't been honest about *me*. There are things I should have told you, things that you have the right to know, and it would be morally wrong for me to marry you when you don't know all the facts. Don't cry, *mon coeur*,' he pleaded, wiping away a tear with his thumb, only to see it replaced with another.

'I don't understand,' she choked. She felt as though she were balanced on the edge of a precipice, looking down into the abyss. Zac had said the words she'd dreamed of hearing, but she found it impossible to believe him. He looked drawn and haggard and if he really did love her, then he clearly did not welcome the emotion.

'Two years ago I had everything money could buy and nothing that really mattered to me—until a shy English girl with green eyes and the sweetest smile turned my life upside down,' he revealed quietly. 'I was drawn to you in a way that had never happened to me before, although I told myself it was simply good sex,' he admitted harshly. 'I wasted no time in making you my mistress and, despite coping with the loss of my father, my mother's grief and an intolerable workload, I was happy.

'You made me happy, Freya, but then you dropped the bombshell that you were pregnant and I was certain the baby wasn't mine because, unbeknown to you, I'd had a vasectomy to ensure I would never father a child.'

'Zac…' The raw emotion in his eyes made her heart stand still. How could she ever have thought him cold, or believed that he didn't care? she wondered.

He shook his head and placed a finger gently across her lips. 'What I have to tell you has been burning a hole inside me for what seems like a lifetime and I need to speak now, while I have the courage.'

Fear settled over Freya like a shroud and she shivered. What on earth did Zac have to tell her that demanded his courage?

'I've already told you that I was in my teens when my mother gave birth to my twin sisters. They appeared to be healthy babies, but died when they were a few months old,' he said flatly. 'Doctors discovered that both my parents carried a gene that resulted in a high chance of their children developing a rare, incurable illness. I did not develop the disease, but my parents were advised that there was a possibility I had inherited the gene and could pass it on to my own children.'

As his words slowly penetrated her brain Freya felt her blood congeal in her veins and her legs buckled as terror swept through her. 'Could Aimee develop the illness?'

'*Non*,' Zac gripped her arms and quickly sought to reassure her. 'A child can only be affected if both parents carry the gene, and if you were also a carrier Aimee would have shown signs of the disease by now. But there is a fifty-percent chance that I am a carrier. I had a vasectomy because I was determined that I would be the last in the genetic link— the last Deverell. But the vasectomy reversed. When I discovered that Aimee is my child I knew she might also carry the gene and I despaired of telling you.' The lines of strain around his eyes were plainly evident and Freya's heart ached for him. He had carried the burden of worry for their child alone in an attempt to protect her.

Finally she could understand Zac's decision never to father a child and his adamant refusal to believe that the baby she had conceived was his, and now that she knew the whole tragic story she wanted to weep for him—for the young boy who had witnessed his parents' devastation when they had lost their twin daughters and for the man who had done everything in his power to prevent another child from suffering.

She looked up at him and caught the flare of pain in his eyes before he quickly masked his thoughts. He'd said that he loved her and he adored Aimee… 'I understand everything you've told me, but not why you want to postpone the wedding,' she murmured. 'If you love me…'

'More than life, *mon coeur*,' he vowed fiercely, 'more than you can ever know.' He slid his hands up her arms to cup her face and she could have died at the expression in his brilliant blue gaze, the faint sheen of moisture that revealed his vulnerability and his deep, abiding love for her.

'When I received the results of the paternity test I was desperate to know if I carry the gene and the likelihood that I had passed it on to Aimee. I contacted medical experts who specialise in genetics and discovered that in the last two years a reliable test has been developed, which means that I will finally know if I am a carrier. If I am, then Aimee will have to be tested and it will mean that I can't risk having another child,' he said in a strained voice.

He broke off and stroked a stray tendril of hair from her face with fingers that shook slightly. 'When you spoke to Camille at the party I saw in your face how much you would love another baby and it hit me like a thunderbolt that I hadn't been fair to you, *chérie*. I've spent the past three days on *The Isis* in abject despair, knowing that it would be wrong to marry you until I know if I can give you other children.

'Waiting for the test results is tearing me apart. If it proves negative then I will gladly marry you, but if it is not, then—' He broke off, his expression tortured.

Freya stared at him. 'And if it's not, what then? What are you suggesting?' she demanded fiercely. 'That I marry someone else? Have children with someone else? Is that what you want?'

'No, it's not what I want,' he denied savagely. He spun around so that his back was to her and ran a hand over his face, but Freya saw the betraying gesture and her heart clenched with love and tenderness. 'It would destroy me to see you with another man, to know that you loved him and to watch you grow big with his child whenever I came to visit

Aimee. But what I want isn't important,' he continued huskily. 'I want you to be happy, *chérie*.'

'Then come here and make me happy,' she pleaded softly. 'You're the only man who can, the only man I want. I love you,' she said simply, opening her arms to him when he jerked his head round and stared at her.

'Don't you understand? I want to postpone the wedding until I know if I can give you more children.' He swallowed when she walked towards him and wrapped her arms around his waist. For a moment he fought against his desperate need to hold her, but he had never been able to resist her smile and with a groan he slid his fingers into her hair.

'I've waited for you to ask me to marry you for two long years and I'm not waiting any longer,' she told him fiercely. 'I don't care what the test reveals. Aimee is healthy and you've said she stands no chance of developing the illness herself. It would be nice to give her a little brother or sister, but I love you, Zac, and that's more important than anything else. All I've ever wanted is for you to love me the way I love you, completely and utterly for the rest of our lives.'

'Freya…' His voice broke and he claimed her mouth with such tender passion, such *love*, that her eyes filled once more. '*Je t'aime, chérie*, for ever.'

'Show me,' she whispered against his mouth and smiled when he scooped her up and carried her over to a sun lounger.

'Do you want me to take you to the bedroom?'

'No time,' she muttered thickly. She had been starved of him for the past two nights and she couldn't wait a moment longer. His clothes were a hindrance and she tugged impatiently at his shirt buttons, murmuring her pleasure when she parted the material and ran her hands over his broad chest.

He dispensed with her robe with similar speed and paused to savour the sight of her in a wisp of black lace before he drew her negligee over her head and absorbed the beauty of her soft curves. His woman—the thought of living without her had almost destroyed him and the knowledge that he didn't have to was slowly sinking in. He would make her happy, he vowed fiercely. He would devote the rest of his life to loving her so that she forgot the lonely years of her childhood and knew beyond doubt that he adored her.

He lowered his head and captured her mouth in a tender caress before increasing the pressure, crushing her soft, moist lips beneath his own as passion quickly built to a crescendo of need. Freya curled her arms around his neck and arched towards him when he trailed his mouth down her throat and over the soft swell of her breast. The sensation of his tongue stroking delicately over her nipple made her cry out.

'I love you so much, Zac,' she whispered, wondering how she could ever find the words to tell him what he meant to her. 'I've wanted to say the words for so long,' and had said them, silently, in the sweet aftermath of their lovemaking. Now she could say them out loud and she smiled when he transferred his mouth to her other breast and then lifted his head to stare down at her.

'The words are special, but I was afraid to say them, knowing that I should let you go,' he said deeply. 'Instead I tried to tell you with my body. When I kissed you, caressed you, my heart was reaching out to show you how much you mean to me. You are my life, Freya—you and Aimee. You mean the world to me.'

He moved over her and entered her with exquisite care, setting a rhythm that swiftly built to explosive passion. Freya wrapped her legs around him and revelled in his strong, deep strokes driving her higher and higher until she could take no more. As she shattered she called his name and heard his answering groan, heard him tell her again and again that he would love her for eternity. She convulsed around him, heightening his pleasure to an unbearable degree, and he finally lost control, gloriously and unashamedly and with a lingering sadness that he had dared not risk making love to her without a protective sheath.

Afterwards Freya hugged him tightly to her and stared up at the night sky. The moon was a pale orb suspended against black velvet and the stars seemed close enough to touch. She loved the weight of Zac's body on hers, but eventually he eased away from her and stared into her eyes.

'If the test results are positive…'

'Then we'll deal with it,' she said steadily. 'All my life I have longed to be part of a family and now I have Aimee; I feel closer to Yvette than I ever did to my grandmother and Jean is more than Aimee's nanny, she's become a dear friend. But most of all I have you,' she said softly, her eyes shimmering with tears as she traced the contours of his face. 'I want to be your wife, Zac, and know that whatever the future brings, we'll face it together. There'll be lows as well as highs, but there will always be love and that's all we need.'

Zac said no more, couldn't when his throat ached with emotion, but he kissed her and stroked his hands over her body, showing her without words that he would love her for the rest of his life.

Three days later they were married and their wedding day was everything Freya had ever dreamed of. A day of joy and laughter that began when she walked across the lawn at La

Maison des Fleurs escorted by Laurent and with Aimee clutching her hand and skipping alongside. Zac was waiting for her beneath a bower of pink and white roses and as she approached he stepped forwards to draw her and his little daughter into his arms.

'Papa,' Aimee greeted him with an impish grin and drew murmurs of delight from the assembled guests when she toddled off to sit between *Mamie* and Jean, the two people she loved most after her parents.

Zac looked so utterly gorgeous in his superbly tailored wedding suit that Freya's steps faltered and she stared up at him, overwhelmed by the depth of her love. He smiled and she caught her breath at the lambent warmth in his gaze, an ache starting deep inside her when he lifted her hand to his lips and kissed each finger in turn.

'You know I will never let you go,' he murmured, his voice shaking with emotion. 'You are mine and I guard my possessions jealously, *chérie*.' He brushed his lips over hers in a gentle kiss that promised heaven and hand in hand they stepped forwards to make the vows of love that would last a lifetime.

EPILOGUE

FREYA tiptoed into the nursery and smiled at the sight of Aimee asleep in bed surrounded by her collection of teddies. At nearly four years old she was growing up to be a bright and beautiful little girl and was a devoted sister to her baby brothers.

At the other end of the room two cots stood side by side, each containing an identical dark-haired baby boy. From the moment Zac had learned he did not carry the gene that had taken such a devastating toll on his family, he had been eager for them to try for another child, and as usual he couldn't do anything by half, she thought wryly.

Luc and Olivier were now nine months old and were quickly discovering how much mischief they could get up to now that they could crawl. Both had inherited their father's strong will and she'd had a tussle to change them into their sleep suits. Now, finally they were asleep and looked so utterly adorable that she couldn't resist leaning over to brush her lips against Olivier's velvet soft cheek and then Luc's.

'Ready?' Zac's voice sounded from the doorway and she glanced up, her heart lurching when his mouth curved in a wide, sexy smile.

'Do you think they'll be all right? We've never left them

for a whole night before,' she murmured anxiously as she followed him into the hall.

'Of course they will. Jean and my mother will spoil them beyond redemption,' he assured her. 'It's about time we had one uninterrupted night.'

'Mmm, I'm sure we'll sleep well.'

'I wouldn't bank on it, *chérie*,' Zac warned her, the gleam in his eyes sending a quiver of anticipation through her. 'I have various plans for our second wedding anniversary, and none of them involve us lying still.'

He held her hand as they rode the lift down from the penthouse and walked along the quayside to where *The Isis* was moored. Freya could not help but glance at him, noting the way his black trousers moulded his thighs and his shirt was open at the neck, revealing the tanned column of his throat. He still had the power to make her heart stop and she swallowed at the lambent heat in his gaze when he lifted her into his arms and stepped aboard the boat.

'Happy anniversary, *chérie*.' He bent his head and kissed her until she was breathless before carrying her down to the lower deck. The master cabin was filled to overflowing with flowers and tears welled in Freya's eyes when she glanced around at the mass of roses and carnations.

'They're beautiful,' she whispered, clinging to him when he lowered her onto the bed. 'Where are you taking me?'

'Nowhere.' He grinned and the gleam in his blue eyes sent a tremor of excitement through her. 'At least, not yet. Later we'll sail along the coast to Antibes and have dinner there. But right now I'm not hungry for food, *mon coeur*.'

'I see.' Freya pouted. 'So I got all dressed up for nothing. Perhaps I'd better take my dress off before it creases.'

'I think that's a very good idea,' Zac murmured, sliding

the straps of her dress down her shoulders until her breasts spilled into his hands. He groaned his appreciation and dipped his head to capture one dusky nipple in his mouth; tormenting her with his wicked tongue until she begged for mercy and he transferred his lips to her other breast.

She was on fire for him instantly, desperate to feel him inside her. She was glad that her body had returned to its pre-pregnancy shape and eagerly helped him to remove the rest of her clothes, her excitement mounting at the burning heat of Zac's gaze. Their lovemaking had been gentle and more restrained since she'd given birth to the twins, but tonight she sensed his urgency and knew that he would couple tenderness with fierce, primitive passion.

'You're incredible,' Zac breathed, his eyes darkening as he ran his hands possessively over her flat stomach and then lower to caress the sensitive flesh of her thighs. He stripped out of his clothes with indecent haste and came down on top of her, taking care to support his weight as he entered her with one slow thrust that filled her and made her groan with pleasure. Each deep stroke sent her higher and higher until she sobbed his name and clung to him while spasms of intense pleasure racked her body.

Still moving within her, he whispered the words she had waited so long to hear, vowing to love her and cherish her for the rest of his life, before his control shattered and he spilt into her, his big body shaking with the power of his release.

'This is for you, to celebrate the second year of our marriage,' he said some while later, sliding his arm from beneath her shoulders for a moment as he reached for a small velvet box. He slid the band of diamonds and emeralds onto her finger to join her wedding ring and kissed away her tears. 'You are my wife, my lover...' his voice faltered fractionally '…mother of my children, and the love of my life. I will love you for eternity, Freya,' he vowed, before he took her in his arms once more and proceeded to demonstrate without words exactly what she meant to him.

MILLS & BOON®

Mills & Boon have been at the heart of romance since 1908... and while the fashions may have changed, one thing remains the same: from pulse-pounding passion to the gentlest caress, we're always known how to bring romance alive.

Now, we're delighted to present you with these irresistible illustrations, inspired by the vintage glamour of our covers. So indulge your wildest dreams and unleash your imagination as we present the most iconic Mills & Boon moments of the last century.

Visit **www.millsandboon.co.uk/ArtofRomance** to order yours!

MILLS & BOON®

Why not subscribe?
Never miss a title and save money too!

Here is what's available to you if you join the exclusive **Mills & Boon® Book Club** today:

* *Titles up to a month ahead of the shops*
* *Amazing discounts*
* *Free P&P*
* *Earn Bonus Book points that can be redeemed against other titles and gifts*
* *Choose from monthly or pre-paid plans*

Still want more?
Well, if you join today we'll even give you
50% OFF your first parcel!

So visit **www.millsandboon.co.uk/subscriptions**
or call **Customer Relations on 0844 844 1351***
to be a part of this exclusive Book Club!

*This call will cost you 7 pence per minute plus your
phone company's price per minute access charge.